THE TIMBER BEAST

THE
TIMBER BEAST

By

ARCHIE BINNS

New York

CHARLES SCRIBNER'S SONS

1944

ACKNOWLEDGMENT

WE ARE indebted to Bob Miller, Inc., for permission to use a verse from the song "Joe Hill" by Earl Robinson and Alfred Hayes. Copyright, 1942, by Bob Miller, Inc.

CHARLIE DOW bought his Seattle mansion in the late fall of 1916. Now, twenty-odd years later, it was old-fashioned and inconvenient, with too many rooms with too-high ceilings, and its shingled surface bulged with unseemly bay windows and balconies. In a later renovation, the rooms facing Lake Washington had been given immense plate-glass windows, peculiarly suited to the climate, but they did little to disguise the age of the house, and nothing to change its size.

Charlie Dow liked to refer to himself as "an old timber beast," thereby absolving himself from any grace or elegance that would not be found in a common logger. He was not conscious of changing fashions in architecture, and he was not inclined to quarrel with the house, which was a mark of his mystifying success. While other independent logging operators stayed close to their holdings until they evaporated in bankruptcy, Charlie had kept his mansion in Seattle through good years and bad; at the same time, he continued to hold on to his large and deserted residence in Thunderbird County, where he logged.

In the twenty-odd years since the Dows' sudden move to Seattle, a good deal of the family's life had happened. Bailey and Paul, who first saw the mansion at the ages of seven and two, had gone to college from there. Myra, the first wife, had died there, and Charlie had brought home a bride younger than his youngest son.

The new wife, Marian, was strong and healthy, but she did

not provide the big house with the second spring which Charlie had expected. After four years, he was still denied the luxury of hoisting a child onto his shoulder and saying, "He's going to be the champion logger of Thunderbird County!" Long ago he had stopped saying things like that about his present sons.

At the moment there were two children in the house, but they were both girls—nieces of his first wife. Myra's brother, Phil, and his wife stayed close to their gold mine near Fairbanks, in Alaska. Their children, Frances, who was sixteen, and Ginger, aged eight, attended school in Seattle and spent long week ends at the big house. Charlie and Marian, having no sons of their own, lavished their affection on other people's daughters. School was out now and the girls were staying at the house until their steamer sailed for Alaska. The same vacation period was bringing Paul home from his last year of college in California. There was a flurry of unpacking and pressing because the girls wanted to wear their party dresses for the hail-and-farewell dinner.

While they were there, the girls gave the house a semblance of home, and they appreciated even its infirmities. There was, for instance, the bellowing in the water pipes that began a few seconds after the hall toilet was flushed. . . .

As Marian Dow came upstairs with an armful of rustling taffeta, there was the sound of the flush; at the same instant the door crashed open and Ginger came flying out and down the hall. She checked herself at the newel post at the head of the stairs and Marian caught her with her free arm. The bellowing in the water pipes began.

"I made it!" Ginger shouted. "I got here before the cow mooed!"

Laughing and holding the child, Marian said, "I'll have the plumber in tomorrow."

"No," Ginger said, "don't let him fix it!" Her dark eyes were flashing in her intense little face and her light brown hair shook with her head. "It wouldn't be any more fun going to the bathroom!"

Marian compromised. "If you promise not to break your neck before the cow moos, I won't have it fixed until after you're gone."

"All right; but don't let him fix it too good."

With Ginger walking beside her, Marian went on to the room where Frances was repacking. The older sister had the well-fed, confident look of a private school pupil, and when Marian came in with her newly pressed dress, she immediately took it from her and said, "Aunt Marian, you should have let Mrs. Wilkes do that!"

"I'm younger than she is, Fran, and she's having a busy day."

Frances had no clear idea of where to put the dress, and after a few seconds of hesitation she put it down in an armchair. She had only taken it out of deference to her aunt's superior age and beauty. Actually, Marian's age did not amount to a great deal, being twenty-four. Her beauty was more impressive, and the strong light from the store-sized window did nothing but emphasize its freshness. She had a great deal of shining, copper-colored hair, with darker unplucked eyebrows, clear ivory skin, and a slow, amused smile that started with her lips and then seemed to come out of her deep blue eyes, giving a feeling of warmth and affection. Marian was beautiful, and Frances was a little in love with her.

While the others went on with the packing, Ginger wandered to the big window and looked out. "There's Cousin Bailey!"

"What's he doing?" Frances asked.

"Burning the brush that the gardeners left. I'm going out to talk to him." In a moment they heard her racing downstairs.

Frances sighed as she folded her slacks. "I'm never going to marry," she said, "and I'm specially not going to marry a man who owns a gold mine! He'll have to have a civilized job in the states—so we won't have all this bother about children going away to school."

Marian said, "People make sacrifices for their children wherever they are. If it hadn't been for the boys, Charlie and your Aunt Myra wouldn't have put the money they did into Home Place—and then abandoned it to come here."

Frances went to the big window and looked down the slope of the lawn, past the feathery cluster of bamboo and the flowering rose bushes, to where her big cousin and little sister were burning brush in the open space among the evergreens. "All that bother about education, and a lot of good it did Cousin Bailey!"

"Why do you say that?"

"What good did it do him?" Frances asked. "He graduated from Yale and then he was in New York for years—and what has he got to show for it?"

"But Fran, you can't judge that by looking at him."

"It isn't his looks—he's almost handsome. But what good is he? He's middle-aged, he's thirty, and what has he ever done? He just putters around and talks."

"He has his business," Aunt Marian said.

"Boat moorings! A parking lot and service station for boats! Is that a man's job—when he could be logging with Uncle Charlie?"

"You sound like your Uncle Charlie, Fran. If Bailey's happiest working around with boats, that's what he ought to do."

"And you know the reputation he has about women," Fran went on.

"You seem to know more about Bailey than I do," Aunt Marian said. "Where do you hear it?"

"Everywhere; at school——"

"The girls talk about Bailey at school!"

Frances giggled. "His reputation has got as low as the third grade."

"No, Fran!"

"Ginger told me about it. You know the crazy things eight-year-olds do. Once when their teacher, Miss Lawson, was out of the room, one of the children said, 'Lawson has suppressed desires.' Soon they were all singing, '*Lawson has suppressed desires; Lawson has suppressed desires!*' Then our little Ginger got up and said, 'If my Cousin Bailey was here, he'd know just what to do for her.'"

Aunt Marian laughed while she looked a little worried. "Where do you suppose——"

"You never can tell with eight-year-olds," Frances said. "When I asked Ginger, she didn't know what it meant or why she said it. It was spreading Cousin Bailey's reputation, all right."

"It certainly was!"

One of the nicest things about Aunt Marian was that you could always count on her laughing at anything funny, and she sometimes told stories that weren't quite proper. With that bond between you, you could discuss anything with her—anything but her own problems, if she had any. You never knew. Sometimes Frances wondered how any one as beautiful and young and loving as her aunt could be married to Uncle Charlie, who was an old man. They never discussed that. But Fran couldn't help feeling that she must have secret problems.

At the brush fire among the circle of trees, Bailey visited with Ginger. Bailey was a little under six feet, heavy-shouldered like his logger father. Dressed in the white shirt and

white duck trousers and yachting shoes which he wore around
the boat moorings, he looked particularly large, and more
capable than he was. His brawny look was carried as far as the
border of his face by his thick, dark brown hair and square
jaw: but at those points it gave up, and left him with a sensitive
face and fine, dark eyes that had a mixture of melancholy and
humor, and an engagingly sad grin.

Giving him the news, Ginger said, "Cousin Paul telegraphed
from Eugene, Oregon. He ought to be here any time now."

"Not quite," Bailey thought. "That's about three hundred
miles, and Paul takes his time; he won't be here until after
four."

"The Darlings are coming to dinner; I'm going to wear
my lace party dress."

"All the Darlings coming?"

"There are only three." Then Ginger said, "Violet King is
coming, too. I heard Aunt Marian inviting her. You like Violet,
don't you?"

"Don't you?"

"Frances says she always looks as if she was in Sunday
school. Do you think so?"

"Not specially," Bailey said.

"The Darlings were invited because Uncle Charlie and Aunt
Marian couldn't be at the graduation."

"That's right," Bailey said.

Ginger looked at the burning branches, which coated with
white ashes as they were consumed. "It looks like snow burning."

She looked at the heat waves in the air above the fire. "The
air looks like glass."

Bailey threw in some dry stakes that had once held up roses,
and the flames wrapped themselves around the wood. "The fire

is loving the wood!" And as it was consumed, she said, "The fire is loving it to death!"

Bailey could do nothing to encourage the chain of clear-visioned impressions, but he wanted them to go on. For him, the vision of early childhood was one of the few sacred things. Most people went blind to the beauty of the world at the age of six or seven—and for the rest of their lives they groped in the dark and drew on fading memories.

When the child stopped saying lucid things, she became a small, determined pest, worrying him about the exact minute when his brother would be home.

Bailey had figured Paul's course on Highway 99 at the forty miles an hour which he expected him to average. By that dead reckoning, he predicted that his brother would arrive after four. Ginger interpreted it in her own hopeful way, and when it was four by Bailey's watch, she towed him by the hand around to the driveway; at a few minutes past the hour she began fretting because Cousin Paul did not appear. Bailey was still reasoning with her when she shouted, "Cousin Paul! Here he is!" and Bailey caught her by the arm to keep her from dashing in front of the old green convertible that rolled into the driveway.

When it stopped beside them, Bailey turned Ginger loose to throw herself on her favorite cousin as he eased himself out of the car. As usual, he was hatless and without a tie, with his shirt unbuttoned at the neck. He had never dressed better than carelessly, though Bailey could not remember any woman criticizing him for it, neither mother nor stepmother, nor nieces nor aunts. It was Paul who mattered, and Bailey had never seen him look more handsome than he did now, sunburned and dusty from travelling with the top of his car down. He was over six feet tall, and just slender enough, with the grace of a good woodsman and a good athlete. His thick hair was bleached to a straw color, with darker hair showing through, and his fine, tanned face was given depth and life by his deep-set eyes and his shy boyish smile.

Before Ginger was through embracing Paul, the others came hurrying out. Frances threw her arms around his neck and kissed him and asked him questions, and kissed him again before he could answer.

When Frances was through for the moment, it was Marian's turn. She held out her hand and said, with her lovely smile, "Welcome home, Paul!"

Taking her hand, he said, "It's nice to be home."

"Why don't you kiss her?" Ginger asked.

As Paul complied, Ginger said, "It's just like the movies!" Frances said, "Don't they look like a technicolor film?"

Bailey didn't think much of the compliments, though there was something in the technicolor idea. In the June sun, his step-mother's fabulous coloring and Paul's pale-and-dark gold hair and deep blue eyes looked too vivid to be real. As they were together for that moment, Bailey thought they were the most beautiful couple he had ever seen. It was too bad that it was only an impromptu thought up by the children. Marian was his father's wife, and Paul, who attracted women of all ages, had never been attracted by any of them.

They had dinner by candlelight, which treated the table and the ten around it graciously, giving them a soft island of light inside the dusk of the big, clumsy dining room.

Dinner was a family affair in the sense that every one around the table belonged more or less closely to the family of one or the other of the logging partners. Charlie Dow, the head of one tribe, had the look of a logging operator even in his dinner jacket. At sixty, he was big-shouldered and steady-handed, with thick graying hair and a thick moustache. Suitable to a business which depended on moving enormous weights efficiently, he gave the impression of locomotive solidity. And because the weights which he moved were cylinders capable of every kind of treachery, his air of alertness hardly ever left him; when any one spoke, he was apt to turn his head and big shoulders quickly in that direction—not nervously, but alertly, as if by chance an enormous log might have broken loose from its flatcar in one of the enlarged photographs on the dim wall.

None of the other members of Charlie's tribe engaged in logging and they were all of a softer breed: the two good-looking sons by his first marriage, the boarding-school girls passing through the house like well-fed, migratory birds travelling on first-class tickets, and his charming young second wife.

Martin Darling, who was the other partner in the business, boasted gently that he was a logger who had never moved a log in his life. Only Charlie knew Martin's precise status; his name was not included in the name of the firm, and presumably he was a partner only in the sense that he had put money into the business. Any one looking at Martin Darling would not expect him to move logs except with capital. He was a small, plump man of over eighty. Time had taken his hair away and merged his round, smooth-shaven pink face and smooth pink head into one sphere; when he was pleased and beamed softly at Marian, who was on one side of him, or at the school-girl Frances who was on the other, pink light seemed to radiate from the top of his head as well as from his round cheeks. But time that had brought about the merger of the head and face had not tampered with his faculties. In business he had a reputation for driving hard bargains, and when he relaxed into his favorite sport of archery, he seemed to find it easier to hit the bull's-eye than to miss. Once he had assured Bailey that he could duplicate the delicate shot made by William Tell, and Bailey quite believed him. He did not, however, offer to hold the apple, because Martin had no great opinion of him, and he had a certain streak of spitefulness.

Mrs. Darling was a gentle, apologetic woman who seemed to have lost her age and identity in a lifelong effort to please. She looked like a woman of sixty, though she was probably younger, having a daughter of twenty-three. But her eyes were nice when she talked to Bailey, who was seated at her right. When she ventured into the general conversation, she prefaced her remarks by saying anxiously, "Now, if I am wrong, I want some one to correct me—" And, as often as not, she was corrected by her definite blond daughter, Bertha, who sat opposite her, renewing school ties with Paul.

The fourth member of the Darling tribe was Violet King, who was on Bailey's right, and she was a member only by courtesy. Violet was a distant cousin of Mrs. Darling, and Bailey had discovered her in Martin's office, where she worked as a stenographer. In a way, she was not much of a discovery. She was as matter-of-fact as her noiseless typewriter, and almost as silent; when she did say anything, it was reliably dull. Aside from that, she was a dark-haired, pretty girl, almost too neat, almost too well dressed, and almost too well behaved, without giving the impression of being particularly well-bred. That Sunday-school look which Frances had noted, puzzled Bailey at first, and he had invited her out once to see if she was like that all the time. After that he had taken her out with fair regularity. Now she sat beside him in her best Sunday-school manner, eating neatly and turning her humorless pretty face when he spoke to her, and saying, "Yes," and "No," and "I don't really know."

Across the corner of the table, Bertha was telling Charlie Dow about the commencement exercises. "You would have been proud of Paul in his cap and gown. He made me think of the Black Prince—the one who wore sable armor to set off his fair complexion. Paul and I photographed each other in our caps and gowns. I have a set of the prints in my handbag; I'll give them to you after dinner."

"I'd like to have them, Bertha."

"I don't know how the ones of me came out." She turned to Paul, "I suppose I look terrible."

He said, "I haven't developed them yet."

"Don't forget to let me see them when you do."

"I won't forget," he said.

"In my favorite one," she told Charlie, "Paul is holding his diploma like a sword, and there's a tall palm tree and people walking in the background, in caps and gowns. It gives the feeling of Crusaders in the Holy Land."

"I'd like to see it," Charlie said.

Frances had taken advantage of the Crusade, and she had Paul telling her about Stanford University. "It isn't my kind of country," he was saying, "but it's nice in some ways. The foothills rise almost from the edge of the campus, and the near ones are bare except for windbreaks of cypress trees. They don't seem like much at first, but when they're green in the spring——"

"And the poppies!" Bertha said. "They're something to see, Frances! We could see them on the Santa Cruz Mountains, twenty miles away—great patches of orange! Once Paul and I thought we'd walk to them——"

At the far end of the table, Marian was silently cutting Ginger's meat. Bailey thought she looked depressed, probably because Bertha was pushing Paul around. He went to the rescue, raising his voice a little and recalling his college days to Violet.

"When I was at Yale, we often went on picnics."

She asked politely, "Where did you go?"

"Different places: East Rock, West Rock."

"What are they?"

"Two little mountains, just alike."

"Were they nice?"

"Yes," he said; "we had fun."

"What did you do?"

"We ate sandwiches."

Her pretty, Sunday-school mask looked blank. "People generally do, on picnics."

"Yes," he said. "They were just like picnics anywhere else."

"What did you do after you ate your sandwiches?"

"We went home."

Clowning did not seem to help; when he stopped, Bertha was still on the Stanford hills.

"Paul, do you remember that night we were coming home from a hike? It was almost dark, and the wind was blowing through the cypress trees, and the hills were so lovely and ghostly. You said you thought it must have been something like that on the hills around Bagdad in the *Arabian Nights.*"

"They were nice hills, all right," Paul said. He felt uncomfortable because of the impression she was creating. He had made the remark about Bagdad to some one else, and Bertha had only overheard it. He had avoided her as much as he decently could at college, and while the separate things she recalled were true, they added up to a kind of lie.

Without interrupting any one, Marian began talking. She was talking partly to Martin Darling, but she was also talking to every one. She said, "Charlie and I are going to open Home

Place this summer; Bailey has promised to bring up his sloop on week ends, and we'll go sailing and fishing——"

"And we'll be in Fairbanks!" Ginger lamented.

Frances said, "Don't make us jealous, Aunt Marian!"

"Maybe you can come back early and stay at Home Place for a while, and maybe we can persuade Paul to help us study the geology and the botany of the neighborhood." To Paul she said, "I'm not trying to sign you up first and ask your permission afterward; but it would be nice if you could help us."

Paul said nicely, "I'll try, anyway."

"And we'll have picnics, and fires on the beach——"

"Am I invited?" Bertha asked.

Marian said, "You are all invited."

From the head of the table Charlie said, "If Paul decides to go logging with me, we'll see a good deal of him at Home Place." To Martin he said, "Paul is going to spend a few days at camp, looking over the works. What would you think if we made a timber beast of him?"

Martin beamed. "I approve of that, Charlie! I've always said you should have a second-growth logger coming along." While he beamed, his little round blue eyes looked at Bailey with cheerful reproach that was somehow disagreeable.

Bailey said, "You don't have to look at me when you say that."

"Dear, no!" Martin said, as if he knew better than to expect anything of Bailey.

Bertha said, "I think it's mean to take Paul away to the woods as soon as he gets here!"

"He'll be there only a few days," Bailey told her. "I'm going up as far as Hewitt with the boat, and dig him out of the woods." After a moment he added, "Then we're going cruising."

"You're a great help!" Bertha said.

Home Place meant different things to the different people about the table, and the very act of talking about it drifted the conversation away. Mrs. Darling brought it back gently. "I may be wrong, Mr. Dow; I've never had any experience living in the country, but if I had an estate like yours, I would want to live there the year round."

Charlie looked pleased. "You could do worse," he agreed.

Ginger said, "I'd go up there and stay forever!"

"Maybe we will," Marian said.

Bailey said, "It's such a sensible idea that nothing less than a disaster will ever make it happen."

"How do you make a disaster?" Ginger asked.

Every one laughed, but there were no suggestions until Frances turned to the chuckling financier beside her. "You look as if you knew, Mr. Darling. How do you make a disaster happen?"

Martin beamed. "It doesn't take any special effort," he said softly. "You just go on in your usual way."

"We'll try to get along without one," Marian said.

The talk about the place in Thunderbird County had put Charlie in the mood for his favorite story, and he said, "I suppose most of you have heard about the time I discovered Home Place?"

Most of them had, and Ginger was the only one with any enthusiasm for hearing it over again. Then Violet said earnestly, "I'd like to hear it, Mr. Dow. I didn't even know you'd been an explorer."

With a willing audience of even one, there was no discouraging Charlie.

"I was an explorer at that time, all right," he said. "It's easy to remember the date, because it was the Dark Day, and that would make it the twelfth of September, 1902. I was a young fellow then, and I hadn't started logging for myself. . . ." He had to go back a little from there. "You know, my father was a sea captain with his eye on the logging game. He didn't live to get into it, but between voyages carrying lumber he acquired timber land——"

Charlie's use of "acquired" was one of the things Bailey admired about his father. Whenever he told about the timber on which the family's fortune was built, he observed that his father had acquired it. Captain Dow's method had been to use a new crew for each voyage, and to have each member of the crew take up a timber claim, going through the necessary formality of swearing that it was for himself. Each member then signed over his claim to the captain in return for five dollars and a bottle of whiskey—and sometimes for only a bottle of whiskey. A more sensitive age might have considered it perjury and theft of timberland from the public domain; but it was acquired in an age in which morality was preoccupied with the bed and the church pew. And Captain Dow had not been alone in his method of acquiring timber.

"I was a donkey puncher at a haywire logging camp on Hood Canal. There were always forest fires out here, but that year was the worst. There was very little rain all summer, and the dry weather lasted well into September. But every one who hadn't been burned out went on logging and setting more fires."

Bertha asked, "Weren't there any laws about shutting down in dry weather? Didn't they watch the humidity?"

"Nobody had ever thought of such things," Charlie said. "It was every man for himself. But that summer was a lesson. Down on Lewis River, one fire burned up a quarter of a million acres of timber, and a lot of settlers. In the Matlock region, there was another fire almost as bad, and the smoke got so thick we couldn't see anything. The last morning we worked, every one carried a lantern, but the light never got beyond the lantern chimney. When we shut down, most of our crew went to fight the Matlock fire, and I thought it was time to look after my holdings."

Bailey suggested, "If there had been fog lights in the woods, you might have had to work half a day longer."

"Yes, and been burned up along with the camp!"

"Anyway," Bailey said, "it shows that people will do the intelligent thing when it's a choice of that or being burned alive."

"It's the way people learn," his father agreed, and went on with his story.

"The only transportation I could get was a dugout canoe, and an old Indian. On the trip across the Canal it was worse than the middle of the night; we never saw anything except the ashes of leaves, and dead birds falling out of the sky."

"Why were the birds dead?" Ginger asked.

"Suffocated," Charlie said. "The smoke was bad enough where we were, a couple of feet from the water; we were coughing all the time. The birds just fell out of the sky and they never moved. Leaves were falling all the time, and they looked perfect, except that they were black or gray, and when you touched one of them, it went to powder."

"What kind of leaves were they?" Violet asked.

"As I remember, salal and alder and pieces of fern. They were falling as thick as snow. . . . When the Indian landed me at Port Gamble, the mill was running with all its electric lights at noon. I expected to catch the Seattle steamer from there, but it never showed up. It was too far to go by canoe, but there was a tug at the dock and I talked her captain into taking me to Hewitt. He wanted a hundred dollars for the thirty-mile trip, and I didn't haggle with him——"

Frances said, "You must have had a lot of money, Uncle Charlie!"

He smiled a little grimly. "As a matter of fact, I didn't. But I thought if I was going to lose everything else, I might as well be good and broke.

"It was a blind-folded kind of voyage: from land to land we never saw farther than the bow of the tug. We steamed through that pitch-black afternoon for about four hours with all lights burning and the whistle blowing. We could tell by the echo when we were close to land, and it began coming back to us clear and sharp from starboard. I was in the pilot house with the captain and he said, 'That's the bluffs just south of Hewitt. In five minutes the echo will give out where they end at the harbor entrance.' We both looked at the pilot house clock, and in five minutes, when he pulled the whistle cord, there wasn't any real echo, just as he'd said there wouldn't."

"He must have been a smart captain!" Ginger said.

"He was a smart young man, and by then he was feeling set up about his navigation. He held his course for maybe a minute longer, then turned in towards the land. We still couldn't see anything, and he had just rung for half speed when the propeller hit something, and we drove hard aground——"

"Were you shipwrecked, Uncle Charlie?"

"We were shipwrecked," he said. "We'd gone aground on a falling tide, and because the propeller had already hit something, the captain just had to lie there until the next tide floated him off. But I was on the right side of Puget Sound, and I knew it couldn't be far to Hewitt. So we lowered the small boat and the captain rowed ashore with me."

"Where were you, Uncle Charlie?"

"I don't think it had a name then," he said; "we were a few miles from where we had thought we were, at the mouth of a little valley; that was why there hadn't been much echo. The captain had tried to run the tug into the valley, mistaking it for the harbor. It was pitch black at five in the afternoon, and the smoke dimmed the light of my lantern. But it was a low shore, with grass and some second growth trees. I noticed two shining eyes about level with my shoulder. I went up to them and found they were the eyes of a buck deer, and he didn't run until I was almost close enough to touch him. There were smaller animals, too—coons or wildcats; I could just see their eyes shining around me in the dark."

Violet asked, "Weren't you scared among all those wild animals?"

"No. And they weren't scared of me. They knew it was a kind of truce. They were worried about what was happening to their timber, and I was worrying about mine. We didn't know it, but help was on the way. I got out of the valley onto the country road, and while I was walking in to Hewitt, the rain started. I was soaked through when I got there, and I've never been as glad to be wet. That rain saved my timber—and a lot of other people's."

Violet was loyal but unenlightened, and while the others relaxed at the familiar ending of the story, she waited expectantly. Then she asked, "But what about Home Place? You were going to tell about how you discovered it."

"I did, Violet," Charlie said, "only I didn't make myself very clear. That was where I landed from the tug—the place where I saw the animals. I couldn't see much of it that day, but I got a nice feeling about it, and when I went back later I liked it still better. I thought then that I'd like to build there. But that didn't happen until years later, when my first wife wanted a place near town, but in the country, where we could raise our boys."

"But you didn't stay there long," Frances reminded him.

"No," Charlie said, "things interfered and we moved to Seattle. We never enjoyed it as much as I had hoped; discovering it was the best part."

"Did you discover any other places?" Ginger asked.

"No, that was the only place I ever discovered." Then he smiled, "But I did make one other discovery."

"A real discovery?" Ginger asked.

"Yes, an important one."

"Tell us about it!"

He said, "That morning I went ashore from a tug, too, but things were different. . . ." Again he had to go back a little. "Most of the timber Father acquired was in Thunderbird County on the second bench, but there were a few odds and ends he'd picked up as a speculation. One half-section was near Illihee, at the head of the Sound. I don't know if he ever saw the property, but when I took over, it didn't amount to much. The adjoining sections had been logged about the time Father acquired this one, and the loggers had used long-handled axes——"

Frances said, "I thought all axes had long handles."

"These were especially long," Charlie explained, "the kind that reached over into other people's property. The good timber in our half-section had been taken out; there wasn't much left but small stuff and second growth. I should have got rid of it for what it would bring; but I've never liked to sell property, so I paid taxes on it and grumbled, without knowing it was the best investment I'd ever make.

"Not so many years ago I decided to take a look at the half-section near Illihee. It didn't look bad; the timber had grown some and I thought of bringing in a couple of 'cats' and logging it off, but other things came up and I let it ride. The next summer I went back—" He paused doubtfully, looking toward the other end of the table.

Ginger said, "What happened?"

"I discovered your Aunt Marian," Charlie said, "but I don't know if she wants me to tell about that."

"You don't mind, do you, Aunt Marian?"

They all glanced in her direction, and Bailey sympathized with her flustered look.

Mrs. Darling said gallantly, "I suppose most of us would be reticent about having our romances told."

Bailey said, "I know I would be."

From the other side of the table, Bertha looked at him wickedly with her crockery-blue eyes. "Even about one or two of them, Bailey?"

The tension was broken and Marian said, "It seems rather personal, Charlie. But I don't really mind, if you'll make it brief."

Charlie cleared his throat and said, "That's about all, anyway, girls. I went up to Illihee to look over that half-section, and I discovered your Aunt Marian."

"Where did you discover her?" Ginger wanted to know.

"In the pasture of a stump ranch," Charlie said. "I discovered her, and I brought her home to prove it."

While the children satisfied themselves that Marian was really there, Bailey looked resolutely across the table, first at the superior Bertha, who had scored on him, and then at his brother. Paul was looking directly ahead and down, with a faint scowl on his flushed face. The brief account of the romance seemed to embarrass him as much as it did his young stepmother.

II

S*INCE THE* middle Sixties, the axe and saw had felled the trees, and the saw had bucked them into logs. And since the Nineties, locomotives and flatcars had taken the logs to tidewater. Big-time logging depended on the intermediate step, and it had been born of improved methods of getting the logs out of the woods and onto the flatcars. One of the methods was the giant skidder, which picked up the logs from where they were bucked and loaded them at a spur track.

Paul and Bailey sat for a while on a comfortable stump, watching the big machine and its crew. Personalized, the skidder was a two-fisted giant who reached out into the woods a quarter of a mile or more with one arm, and grabbed a handful of logs which he brought in and set down in front of himself. With the other hand he picked up the logs one at a time, like counting them, and stacked them in neat pyramids on the flatcars. Just now, with logs of average size, the giant brought in six logs to the handful, or "turn," and put a layer of three on a flatcar, then a layer of two, and added the sixth for the peak log. He then nudged the loaded car ahead on the spur track and brought the next empty into place for loading.

The mechanism by which the giant skidder reached out for logs had three main fixed parts: a hundred-and-eighty-foot spar tree near the end of the skidder, a smaller tail spar tree a quarter of a mile away in the woods, and a taut two-inch cable, or "sky line," stretched between the two. The main moving part was a one-ton steel carriage which ran back and forth on the sky line. Attached to the carriage were the outhaul cable, which pulled the carriage out along the sky line in its reach for logs; the hooked rigging, representing the giant hand which picked up the logs, and the skidding line, which brought the carriage and logs back to the giant. The cables which operated the carriage and its rigging led through blocks on the spar tree to revolving drums on the machine, and they were controlled by the skidding lever man.

To assist the giant in picking up the logs, there were six "choker men" who noosed short cables around the logs which were to be brought in, and a "hook tender" and "second hook tender" who hooked the ends of the short cables or "chokers" to the two hooks on the carriage rigging. The hook tender then yelled to the "whistle punk," who squeezed the handles of an electric "Tootse" which tooted the whistle of the skidder. At the signal, the skidding lever man moved a lever and opened a throttle; the big machine shook with a rattling roar; the six logs came to startled, separate life, swung towards each other, bumped, and became one homing pack, with their heads up and their tails tearing the earth, knocking down small trees, walloping over logs that had not heard the call, and finally swinging through the air with the awkward joy of wooden tons that had never dreamed of flying.

The turn of logs came rushing in, with blocks and cables whining and slapping, and the skidder trembling with its staccato thunder. The machine calmed as the lever man dropped the logs at the landing. While they were still falling and rolling, the chaser was ducking among them to loosen the chokers.

The arm and hand with which the giant loaded the logs were represented by a platform-shaped boom which swung on the base of the spar tree, and a cable with a pair of giant tongs.

These were operated by the loading lever man, who swung the boom out over the landing, and lowered the tongs. The head loader guided the tongs to the log which he had chosen and flipped them over the center of it. As the lever man hoisted away, the tongs bit in through the thick bark, the log lifted in the air, and the swinging boom carried it over to the flatcar and added it smoothly to the load. The second loader shook the tongs loose from the log, and as they were free, the boom and tongs swung out over the landing for the next log. On the flatcar, the third loader stamped identifying marks on the ends of the logs with a branding hammer. When the car had its load, it was moved ahead on a cable and an empty "spotted" into place under the boom.

In his mind, Bailey could see where every one was and what he was doing. Actually, most of the crew were out of sight in the distance of brush and tree rubbish and snags. There was also smoke and steam from the skidder, and a great deal of noise. In actuality, he saw much less, but saw it more dramatically.

As the carriage went whining away on the sky line, with its dangling rigging and freed chokers, the head loader flipped the tongs over the first log of the turn at the landing.

Bailey looked at his watch and said, "Thirteen and a half minutes since they started loading the last turn."

"That's hitting her up," Paul said.

Above the rattling roar of the machine Bailey said, "They should average better than thirty cars today—a quarter of a million feet."

Paul said, "That's a lot of work for twenty-two men." He seemed unimpressed by production, or he was thinking of something else.

"Twenty-two men, and a skidder," Bailey elaborated; "the unmoral machine that can rape five acres of virgin timber in a day."

"I suppose it depends on how the machine is used."

Bailey said, "In the last two days you must have had a good look at the joys of logging."

"Everything from the survey gang to the boom men," his brother said.

"Have you decided to get into the game?"

"I'm still thinking about it." Then he said, "There's Father."

Their father was standing with the head loader and head rigger, watching the loading operation. He was a big man, but he, too, was dwarfed by the skidder and the enormous spar tree. When they went over to him, he was his proper size again. He had big shoulders and he looked tough for a man of sixty, and his business suit did not seem out of place there; it looked just battered enough to have been tried and stood the test. He was evidently criticizing the third riggers, saying to the head rigger, "They've been farting around too long with that tail spar." When the brothers came up to him, he said: "I was looking for you boys. I'm going down to headquarters on the speeder; I'll go home from there. Want to come with me?"

The brothers looked at each other, and Paul said, "There's a picture or two I want to get in the morning."

"I'll stay, too," Bailey said. They were going sailing together the next day, and it would be more sociable than going back to his boat alone.

"All right," the father said. "You know what the chow and the beds are like."

"They're all right," Paul said.

When their father had gone, they watched the skidder for a while longer. The next turn of logs came rushing in, with the skidder shaking and roaring; blocks and cables whining and threshing on the spar tree overhead. The turn came in fast, with the head loader just reaching for the tongs. He swung them and flipped them into the last log of the previous turn as the skidding lever man set down the next, in an awkward, thundering heap, with one log lying crosswise near the end of the others. Before the logs had settled, the stocky little chaser was ducking in to loosen the chokers, and the load lever man was picking up the last log of the previous turn. As he took it up fast, it swung off balance, and the lean head loader ducked back. At the same instant the crosswise log on the next turn came to life as the skidding line slacked, and lunged off the end of the heap, at the chaser. He danced out of the way, colliding with the head loader, and for an instant they were stopped, back to back, with the end of one log swinging through the air just above their ducking heads, and the end of the other log grazing the toes of the chaser's calked boots.

It was nothing: an awkward moment at the landing; two margins of safety, both of them too narrow, colliding and reaching the vanishing point. In another moment the quick-footed chaser was in among the logs, loosening the chokers, and the head loader was in his usual place, scowling at the log in the tongs as it was lowered to make the peak of the completed load on the flatcar. Work went on, and lives went on; the sun felt good, and the air was good with the wild, sweet smell of drying fir branches and the bitter sweet of crushed bark. And a childish group of young fir trees that had escaped the devastation of logging looked wild and lovely, blowing in the wind.

It was nothing, Bailey told himself; no one hurt, and a few seconds had been saved by snatching the log from under the nose of the incoming turn. The little chaser would eat at the mess hall and go to the bunk house as usual, and the red-haired, lean-faced head loader would go home as usual to the cabin at headquarters camp, where his plump wife and two little red-headed boys would be working in the garden while they waited for him to come home to supper. That was probably why he took chances to keep up the pace and hold his job.

It had been almost nothing. But what it could have been was one of the reasons why Bailey had never gone into logging with his father.

The brothers did not discuss the awkward moment at the time, although it had stirred Paul to an angry one-word comment: "Highball!"

At Camp Two, where the brothers spent the night, they had a bunk house to themselves. It was a cabin with four single beds and a wood stove. Inside, it was like being at a rough cabin camp, and the similarity was even greater outside, with a row of identical cabins on each side of the short street, and a stack of firewood beside each door. The main differences were the big mess hall with its attached cook shack, and the steel rails which ran along the street and disappeared into the woods. There were also the runners under the cabins, which could be hoisted on board flatcars when camp was moved.

Night life at camp was limited, and sociability was largely saved for the week end, when the loggers went to town. Bailey had brought a bottle of whiskey, and earlier he had had the idea of visiting some of the skidder crew; but he had thought better of that, and only shared his whiskey with the bull cook, who had brought them firewood, and the bed maker, who brought blankets and sheets and made up two of the beds for them. "A drunken bed maker," he thought, "isn't likely to meet with a more serious accident than falling into a bed."

But the bed maker was too deferential to the brothers, whom

he looked on as big shots; he accepted only two drinks and went out, wishing them "Good nights" that were altogether too cheery and respectful. Around nine-thirty they heard a logger in the next cabin playing softly on a harmonica, but that stopped in a little while. Except for themselves, Camp Two, with its one short street, was asleep in the bosom of the woods.

At their elevation the air had a mountain quality, and the fine smell of evergreens came into the cabin; but Bailey could not enjoy it thoroughly. He was lonely and gregarious by nature, and not having done a day's work in the woods, he was not ready for a logger's sleep. He did not know about his younger brother, who was stretched out on his narrow bed, long and easy and tough-looking, with his feet crossed and the soles of his borrowed calked boots showing their vicious steel fangs. At the other end of him, his arms were crossed under his head, and his fair, grave young face was looking up at the ceiling, self-contained and without boredom.

Bailey said, "Well, Paul, thought of anything exciting to do?"

"Nothing definite," Paul said. "I was playing with the idea of setting up my camera somewhere and taking a long time exposure of the stars."

"Up here in the woods?"

Paul said, "The air is clear, and I don't need the whole sky. I'd want the edge of the woods to show in the picture, and if I could find a big tree without too many branches, I'd like to try one looking straight up through the branches at the sky."

It was not Bailey's idea of what the evening should be, floundering through brush and standing in the cold while Paul fiddled about with a foreign camera aimed at still more foreign stars. For most of eight years Bailey had been away at college and in New York, and when he did come home at last, Paul was away at college in California. On the few occasions when they had been home together, he had seen his brother mostly going away somewhere: to Mount Rainier or the Olympics, or the rain forests beyond the Olympics; a brother who was ninety per cent stranger, coming home about his own obscure affairs, and going away again. This was their first evening alone in years, and Paul mustn't slip away among the cold, meaningless stars. It was an evening when they should sit in the cabin and get drunk together, and talk their hearts out. "The stars wouldn't sit still for two hours," Bailey objected; "they'd move and only make a blur."

"They'd move," Paul said, "but they wouldn't blur; they'd make geometric lines of light. If the picture turned out, it'd be a record of a few hours of their orbits."

Bailey said, "Couldn't you let them go till another time? They'll keep, won't they?"

"They'll keep," Paul said, "if there's anything else you'd rather do."

"I'd rather get drunk, and talk."

Paul's voice went uneasy: "I don't drink," he said, "and I'm not much good at talking; but I'll do what I can."

"I didn't mean roaring drunk," Bailey said. "But it's cold outside, and the stars make me feel sad. I want to be warm and a little drunk, and talking to some one who believes that things matter."

Paul said, "We don't know each other very well, for brothers. I don't know whether that gives us more to talk about, or less."

The older brother poured whiskey into a thick white mug from the mess hall, and added a little water from the bucket which the bull cook had brought. Looking at his brother he asked encouragingly, "A drop?"

"No, thank you." Then he changed his mind. "Well, just a drop, with plenty of water."

Bailey poured a few drops in the other mug for him, and added water. Raising his own mug, he said: "To highball logging."

"I won't drink to that," Paul said.

"Neither will I," said Bailey; "but it's something I have to get off my chest. It's stupid of me to keep thinking about that awkward moment at the skidder landing. All the other moments were potentially as bad, because every one was being pushed. And the Old Man was kicking because the third riggers were too slow with the next tail spar."

"I know," Paul said. "Yesterday I asked Father if he didn't think the crew was being pushed."

"What did he say?"

"He said, 'Hell, yes! We're logging now!' " After a minute Paul said, "I can understand a little how he feels. This is the first good year since some time in the Twenties, and he wants to make the most of it. I suppose Martin Darling wants something out of the money he's put into the business, too. Father's being highballed, or thinks he is, and he highballs his crew. That's what I hate about logging. No one has the right to take chances with other people's lives."

Bailey clicked his crockery mug against his brother's. "We can drink to that!" Then he said, "When you gamble with other people's lives, you can't always return them in good condition. They killed a man the week before you came home, and two in May."

Paul said thoughtfully, "They killed too many even in the bad years."

"Sure. In the bad years you highball to keep from going broke, and in the good years you highball to make something; it's highball all the time."

Paul said, "If they all had Father's instinct, there wouldn't be many accidents. But when he's pushing the men, they take chances he wouldn't."

Bailey poured himself more whiskey. "He wouldn't have taken the chance Steve did with Tag."

"I know he wouldn't," Paul said.

The long-ago incident was something of a family skeleton, even though the father was not directly responsible. It had come of a highballing hook tender who signalled the donkey the moment the chokers were hooked on—and left any one who was in the way to look out for himself. On this occasion, a choker setter was caught between a swinging log and a stump, which almost severed one of his legs and crushed him badly otherwise.

When there was an accident, the procedure was to blow a series of five blasts on the donkey whistle, to summon a locomotive to serve as an ambulance. In this case the nearest locomotive was on its way down with a train of logs, and the engineer would have to run the train onto a siding and uncouple the cars before returning to camp. Then there would be the twenty-mile trip to town, while the logs waited on the siding. And they would have nothing to show for it but a dead man in the cab of the locomotive.

In the interest of production, the "side push" had the broken logger moved to the shade of some bushes, where he was left to die. The body would be taken to the morgue on the evening log train, without any loss of time.

Unfortunately, the logger was still alive and cursing at quitting time, and he was still alive when he was finally taken to the hospital. He was a big, radically inclined Swede with the name of Tag Sorenson, and his powerful constitution brought him through without any more apparent damage than the loss of a leg.

Highballing had overreached itself, and Charlie Dow was responsible for leaving a man to die without medical attention. He settled in the hospital, with an agreement to pay Tag's bills, and give him a job for life. The job was caretaker at Home Place, on the Sound, and it amounted to his being watchdog for an empty house. He did little work, but since the family went there only occasionally in summer, it did not matter a great deal; it turned out to be no more expensive than hiring a caretaker.

"No," Bailey said, "the Old Man wouldn't have dragged a logger into the brush to die while he went on working; but when you're pushing your crews all the time, the ones who stick are apt to be the kind who'll go you one better."

Tasting his whiskey and water, Paul asked, "How is Tag getting along?"

"About as usual," Bailey said; "a little drunk and disheveled, like the grounds. He's bought himself a record player for his radio, and it seems to give him a good deal of melancholy pleasure."

Paul said, "I always liked him."

Bailey said, "I go there now and then and bait him about the I.W.W., and he insults me; he rather likes it. Maybe we'll stop there tomorrow."

Paul was thinking of something else and did not answer. The bunk house was getting chilly and Bailey built up the fire until the stove roared sociably. When he was sitting on his bed again, pouring more whiskey into his crockery cup, his brother said quietly, "I'm not going into logging with Father; not now, anyway."

"I used to think about doing it, but I could never convince myself." Bailey drank and went on, "We must be a great disappointment to the Old Man. When we were children he used

to say we were going to be the champion loggers of Thunderbird
County; I turned out to be the proprietor of a boat mooring,
and you an amateur photographer!" After a while he gave a
snort of a laugh: "Anyway, I was once a well-known logger!"

"A logger?"

Bailey nodded. "I had a book shop in Greenwich Village."

"I heard about it," his brother said.

"It was the PAUL BUNYAN; I had the head of a blue ox over
the door and I plugged the books of Jim Stevens and other
western writers."

"What about your being a logger?"

"You should have seen me in my Paul Bunyan days! I wore
a stag shirt and tin pants sagged off at the top of my logging
boots; I let my beard grow and chewed Copenhagen and talked
logger style——"

"You did!"

Paul's voice was so shocked that his brother became self-
conscious. Drinking, he said, "It was Greenwich Village, and I
had to do something crazy; I didn't want to be conspicuous."

"It's all right," Paul decided; "only it seems a queer way to
sell books."

"That was advertising," Bailey said. "I didn't depend upon
it altogether; when I was choosing a book to plug, I would get
the opinion of some reliable critic, then reduce it to simple
logger's terms. That was the fresh western approach to literature."

"It worked?"

"At first," Bailey said; "for a while it was quite the thing.
Then a rival opened a shop near me on Washington Square. He
was a cowboy from Taos, New Mexico; he wore chaps and a
sombrero, and a silk handkerchief knotted at his throat, and he
carried a heavy Mexican saddle wherever he went——"

"Didn't he have a horse?"

"No," Bailey said. "Perhaps he hoped to meet one. He carried the saddle to Village parties and used it for a pillow when he passed out. That's aside from the point, though. He was my immediate rival and he claimed to be able to judge books by the side of the cactus on which the spines grew. That was the fresher western approach to literature, and my following declined."

Paul asked, "You haven't a photograph of yourself in your logger's outfit?"

"I don't know." Bailey thought, and added, "I hope not."

Drinking straight whiskey, Bailey became gloomy. "It sounds funny, doesn't it? It's also a tragedy: the Old Man wanting, and needing, a logger son—and getting a Greenwich Village clown."

"I'm no better," Paul said.

Bailey looked at his brother morosely. "No, you're no more useful than I am, but you're the apple of the Old Man's eye and he'll never feel disappointed in you."

"I don't know why he shouldn't," Paul said; "he has a right to be." He looked thoughtfully at the half-empty bottle. "What do you say to turning in?"

"You turn in when you like," Bailey said. "I'm going to stay up a while longer."

Paul did not seem to hear.

"You turn in," Bailey repeated.

"I thought you wanted to talk."

Bailey looked at him and remembered. "That's right: get drunk and talk. But I'm not drunk yet; it takes a long time in sober company."

"I'm sorry," Paul said.

"Oh, I'll get there," Bailey said; "I'm in no hurry."

Paul said, with sudden directness, "You haven't told me yet what's bothering you."

"Homesick," his brother said.

"You were home this morning," Paul reminded him, "and we'll be at Home Place tomorrow."

Bailey looked at him craftily. "Right now we're in one of Father's many mansions." He drank, and asked, "Weren't you ever homesick?"

"A little," Paul said, "when I was young and away from home for the first time or two."

"That isn't the real thing; that's only a childhood ailment, like chickenpox or whooping cough. Haven't you ever been homesick since you grew up?"

"I don't think so."

Bailey looked at him curiously. "You are cold-blooded."

"I'm not," Paul said earnestly. He searched in his mind and said, "I've never been as far away from home as you."

"It isn't a matter of distance," Bailey said. "You can be terribly homesick for the very place where you are. Hasn't that ever happened to you?"

"I've been in a place I once knew very well, and felt sad, thinking of the past."

"That's the nostalgia of time," Bailey said, "and it's incurable. The childhood nostalgia of distance can often be cured by a ten-cent bus ride; it's in two dimensions, like a map. The other kind is in three dimensions, with a fourth dimension of time." Bailey drank generously from his coffee mug of whiskey. "Where does the bus leave for home in the secure world where Mother is waiting for us with a good dinner, and maybe a good scolding for being late?"

"I hadn't thought of that as homesickness," Paul said, "but I see what you mean. I have been homesick."

"That's one of the incurable forms, but it's a part of growing up," Bailey said. "It's not so bad because it's inevitable. It doesn't bother me often."

"It's bothering you now, isn't it?"

Bailey was beginning to feel his liquor, and the need of justifying himself to his brother; proving that his expensive education had not been entirely wasted. "I've made a study of it: Homesickness is the great American malady!" He drank inclusively. "I'm being homesick for all of us."

His brother said, "I don't see why Americans should be more homesick than any other people."

Bailey said, "Because America has never come home."

"Why not?"

"Because it's impossible," Bailey said. "What else would stop Americans from doing what they wanted? Home is in the past as well as the future, it is scattered over thousands of years of time, and scattered over the face of the earth. Because of our British-Christian-Negro heritage, home is scattered over England and Palestine and Egypt. Egypt because the children of Israel were there in captivity. Each place leaves its sting of homesickness. Indian campfires and Indian shadows lurk at the edge of the land which is our home, and Pharaoh's army hunts along the Red Sea; Negro tom-toms boom in the dark and the River Jordan rolls through our home land. The Jordan is one of our rivers as much as the Mississippi or the Columbia. It is our river because slaves in the South were homesick for the River Jordan, which they had never seen. Now we are the slaves of dreams of our slaves. Because of Negro spirituals which have become a part of us, we see ancient Israel and Egypt through Negro eyes. We see alien countries through the eyes of a people alien to those countries and to us; their imagination becomes a part of our imagination, and we are homesick for lands we never saw." He poured whiskey into his cup and, as an after-thought, added a little water. "Poets have played the same trick on us and made long-ago foreign things a part of us. The corn harvest of Iowa, cotton picking in the South, the maple sap gathering in New England, the apple harvest of Yakima, belong to us, but so does the barley harvest outside Bethlehem. A consumptive English boy did it with a few words about a Moabite girl, dead thousands of years: *'sick for home, she stood in tears amid the alien corn.'* He said those few right words, and the alien corn became ours forever, and yet alien forever, and Ruth's homesickness became part of our homesickness."

Paul stirred and looked at his brother with concern and shy affection. "It's a good kind of homesickness," he said. "It makes history and the world come alive. It's probably the purpose of education to give people that feeling about other peoples and other countries."

"Education is only part of it," Bailey drank and hiccoughed. "Imagination begins at home, if you are going to have any. It was Mother who read to us from the Bible and the English poets."

Paul said, "You used to criticize Mother and say she was one of the good women who helped ruin the Northwest."

Bailey said vigorously, "I'm criticizing her now!" He frowned into his cup, then his face softened. "Dear, didactic Mother! She wanted to make us into civilized Christian gentlemen. We aren't civilized, we aren't Christian, and we aren't gentlemen. We're spiritual aliens whom Father doesn't understand, and who won't work for him. By rights, we should have grown up in the logging game and gone into the business with the Old Man. What stops us? The imagination that Mother gave us. When the Old Man sees a log drop on a man, he thinks, 'Now

I have to get a new loader.' When we see it happen, we think, 'That was my brother, and a man has no right to kill his brother to save two-bits' worth of time.'"

"He hasn't the right!"

Bailey said gloomily, "But at least the Old Man produces something, and gives people jobs; he helps keep the haywire world going. That's more than we can say for ourselves."

"It is."

"Suppose the officials at Olympia called the Old Man in and said, 'What about those sons of yours? You've wrecked thousands of acres of timber and burned up thousands more, and killed dozens of men, to produce them. That's a big investment for the State. What have you got to show for it? Do these young men produce anything, do they run a donkey engine, or a concrete mixer, or play the fiddle?'" Bailey shook his head gloomily. "If I were put on trial as a bad investment, I wouldn't defend myself."

"I don't know what I'd do," Paul said. "I'm glad I'm not going to be put on trial."

"Haven't you ever imagined yourself on trial and thought of the straightforward answers you'd make to prove your innocence?"

"Yes," Paul said deliberately. "But there isn't any reason for it. I haven't done——"

"There you go!" Bailey interrupted, "I ain't done nuthin'. I think every one has a secret desire to be put on trial in a solemn court of law."

Paul looked doubtful. "On trial for what?"

"Oh, murder, or treason. It must always be serious to make it worth while defending yourself, and it must be something you haven't done, so you can defend yourself with straightforward innocence."

"But why should any one want to go to all that trouble for nothing?"

"Conscience, maybe."

"But you said we all imagine ourselves being tried for things we haven't done."

"Yes, but that might be a smokescreen for things we have done. You imagine yourself innocent and righteous, impressing the Court tremendously—but if the charge were something else —something you'd done or contemplated doing—would your replies be so straightforward?"

"I suppose not," Paul said. "No, they wouldn't be."

Bailey started to pour more whiskey into his cup, then set the bottle down with the air of needing his faculties. "I'm going to put you on trial now," he decided.

Paul looked disturbed. "Why should you?"

"For one thing, because you want a trial."

"But I don't; I'd rather turn in and get some sleep."

"You admitted to imagining the event."

"That doesn't mean I want it. More likely, it's something I'm afraid of."

"It's all the same thing," Bailey said. "Are you ready to defend yourself?"

Paul said, "I ought to know what I'm being tried for."

"You're on trial for being a worthless son-of-a-bitch like myself, and a burden on the State."

"But I don't think you're worthless!" Paul said earnestly.

"Thank you," Bailey said judiciously. "Are you ready?"

"Do I have to answer all your questions?"

"You can answer any way you please, but I'll know when you're lying."

III

S*ITTING ON* the edge of his bunk-house bed with alcoholic dignity, Bailey began: "What is your name?"

"Paul Dow."

"What is your age?"

"Twenty-five."

"Your occupation?"

"I have no regular occupation."

"Your irregular occupation?"

"Photographer."

"You take photographs for money?"

"No, but I sometimes sell a photograph, or win a competition."

"Have you any other irregular occupations?"

"Occasionally I work as a logger, or fruit picker, or harvest hand."

"You are a migratory laborer?"

"I have never thought of it that way; I suppose I am."

"Are you a bindle stiff?"

"In a way; I usually have a sleeping bag with me."

"Is there any way in which you are not a bindle stiff?"

"I travel by car."

"Do you often drive at an excessive rate of speed?"

"Hardly ever more than forty miles an hour."

"You are never in a hurry to get somewhere?"

"Hardly ever; I am almost always there."

"Why do you drive at all when you are already at your destination?"

"A destination can be a big place. All country is interesting. When a part of it attracts me particularly, I stop."

"You get out and walk?"

"It may be the end of the road. Then I leave the car somewhere and pack in."

"Is that in search of employment as a migratory laborer?"

"There is no employment in the mountains."

"Tell us, Mr. Dow, have you had training in any special field?"

"At Stanford, I majored in Geology."

"For what purpose?"

"I was interested in rock formations and minerals and meteorites; they are a part of nature, and I wanted to know more about them."

"On your trips to the mountains, have you found deposits of useful minerals?"

"I once found a deposit of tungsten on Mount Olympus."

"That is interesting."

"No more interesting than rock crystal or slate."

"You are a geologist, and you do not distinguish between valuable minerals and rocks?"

"I can tell them apart, but they are equally interesting parts of nature."

"That is your attitude off Mount Olympus as well as on?"

"It is."

"Tell us, Mr. Dow, what would your attitude be if you were to find a rich deposit of gold in the mountains. Nuggets you could pick up by the handful?"

"I should probably be tempted to make a fool of myself."

"In the opinion of the Court, that would not be a bad idea."

"Thank you."

"We shall now go into the matter of your social adjustment. Do you like people?"

"Yes."

"What kind?"

"All kinds of people."

"Men who get drunk?"

"Yes."

"You get drunk with them and make a disgrace of yourself?"

"I do not drink."

"But you like bad company?"

"Men who drink aren't always bad company."

"You prefer the company of drunks?"

"I didn't say that."

"You disapprove of drinking?"

"For myself, yes."

"Why?"

"For one thing, whiskey is bad for the stomach lining."

"You are careful of your own, but you don't care what happens to other people's?"

"I use my judgment, and expect other people to use theirs."

"In other words, you are not your brother's stomach lining's keeper?"

"I have never even seen my brother's stomach lining."

"What about your own?"

"I have never seen it, either."

"But you take good care of it?"

"I don't try to ruin it."

"That is your own affair; but my stomach lining has had more fun than yours."

"Mine does not complain."

"Don't boast. . . . You told the Court that you love all kinds of people. When you were attending Stanford University, in what way did you express your love of humanity?"

"I wasn't aware that I had to do anything special."

"What was your fraternity?"

"I didn't belong to one."

"You didn't get a bid, eh?"

"I got several."

"But not from the one you wanted."

"I didn't want any."

"You thought they would rope you in and then want you to donate lumber for a new frat house?"

"I never had such a thought!"

"What, then?"

"It seemed to me that fraternities were a kind of ready-made aristocracy; I couldn't see any reason for them."

"You wanted to appear outstandingly democratic?"

"I did what I wanted to, and I wasn't interested in how it appeared to other people."

"Mr. Dow, is it not true that you entered Stanford University because Bertha Darling was enrolled there?"

"That is ridiculous! I don't think she decided to go until after she knew I was——"

"Mr. Dow, is it not true that this Bertha Darling entered Stanford University because she doted on you, and you disappointed her cruelly by avoiding her company?"

"I can't answer for why Bertha went to college, and I didn't specially avoid her."

"You admit to encouraging her by accompanying her places?"

"I do not admit to encouraging her, though we were occasionally together."

Bailey hiccoughed and drew himself up with severe dignity. "Will you mention instances?"

"Well, after an eleven o'clock class, I sometimes walked with her as far as the post office."

"Was that accidental, or arranged?"

"We were both going in the same direction."

"From the same class?"

"We had the same eleven o'clock class for one quarter."

"And you timed your exit from the class so you could walk with her?"

"I did not."

"She waylaid you at the door as you were going out?"

"I don't think it was exactly that way."

"Why were you going to the post office?"

"To see if there was any mail for me."

"Was there?"

"Not very often."

"But that did not discourage you from walking there with Bertha?"

"I could always hope to get a letter."

"From whom, for example?"

"Well, from you."

"Did you?"

"Two or three in four years."

"Tell us, Mr. Dow, was there no place where you could have turned off without walking all the way to the post office with Bertha?"

"Yes, there was the Union, and the book store——"

"But you didn't duck into one of those places?"

"Sometimes I did."

"That is most significant. . . . Now, is it not true that another young woman wrote a poem about your golden physique? It had something to do with your throwing the javelin at a track meet, and it compared you favorably with the Greek heroes whom educated young women adore?"

"I don't know."

"Is it not true that you saw the poem which was published in one of the college magazines?"

"Even if I did, that is no proof that it was about me."

"Mr. Dow, you have testified that you love all kinds of people. That includes women, of course?"

"It would have to."

"Will you tell the Court the way in which you show your love for women?"

"I was speaking in a general way when I said that. I wasn't thinking specially of women. I don't do anything about them."

"You are undemonstrative?" Bailey pronounced the word with great care.

"You could call it that."

"Do you admit that you are particularly attractive to women?"

"I don't think so; not specially."

"Haven't you often been told that you could make some woman very happy?"

"I suppose every man has been told that, but very few have done it."

"It's easy; I have made a number of women happy."

"Permanently?"

"There is no permanent happiness."

"I prefer to think so."

"That is generous of you. Now, Mr. Dow, you have a brother. If he attracted a woman, he never ran from her; and if one attracted him, he did his best. How do you account for his being your brother, or you being his?"

"Heredity, I suppose."

Bailey did not seem to hear at first. Then he touched Paul's shoulder, with the air of having made an important discovery. "That's one of the interesting things about brotherhood?"

"What?"

"By having brothers, you get to know the strangest people!"

"You are making fun of me."

"It's heredity, of course. You're a throwback to some ascetic ancestor."

"If it was that way, all right."

"But there's a joker in it."

"What is that?"

"How do you suppose this ascetic became your ancestor?"

"I hadn't thought of that."

"Probably he didn't think either, until it was too late. He was a hypocrite, or she presented it as a religious rite."

"I can see how it might be that."

"You are broad-minded."

"No."

"You are also in danger of women by not knowing them."

"Do you think you know them?"

"I at least try and try, and I am not proud."

"You think I am?"

"I know it. You have the kind of pride that goes before a fall. The first little dilly who trips you up will tie the old logging chain around your neck, and you won't go to the mountains any more."

"You seem very sure of everything."

"No, but I am only a drink or two away from it. Where were we?"

"I was on trial, and then you began talking about women."

Bailey's flushed face was suddenly angry, while he pounded his knee, in place of a table. "You are still on trial, and we are still talking about women. You want to be close to nature; you explain nearly everything that way, even your avoiding women. You should know that the closest you'll ever be to nature is with a woman."

"For you, nature means only one thing."

"For nature, nature means only one thing. You pretend to worship nature when you go to the mountains, but you go there to hide from her."

"Do you mind if I open a window?"

"Open them all, the door too, if you like. The bunk house stinks like an old barroom. I think we'll bring the trial to an end. When the fresh air hits me, I'll probably go out like a star that hasn't been there for a million years." He staggered to his feet, addressing an imaginary jury. "Gentlemen, I hope you won't believe anything the prisoner says in's own defense. Look at him: this one-time baby, this former child, this ex-boy, this— this person who's on's way to being in his dotage—" He hiccoughed, and looked severely at his brother. "What 'n hell have you got to say for yourself?"

"Only that I agree with you and don't want to defend myself. It hadn't even occurred to me that I had to be of any use. I have no ambitions that will ever take me farther than the mountains and woods and harvest fields. I love this state, and I have never wanted to be away from it. I have never— That is all."

Wavering solemnly on his feet, Bailey thought it over with the look of trying to find some offense in the statement. When he could find none, he made a helpless gesture, with a cup in one hand, and the empty whiskey bottle in the other. "What can the state do to some one who loves it? Acquitted, but don't do it again." He flourished the bottle out of the window, and they heard it thud against the next bunk house.

Paul took a deep breath of the fresh air that was clearing the cabin. "I didn't know how I would answer some of your questions until I answered them."

Bailey stumbled uncertainly towards the door. "I'll pump the bilges and then turn in." When he came back he said, "Going to turn in all standing." He sat on the edge of his bed long enough to kick off his shoes, then crawled under the company blankets. "Christ, I'm tired!" He closed his eyes and seemed to be asleep, but after a minute he opened them again and looked at his brother, who was peeling off his clothes. Paul's fair skin was tanned darker than the brown-gold hair of his body, and he was beautifully muscular, undressing with the easy confidence of a crack athlete in a locker room.

"Tanned all over," Bailey said. "You sun bathe, eh?"

"Whenever I can," Paul said.

Bailey said, "That girl knew her stuff, you and the Greeks." When his brother did not answer, he said, "You're a hell of an ascetic, sound and in good health, and beautiful all over; inside, too, with your beautiful stomach lining."

"Shall I turn out the light?"

"Go ahead; throw a shoe at it, break it with a bottle! Aren't you going to put on your pajamas?"

"I don't own any," Paul said, and turned out the light. There was the sound of him crawling into his bed.

Bailey said thickly, "It'll be colder'n hell in the morning."

Paul's clear voice said, "I expect it to be."

"You like to be cold?"

"Why, yes. Don't you?"

"I don't like to be anything I don't like."

"Being warm wouldn't mean anything without it," Paul said. "Things don't mean anything except in relation to something else. Food and warmth and shelter don't mean anything without hunger and cold and exposure."

"You're prob'ly right," Bailey said.

"If you're always well fed and warm and sheltered, you aren't related to anything except your comforts."

Bailey said with an effort, "Unpleasant things make pleasure possible——"

"It's more than pleasure—it's a matter of balance. You can't hoard more than you need without getting diseased; you pile it on, like fat, and it weakens you and makes you ugly. And it deforms other people, too. That's because when one person has too much, there isn't enough for some one else, and that's another kind of disease. People are not specially good or bad; it's only that some of them don't understand how to live and others never have the chance." He paused and was answered by the loud, drunken snoring of his brother.

That was another waste, Paul thought. His brother had tried so hard that he had defeated himself. He had drunk most of a quart of whiskey and talked eloquently and cross-questioned his brother like a criminal lawyer, trying to get better acquainted with him, and trying to find out what was in his heart. Now, when Paul was ready to talk at last and tell his deepest convictions, there was no one to hear him and he was alone, as he had been so much of his life.

From the warmth of his bed he looked out of the square of window at the bright stars above the treetops, and listened to his brother's steady snoring, and he felt more at peace. This night was a beginning, and they would talk again. If they had gone on long enough, he might have explained something to Bailey, something deep and terrifying, like a charge of explosive buried under their quiet lives; but the opportunity had gone away without ever being quite close enough to be real. . . . Bailey, snoring like a pig, and no wonder, after all he had drunk. The difference between the same person, conscious and unconscious: talking like an angel and snoring like a pig.

Maybe Bailey was right that every one has the hidden desire to be put on trial. It was bracing, anyway, and afterward you felt clearer and more confident. How much of it would Bailey remember when he was sober? He said he would know when Paul was lying, but maybe he was too drunk to notice. Paul hadn't told any lies—only evaded a little. But there was one gaping contradiction in his testimony. He had cleared himself by saying that he loved his native-state and had never wanted to be away from it. That was true. But a soberer or less clever man than his brother would have asked why, then, had he chosen to spend four years in California?

IV

IT WAS true, what Charlie had told about discovering Marian in the pasture of a stump ranch on a summer morning. But it was only a moment of the truth, and behind that summer morning there were other times of the day and other seasons of other years. And other truths. And "discovery" is an egotist word. Charlie had not been the first to discover Marian; he had not even been the first to discover her in the pasture of the stump ranch near Illihee.

Her first memory of the stump ranch was one moment of an evening back near the beginning of time. She and her brother, Jerry, were walking towards the house through summer dusk, along a footpath through a mown hayfield. The air was fresh and still, the earth warm under her bare feet, and somewhere her tall father and mother were walking towards her, with her father's arm around her mother's waist. They seemed far away, but only as people can seem far away in a picture that is close enough to touch. As she and her brother walked towards their parents through the dusk, a wave of warm air rolled over them like an invisible breaker, piercingly sweet with the smells of stubble and clover and summer, and reassuring with the sounds of distant bells, the comfortable, clear twittering of birds going to bed, and the voices of her father and mother talking together. She and Jerry walked to meet them—and the memory faded and blended with all summer dusks: the warmth of the earth under her bare feet, and a feeling of well-being in which the

50

children and the man and the woman, summer and the warm earth, were intertwined. That was her first memory of what she thought of afterward as "The Land of the Vine and the Fig Tree."

Most of her early memories were of evenings. It was then that her father was home from the shingle mill in Illihee; his late afternoons and evenings were devoted to the stump ranch, and it was then that things happened. There was one evening when she and Jerry watched their father build a bench in the front yard. It seemed to the children that the bench had been finished hours before; time and again they asked, "Isn't it done now?" and their father answered patiently, "Not yet, children," and went on rounding corners and edges with his drawknife. Finally he said, "It is done." Then he called, "Mother, will you come and sit on the new bench?"

The screen door slammed and their mother came from the house to admire the new bench. She, too, was tall, with black hair and fair skin that sometimes came into faint bloom with color from inside, but was never much changed by the sun, and she had a fine, comfortable bosom and arms that could be very loving.

"It's nice," she said. "A place to sit in summer evenings when our work is done."

"We'll sit on it now," the father said. "I made it big enough for all of us, and maybe a visitor or two."

They all sat on the new bench. Nighthawks fell through the sky with a booming sound; yellow light filled the windows and open doorways of a tugboat that was creeping out of the inlet. At the end of the tow of logs, dark against amber water, a man hung out a lighted lantern, and beyond the forested far shore the Olympic Mountains climbed out of the dusk, blue and pink in the upper air.

The man and the woman and the boy and the girl sat on the new bench in the fine summer evening, and the father said, "No one is luckier than we are. This is our country and our place, in the shadow of our own vine and fig tree." The grape vine was beside the bench, on a trellis of split cedar, with its familiar leaves and tendrils and clusters of round dull green grapes, but Marian could not remember having noticed the fig tree until her father began talking about it. "The fig tree is one of the oldest trees on earth, and it has always been known as peaceful and friendly. It grew in the Garden of Eden and supplied food for the first man and woman. Along with the grapevine, the fig tree has always stood for contentment; it is as pleasant to touch as it is to see, and in its shade man remembers Paradise."

While her father talked, the fig tree seemed to stand out more beautifully in the dusk. It was not a big tree, but its trunk was smooth and straight, holding up its cloud of mysterious leaves. At the ends of the branches and among the leaves, in the green dusk, there were green pear-shaped fruit standing out with gentle stiffness. As her father talked, the tree became more real and precious, like the meaning of all fig trees, and it became the tree that stands for contentment.

The bench had been built only a few yards from the front door, in the heart of the land of the vine and the fig tree, and it seemed easy to find; but Marian could not recall the family's being there more than a dozen times in all the years that followed. With her father working in Illihee and farming in the scraps of days that were left, and her mother working from early morning until long after dark, there was not much time for sitting.

One of the few times when they were all there together, Marian and her mother and Jerry had a picnic supper waiting for their father when he came home for the last time from the shingle mill. Marian and Jerry were there to greet him as he climbed down from the high old Ford. Marian reached for his lunch box, to carry it into the kitchen as she had always done; but this time her father tossed the box recklessly into the grass and picked her up with one arm, to kiss her, while he hugged Jerry with the other. "The heck with the lunch box!" he said. "Your father's a free man." He gave each of the children a hand and they marched to the place where the mother was fixing the last things for the picnic. She was fine and smiling, with a spoon in one hand and a pot cover in the other. Before being kissed, she brushed a lock of black hair away from her forehead with her arm and said, "Welcome, home, Father!" He held her in his arms and said, "We're beginning to live, now!"

Jerry was about ten at the time, and strong and clever. He had spent hours going back and forth to the beach, bringing up flattened, sea-worn stones and fixing a place for a fire. He made it round, like the bed for a clam bake, and, with a fire in the middle, there were flat, smooth stones all round where things could be set to keep hot.

While they ate and talked and planned, smoke from their fire glided up in a fragile blue column, into the bright, misty autumn sunshine. On the right there was the Island Belle grapevine, with its heavy purple clusters hanging under gold leaves; and on the left there was the fig tree, with its slender, gently proud trunk holding up its cloud of mysterious-shaped leaves. Under the leaves were yellow-green figs of the second crop.

The talk was mostly about the change that had come to the family, and plans for the future. The father said, "When the mill failed, it was just as if fate had given me a nudge and reminded me that I couldn't wait forever to do what I was going to do. That nudge woke me up! I knew that I couldn't go on being half a farmer and half something else."

The mother said, "When you work for some one else, it's like living on rented land, where anything you build belongs to some one else. Even while you were a foreman you were never paid what you were worth. Of course, we'll have to economize and we won't have as much ready money; but what you build will belong to us, and we're going to build the finest farm in the county."

The way the mother spoke of economizing and working made an adventure of it, and they all seemed richer instead of poorer. The father bought another cow and a team of gray horses, and he did his own fall ploughing with his own team. During the summer he had slashed two acres, and after the ploughing they all cleared land, and Marian and Jerry discovered the night. They had always gone to bed early, but now they often stayed up until ten o'clock, dragging brush and carrying chunks of wood to the fires. The clearing at night was another world. Fire-colored smoke rose, and sparks went up like gold snakes that shot out of sight into holes in the night sky. Around the fires the earth was not the earth; it was the floor of an enormous room, littered with bark and rotten wood and charcoal from old fires. Beyond the edge of the firelight it was still like a great room, shadowy or in darkness, with the floor littered with things which were being cleared up because they did not belong there.

When it was very late they went home; sometimes all of them, and sometimes Marian and Jerry, while their father and mother stayed in the clearing a little longer. Once or twice, going home across the field to the still, dark house, the children stopped on the path to look back. Log and stump fires blazed and glowed in the darkness; sometimes their father's tall, shadowy figure threw a chunk onto one of the fires and a great burst of sparks went up like new-made stars. The children said, "The volcanoes are going good tonight." That was because Jerry had once seen a picture of blazing volcanoes, and the clearing fires reminded him of it. He promised to show Marian the picture. She could not remember that he ever did, but when she was grown up she could still see the picture in her mind: out of darkness over the earth, ranks of firelit cones spouting smoke and flame and storms of sparks in the passion of creation. Clearing the land was the story of creation over again, and in the memory of it there was a solemn satisfaction which linked one with the busy night before the dawn of the world.

Their father and mother had foretold that there would be less money, and the need to economize—and those things came true. When they bought things at Shaeffer's store in Illihee, or farther away in Olympia, the storekeeper said, "The price is so and so," and it was. But when they took what they raised to the store or cannery, they asked, "What will you pay for these things?" And the price might be half a cent a pound for string beans or cabbages, or maybe a cent a pound for blackberries. Sometimes, if they had the right thing at the right time, the price might be better and they would come out a little ahead on the crop. Again, there might be no sale for it at all.

From the years of economizing, Marian recalled that her summer underwear had been made from flour sacks. Once, when she was about eleven, there was a pair of panties with a printed rosette and ribbons and the legend, "First Prize Flour," large and legible on the seat. Her mother laughed about it and her father gave her an affectionate spank and said, "Quite right; your bottom would take first prize anywhere!"

One of the few things they could always sell were eggs, which represented money, and they had to be used sparingly. That economy only increased Jerry's passion for fried eggs, and his mother put it to use. When there was some chore to be done outside of Jerry's usual work, he would always undertake it for the bribe of an extra egg, which he fried and ate in a sandwich as soon as he collected. The egg was always the largest he could find, and breaking it into the pan was an important moment. If it turned out to have two yolks, his gray eyes would light up in triumph as he announced, "A double-yolker, Ma!"

Once in the kitchen Marian saw the triumphant look as he was about to fry an egg for which he had bargained. She noticed that the egg was already cracked, and he broke it silently into the pan. Then he produced a second egg from the concealment of his hand. Breaking it smartly on the iron rim and spilling it into the pan, he announced, "A double-yolker, Ma!"

Marian gasped, then clapped her hand over her mouth; the second egg *was* a double-yolker, and the three naked yolks looked as conspicuous as golden hills.

Nothing might have happened except for the gasp of surprise which the girl stifled too late. The mother turned from the sink to look shrewdly at her children, then into the frying pan, and back to Jerry's chagrined face. "You cheat!" she cried. "You sneaking cheat!"

Jerry already had the opinion that women are not wholly responsible for the things they say, and he looked just pained enough. "Aw, don't carry on so, Ma," he said. "I knew you kind of liked it when I got a double-yolker, and I thought I'd cook one up. Anyway, I was hungry."

But his mother continued to carry on. "It's not the egg," she said, "it's the principle of the thing."

"The principle of an egg," Jerry said.

"The principle of cheating because I'm too busy to notice what you're up to, and laughing at me behind my back!"

"I wasn't laughing," Jerry said. "Ask Marian if I was."

Marian listened unhappily while Jerry finished frying the eggs and made them into a clumsy sandwich between two large slices of bread.

"That's all you think of," the mother said, "stuffing yourself!"

Eating large bites while he leaned comfortably in the doorway, Jerry said, "When I was cleaning out the wood shed, all I thought of was doing a good job. If it made me hungry, can I help it?" He could have saved a good deal of fuss by eating his sandwich outside, but he enjoyed arguments almost as much as eggs, and while he ate he went on defending himself and making his mother madder.

"I like eggs as well as you do," she cried, "but I don't eat any because they're something we can sell! I'm ashamed to admit that I don't even eat decently, but you might as well know, while you're making a pig of yourself!"

Marian thought her mother was exaggerating, but she saw Jerry wince as the shower of harmless words changed to words that stung. Scowling, he took one more small bite, then stopped. "Oh, hell!" He threw his half-eaten sandwich on the table and tramped away.

The mother went on scolding after he was out of sight. "Fourteen years old and he can't even clean up after himself!" She swept the remains of the sandwich into the garbage, and the plate clattered into the sink. "If I had done what I should, I would have taken it away from him before he had a bite!" She went on for a long time. Then, unexpectedly, she sat down at the table, with her face buried in her arms. "What kind of a mother am I," she sobbed, "making him miserable about an egg and driving him out of the house? That wasn't me; it was what's left of me when I'm worried and worn out. I only want us to get ahead so you and Jerry can have the things you should. Even when I'm mean about small things, it's because I want you to have the big things of life."

In the years of growing up, the girl sometimes recalled the moment from early childhood: she and Jerry walking across a field in the dusk, and a wave of warm air rolling over them, rich with warm sounds and scents, like a wave from the shore of all summers. She was in the same place, and sometimes she walked across the same field in the dusk, but the scene had changed with the new acres they had cleared; the path had been obliterated by the plough, and the field of childhood was a far-off, half-remembered land. She could never quite bring back that feeling of well-being in which the children and the man and the woman, summer and the earth, were intertwined. Even while they had been in that embrace, the parents had had different dreams of the meaning of life, their bodies had had different degrees of endurance, and in time those differences tore their world apart.

A fragment of a Saturday in February stayed on in the girl's mind like a fragment of stopped time. She was at the sink, drying dishes that were pleasantly warm through the towel. Her mother was at the kichen table, cutting floured dough into blocks that looked like snow on fence posts, and tucking them into bread pans. The kitchen had had its Saturday scrubbing and it was full of the clean smells of flour and yeast and fir wood that crackled in the fire-box of the range. Another time the kitchen might have seemed too hot, but it was made luxurious by a squall of sleet dashing against the south window. Jerry was working in the barn, while his father hauled manure to the west field. Seeing him there added to the coziness of the kitchen. Carrying a plate in the flour-sack dish towel, she went to the window and looked out again. Through scattering sleet she saw the wagon stopped on the hill, the wet gray horses with their rumps turned towards the wind, and her tall father standing in the wagon, against a background of second-growth fir forest, scattering forkfuls of dark manure to the earth. While she watched, the falling sleet changed to great flakes of snow that blurred the man and the wagon and horses, and painted out the dark manure almost as fast as it was scattered on the ground. The squall passed and went away over the hill, and the man and wagon and horses moved after the retreating snow, and the man took up his fork again and scattered fertility to the earth.

Marian said, "I don't believe Father minds the sleet at all; he seems like part of the weather."

Her mother turned to the window with a bread pan in her hand and looked at the wagon and horses halted on the hill, and the man scattering manure. "Your father can throw it around," she said coarsely. "He's good at that; he could always shovel it out and throw it around; but he's a failure; nothing ever comes of his plans." When she had gone back to her bread-making, she amended bitterly, "When I've killed myself with work, your father'll get a young woman for nothing. He can throw it around, and he'll take in some one else, the way he took me in."

Afterward the mother took back what she had said that blustering February afternoon. She explained to Marian that she had only talked that way because she was too tired to know what she was saying. She had the best husband in the county, and the hardest worker, and he was not to blame for farm prices that made so much work and scrimping for so little. Still later the mother repeated all the bitter things she had said, and they had grown more bitter with being held back for a while.

Marian did not believe her father was a failure, but she was unhappy on her own account. It hadn't mattered at the district school, where every one was poor, but now she was attending high school. In Illihee the logging people and storekeepers were the aristocrats, and even Mr. Barton, who greased cars at the round-house, had more money than a farmer. From the first day of high school Marian had been conscious of her shabby clothes.

Jerry was tolerant of the farm, but not of his mother's nagging. Near the end of his last year in high school he talked it over with his sister. "We have a pretty good start here," he said. "Maybe we could make something of it, but it's like working in a nest of yellow jackets all the time; you don't get any fun out of it that way." He left when he was eighteen and never came back to work on the farm.

After Jerry was gone there were changes. Marian had never cared much about farm work, but it seemed natural that she would have to do more of it, and she accepted it because that was the way things were. The first test came one day that summer, after an almost silent dinner. Her father pushed his plate and chair in opposite directions and got up. "Well, Marian," he said, "it's time the potatoes had their last going over. When you're through here and it cools off a little, you can get yourself a hoe and give me a hand, if you like."

"All right," she said; "maybe in an hour. And I'll bring something cold to drink."

The father was silent in the house, but the girl knew that in the field he would loosen up and begin to talk. If he decided the sun needed a little time to cool off, they might go to the stream in the pasture and look for the trout he and the children had once turned loose there, or they might go to the beach and sit in the shade of the bank under the vine maple trees. There, watching the moving tide, it was easy for the fullness of summer to overflow into dreams. If there was the right perfection in the day they might talk of building the Little Ship. Years before they had planned to build a little ship with white sails and launch her from their own shore. It would be big enough for all of them to live in comfortably, and they would spend the whole summer sailing and drifting on Puget Sound, anchoring at evening in some green cove or in the shelter of an island. When they found a place to their liking they would stay as long as they pleased, exploring and fishing and swimming. . . .

The children had always taken part in planning the little ship and her voyages. The time when their dream might have blossomed into reality had come and passed in hard work and disappointments. There were changes in the crew, too: the slender, enthusiastic father dulled a little by the heaviness of the earth; the affectionate mother bitter from overwork and disappointments; Marian full of troubled questions, beginning to lose faith in dreams. Jerry would not be there at all, except perhaps as a white seagull flying after the ship. Things happened to people, and they changed or were gone. Only the little ship they planned remained unchanged, immortal. It was planned for four happy people, and it would always be for them. . . .

That afternoon, when the dishes were done, she put on a straw hat and canvas gloves and went to the woodshed where the hoes hung on the wall. She took one down and went out of the gloom of the shed into the bright sunshine.

Her mother was waiting on the side porch. "Marian."

"Yes, Mother?"

"Sit down; I want to talk to you."

Marian sat on the edge of the low porch, idly taking off the cotton work gloves and wondering what had happened.

"Look at your hands."

She looked at her hands, rounded palms that tapered to long fingers, and saw nothing unusual about them. They were lightly touched with work and tan and berry stains, with pink showing through; they did not have the expensive, hot-house look of the hands of movie actresses, but they looked young and companionable; good enough, but not too good for life. "They look all right to me."

"Look at mine." The mother held out her hands, palms up, like an open book. They were long, generally triangular hands, but big-knuckled and cross-hatched with deep lines that looked as if acid had been poured into them, and where the inside edges of the palms were smooth they looked old and polished, as if part of them had been worn away. It was the first time the girl had noticed how bad her mother's hands looked, maybe because they were always in motion. She took one of the ruined hands in hers. "Less work," she prescribed, "and more gloves and hand lotion."

Her mother answered with faint pressure, then withdrew her hand and put it beside the other. "There is my face, too; and my heart and my soul. Hand lotion won't help them."

"I'll help you more," the girl said penitently. "I know I'm not always very good——"

"You do more than you should, Marian. I'm not complaining for myself. I tried one kind of life and it didn't work. You're all I have left." She took her daughter's hand and held it fiercely. "Mother used to say everybody should have two lives, one for practice and the other for the real thing. I've had the practice, and I have you. You're all that matters, and I'll be satisfied if you have a good life."

The girl had never thought of the possibility of having any other kind, but her mother gave significance and excitement to what she had been taking for granted. With sober mockery she asked, "What should I do to have a good life?"

"For one thing," her mother said, "you're not going to marry a stump rancher."

Marian had already decided on that. "I don't intend to."

"You aren't going to marry a poor man of any kind."

The girl had rather hoped she wouldn't, but she did not like having it made so definite. "I don't expect to marry any one," she said; "but suppose I loved a poor man?"

"If you thought you loved some one with an incurable disease, would you marry him?"

"Do you think being poor is like that?"

"I know it is."

The girl felt something like a physical jolt, bumping against her mother's iron conviction. "Suppose I had to choose between a poor man I loved and a rich one I didn't love?"

"You would marry the rich one."

"That would be immoral."

"It wouldn't be as immoral as marrying the poor man you loved."

Marian was bewildered by her mother's reasoning. "How do you mean? That doesn't make sense."

Her mother said, "Being immoral is doing wrong. Which do you suppose is worse: killing your love for some one and his love for you—spoiling something fine and making both of you miserable—or starting with some one you didn't love and having something nice come out of it?"

"You think money is everything."

"I know it is."

"It isn't health, or love, or happiness——"

The mother interrupted. "You can't have any of those things long without it." Her voice became more passionate with conviction. "Marian, you must listen to what I am saying. I've made enough mistakes for two of us. I'm telling you the facts of life, and I expect you to be smart enough to remember them. The one to remember first and last and all the time is that the world is a store, like Fredericks or the Bon in Seattle, only bigger, and everything is for sale. That's the size of it. If you're young or strong or good-looking, it's like having a little credit; but if you don't pay up, you don't get anything more."

Marian said doubtfully, "I can't believe everything is for sale."

"The best and most expensive things often have no price tags on them, but you'd be a fool to think you could get them for nothing."

"That's disgusting!" the girl said. "It's a disgusting world!"

Her mother said quietly, "Do you think you can change it into the kind of world you want?"

Marian suddenly felt old and defeated, shaking her head. "I don't see what I can do."

"If you can't make the world over to suit yourself, you'll take it the way it is," her mother said grimly. "You'll run with the hounds instead of the hares, and you'll remember that only a fool thinks he can afford to be poor."

The girl wanted their talk to end, but there were still loose ends in her mother's reasoning and she was curious. "According to you," she said, "there isn't anything I can do about it; if I'm poor, I'm poor, and I always will be."

"If there wasn't anything you could do, I wouldn't talk about it. You know how a man will be while he's still a boy. He starts with nothing and ends with nothing, or he kills himself getting ahead and it doesn't do him any good. With a woman, you can't be sure until the day she marries. She can change everything along with her name. You're nice-looking and not too gay, and you have sense. You can have the kind of life you want, if you want it enough."

"It can't be as easy as all that!"

Her mother said, "It's been done on a borrowed shoestring— but you must want a thing enough to know how to use the shoestring. Other people may think you're being reckless or crazy—until you've done what you set out to do. There was a case like that in this county in the early days."

"What was that?"

"A young woman was left a widow with three small children," her mother began. "They were destitute, and in those days there wasn't any poor farm, or anything like that. It was up to the county commissioners, and they voted a hundred dollars cash to relieve the distressed family. The neighborhood expected that she would rent a little cottage, buy enough beans to last a year, and outing flannel to make warm clothes for herself and her children. Instead, she went to Olympia and spent the hundred dollars on herself in one day. She bought the most expensive silk dress she could find, and she paid ten dollars for a hat at a time when other women were wearing sunbonnets. She came back looking like a queen, and the neighborhood was wild; the women talked about tarring and feathering her, and the commissioners slunk around, trying to keep out of sight. The scandal lasted a week; then the young widow married a wealthy stock farmer from Chehalis County and went on having fine clothes for the rest of her life. She hadn't been sensible with the hundred dollars, but she had been wise, and she made it go a thousand times farther than if she had spent it on beans and outing flannel."

Marian had heard the story before, but she could never quite get to the bottom of it, because it was so much more than its few common ingredients. "She was a smart woman, all right, but it wouldn't work nowadays."

The mother said, "You have to see behind what she did. She got into the kind of company she wanted to keep by making herself that kind of person. Nowadays, it would take more than a silk dress and expensive hat, but the idea is the same. You're going to train yourself for the kind of company you want to keep."

"I don't quite see how, Mother."

"I can see part of it," her mother said, "and we'll work out the rest. To start with, you'll never get anywhere in a potato patch; you're through with that from this day."

"But I promised to help Father with the hoeing——"

"I've done it before, and I'm still a good hand at it." The woman rose from the edge of the porch and took up the hoe. "There are a lot more important things. You've been neglecting your piano practice, and that won't do. If the house is too warm right now, you can go to the beach, or take a book out under a tree. One way to make yourself nice is to feel nice and at ease."

Sometimes Marian thought her mother was a little crazy, and she was amused and ashamed by turns at the decision to groom her for a life of ease. She fought against the idea, knowing that her mother was already overworked, but she took kindly to comforts and luxuriated in sleep. Sometimes she worked harder than ever to make up for her comforts, and she found work less of an effort because ease was at her disposal. Now there was never any question about time for parties or visiting, or time to look after herself and her clothes. The mother, who had no time to think of her own appearance, gave shrewd professional advice. "Any one," she said, "can wear clothes and powder and rouge. But if those things hide blemishes, you're paying blackmail to them and you're always anxious and afraid of being found out. You can only be confident when they hide something finer than themselves. One way or another, some of you is bound to show through, and what you are depends on whether it makes more or less of you."

By the mother's theory, clothes were always secondary to health and mental ease and physical perfection; but in practice she could not take her daughter's clothes casually. Once Marian woke at night and heard the sewing machine running. In the still house, it sounded as tireless as the mill of the gods. Above its whirring rumble she could hear the somber crowing of roosters; when she looked out the sky was paling with morning, and between its dark shores the inlet gleamed dully in the first invisible rays of light. She crept down the dark stairs and opened the living room door. There sat her mother at the machine, muffled in an old winter coat, and glassy-eyed, finishing a dress that Marian was to wear at a town dance next evening.

The girl put her mother to bed, then sat by the window thinking contrite thoughts until it was time to make breakfast. Her mother had said that unless clothes hid something finer than themselves you paid blackmail to them and were afraid of being found out. Behind her new organdie dress there was the ghost of a haggard woman in a moth-eaten coat, with roosters crowing outside and a wide gray streak of dawn in the sky. She took no pleasure in thinking of the dress, and decided it was spoiled for her. The feeling lasted all day, but at the dance she forgot about it and was a great success.

In the comfort of that summer, Marian found contradictions of life which she did not try to explain. One of them was that by different paths and at different times her conflicting parents sometimes led her to the same place. Sometimes her mother would say, "Why don't you take your book or sewing out to the old bench in the front yard? It's shady there, and not many country estates have a finer view." To the mother's practical mind the bench between the grape vine and the fig tree was just a sitting place for the one member of the family who had time to use it. But it gave the girl the feeling of having lived a long time, and of coming back to the ruins of an earlier civilization. She used the bench for its intended purpose, but something was missing—the spirit in which it was built.

But the tree was still the meaning of all fig trees, with its gently proud trunk holding up its cloud of mysterious leaves and green fruit that stood out expectantly with gentle stiffness. Once, with an obscure feeling of guilt and excitement, the girl picked one of the mysterious-shaped leaves and hid it between the pages of "Lord Jim," which she had been reading. That night, when she was about to do her exercises, she took the fig leaf and held it in front of herself, and considered the effect in the full-length mirror which her mother had found in a secondhand store in Olympia. In soft lamplight and the dusk of shadows, her vivid face and supple smooth body looked like the meaning of all young faces and young bodies. Marian decided definitely that she was beautiful, and she was pleased. Later, when she could not sleep, her mood changed and she was depressed, wondering if it had been the beauty of a flying moment in which she was virginal and touched by sin that was still only in her mind.

At the close of her last year in high school, Marian got ten votes out of thirty for the best-dressed senior, and she was voted the one most likely to succeed. She also got two proposals of marriage that were quite unexpected, because her mother had ruled out anything that suggested going steady with a boy. Both boys were the sons of poor stump ranchers, without means of supporting wives, and probably their declarations were as much of a surprise to themselves as to the girl. When Marian fell in love a few weeks later, economics and her mother's calculations had nothing to do with it.

V

THAT JULY morning brought back the childhood feeling of being a part of summer and the earth. Even when breakfast was over, the crackling fire in the kitchen range was grateful, but the sun was bursting gloriously through fog and dew. The chill of that hour was like the intoxicating luxury of being naked and penniless, with the promise of untold wealth. While Marian was making her bed, the open window let in the smells of salt water and stubble fields and mist and apple leaves. Beyond the east field and the pasture, there swelled the alder woods, with three dead cedars stabbing out of the rich green mass. One of the bleached trees was a snag, but the others tapered to spear points, with their few high stripped branches curved back and down, like barbs. There was nothing special that Marian could name about the dead trees rising from the alders, but they affected her strangely. As far back as she could remember, when she glimpsed them right, it was like a whispered story of something magnificent that was happening, though she could never quite make out the words. . . .

That morning something was happening. The alder woods were on the far side of a cove made by the stream that flowed through the pasture, and a strange vessel was looming out of the mist as it burned away in the cove. It was a large black tug, with white upper works and a buff-colored smokestack, lying at anchor where nothing larger than a launch had stopped within the girl's memory. Tugs passed daily, going to and from

the booming ground at Illihee. But when one stopped mysteriously in the farm cove, it immediately became larger and more
important than an ocean liner passing at a distance. While the
girl wondered, she saw a four-oared boat with three extra passengers, rowing smartly towards the land. There was just a
glimpse of the boat and the men and the regular-dipping oars,
and then they disappeared under the brushy pasture shore, like
explorers reaching a new continent. Marian knew just what they
would find—a cow pasture between a farm and logged-off land
that had gone back to second-growth; but that did not affect the
romance of their rowing ashore in the morning to a strange
coast. In a little while the rowboat returned to the tug, without
its passengers. Soon after that, two men appeared in the pasture,
walking uphill along the dim track of the skidroad. In the girl's
mind, that too became a romantic circumstance. The skidroad
was the ghost of a trail through the pasture, crossed by rotting
skids that sometimes caved in when you stepped on them. Fifty
years before, when the skids were new and well greased, ox
teams had dragged the best of the timber over that road, to be
dumped in the booming ground in the cove. Now, it seemed,
the strangers were turning time back, re-exploring the cove and
the road over which the first wealth of the country had been
hauled away.

Marian watched the strangers out of sight, the big man with
the purposeful walk, and the slenderer, deferential one. They
disappeared where the ghost of a road vanished into the dark
second growth firs at the upper end of the pasture. From there
on, the woods were so dark and the track so overgrown that you
could imagine buried treasure and old clues, undisturbed for
half a century.

When the expedition disappeared inland, the girl reached a
sudden decision to go exploring on her own account. To the men

from the tug, the strange shore was adventure, but for one who had grown up on that shore, adventure was the strange craft anchored in the cove. In a way, that made romance a matter of ignorance, but it did not make it less romantic.

In the east field the sun was already drying up the dew from the stubble and clover, but in the pasture it was like an earlier hour of the morning. The delicious chill clung to the earth along the half-obliterated skidroad, and in the lee of stumps and bushes thick dew glimmered like frost on grass and stones and spider webs. And through the luxury of chill and damp, in the smell of the morning, there was the faint scent of burning evergreen woods, and the glory of the rising summer sun; the power and the glory.

Swinging down the skidroad, the girl breathed deeply and repeated to herself, "What a morning!" Then she sang to herself and the pasture, *"My Lord, what a morning!"* She sang, and stopped abruptly, remembering that three passengers had come ashore from the strange tug, and only two had reappeared in the upper pasture.

The third was crouching in the hollow between the skidroad and the stream, kneeling over some dark instrument set close to the ground. He was only a few rods away, a figure of soiled buff and faded blue, with his face averted, but he had not heard her or did not want to be disturbed in his calculations.

Marian waited in a quandary. She did not want to speak to the unsociable stranger, and neither did she want to go away rebuffed by some one who had less right to be there than herself. She waited a minute, then the stranger turned his bleached yellow head and looked towards her; he spoke with belligerent shyness: "Good morning."

"Good morning," Marian answered. "It's a fine morning, isn't it?"

"It's a beautiful morning." When he stood up, painfully, the girl's first impression was of a crippled young man, but he improved by the moment, standing first on one foot and then on the other, shaking his free leg to bring back the circulation. Probably he had been crouching over the instrument for some time, too absorbed in what he was doing to notice the cramping of his back and legs.

Marian looked down at the black instrument, and asked, "What are you doing?"

"Trying to get a picture," he said grudgingly.

It had been stupid of her not to recognize a camera, but she had never seen one used that way before, with its shortened tripod legs sprawled ridiculously and its chin almost level with the ground. "May I look?" she asked.

"There isn't much to see." Then he said, "All right."

She stepped down into the little valley and stood beside him. "I'm Marian Clark," she said; "we live over there." She nodded towards the farm.

"How do you do?" The boy was still shy. In a few seconds, like an afterthought, he said, "I'm Paul Dow." He might have been eighteen or nineteen, and Marian thought he was the most attractive boy she had ever seen. He was taller than her father, who was nearly six feet, and in spite of his shyness, he was easy and active-looking; not like an athlete who wants people to look at him, but as you might imagine an Indian who makes himself a part of nature, from whom he gets his strength. His tan skin made her think of a blond Indian; his thick hair was bleached to straw color on the outside, with darker hair showing through, and his deepset blue eyes and thin face had a youthful sternness which she did not understand. There was also something Indian-like in Paul's few clothes. His faded shirt, open half way down his brown-gold chest, gave no hint of underwear, and his tanned, sockless ankles showed between his faded corduroy trousers and old, expensive, rubber-soled oxfords. Altogether, there was a look of his not having committed himself to anything when he put on a few clothes for convenience. His appearance stirred the girl to strange thoughts and feelings, and his grudging conversation left her puzzled. But at least she knew he was taking a photograph, though she could not imagine of what, with his complicated camera telescoped to the earth among dew and grass and spider webs.

"What is the picture of?" she asked.

The boy pointed at the shimmering ground just in front of his camera. "What you see there," he said. "That spider web, with blades of grass for a background."

She knelt beside the camera. The dew-covered web was the irregular kind, spun over a branched twig on the ground, with the ends of the twig holding up the sagging fabric in points. Her hand could have covered the whole structure without disturbing the dew on it, and it was not much to look at until her eyes became used to it. Then she said, "Why, it's like a tent; a little circus tent with the ends of tent poles showing through!"

"That's what I want it to be like; a circus or carnival." He studied an exposure meter and knelt to make some delicate adjustment. He was close to the girl, but she knew that he was kneeling beside the camera exclusively.

"It's lovely," she said. "I didn't know you could photograph anything so fine."

"I'm using a microscope lense," he said. "If it comes out the way I want it to, it'll show up as big as a circus tent in a landscape. The dew on those blades of grass can be lights, or balloons."

Marian was enchanted. "Part of a little world!"

"A bug and spider landscape," he agreed.

"A perfect little world."

The camera clicked, and he said, "It wouldn't be so perfect for an insect that bumped into the tent."

She had forgotten the purpose of the web. "It's queer to think about: a lovely little landscape in the morning, and the center of it is a trap."

"For the insect, yes; for the spider, it's a living."

"Do you think the insect would have any suspicion of the web?"

"I don't think so. It would either get into it, or blunder by without knowing the danger."

"That's horrid," Marian said. "It's worse to think about than being eaten—not knowing and being so helpless." The boy went on fussing with the camera without answering, and she laughed apologetically: "That's foolish of me; I can't think of two different kinds of insects without taking sides."

He glanced at her, absent-mindedly, or sternly. "You don't like spiders?"

"It isn't that," she said. "It depends. We had a spider I nearly liked. He was yellow and black, with a body as big as a marble. He had a web outside our porch window, and he caught flies by the dozen and wrapped them up in little packages. He wasn't afraid of anything. When a big hornet flew into his web, he wrapped it up as if it had been a fly. He was brave and useful—and then one of our neighbors came along and held a lighted match under him."

Paul made a sympathetic sound, and the camera clicked again. "It would be better if people could learn about all the insects before killing any of them."

"Are there any you'd kill?" she asked.

"A few; mostly parasites, and flies that come into the house with dirty feet."

"You say things so nicely."

The boy frowned and looked ill at ease. "I wasn't trying to."

She knew that was so; since she had first intruded on him, he hadn't done or said anything intended to attract her or encourage her to stay. It wasn't flattering, but he was being honest with her, and honesty lasted longer and kept faith with life. "Am I bothering you?" she asked.

"No," he answered, fussing with the camera, "no, you're not bothering me." After a minute or two he looked at her as if something more were expected of him. "This is your land, isn't it?"

"It's ours."

With unexpected formality, he said, "You're my hostess, in a way."

She warmed to the suggestion, then felt a hollow doubt, not being sure how it was meant. "I'm not trying to trade on it," she blurted. "If I'm bothering you, say so, and I'll go away."

He looked startled and helpless. "Why? You don't have to go."

"A hostess should know when to leave her guests alone. You were taking pictures, and I came along and talked and bothered you."

"No," he said. "I came in here without asking permission, and I was rude to you, although I didn't have any right to be here."

"Father says that beauty belongs to whoever has the eyes to see it, even if it is on another's property."

Paul thought it over, scowling down at his camera. "It's true, in a way." Then he said, "Your father must be nice."

"Oh, he is!" Out of loyalty to her mother, she added, "He isn't very practical, though."

The boy made no comment, but he looked so troubled that the girl wished she hadn't said it. Maybe he wasn't practical, either. It came to her, vaguely, that he was something like her father; that was why she was so drawn to him. Paul began packing up his camera. "I suppose we could talk," he suggested.

If he had said that in the first place, the girl would have waited patiently for hours. "Don't you want to take more pictures?"

"Not now," he said. "The dew is almost gone. I've got seven exposures, though I won't know if any of them are good until I've developed the film."

"You develop your own?"

"Of course," he said. "Roll them, too. I buy my film in bulk."

She looked at him admiringly. "You must know a lot about photography!"

"There's nothing to that part of it. I make my own high-speed film, too. I put the film in a jar with a drop of mercury. Sometimes the film streaks, though, and I haven't found out what does it."

"I'm sure you will find out," she said.

They were walking along the skidroad like old friends, in the glory of the summer morning. Now it was nine-tenths triumphant warmth and light, made perfect by one last part of evaporating chilliness, the smell of salt water, and the blue incense of distant burning woods. To Marian it seemed like a morning at the beginning of the world. She had the happy, buoyant feeling that the old world had burned away with the mist, leaving her and the tall boy striding through a new world, with golden light on their faces. The feeling was so strong that she asked, easily, "What would you do if you found every one else in the world—everything—gone?"

He walked more slowly, looking down at her sternly, but

with interest, as if he had already thought of the possibility. "Why, I'd make the best of it and get me food and warmth and shelter."

"Just how would you go about it? How long would it take?"

"Not long," he said. "I'd have them all by the end of the first day."

"Really?"

"Really," he said with quiet assurance.

"You are clever!" Marian never doubted his abilities, but she had a lively interest in hearing how he would manage. "What about food, for instance?"

"Old mother nature always has something in the cupboard; it depends upon the season. Just now it would be clams and blackberries, and camas on the prairie." From the way he spoke, he might have been fifty years old, and he was so young and serious and beautiful to look at that the girl loved him, quietly and deeply and almost without excitement. It did not disturb anything, only made everything as it should be, and it did not even interrupt conversation. "What about shelter?" she asked. "How would you manage?"

He answered, "For the first night, anyway, I'd thatch a lean-to of fir boughs. If the weather was cold, it would have sides, but either way it would be open in front. I'd have a small fire just outside, and the roof, coming down to the ground, would reflect the heat like a Dutch oven. You have no idea how much warmth you get that way from a small fire."

"But how would you make a fire without matches?"

"Bow-drill."

"What would you use for a bowstring?"

"One of my shoelaces, if I had shoes."

"What if you didn't have shoes?"

"I don't know; I'd think of something." But he walked a

dozen slow steps beside her without having a thought of anything.

"You could braid a lock of my hair," she suggested, pleased that the fact of her long hair suited the hypothetical adventure.

"Braided hair would make a good cord. It would solve the problem, all right."

"It's a good thing I didn't have it cut," she said. What they were talking was not what they were saying. They were talking about an adventure that could never happen, and almost invisibly blazing the possibility of one that might. She had offered to go with him, and he had accepted her company at least on the imaginary journey. This side of both, there was the third and real journey of the present in which they were together. It consisted of walking along the skidroad towards the salt water in the summer morning. Not that it mattered in which direction they walked, or whether they walked at all, having already arrived. She did not know how much of her feeling he shared; some of it, probably, because he slowed his steps to hers, naturally, and asked, "Were we going anywhere in particular?"

"We were going to talk," she reminded him, "and we're already here."

They sat on a broad stump beside the trail and exchanged information. Between them, across the stump, there was a narrow boundary where the wood had neither been chopped nor sawed, but had torn apart as the tree fell, leaving a row of upstanding splinters, like a little picket fence. On Marian's side there were the weather-darkened scales of fir cones gnawed by squirrels; near her dangling feet were the coarse, rounded leaves of salal, with strings of berries turning from red to purple-black; down the hill beyond the end of the pasture, the smokestack and mast of the strange tug lifted above the bank into the morning sun. "Did you come on the tug?" she asked.

"Yes," he answered. "Father had business here, and I came along."

"Your father's captain of the tug?"

"She's ours," he said. "She's Father's. He's a logger, and he sometimes uses one of his tugs for a business trip."

"It must be fun travelling that way; like having your own yacht."

"Better," he said. "I always have more fun on work boats. On yachting trips, people seem to think they have to have a good time if it kills them, and they have to have it right away. As likely as not, they drink too much and make a mess of themselves and don't have any fun at all. At least I don't see how they can call it fun. On a work boat, you have things to do that mean something. It's all natural, and when fun comes along it's something you've earned."

"That must be the nicest way to travel."

"It is," he agreed. "If we'd come by car, it would have been just highway and gas stations and a dirt road leading to the bay. On the tug, it was like coming in to a strange coast. We came in and anchored here last night. There was just the still water and the dark shore and one lighted window on the land."

"My window," she said. "I'm the night owl of the family." Inside she thought, I was probably doing my exercises, keeping healthy and beautiful for some one I'd never seen and feeling discouraged—and all the time the boat was anchored off our shore, and he was looking towards my window. . . .

"It seemed like a friendly shore," Paul said. "While I was on deck, one puff of land breeze came out to me. It was so warm and solid that at first I didn't know what was happening; it was like a warm wave I couldn't see because of the dark, and it had the smell of the sun on hayfields——"

Marian felt tears come to her eyes, remembering a footpath

through the field in long-ago summer dusk; a wave of warm air rolling over her like an invisible breaker from the shore of all summers; the warmth of the earth under her bare feet, and a feeling of well-being in which the children and the man and the woman, summer and the earth, were intertwined.

On the stump beside her, Paul said, "I've been talking a lot. Am I boring you?"

She shook her head. "That's the first thing I remember—a wave of warm air like that coming across a field at dusk."

"Where was that?" he asked.

"Here," she said. "I've always lived here." She might have said it was the same field, but even though that was true, it seemed remote and improbable.

"Do you go to school here?"

"I went to high school in Illihee. I graduated last June. I'm going to the University in the fall."

"We live near the arboretum," he said. "That belongs to the University."

"I know," Marian said. "Father went to the University. He remembers when the campus was in the woods and they were clearing land for the Exposition."

"That was before my time," Paul said gravely.

"Do you go to the University?" she asked.

He shook his bleached head. "I graduated from Lincoln last year, but I don't know if I'm going to college." As if it might be of some help, he added, "My brother, Bailey, goes to Yale."

"That must be grand!"

"I don't know," he said doubtfully. "It's a long way from Puget Sound."

"But it's a great college," she said, "like Harvard."

He was leaning forward, absently prodding the bark of the stump with the tripod. "Bailey says it's better; I suppose it's a matter of opinion." Then he recalled, "Mother put up quite a battle for me to go to Yale."

"Doesn't she care now?"

"She's dead," Paul explained; "she died in April."

"I'm sorry," Marian said.

He was looking down at the tripod, or at his bare, tanned ankles. "Mother was a woman of character," he told her solemnly. "I miss her a good deal."

Marian said, "I'm sorry, Paul." She was sorry, with a quick warm sympathy, and without thought of personal advantage she was aware of a door open to some emptiness in him. If she knew how, she could fill the empty place before the door closed. She couldn't be his mother, but it would help if she knew what kind of woman his mother had been. At least, she had argued with him about Yale. "Don't you plan to go to college at all?" Marian asked gently.

"I don't know," Paul answered.

The talk of college had come about because she had hoped to find him at the University in the fall. Now everything had changed, and for the moment she was grown up, playing the part of his mother and trying to be disinterested and wise. "If you don't know whether you want to go to college," she decided, "I think you should wait until you do."

His voice brightened. "That's the way I feel."

"There must be things you want to do," she said.

"There are; enough for a lifetime."

"Travel?" she suggested, enviously.

"Travel, for one thing, but not far. It wouldn't have to be any farther than from the Pacific to the Cascades." He gave her a troubled look. "I don't know if you understand what I mean. I want to know this part of the world where I live; not the cities; I don't care anything about them; I want to live in the mountains and woods and prairies, and on the rocky little islands at the edge of the coast. I want to study all the trees and plants and birds and animals—everything that lives and grows; the mountain ranges and streams, too, and the storms and weather." He scowled down at his bare ankles. "I don't know if it makes sense. I never tried to tell any one before. I don't know why I'm trying to tell you."

She thought, because I love you. Out loud she said, "It does make sense, Paul."

He went on as if he had not heard, or did not believe her, "There isn't even a name for what I want to do."

"Does it matter?" she asked.

He looked at her sharply. "It doesn't as far as I'm concerned, but it's not so easy when you have a father and relatives who expect you to go into the logging game. They at least expect you to make money."

"In time, maybe you'll make a lot of money out of your photographs," she said. "Then there won't be anything to worry about."

Paul looked gravely doubtful. "I don't think you make money out of anything unless that's what you're after."

The girl, who had been trying to cheer him, began to feel his gloom. "I don't see why every one has to make money," she lamented. "People don't really need so much."

"Food and warmth and shelter; that's about all."

She remembered what he had said earlier. "You said you could get those things in one day—and most people work all their lives without getting anything more."

Paul said, "Even the ones who have too much to start with. They get mixed up between what they need and what they think they need, and they never get out of the tangle."

It was almost hot in the sun, and the girl was getting tired of words and theories. "You said you could find food and warmth and shelter in a day, starting with nothing. You don't have to think about warmth or shelter today, but what about food? If you don't have to go anywhere, why not see what we can do about lunch, starting with nothing?" He did not answer at once, and she added hastily, "Of course, you'll be very welcome to come home with me for lunch."

Paul's alarm was visible. "Thank you, I wouldn't want to bother your parents." Then he asked, "Don't you have to be home for lunch?"

"Not specially. I started with the idea of walking into town, and Mother doesn't expect me."

He frowned in thought and said, "It's what I would have done, anyway, if I got hungry. We'll see what we can find."

Her heart pranced to be off on the adventure, but her voice had a ladylike qualm. "Of course, it's hours until lunch, and I'm not hungry."

Paul did not think much of that. "There are no servants and no refrigerator," he said. "If we have anything substantial, it'll have to be baked clams; and the tide is coming in."

The simple decision about lunch had sunk the modern world, and nature's clock had taken charge. Marian slid off the stump with a feeling of urgency. "The tide isn't going to beat us."

"Do you know where there's a good clam beach?" Paul asked.

"Just around the point," Marian told him.

Paul was already working on the details of their adventure. "Am I allowed to use my knife?"

"There's no harm in using what we have," she said.

"It wouldn't be much of a trick to manage without—but it will save time."

"And we need to save time," she said. "We don't even have twenty-four hours to found a civilization."

Near the lower end of the pasture, Paul left the skidroad to tear a strip of bark from a dead cedar and separate the inner layer, which came away in dry brown ribbons. "Tinder," he explained, stuffing the fibers into his hip pocket. Farther on, when they had climbed the rail fence, he paused again to whack off a slender shoot of hazel, which he trimmed and notched as they went single-file along the cool, damp trail. "Bow for a bow drill," he said briefly, like an Indian.

"It makes good bows for shooting, too," Marian said. "Jerry always used hazel."

"Who's Jerry?"

"My brother; he was killed two years ago."

"I'm sorry," he said. "How did it happen?"

"He was a brakeman on a logging train; he slipped and fell under the wheels." She saw him wince as he walked on ahead of her.

"I'm sorry," Paul said, walking more slowly. "It's a dangerous business. You have to be so careful, and even then—" After a few more steps, he asked, "Was it around here?"

"Illihee," she told him, "in front of the high school. I was there while they were getting him out from under the train."

Paul muttered sympathetically as he walked on.

The girl hadn't intended to talk about Jerry, but it had happened naturally, on the familiar trail. Only a few summers before, Jerry had stalked along the trail ahead of her with a bow and arrow, and still later with a twenty-two. Sometimes in the fall, after school, they squished through the bare woods to the fishing shack. If they got there at the right time, they saw the men of the Winters tribe rowing out into the gray tide, with folds of beach sein falling smoothly from the stern of the boat and leaving a dotted line of corks that followed the boat back to the beach. Jerry would help haul in the net that suddenly churned with life crowded into shallow water. After the salmon had been tossed into the boat and the enemy dogfish killed, there were fish left—porgies and bass and salmon trout. Jerry would lug home as many as they could use. The first time, he staggered under half a gunnysack full and would not let Marian help. When she protested that it was too heavy for him, he said, puffing, "Food is never too heavy when you're carrying it home to the family." That was Jerry, the boy. When he graduated from high school and became a man and a brakeman, he was salty with logging jargon and mysterious with his own important affairs. After the first pay day he showed his sister a roll of worn bills. "Five dollars a day," he said. "The farm doesn't bring that much in a week. And I'm not spending any of it on dames." Then he said, "You'll be through high school in two years. When you're going to the University, I can help you now and then."

Jerry showed her the roll of bills in the spring, and his life was over in the fall.

That noon, she and some of the other girls were watching the football team practice kicking and passing. The fullback was Karl Weber, a big, square-built fellow who walked four miles to high school from a lonely lake back in the hills where his family farmed. Most of the boys were at the north end of the gravelly playing field, and Karl was at the south end, booting the ball to them. A logging train was passing a block away, and you could not hear the thud of Karl's big work shoe against the ball, but it went up and up, spinning in the sunshine of the blue sky as if it would never come down. Maybe it never did. While it was still up there, spinning, auto horns on the next street blared, the heavy galloping of the logging train changed to a grinding shriek and bucking crashes, and then the locomotive whistle was wailing doom, and the boys were racing off the playing field and across the unpaved street. Some of the girls went. Marian hesitated; then she, too, was running.

Deserted autos were standing in the street, and people were still hurrying towards the flatcars pyramided with logs that were thick with snow, like the big guns of winter come to terrorize a valley that was too fearfully bright with sunshine. Marian was only one of the crowd that was being swept together beside the third car from the last. Then Mr. Swenson, the tailor, barred her way gently. "Your brother's hurt," he said. "Yust you wait, and be brave."

When she brushed past him with a cry, and broke through the arc of lookers-on, her terror went away. Beside the log-stacked flatcar, it was like the clear calm at the center of a storm. Members of the crew were working like silent giants. The only sounds were the steady clank of logging-jacks, the deep outrush of air from the mouths of men who were breathing like swimmers, and now and then an undertone word of direction or agreement. The only one talking was Jerry, looking young and calm and unhurt, with his head bare and his heavy stag shirt open at the throat, and just a slight cut high on his forehead. Jerry was propped up on one elbow, close to the wheels of the flatcar, smoking a cigarette and talking pleasantly to the laboring train crew. "Don't kill yourselves," he was saying; "there's plenty of time; I'm not going anywhere tonight. Don't try to do it all by yourself, Larson." It was nearly a minute before he noticed his sister kneeling beside him in the dust and weeds. "You here, Marian?" he said. "You should be in school, shouldn't you?" Then he said, "Don't cry, sister. I'll be laid up for a while, but I'm all right." He took her hand the way he used to when they were children going home across the dark field, away from the volcanic fires of land clearing. "It was just a bad break. We were passing the school and I saw a football go up over the treetops; a beautiful kick! Made me think of last year when I was on the team. I turned my head for just a second, to watch the ball, and I lost my balance. I'd have been all right except for the snow on the logs—there wasn't anything I could get my caulks into."

"Don't think about it now," Marian said, holding his head in her lap. "It could have been so much worse." But it was bad enough. One of the brutal iron wheels had stopped on his legs just below the knees, and they had to jack up the car, with its tremendous weight of logs, before he could be freed. "Does it hurt very much?" she asked.

"It's funny," he said, lighting another cigarette, "it doesn't hurt at all." Then he frowned ruefully. "I'm worried about my car. I still have three instalments to pay."

Pain came afterward, and Jerry died of shock late that afternoon.

Walking ahead of her through the woods, Paul said, "When a person has lost some one, there are things you want to say, but you can't find the words. At Mother's funeral, everything the minister said sounded so empty. I kept saying to myself, 'These things haven't been very well thought out,' and that was as far as I got."

Marian agreed soberly, "They haven't been very well thought out."

The memory of Jerry faded from the familiar trail, and they did not refer to him again.

From its little clearing of thin dry grass, the fishing shack faced the beach and the incoming tide, with the still dark woods so close to its back that fir cones had fallen on the mossy roof. The rough, vertical boards of the walls were dry and silvery in the sun, like a deserted bird's nest. On one side, near a pile of driftwood, the sein boat was propped up with one gunwale against a stump, and its seams open in the sun. On the other side, there was a big Juneberry tree, with two robins feeding on its blue berries. It was a sweet, lonely place, with only the boy and girl in the morning sunshine, the smell of deep woods and salt water in their nostrils, the feeling of light dry grass under their feet, and the pair of birds in the magic tree. They forgot their hurry for a minute, exploring the little clearing. Marian would have liked the minute to last forever, but she did not know the right words.

Even Paul sounded regretful when he said, "The tide isn't getting any lower, and we have to find something to dig with."

They got pieces of board from the pile of driftwood, and Paul kicked off his old oxfords and rolled up his cords. "Better let me do the digging; you aren't dressed for it."

"I soon will be." She sat on the low bank to take off her shoes and stockings, then stood to tuck up her dress. "Now," she said triumphantly, "if we have to wade, I can go deeper than you without getting wet."

The boy looked at her perfect legs, blushed, and was stern again. "We'd better get going," he said. On the beach his embarrassment went away. They dug like children, racing the tide and scrambling for clams in the sides of their diggings, that filled with water and crumbled as they worked. The girl's hair was coming down, she had a blister in the palm of one hand, and her legs were warm with the beginning of sunburn; but discomforts could not touch her happiness, and she forgot them altogether when Paul said, approvingly, "You'd make a good squaw." At the moment, that seemed the noblest estate of womanhood.

Later she did more squaw work, gathering flat stones while Paul made the parts of the bow drill. He sat companionably near to where she was building the bed for the clam bake, and at the end of each trip she paused to see how he was making out. Every time she came back, with her long thick hair over her shoulders, she carried a round, smooth stone in each hand—one for him and one for herself. When they were added to the hearth by the sea, they were no longer his and hers, but theirs. . . .

What would Mother think if she saw me now? Mother, Mother, I am older and wiser than you! All your hardboiled wisdom comes from twenty years of disappointments. I remember back to the Stone Age by the sea, at the dawn of time. I remember what you have forgotten, or never knew: that the only good of life is a man and a woman doing things for each other and sharing all they have and all they are and all that happens.

She put the familiar-feeling stones in place, digging them into the sand to make them lie evenly, and filling the crevices with pebbles. When she had finished, and brought dry wood for the fire and pieces of cedar shake for kindling, she settled herself on the bank beside the boy. Perhaps her face reflected her feelings of ancient time and tenderness; he responded with a lovely look and said, "We got through at the same time. The bow drill's about ready for a trial."

She said indulgently, "If it takes too long, you can use a match; we decided there was no harm in using what we have."

"But we haven't any matches," he said. "I don't smoke, and I don't usually carry matches unless I'm spending the night in the open."

"I'm glad we haven't any," she said. "I'm glad this is the real thing!"

He reached for one of his shoes and began taking out the lacing. "It won't take much longer than lighting a match."

That was not entirely accurate, and there were mechanical

difficulties. The shoelace was old, and it broke while he was stringing the bow. "We'll hope the other one is stronger." He reached for the remaining shoe.

"It won't be," Marian said, "not if they're the same age. I've noticed that shoelaces are like old couples who've lived together for a long time. They look strong and healthy, but if something happens to one of them, the other is likely to go in no time."

Paul looked gravely amused as he untied the broken pieces and put them in his shoe. "So much for the old man." He took up the other one, "We'll see how the old woman makes out."

The girl laughed, "You're heartless!"

"No. I'm giving them a chance to die on the same day."

"They did!" Marian said as the second lacing snapped while he was looping it around the drill.

"I'll have to think of something else," he said.

Thoughtfully, the girl combed her long silky hair with her fingers and separated a strand from where it would show least. She hesitated a few moments, then picked up the open knife and sawed off the strand close to her head. The boy, who had been considering ways and means, did not even notice. She gave him the severed ends: "Hold this while I braid it."

"Your hair!" Paul's voice was shocked. "You shouldn't have done that!"

"I have plenty more," she told him, dividing the long strand into three. "Is this enough?"

"Plenty," he said, "only you'll have to braid it tighter."

She stopped and changed ends with him. "You braid while I hold it. You know better what we want."

"You shouldn't have done it," he said again, braiding the shining strands into a tight cord. "It's such nice hair; it's the color of copper."

Probably he hadn't even noticed her banner of hair, but when she cut some of it off and put it in his hands, he saw it was nice.

"You are very observant," she said.

"You are laughing at me."

She met the stern gaze of his blue eyes and laughed again. "I am laughing because I am having fun; and you certainly know how to flatter a girl."

He looked doubtful, intently braiding. "I didn't think so. How?"

"Oh, by admiring her hair."

"You *are* laughing at me."

"A little," she said, "but only because I like you. If it bothers you, I won't do it any more."

"It doesn't bother me." He finished the braid, and said, "I don't know much about girls."

"How is that?"

"Never had time for them," he said, stringing the bow with her bright hair. "And—girls bother me."

"Do I bother you?"

"No, you're all right."

In some clear part of her mind she knew that it would be a great gain if he were to tell her and himself just how girls bothered him, but she was in a glow from being told she was all right, and they were ready to try out the bow drill.

"It works this way." Paul twisted a loop of the bow-string around a straight shaft of wood, and set one end of the shaft in a socket carved in a piece of board and packed with cedar-bark tinder. He put a smaller piece of wood over the other end of the shaft and pressed down on it while he sawed back and forth with the bow. He sawed away until his bleached hair hung down over his sweating face, and Marian felt sorry for him. "Can't I do it for a while, Paul?"

Struggling with the fire-making apparatus, he panted, "Can't stop; I'd lose the friction. Be ready to blow when it starts smoking."

There was barely a foot of room between the ground and the bow, but the girl lay flat on her stomach, with her face close to the rotating drill, and waited tensely. As she watched, the slender drill seemed to grow until it was as big as a ship's mast, spinning on the parched deck of the board. An occasional drop of sweat splashed down from the boy's forehead, and nothing else happened for a long time. Then a miraculous curl of whitish smoke rose from the tinder about the drill.

"Blow!"

She was already blowing, while the drill whirled and the wisp of smoke thickened. Suddenly the fire-making apparatus disappeared from her worm's-eye view as Paul threw the bow and drill aside and caught up the board. "Got it!" he called triumphantly.

The girl was disappointed at first because there was only smoke, but Paul was assured and confident, breathing life into the smoldering tinder.

When the driftwood fire was snapping and blazing on the bed of stones, Paul was as pleased as God creating the world in one day instead of seven. Shaking the damp hair off his forehead and looking up at the sun, he said, "Now we have food and fire, and it isn't noon yet. You can see it's not much of a trick to make a fire without matches."

"It was exciting," Marian said; "but I wouldn't want to do it three times a day."

He saw no reason for that. "With a little looking after, this fire we've started would burn forever."

She said, "I want it to."

After their race with the tide and their race for fire, the world became leisurely again. They went to the spring, inside the border of the woods, and lay on their stomachs to drink. The girl had one glimpse of her happy young face and disheveled hair in the dark water, and then as its mouth came towards hers the image went away, as if it knew the kiss was for the boy who was drinking next to her.

From the spring they followed the trail to another old skid-road. It, too, had become a narrow trail, with branches almost meeting above the rotten skids that were overgrown with moss and Jacob's ladder ferns. As always, the woods were very still, and there were no birds. Paul stopped to examine some big, yellow-spotted mushrooms, and Marian knelt beside him. The mushrooms were funnel-shaped, stiff and fleshy, with milky drops where they had been nibbled by squirrels.

Marian said, "I thought toadstools were poisonous for animals, too."

"Rodents can eat things we can't," Paul said gravely. "But these aren't what you think of as toadstools." He broke off a piece and tasted it. "Peppery Lactarius."

"Paul! Be careful!"

Nibbling thoughtfully, he said, "They aren't poisonous."

She could not quite believe it, but she wanted to share everything with him; she broke off a piece of the forbidding-looking mushroom.

"I don't think you'll like it," Paul said. "The milk is like red pepper."

With its hot taste on her tongue, she said, "I don't, but I wanted to taste it, and I'm glad I did." Marian saw for the first time that this is a different world with each different person. With Paul it was most different of all, and she touched and tasted things which she had always thought were death.

They turned back to the path that led beside the spring.

Then they were in the blinding sunshine of the clearing, with dry grass under their feet, walking towards the airy shade of the Juneberry tree, and the whole world seemed to lighten and open away, with upward gliding smoke from their fire, the smell of the sea, sunshine sparkling on blue water, and the magic feeling of newness in their young hearts.

For a while they had nothing to do but talk, and at first they hardly talked at all. The boy lay on the grass, with his eyes closed or looking up at the leaves and branches of the tree, while the girl sat beside him playing with little stems of dry grass. In one of the most silent and idle moments of her life, she had a feeling of confident well-being. This is it: I am not waiting for time to pass or for anything to be different from what it is; there is no more loss or waste or waiting; this is here and now, and it is enough.

After a while Paul asked, "Did you ever happen to hear of a logger named Tom Horton?"

She thought and said, "Not that I remember. Why?"

"I just thought you might."

"There are always loggers around Illihee," she said, "but usually you don't hear their names."

Paul said, "He might have been driving a cat, or working as a mechanic; he was very good with cars."

"I don't believe I ever heard of him. When was he around here?"

"I'm not sure he ever was," Paul said. "I just thought he might have been." He seemed willing to let the matter drop, but it was something that interested him and she wanted to share in it and be of help.

"What does he look like, Paul?"

He said, "I don't exactly know; I never saw him. At least, I was too young to remember when I did."

"Could you tell me anything about him?" Marian asked.

Paul said, "He was our chauffeur when we lived in Hewitt, and before that he worked in the woods. But that would give you the wrong idea of him. He did things like that because he wanted to. Bailey says he was a wonderful person, and Mother thought there was something very fine about him; she talked about him a few days before she died."

Marian would have liked to be of help, but could not. She had never heard the name and Paul did not know what Tom Horton looked like.

When their fire had died down they swept away the last embers and put their clams on the hot stones. White steam went up in a solid puff as Paul covered them with a big armful of ferns dipped in salt water—and again the world became leisurely. Only now they were beginning to feel hungry. Neither of them mentioned it at first, but after a while they began picking and eating Juneberries, with Paul bending down the branches for his smaller partner, like a considerate father bear. "This is one of the best specimens I've seen in the Sound country. East of the mountains you could live on them in summer; they call them 'sarvice berries' there."

Picking and eating the buttery, sky-blue berries, Marian asked, "Is it nice east of the mountains?"

"Not the way it is here," Paul told her. "It's hot in summer and cold in winter, with very little rain. Farming's mostly irrigation ditches. If it weren't for the ditches, the country would go back to desert again. It's all right for the people who like it, but I always feel good when we start down this side of the mountains."

Marian said, "You love this country, don't you, Paul?"

"You love what you know, or you don't really love anything," Paul said, picking and eating Juneberries again. "A friend of ours from the Horse Heaven country doesn't see how we can live here. He calls this side of the mountains the 'Green Hell' and after he's been in Seattle for a few days, he gets homesick for the sun and the burnt hills and the empty sky."

The girl felt humble and elated. In the hours they had been together, he hadn't so much as touched her hand by accident, but when he talked what was in his heart she felt close to him, and he no longer seemed cold or stern. It was like a distant star becoming less distant, until warmth mingled with light and you were thawed of all doubts. . . .

At the beginning of their day, the clam bake had been the important thing; afterwards at times they had forgotten it altogether. It became important again when the boy laid back the cover of wilted ferns and they began devouring the clams. They had baked until they had absorbed most of their nectar and begun to turn golden-brown in their open shells, and all you had to do was lift out the meat, using the neck for a handle.

"These are the sweetest I've ever tasted," Marian said. "When I was small, I used to scramble for the ones that were baked right on the hot stones, and when I was older and more polite I hoped I would get some; but these are all baked that way."

Hoisting a clam by its convenient handle, the boy said, "It's the only right way." He swallowed, and added with a touch of scorn, "It was probably women who turned clam bakes into steamed clams." Afterward, still eating and shamelessly piling up the empty shells beside him, he said, "If we ever give the country back to the Indians, we'll hold out on the clams, won't we?"

"Or go live with the Indians."

"Anyway," he agreed, "we'll go with the clams."

They were still eating when the rich blast of a steamer whistle swelled and filled the afternoon air.

The boy picked up another clam. "Father must be back from the woods."

From habit, the girl looked around for picnic things to pack, but nature had provided nearly everything and there were only her shoes and stockings to think about.

"We'll finish the clams, first," Paul said easily.

"But the tug's waiting for you, isn't it?"

"It can wait," he said; "there's no such hurry."

Marian would have liked their picnic to go on indefinitely, but for her it was already over. She had never been in a position to keep a train or steamer waiting; the idea gave her a feeling of sacrilegious guilt, and she was already pulling a stocking over one of her sunburned legs.

When the boy saw it was no use, he sat on the bank near her and put on his shoes with the broken laces, which he knotted together. After that there was only his camera, and the fire-making equipment which had served its purpose. Methodically, he put the pieces of board and the drill on the bed of stones, where they could be burned in another fire, and unstrung the bright cord from the bow. Holding it out uncertainly, he said, "Your hair," and when Marian did not take it he became self-conscious and blurted, "Don't you want it?"

"If you can put it back," she said.

"I can't do that."

"Then you might as well burn it."

"It's such nice hair," he said regretfully, "it's really the color of copper!"

His detached praise of her hair made her feel helpless against tears or laughter, whichever one might reach her first. To escape both, she said, "If you like, you can keep it. Then, if you ever want to see me, you can burn a little of it and I will appear."

Paul shoved the embarrassing braid of hair into his hip pocket and they started back, single file, on the narrow trail at the edge of the shore. Neither of them said anything until they were going through the alder woods, where the green dusk was dappled with sunlight. As if to explain some imagined fault, Paul said abruptly, "I guess I'm not much of a hand with girls; I've never had much to do with them."

He had said that once before, like gold apologizing for not being polished brass, and the girl had let the opportunity slip. "Why haven't you, Paul?" she asked, trying to consider his loss rather than her gain.

"They bother me," he said as before.

"How?"

"Oh, trying to attract my attention," he floundered. "Trying to get me to take them places——"

She said, "You can't blame them; you're very nice, and attractive. You shouldn't let that bother you."

"It hasn't anything to do with me," he said. "They don't care about me or the things I'm interested in. Father's supposed to be a big shot in the logging business, and that means money." He made a gesture of throwing something unpleasant away. "You know the rest."

"You haven't much of an opinion of girls," Marian said unhappily.

"Oh, girls are all right; it's mostly their mothers."

"I think I know what you mean," she said. "Mothers do things for their daughters that they wouldn't do for themselves."

"Maybe that's it," he said gloomily.

"Girls are human beings," she said, "and they're as nice as other people. You ought to remember that."

"I've tried to, sometimes," he said; "but I can't keep it up when I know there's some woman scheming in the background."

"Mothers aren't all like that; even when they are, the girls can't help it."

"I know," he said, "but I hate it."

In a way, it was a gloomy ending to their expedition, but that was only by the accident of its being the last thing they talked about. When they were in the pasture again, the whistle bellowed a second time, and after that there was the hollow roar of the tug blowing off steam. It wasn't a good time to talk or think, and at last Paul seemed to have a feeling of urgency. He adjusted the strap of his camera case and said, "Well, I suppose I'd better go on board before they make any more noise."

Marian said, "I'm afraid I spoiled your day for taking pictures."

"Morning's the best time for what I was after," he said; "and I got quite a few."

"I hope they turn out well," she said.

"Some of them will; there'll be good and bad—but you never know which until they're developed." He hesitated, then said, "If you like, I'll send you one."

"I would like that very much."

"We proved our point about food and fire, didn't we?"

"We did, Paul, and it was such fun—for me, anyway."

"For me, too."

They stood for a minute without saying anything, uncertain, as if the meaning of their day together were being weighed in invisible scales. The boy made a half-gesture towards the pocket in which he had put her braid of hair. Then he held out his hand. "Well, good-bye, and thank you." His tough, abrupt grip hurt for a moment, and then he was striding down the skid-road trail to the salt water.

It was past the middle of the afternoon, but Marian did not

go home at once. She sat in the grassy hollow by the stream, where she had first seen Paul with his camera. "I'm in love," she thought. "How handsome he is. There isn't anything about him that I would change. I'm the one who would do that. I'd change all of me if he wanted me to. I've changed already. Even Mother won't find any fault with him when there's money in the family. Not that it makes any difference, because I want us to live like Gypsies, exploring the Sound and the woods and the mountains, learning the meaning of things and finding our living wherever we are."

She was certain of that, even while she took comfort in knowing that the two of them, who needed so little, would never have to do with less. Then she remembered, like an uneasy waking, the last thing they had talked about. Mothers scheming to trap Paul because there was so much money in his family. She had tried to be wise and fair, talking over something which didn't touch her personally—and they might have been talking about her mother and herself. When she told about Paul, her mother would probably scheme all day and dream all night, perfecting a fool-proof trap for the boy, who would be scared away. That was unfair to her mother. More likely the trap would be so subtle that the only part of it he would see would be his own trustingness. But love is too terrible and proud to be treated that way. Without knowing it until now, she had broken with her mother's teachings at the moment of falling in love. She would say nothing about Paul until they got to know each other better and came to some kind of an understanding.

In fantasy, her day with Paul had been the gateway to living. In fact, it was a triumphal arch set up in a potato field, and when she marched through, with eager steps and a beating heart, there was nothing but more potato field on the other side.

That fall she went to Seattle and enrolled at the State University. She hoped to find Paul there; even if he didn't go to the University, the chances of meeting him in Seattle seemed much better.

She did not see anything of him until the second semester, and then it was an unsatisfactory glimpse. She and Rosemary Smith were driving with Joe Field and Brocky Wilson of the Beta house. The plan was to drive somewhere along Lake Washington, where they were going to feed the ducks and take pictures. It was a simple and proper date, but the boys had just passed a dreaded examination and were in a carefree mood. Something was wrong with Brocky's car, and he and Joe called for the girls in a borrowed vehicle—an outlandishly high model-T Ford painted with rowdy slogans such as: DON'T LAUGH, LADY, YOUR DAUGHTER MIGHT BE IN HERE.

The car set the mood of the expedition and Brocky clowned his way through the Montlake Bridge traffic, with Rosemary hanging on with one hand and shielding her eyes with the other, like a comic opera sailor, while she called directions and encouragement. In the back seat the usually inhibited Joe kept one arm around Marian and promised fervently to point out a cow as soon as they were out in the country. Brocky asked pedestrians the way to the campus and continued in the opposite direction. In the Arboretum he came to a dramatic stop opposite a parked car with a boy and girl locked in fervent embrace; he gathered Rosemary swooningly into his arms, and Joe followed his example with Marian. Then he drove on.

Near the Avenue, where there were pine trees and grass beside a marshy pond, Brocky drove the car off the road to bestow his blessing on a tall young man who had just come up from the pond, bare-footed, with his trousers rolled up, his shoes in one hand and the root of some water plant in the other.

Marian's heart leaped! It was Paul, standing there easy and preoccupied and absolutely beautiful, with the spring sunshine coming through the pine trees to light up his fair hair and grave blue eyes. She saw him for a few seconds while Brocky declaimed,

> Blessings on thee, little man,
> Barefoot boy with cheeks of tan—

and then the engine roared and the car jumped ahead and staggered onto the road, while Marian freed herself from Joe's embrace.

The day was spoiled. Spring and the carefree outing, the boys' clowned love-making and the intense embrace of the couple in the parked car, had warmed her with confused excitement. They were fragments of some poignant and compelling thing. Only they had been mixed up like the parts of some beautiful machine. In moments when she had been close to Paul, the scattered parts had fitted together; the engine ran swiftly and fiercely, and she had the feeling of flying. But it was a power over which she had no control, and it left her with nothing but loneliness among the bright and scattered parts of love.

VI

GOING HOME for summer vacation was like putting on childhood dresses and shoes. Home was smaller than she remembered it, and more intimate and worn, and her mother made her feel naked when she questioned her minutely about the boys she had gone out with and their prospects. After considering them all, the mother favored Brocky Wilson, whose father was a commission merchant.

"If you don't find any one better," she decided, "you might set your cap for the Wilson boy."

Marian said, "But Mother, I'm not in love with Brocky, and I never expect to be."

Her objection raised the old dispute and the mother said, "As for that business, you'll do yourself the best turn by never falling in love at all. If you do, you have that much less chance of making a good marriage."

"You can be as hard-boiled as you like," Marian said, "but all the girls at our house believe in love, and I believe in it more than I ever did."

"You won't when you get to be my age, or even after you've been married a few years."

"Not even to the sweetest boy in the world?"

The mother smiled bitterly. "Joan Albright at the store once said your father had the sweetest and most sensitive nature she had ever known! She told me that as if she were trying to sell him over the counter to me. 'The sweetest and most sensitive nature!' "

The girl thought back to the time before her father had shrunk into timid silence. "I think so, too, Mother."

Her mother was only upset for a moment. "Neither of you has been married to him, and I have been for over twenty years. Once I loved him, or thought I did, and that's the only thing I can't forgive myself for."

"I don't see why, Mother; I don't see that at all."

"You will if you make a fool of yourself in the same way. The best of men are beasts, and if you make the mistake of falling in love, you put yourself in a man's power and he uses you and takes all kinds of liberties with you and afterward you hate him and you hate yourself for everything you've ever let him do!" Her voice grew scalding, "And there's no end to it. It's only in the last year that your father has really let me alone. For fifteen years, after I was done with that business, nearly every night in bed he would start making his sly advances that would always have led to the same thing, if I'd let them. When I stopped him he would turn away and sulk, or go downstairs and sleep on the sofa. In a few nights he would be back, and it would be the same thing over again. Think of having to put up with that for all these years."

"I can't imagine putting up with it!"

Her mother missed the irony. "I wasn't going to tell you these things, but you've been to college and met young men worth thinking about. It's just as well for you to know what to expect if you ever give in to a man."

The girl tried drawing on her slight knowledge. "I've heard of it being the other way round, where the woman complained that her husband didn't pay enough attention to her."

"I don't believe those things really happen," her mother said. "If they do, there is something wrong with the woman."

"And there are men who don't care about women that way. You should have married one of them."

"That wouldn't do at all," her mother said; "then you wouldn't have any real hold on a man."

"It's a queer way to look at it," the girl said; "wanting something you don't want."

"It isn't wanting, Marian; it's being wanted. That gives you a hold on a man; you're sure of what he has, and unless it's enough, you don't have to give him what he wants."

Marian said, "That sounds too cold-blooded for me."

"It's practical, and if you aren't practical, God help you in a world like this! I've never seen the government or any one else lift a finger to help people who married for love." Then the mother softened a little. "Of course, if a man had money to burn, and he insisted, you could afford to humor him. Even now, if your father made good and I could have things and take it easy, I would put up with a good deal from him."

The girl stared at her mother's lined face and gray hair and tried to comprehend the fantasy—her father, after twenty years of labor, still on probation. It had taken Jacob in the Bible only fourteen to get Rachael, and Leah had been thrown in at the half-way mark. "It seems a long time to wait for a woman to live with."

"Well, I've waited as long to have some kind of life, and I'm still waiting."

"Fifteen years!" Marian tried to imagine living that long in the same house with Paul and not having him. That would wear any one out and drive him to anything. "I don't suppose Father has had other women, either."

"Of course not," the mother said. "I've never had to give

that a thought, with him always after me. And he's hardly ever away, except to go to the store."

"He isn't the kind," Marian said quickly. "That's why I think you could be nicer to him."

The mother was holding one hand palm up on the table, moving her fingers as if she were testing invisible dice to see if they had been tampered with. "Lately, though, he's let me alone——"

Marian was uneasy because of her stupid remark about other women, and the hunting light of suspicion in her mother's eyes. It was only a flicker, and there was nothing to find, but she did not like to see it there. "You've had to work too hard, Mother, and so has Father. It's mostly my fault, because I haven't been anything but an expense. Next semester I'll work, or stay at home——"

"I haven't been paying so much attention to your father," the mother went on, "but I can't think of any woman who would give anything away to a man like him."

The girl said, "I wouldn't have mentioned it if I had thought there was any one."

"I would know it if there were."

"I'm sure you would, Mother."

"Not that I would be any worse off if he did make a fool of himself."

"Do you want to show me how this goes, Mother? No one can make a French seam the way you do."

For a few days, Marian thought, her mother was in a better mood towards her father. Then he went to a Lodge meeting, and a fierce quarrel broke out when he came home late. The girl had gone to bed, but from her room she could follow the track of the storm through the downstairs rooms. It reached its climax with the mother trying to drag the father to the telephone, and then the instrument was being cranked while the mother called up neighbors and demanded to know when the meeting had broken up. Apparently the answers left room for doubt and the storm raged again; then it swirled upstairs, where it sank to fierce whispers and muttering. Then it moved downstairs again as the woman followed the man, and grew louder as it receded into the distance.

When Marian woke after a few hours of uneasy sleep it was still going on. While she dressed hastily she tried not to hear the voices: the woman's fierce whispering that seemed trying to tear the heart out of some mystery, and the man's sleepy and exhausted muttering.

Marian had not quarrelled with any one since childhood days, and the night-long wrangle was as incomprehensible to her as roaring drunkenness to a teetotaler. At first she planned to make breakfast as a kind of peace offering, but when she got downstairs the voices upstairs had grown louder, and something told her there would be no breakfast and no peace in the house that day. Instead of making a fire, she took a coat from the downstairs closet and went out into the blessed peace of the morning.

She hurried until the second growth fir woods were between her and the house, and from then on she walked more slowly, thinking: What a mess! Quarrelling all night! What's the matter with men and women that they can't get along together? Wouldn't you think they'd learn how in twenty years? They knew once without having to learn, and they've been fifteen years unlearning it. Fifteen years! In that time I'd only love Paul more!

She had left the house to get away, but now she had to go towards something, and she decided to continue on to town. She could have some breakfast at the lunch room by the bus station;

then she would visit the Petersons and talk things over with Hedvig—not necessarily the things that bothered her—anything would do. The Petersons were all sceptical and full of gusto; they did not attend Lodge meetings and would not know anything about the rumpus of the night before, and even if they did they would not care at all. Walking along the country road in the fine, reliable morning air, Marian saw that the world was a likable place the way it was; you had only to choose the company of people who believed in life rather than those who were tangled in their ideas of what it should be.

Near the Harveys' mail box the girl stepped off the narrow road for a car which overtook her. She was in no hurry and she wanted it to be a stranger who would pass without offering her a ride; but the car slowed and stopped beside her. It had a familiar sound and there were her parents, strained and grim and sleepless, with her father holding the car door open for her.

Getting in, she said, "You shouldn't have worried about me; I was just going to take a walk and call on Hedvig."

The father cleared his throat. "You shouldn't have gone without breakfast."

Her mother said, "There's no reason why you should be punished, but that's the way things go; when one does wrong, every one suffers."

Marian had supposed that her parents had come looking for her and that her father would now turn home; but the car chattered on towards town, with the father and mother stiff and grim in the front seat, like people intent on some deadly errand. They did not speak to each other, but the storm was still going on; it had overtaken Marian on the road and gathered her into the deadly electric silence of its heart. Apprehensively she stared at the robe rail with its worn nickel-plated fastenings and she thought: You can't trust anything in this world to stay peaceful.

Even the air you breathe, or the water in which you bathe, can become part of a dreadful hurricane. I never would have thought it of the old Chevrolet, but it's become a black storm cloud descending on Illihee, and God knows where it will strike or what damage it will do!

When the car rolled into town it was a few minutes after eight by the clock at the Evergreen Service Station, and Illihee was awake and at work. At Sixth Avenue the Chevrolet had to pause for a battered logging truck with a trailer as long as a freight train, and at Fifth, passengers were flickering into the Shelton stage and sitting down with the comfortable air of knowing just where they were going and why. At Fourth, half a dozen out-of-town cars were parked around Shaeffer's General Store, and Mrs. Shaeffer was putting gas into the tank of Axel Larson's dust-gray Dodge. In the glass of the pump the level of red liquid sank smoothly, like blood going in during a transfusion. It stopped at ten, and the slow, gray-haired woman was raising the hood of the car to check the oil and water when Marian's father finished parking.

There was nothing the girl wanted in the store, but she had been gathered into the storm and she was too hypnotized to think of escape. Inside the store there was the nostalgic, blended smell of bran, ground coffee, kerosene, ripe bananas, oil cloth and yard goods. Mr. Shaeffer was coming from the back of the store with a sack of scratch feed on his shoulder; at the grocery counter, fair-haired, pink-faced Fred took a pencil from behind his ear and began adding up an order for a family of Indians— corn flakes, sugar, candy bars, and Enterprise Brand canned clams. In the wake of the family, old Mrs. Winston fretted with a can of Instant Postum in her hand. Apparently the instantaneous nature of the beverage was being spoiled for her by the delay in purchasing it. Tottering beside her on his long, thin legs, Mr. Winston remonstrated gently: "But, Mother, the Indians were here first."

At the drygoods counter, Joan Albright was showing yard goods to Mrs. Dickinson and her little girl from Tyee Valley. "I wouldn't be afraid of yellow," she said; "it's the color of sunshine, and we don't have enough of it in this climate. It will go nicely with Drucilla's dark hair, and I think you'll find pleasure just looking at it, because it supplies something that is missing."

The customer was doubtful about sunshine and climate being tied up with dress goods, but she was loyal. "It seems kind of sallow to me," she said; "but if you say so, Miss Albright, I'll take it."

Joan Albright was a niece of the Shaeffers and she had come to Illihee only the summer before; but Marian thought of her as one of the civilized people of town. Joan was in her thirties; she wore glasses and her light brown hair was already streaked with gray; but there was something young about her and she had a sympathy which reached out to find and encourage the hopes of others—perhaps because her own had not been realized. She had spent most of her life in San Francisco and worked for one firm for fourteen years—then left for nothing better than hard-working relatives in a country store. According to rumor, it was at the time her employer became a widower and married again, and she was disappointed in love. However that might have been, she did not give the impression of being disappointed, and there seemed nothing mysterious about her except the secret of how something tender and hopeful kept alive with so little to feed on.

Cutting the yellow cloth, Joan said, "I think it would be nice to use buttons of the same color." Then she looked up and saw the gathered storm cloud of the Clark family and the lightning in the mother's eyes, and her hands were unsteady as she folded the cloth that was like a dwindling patch of sunshine on the dark counter.

"Good morning, Mr. and Mrs. Clark," she said, "I will be with you in a minute." It was not her usual voice and it was like saying that since she was in the storm path she would like to get other people out of the way and face it alone.

Storms know nothing but ungallant destruction, and the mother's voice blazed through the store. "Why, it's Joan Albright, the whore of Illihee!" She pointed scornfully to the price ticket on a bolt of cloth marked "Special." "That's your price, I suppose; ninety-eight cents! You think yourself a bargain, but my husband never has ninety-eight cents to spend on his own wife, let alone on a whore from the Barbary Coast!"

By then the others were becoming unparalyzed. The woman from Tyee Valley hurried her little girl away without waiting for her package, and Joan stepped from behind the counter.

"Please, Mrs. Clark, that is no way to talk."

Marian took her mother by the arm. "You are making a scene," she said and tried to lead her away. She might have succeeded, but the father put his hand on her other arm and she dashed it away, screaming, "Don't touch me. If you touch me I'll cut your hand off!"

"Now, Mrs. Clark," the big storekeeper lumbered between the furious woman and his niece. "Joan's a good girl, and we won't have such talk in this store."

"So you're Joan Albright's protector!" the woman yelled. "I suppose you take your share of her earnings! Get out of my way, you old pimp! You can't protect her from what an honest woman has to say!"

Mrs. Schaeffer broke through the fringe of staring customers, with gas money in her hand and her big bosom rising and falling under her soiled white apron. "Clara," she panted, "you don't know what you're saying." She took the woman by the wrist, but her hand was shaken off.

"You brought the creature, you old madame; I want you to hear me, too; let the whole town hear!" Glaring at her enemy, with her face changed and poisoned by hate, she yelled, "I'm talking to you, Joan Albright! You can peddle yourself to all the loggers and Siwashes on the peninsula, but if you ever look at my husband again, I'll tear your eyes out! You cheap, Barbary Coast whore!"

The raging grew coarser while Marian wondered numbly how her mother knew every obscene term that had ever been spoken or written anonymously on outhouse walls. As the words tumbled out, her saliva began spinning threads between her lips, and then it was flying out of her mouth in fragments like dry cotton.

The diatribe ended with the mother suddenly dashing out into the street and throwing herself in front of a milk truck. The truck missed her by a fair margin, but it grazed the father and Marian and swerved up on the sidewalk, where it struck the fire hydrant. As they were lifting the woman, water from the broken main geysered over all of them. Drenched and bruised, Marian thought bitterly that it was Mother's big day. But the day was almost over for her and she moaned exhaustedly as they carried her to the car and took her home, where Marian put her to bed.

It was mostly nerves and change of life, the doctor said. He left bromides and said rest would be good, if it was possible. He did not take the case very seriously, but the mother kept to her bed and made no protest about being waited upon.

Sometimes the mother thought she was dying or going mad,

and once she had a reconciliation with her husband and insisted that the blame was all hers. But the reconciliation blew up when the father suggested that she had been unfair to Joan Albright, and she screamed reckless accusations and tried to jump out of the window.

Those were the off moments; mostly the mother did nothing worse than complain. Marian kept her room as cheerful as she could, and took up her mother's work. She got up at five and cooked and cleaned and baked and ran the separator and fed the calves and took care of the chickens, washed and ironed and mended and worked in the kitchen garden. Around midnight she finished the supper dishes along with the last batch of canning for the day. Her father spared her all he could during the day, and he began helping with the housework in the evening. After supper, while he dried the dishes or helped with the canning, he talked science and natural history and recalled things he had learned at college.

That summer the girl learned some of the depths of her father's forbearance, but she was usually too tired or busy trying to develop forbearance of her own to be appreciative, and sometimes she did not have forbearance enough. Like the hot evening when she was cooking supper and making pies and trying to fix her mother's tray daintily, while she decided not to go to Hedvig's picnic because her parents might get into a row if they were left alone. As a last straw her father came in noisily with an armful of wood and put a piece in the range, which was already too hot. He asked, "When will supper be ready?" and she heard herself shout, "When it's done! Who do you think I am? I can't do everything for everybody and have it on time!"

The father had only asked so he could arrange his chores accordingly, and he went out looking hurt and startled. But he was not as startled as the girl. She had sometimes told herself that her mother was a dracula who drained the color and warmth out of other peoples' lives. Six weeks after they had changed places, her own menacing shout had been indistinguishable from her mother's.

It was a hard life, but Marian had a good constitution and she was young. Death by exhaustion each night was followed by resurrection in the morning. Then she often had the feeling of being tireless and immortal as the sun, and whether it came up golden or was a muffled burning in the white mist, she thought she could keep up with it forever. While she was dressing she always looked towards the east. Beyond the field and the pasture was the swelling green of the alder woods, and stabbing out of it were the two bleached cedars tapering to spear points, with a few stripped branches curving down like barbs. When she glimpsed them right, it was like a whispered story of something magnificent about to happen. One morning when the open window let in the smells of salt water and stubble fields and apple leaves, mist and the incense of some distant forest fire, everything was so bright that the whispered promise became a shout and the dead trees stabbed out of the misty alder woods like lightning; Marian could almost hear the significant crash of thunder.

The feeling of expectancy lasted through breakfast and through her mother's ritual of accepting her breakfast tray grudgingly and doubting if she would eat more than a bite. The steady glow lived on until the girl went to her own room to make the bed and, as she looked out of the east window, it leaped to a burst of glory. On the near side of the alder woods the white mist was burning away from the cove and out of it an anchored vessel was materializing: a large black tug with white upper works and a high bluff-colored stack. While she watched a small boat was lowered into the smoke of burning mist on the water and men began getting in.

Marian had lived many lives and died many deaths since the first landing at the cove, and she had sometimes told herself that Paul did not matter any more; but now the year's clutter of lives and death went from her like fallen leaves from around a tree that is immortal again with spring. She was young and in love and nothing had changed. Giving her bronze-colored hair a few swift brushes, she glimpsed herself in the mirror and remembered a little of how she had looked the summer before. The same vivid coloring was there, and the same life and glow; only now there was less of soulless perfection. Exhausting work and disappointments and anxiety gave her young looks a touch of poignancy. In that flying moment, at least, she was beautiful.

She did not change her gingham house dress, or touch anything but her warm banner of hair, which was as much disordered as tamed by the brush, and then she was on her way downstairs, with the old wall paper of the stair well flying past her like familiar, outgrown scenery whisked away in preparation for some great event.

In the east field the sun was drying up the dew from the stubble and clover, but in the pasture the delicious chill of early morning clung to the earth along the old skidroad. Thick dew glistened like frost on grass and stones and spider webs, and through the mist and the fresh smell of the morning there came the distant scent of burning evergreen woods and the glory of the rising summer sun.

The year before, on such a morning, swinging along the half-obliterated skidroad to her first meeting with Paul, she had sung out loud, "My Lord, what a morning!" Now, with the loveliness intensified, given meaning, she did not trust her voice, but the same music and words swelled through her.

In the middle of her voiceless song, at a bend in the road, Marian was suddenly face to face with a big man in his fifties, dressed like a businessman except that his clothes looked more comfortable and he was wearing loggers' boots and a slouched hat. Everything about him had the reassuring look of comfort and prosperity, even his smile, which exposed strong even teeth lighted here and there with gold fillings, and the expensive aroma of his cigar became one of the fine smells of the morning.

"Hello," he said. "It's a fine morning, isn't it?" He seemed pleasantly surprised by the meeting, but he gave the impression of knowing what to do in any emergency.

Marian agreed that it was a fine morning, and the big man continued to look at her with hearty and open admiration while he addressed his companion. "Isn't she pretty, Ivar?"

The companion, who was lean and Swedish and slightly younger, said politely, "*Ja*." Then he looked at the girl more attentively and said "*Ja!*" with enthusiasm.

"There's nothing like introducing ourselves," the big man said. "I'm Charlie Dow and I do some logging now and then, and this is Ivar Olson."

Marian introduced herself, and Charlie knew immediately where she fitted into the pattern of the neighborhood. "You're the daughter of John Clark who owns this forty and the old Ludlow tract." While he talked he kept on looking at her as if he never wanted to take his eyes away.

Marian was still in a smiling glow because she was talking to Paul's father, who approved of her, and Paul could not be far away. "I know your son," she told him.

The big man looked chagrined. "You do, eh?" Then his eyes became wryly quizzical. "Bailey gets around, doesn't he?"

The girl stammered, "I mean Paul; I met him once."

Charlie's ruddy face cleared. "Oh, Paul! He's a fine boy."

Marian said earnestly, "I think so!"

"But he's not much of a one with the girls, eh?" Then he said, "Paul didn't come with me this time; he's away in the mountains. That's more his style."

She would have liked to talk more about Paul, but Charlie was already going on comfortably about his own affairs.

"I have a tract back of here. I'm playing with the idea of bringing in a couple of cats and getting out piling." His eyes twinkled, meeting hers. "Think it would be a good idea?"

The girl knew nothing about logging, but the project would certainly bring Paul, and she answered with confidence, "Yes, sir."

Charlie laughed. "It's just an idea, Marian." He used her name naturally, but in a special voice, like touching her. "And there's the matter of a right of way. Think I could arrange that with your father?"

She answered, "I'm sure you could."

"That's for the future." He was still looking at her with open, smiling approval, and while he looked his ideas seemed to change and take form.

"There's nothing like knowing where you're at, eh? Maybe I'll drop around this afternoon—if your father's at home—" Then his ideas developed again. "Look, Marian, Ivar and I are going to be starved after a morning of cruising in the woods. Suppose your mother could have some dinner for us, a little after noon?"

Marian said, "I'm sure we could."

"That's fine." Then he asked, "Sure she won't mind a couple of hungry loggers?"

"Mother isn't very well," she explained; "I do the cooking, so I know it will be all right."

Charlie was voiceless with admiration; then he turned on

his companion: "Ivar, she's beautiful and she can cook! Why are you standing there like a dumb Swede? Why don't you grab her? No, I saw her first!" Then he was serious and friendly again. "If you're sure it won't be too much bother, Marian, we'll be in right after noon."

Going home across the field she thought the morning had been more complicated than she had imagined it, and it had fallen a little short of fulfillment; but she felt a buoyant certainty that this was a turning point in her life.

The first manifestation came a few minutes later when she told her mother about the guests who were coming for dinner. In answer the woman called for a comb and brush and mirror and began putting up her hair, which had gone evenly gray during the summer.

"You can get out my clothes, too," she said, brushing vigorously.

Marian asked, "You're going to get up for dinner?"

"Get up to make dinner, you mean."

"But you can't!" Marian protested. "You've hardly been out of bed for months."

"And I've had a good rest, too."

"But you're sick!"

"What's being sick?" the mother asked. "It's mostly being bored, with nothing to look forward to. Sick of work—work that doesn't mean anything. I'm well enough when there's work that means something."

"But it's only two extra men," the girl said; "and Mr. Dow doesn't want anything special. I can manage all right."

"You can kill a couple of red fryers," the mother said. "Or I'll do it myself. It's not too late for the sugar peas, and not so early but what we can find some new potatoes. Then there's a salad——"

"They don't expect six courses," Marian said. "I told them I was doing the cooking."

Pulling on her special occasion girdle, the mother said, "And so you will; at least you will get the credit. But it has to be worth something."

The girl caught some of her mother's excitement, along with her own, but still she was puzzled. "Mother, this isn't a competition. The way you're going on, any one would think he was a young man you wanted me to catch with a frying pan."

"He's a widower," the mother observed; "it was in the paper a year or two ago when his wife died. If I know anything about men, he's looking around by now."

"Nonsense, Mother!"

"Likely he had something of the sort in mind when he asked himself to dinner, with you looking so young and pretty in the morning."

Marian was troubled because she had been trying to keep away the same thought. "Why, he's an old man!" Then she added boldly, "Anyway, it's his son that I love."

The mother looked at her sharply, "Then he was the one!"

"Who, Mother?"

"The boy who was here last summer."

She felt relieved, discovering she had no secrets from her mother. "He's the one; Paul; how did you know?"

"That's the name, all right."

"But how did you know?"

"I saw him, of course."

Marian was puzzled and suddenly hollow. "You saw him! When?"

"It might have been late August—one day when you were in town."

"Paul was here and you never told me?"

Dressing, the mother reminded her, "You never told me you'd met him. Besides, how did I know who he was? He came here like a tramp, with his shoes in one hand and some wild flowers in the other."

The girl felt stricken. "That was Paul! And I missed him!"

"For the life of me I couldn't think of anything but your father when I first knew him. We'd go for a Sunday walk and the first thing I'd know he'd be botanizing in a swamp and looking a sight. As soon as I set eyes on this boy, I thought: There's another worthless one for a girl to make a fool of herself over——"

"Mother!"

"I had no way of knowing he could afford that kind of thing."

"And I suppose you were rude to him?"

"I was only careful," the mother said. "There was a young tramp I'd never heard of, barefoot at the kitchen door, asking for you. He said he had met you in the woods."

The girl was crying. "And you were rude to him and drove him away!"

"Marian, don't keep sniveling and saying that. I wasn't rude. A mother has to be careful. I said the truth, that I didn't know anything about his having met you. Did I, now?"

The girl checked a sob, "I should have told you——"

"And I told him the truth—that you weren't at home."

"What did he say, Mother?"

"He said he'd be going along; that he just happened to be down this way; he didn't make much of it."

"He's so shy," the girl blew her nose into her wet handkerchief. "It was probably the first time he'd ever called on a girl! Didn't he say anything about coming back?"

"No, he just said he happened to be down this way and thought he'd drop in. When he was leaving I said I'd tell you he'd called and he said it wasn't necessary——"

"Mother, he wouldn't have said that if you'd been nice to him! He wouldn't have gone away and not come back."

"Well, if he'd been a man and really interested in you, he wouldn't have been scared away by my being careful."

The girl did not answer because she had already thought everything would have been so much easier if Paul had been more like his father.

"And you would have saved yourself trouble by trusting me. Why didn't you?"

Marian blurted fiercely, "Because I thought if I did, you would scare him away by turning yourself inside out for him, the way you're doing for his father!"

The mother was tired with the effort of dressing, and she sat on the bed a minute, resting. "You might have trusted me," she said. "You might have known there'd be a difference between the rough idea I give you and the way I'd do something. Maybe I will turn myself inside out, but Mr. Dow won't know it. We'll use our everyday dishes and maybe eat in the kitchen, the way we're used to. We have to feel comfortable, so he can. And if you change your dress, it's going to be another gingham one. We can't compete with millionnaires' china and silver and silks, and the harder we tried, the worse for us. We're going to give him the things he hasn't got: the nice homey things about a farm. We'll eat in the kitchen because it looks real, and men like kitchens best. No matter how many rooms there are, they want to sit in the kitchen and have good food and see women waiting on them."

The girl thought her mother was right, but still it seemed to her that things were mixed up. "It's Paul I want," she said, "and you talk as if I was supposed to win Mr. Dow with home cooking and a gingham dress!"

"It's all the same," her mother said. "I don't know of a better way for you to see Paul than for us to make friends with his father. You'll have him, if you want him enough. Now, wash the tear stains off your face and catch me two red fryers. If Mr. Dow is going to log here and be our neighbor, we're going to start off on the right foot."

The Illihee project was only one of many irons that Charlie Dow had in the fire, and it never got hot. Nothing came of it, but dinner in the farmhouse kitchen was a great success. The logging operator stayed in the neighborhood another day and came back for other meals. His stories of early logging days were enchanting, and it seemed to Marian that at last the larger meanings and the drama of the logging country had come to the house, where there had been only echoes of great things.

Marian and her mother refused firmly to accept pay for the meals, and Charlie did not insist. Instead he thought of a graceful way of returning their hospitality. He invited the family to be week-end guests at his mansion in Seattle.

The father stayed because he was troubled by the whirlwind courtship and because some one had to look after the farm. But Marian and her mother made the trip on the tug. From the moment of meeting in the pasture, things never really stopped for Marian. On the half day's voyage, she had only one regret about the visit to Seattle. Paul was camping in the Olympics and his father did not expect him home for another week.

Even the thought of missing Paul had its wistful beauty. Loving him as she did, she thought something of her would linger in the house as a message, in addition to a beautiful one she would leave in writing. When he came home, he would know before he was told, and remember their day together. It would be most certain of all, she thought, if there was an opportunity to slip into Paul's room. There she would touch his pillow and pray: "God make him bold enough to come back and this time I shall not be away."

Paul's father might have guessed her plan, and everything else seemed to play into her hands. When they reached the cream-colored shingled mansion, the housekeeper was out and Charlie showed the mother and daughter to the guest room. To make them feel at home, he showed them about the upstairs, opening doors to rooms with old-fashioned furniture and newer plate-glass windows, with a view of Lake Washington and the Cascade Mountains. Briefly they glimpsed an enormous bathroom with a ceiling high enough for a church, white tiled walls, and the monumental fixtures of an age when bathrooms were magnificent. They stepped into the room that was waiting for Bailey to come home from New York, and saw the light veil of dust on the books that lined one wall and on the ship models and on a round painting overflowing with voluptuous, golden-skinned beauties amusing themselves languidly in a harem. They were introduced to the linen closet and the dumbwaiter, and they looked into the master bedroom with its heavy dark furniture and enlarged photographs of logging locomotives, spar trees, and flatcars straining forever under the segments of a gigantic tree. Farther on in the hall, as Marian had known prophetically, Charlie said, "This is Paul's room," and swung open the door.

Her first impression was of a laboratory rather than a place to live. The big yellow-walled room was almost bare except for photographic apparatus and nature specimens, and the east wall was not much more than a frame around plate-glass as big as a store front. The window looked out on treetops and a few roofs that ended against the blue of the lake cut by sharp, triangular white sails. At the far edge there were a few mystical white houses, dimly reflected in the water. Above and beyond them the afternoon sun lighted up a green-gold tapestry of trees and high, distant fields that ended against the endless blue wall of mountains splashed with snow.

That first picture of the room lasted no longer than it would have taken for a camera to record it, and then she was aware of the knapsack and sleeping bag on the floor, and the tanned young body in khaki shorts sprawled on a cot at the near side of the window.

Paul got up hastily, tall and tanned and blue-eyed, with his thick yellow hair rumpled, and the confused guilty look of having been asleep or day dreaming; in the room there was the sharp, primordial smell of burned hair or horn.

When the girl cried, "Paul!" her voice filled the room with a soft puff of sound. He seemed more confused, meeting her eyes with an incredulous, somber-triumphant look. It was a beginning that never got beyond that moment, and the father's big everyday voice came in like a logging tractor, knocking down mysterious trees.

"Excuse me, Paul," he said; "I thought you were still in the Olympics."

Paul said, "I came in half an hour ago; I haven't unpacked yet."

"I didn't expect you until next week," his father said. "Anything wrong?"

"No. I just came back." The boy did not look confused any more, only a little annoyed by the guests he had not been expected to see.

"You picked a good time," his father said. "Marian tells me you have already met, and this is her mother, Mrs. Clark."

"How do you do?" Paul nodded and explained, "I've met both of them."

"Mrs. Clark and Marian are going to be our guests for the week end," his father said. "We'll have to think up something special. But now you need a chance to unpack, and we'll see you at dinner. I'm asking your Aunt Phoebe——"

"I don't know," Paul said, "I was going out." Then he added, "I guess I can make it."

At dinner Marian sat next to Paul, but there was not much comfort in it. Charlie did most of the talking. Paul looked very nice in proper clothes, but he was subdued and ill at ease, and all he seemed to think of was getting away. His meeting with Marian had gone dead, and though she tried, she could not bring it back to life again.

On other visits to the yellow-shingled mansion it was the same, except that sometimes Paul stayed away altogether. It was a pursuit in which there seemed no change; but while she followed at a fixed distance, life closed in about her like deepening woods. When she finally admitted the pursuit was useless, there was no way out. By then she was used to comforts for which she had been prepared since high school, and she was used to the big house. And whenever she tried to turn back, her mother's tongue was like a flaming sword between her and the past. The mother's health was an even more efficient weapon. It remained good while nothing went wrong with Charlie Dow's courtship. But the time Marian refused to make a week-end visit to the Dows, the mother worried herself sick and took to her bed. By then the girl was quite out of training for endless drudgery complicated by an invalid—and she knew her mother was capable of remaining genuinely sick as long as her will was opposed.

Really it was all more complicated than that. Even when Marian agreed to marry Charlie Dow, she still thought of Paul, not with hope of revenge, but with the stubbornness of both. She had already conceded that she would never be closer to Paul than she was, but neither did she want to be any farther away.

VII

AS THEY worked the sloop out of Hewitt harbor, alternate tacks gave them a good view of the town, with the rigid smokestacks and trash-burner domes of sawmills, and the square shapes of downtown buildings. It was only a big logging and sawmill town, but seeing it from the water gave it impressiveness; it was also the metropolis of the brothers' childhood.

They had bought supplies ashore; Bailey was smoking a cigar; and the Seattle morning paper lay unopened on the narrow bridge deck. Bailey had bought the paper out of habit, only to find that the daily news habit has shallow roots. After two days on the water and in the woods, a glance at the front page was enough. Nothing special had happened in Seattle or the nation; the big headlines were about Germany and Russia locked in battle somewhere far away in another world—like a chapter in a history book of some one else's country. But it did seem to justify the Old Man's belief that war would keep the log market booming.

From the other side of the cockpit, Paul said, "It bothers me that I can't quite remember when we lived up here; I feel as if I had missed something."

With one hand on the tiller, Bailey said, "You've just seen the town; it hasn't changed much. And Home Place has changed still less; nothing but the trees growing taller."

"I can't get myself to believe that. There's a mystery about the days before I can remember. They're just around the corner, but I'm going the other way—I can't turn back."

"You can take my word for it that it hasn't changed much."

Paul still was not satisfied. "What about us? Would we have been any different if we had gone on living up here?"

"We'd have had more money."

"It doesn't matter." But after a minute the younger brother showed a spark of interest. "Do you really think so?"

Bailey shifted the cigar in his mouth. "Bound to. The Old Man would have been close to the home camp, and he wouldn't have sunk the money he did in the Seattle house."

Paul was still trying to get facts straight in his mind. "Even now," he said, "I can't think of Mother as a woman who would be frightened away."

"She wasn't."

"But she talked Father into moving the family to Seattle, didn't she?"

The older brother snorted. "Talked him into it? I can remember battles that jarred the house."

Paul looked surprised. "I can't imagine Mother providing much of the noise."

"She provided most of it," Bailey said. "Quietly, if you like. The Old Man blustered, but what defense has a man against a determined woman?"

"If Father knew it was a bad move, I'd think he would have refused."

Bailey looked at his brother with wonder. "With a woman there are times when you put up, or shut up. That was one of the times for the Old Man."

"But why—if she wasn't scared?"

Bailey said, "Things got rough during the Wobbly trouble.

Mother thought it wasn't the right atmosphere for growing children."

The younger brother thought it over. "That was when Tom Horton got hurt, wasn't it?"

"Yes, but he wasn't driving for us then."

"How did he get hurt?"

Bailey said, "Hit with something or other. There were plenty of pick handles flying in those days."

"That must have been over twenty years ago."

"All of that."

"Mother made a hero of him as long as she lived. He must have been quite a person."

Bailey said, "I remember him as the perfect human being. Of course, I wasn't critical at the age of five and six, but other people share my opinion of him."

Paul asked, "What was there about him?"

"He'd gone to college, for one thing," Bailey said. "And he'd done a good deal of reading and thinking. Mother was still trying to educate herself so she could educate us, and Tom helped."

Paul said, "You'd think some one like that wouldn't have been satisfied with being a chauffeur."

"Chauffeur, gardener, handyman, and sometimes nursemaid. As I remember, Tom had started working in the woods for his health, and then the Old Man discovered him as a chauffeur—and Mother discovered him as a mind."

Paul said, "I can understand working in the woods, but chauffeuring——"

"He was strong on sociology," Bailey said. "Maybe he took the job to study the capitalistic class from the inside."

"I don't believe that."

"It might have started that way, but Tom had a heart. Without hearts people would go far."

"And what would they be when they got there?"

"Hollow, I suppose. A burnt-out rocket ship, with no one on board, alighting on the cold moon."

"That's all words," Paul said. "You still haven't told me anything definite."

Bailey said, "You owe Tom your interest in botany and geology, and your love of nature."

"It was you who started me," Paul said.

"What you got from me, I got from Tom. He started me collecting specimens when I was four or five. I started you, only I lost interest while you went on."

"That's definite all right."

"Tom was your spiritual father," Bailey said. "He foresaw your devotion to your native state when he planted the shrubs at the Home Place. Other people were going in for deodars and bamboo and umbrella trees, but Tom brought things from the mountains and woods: rhododendron and heather and flowering currant and dogwood; things that looked right because they belonged."

Paul said, "You understand something about nature."

"A little, even about your kind. But that's mostly because I was thinking about Tom."

"I used to be certain I would recognize Tom anywhere," Paul said; "I still have that feeling, but actually I haven't the slightest idea what he looked like."

"Oh, he was a good-sized, husky fellow; you would never think his lungs had been in danger. But there was a gentleness about him, a sweetness that never wore off. The loggers liked him, and so did women and children and cats and dogs. He was just the right person to have around if you brought in a baby flying squirrel, or a bear cub, or a lady novelist, or a drunken Swede. Tom would do just the right thing for every one and everything. He was the perfect servant; maybe too perfect."

"Mother didn't think of Tom as a servant."

"No; she let him be our spiritual father."

Paul stirred uneasily on the cockpit seat. "It bothers me when you say that."

"It bothered the Old Man, too; he was glad to get rid of Tom."

"I thought Tom left us."

Bailey shifted the cigar in his mouth. "It was a coin-flip. The Old Man was beginning to feel the irony of his position—and Tom was listening for the sound of a distant trumpet."

"He heard it, didn't he?"

"He thought he did; and the tune it played was 'Workers of the World, Unite!' So Tom became a Wobbly organizer."

"It's funny that a man of his education would be attracted by a crazy outfit like the I.W.W."

Bailey said, "They attracted some good minds; educations, too. One of the men killed on the *Verona* was a university graduate from New York—Columbia, I believe. Nothing much was said about it, of course, and a man can't go around waving a diploma after the back of his head has been blown off."

Paul swallowed uneasily. "I'd always thought of them as ignorant and fanatical."

"They were fanatical," Bailey said, "like early Christians who stuck to their principles—and were thrown to the lions. Lots of them could have saved their hides by denying they were Wobblies—but they proclaimed the fact even though it meant having their teeth knocked out, or their guts ruptured, or their fingers crushed, one by one, under the iron legs of a jail cot."

The younger brother looked as if his stomach were about to turn over. "That didn't really happen, did it?"

"If you like, I'll name the pillar of society who jumped on the cot for each of a boy's fingers."

"It wasn't——?"

"It wasn't the Old Man, if that's what you want to know."

Readjusting the subject, Paul said, "Do you really think of their beliefs as a religion?"

Bailey said, "They had a vision, however wrong; they suffered in the faith that their fellow men would suffer less—and they sang. Doesn't that define a religion?"

"It seems to," Paul said.

"It's the damndest job to get Americans to sing out loud without looking shamefaced, but the Wobblies did it. I can remember hearing them singing in jail; good, rough voices, steady and triumphant, even though the men knew their singing would bring the deputy sheriffs with oak saps."

"What did they sing?"

"That time they were singing 'Hold the Fort.' A lot of their songs were written by a young Swede, Joe Hillstrom, known as Joe Hill. He wrote 'Hallelujah, I'm a Bum.' But Joe Hill died young—shot by a firing squad for the murder of a Salt Lake City grocer."

Paul asked, "What about Tom? Was he much of a leader?"

"He seems to have been a good organizer," Bailey said, "and he was a good speaker. I heard him for a minute or two when I was a child. He was addressing a big crowd at the corner of the Avenue and making a good job of it."

Paul said, "It would be embarrassing to have your former chauffeur come back to lead the fight against you."

"He showed more delicacy than that suggests," Bailey said. "Tom didn't come back until there was a ban on public speaking in town. He thought it was his duty to uphold freedom of speech."

"It sounds free enough, from what you say."

"It wasn't really," Bailey said.

"What were people so afraid of?" Paul asked.

"Words."

"I suppose Tom was beaten up by some of the ones who were afraid of words? You don't have to tell me about it unless you want to." Then he added, "It seemed to worry Mother as long as she lived. When I was younger I used to ask about Tom in logging towns. Some people had known him, or heard him speak in Wobbly days, but no one knew where he was. I had the romantic idea of going out in the world and finding him."

"I had something of the idea myself," Bailey tossed the chewed butt of his cigar into the passing water. "Mother's dead, and the Wobblies are gone, and if Tom's alive he would be near sixty."

Paul said, "You can't go back."

Bailey said, "Sometimes I think you could but you might not care about going on living."

"I don't understand that."

"Well, when you're a child, you see more clearly than at any other time, but you don't know the meaning of what you see. If you could go back over the things you remember and find their meaning, you would understand the pattern of life."

Paul said, "That ought to make it more interesting."

"We're made to live through a cycle. You can live through it actually, or in your mind. Either way, you're tired and you don't care so much about going on."

"That's only a theory; you don't know."

Bailey said, "I know it partly because I've done part of both, and I have that much less enthusiasm. I've seen some of the pattern of life, and when familiar parts happen over again, I'm not as much impressed; sometimes I'm bored, as I am seeing a picture for a second time."

"There's a lot you haven't done yet."

"Probably less than you think."

"You've never married, or raised a family."

"It depends on what you mean by marriage. Living with a woman is the same idea."

"I suppose you've lived with lots of women, but that means you didn't love any one of them."

"But I did," Bailey said, "and she wasn't just another woman."

"Anyway, nothing came of it."

"It depends on what you mean. I got her with child and that's part of the cycle of life."

"What happened then?"

"I bought her an abortion." After a minute he said, "You don't have to look so finicky about it. Such things happen oftener than you might think."

Paul said, "I don't see how its happening often makes any difference."

"It makes custom," Bailey said, "and you do the customary thing."

The younger brother still looked shocked. "You said you loved her."

"I'll say it again."

"And she loved you?"

"Yes."

"And she wanted an abortion?"

"Of course. At least, I suppose she did."

"You didn't ask her?"

"Not in so many words."

"You aren't sure, then, that she wanted it?"

"If you want to be technical about it, I suppose not, but they generally do."

"That doesn't make her sound any different from the other women you sleep with."

Bailey scowled, "I didn't mean it that way. She was very special. If I'd gone on living with her, I wouldn't have wanted any of the others."

"Why didn't you go on living together?"

"One thing and another," Bailey said. "We quarrelled and I'd had enough of New York for a while, and I came home."

"It sounds like New York," Paul said. "I don't know much about eastern girls, but I shouldn't think you'd find one of them suitable."

"My provincial brother!" Bailey said. "If you had seen Louise, you wouldn't have asked where she came from, and you wouldn't have cared, Brother, you wouldn't have cared!"

"Beautiful?"

"She was beautiful, all right." Then he said, "I don't know whether she was or not. It depends upon what you mean. Our stepmother would make a better showing in a picture. If a good painter did her portrait, you could forget her for a hundred years, and when you dusted off the picture she'd still be beautiful and you wouldn't have lost much."

Paul said, "You have faith in painters."

"It would have to be a good job, of course," his brother admitted. "She should be painted alone in a grape arbor with other people drinking and making love in the sunshine of the background. Marian would be in the shadow of vine leaves, but she wouldn't be drinking; her hands, resting on the table, would be strong and tender, but there would be no one there to caress —only a pomegranate broken open to show that she had eaten some of the seeds and belonged to the King of Hell. She would be alone in the dusk of the arbor, with that still waiting look of hers——"

Paul interrupted, "You were talking about your girl in New York."

"I'm still talking about her," Bailey said. "I had to take you from the known to the unknown. Marian's a subject for a painting. You couldn't do anything with Louise static, in two dimensions. She was all life and motion. Most people are only a little alive, but Louise was all so alive that it hurt, and the pain made other people more alive when they were near her. But there's no use trying to explain to some one who's never been in love."

"You can try, anyway."

"No," Bailey said. "I talk and talk and tell you everything; I make a diagram of my heart on the blackboard and lecture on the scars with the aid of a pointer. You listen and tell me nothing."

Paul looked unhappy. "I don't talk easily," he said, "I never learned. It isn't because I want to keep anything from you."

"You're so healthy, and you've never been in love; you've nothing to tell." Then he said, "This is all nonsense. Every one's been in love; every one's done something romantic, even if he won't admit it."

"I suppose you're right."

"Then you could think of something if you wanted to."

Paul said, "Once I had a braid of a girl's hair."

"A whole braid! She was generous."

"It wasn't a very thick braid, and I got it by accident."

"I know; she was sitting in front of you in school; you had a sharp jackknife, and the braid just came off in your hand."

"It wasn't like that. It was already cut off and she said I could keep it."

"And you kept it?"

"I didn't know what else to do with it; besides, she was very attractive."

"Then you still have it?"

Paul said hastily, "It was a long time ago."

"It was something, anyway; your first scalp." After a minute he looked at his brother expectantly. "Is that all? Didn't you go back to see how her new crop of hair was growing?"

Paul said, "I tried to see her once, but she wasn't at home."

"And you never tried again?"

"Not for a long time."

"But you did?"

"In a way," Paul admitted.

"What do you mean—in a way?"

"When she gave me the hair, she said if I ever wanted to see her, I could burn some of it and she would appear. It was just a fancy; she didn't believe it and neither did I."

"Did she tell you that?"

"No."

"Then how do you know?"

"It couldn't have been anything else."

"Naturally. But she wouldn't have said that if she hadn't wanted to see you again."

"She might have."

"You wanted to see her and you didn't even take the trouble to burn some of her hair and see what would happen?"

"I didn't say I didn't."

"Then you did."

Paul said, "I did, only it was a long time afterward—a whole year since I had seen her."

"And nothing happened?"

"I didn't say that."

"Well, what did happen?"

"I saw her that day—with the man she was going to marry."

"So you waited too long."

"Nothing had been said about the conditions under which I would see her."

"How did you feel about it?"

"About what?"

"Seeing her so soon after you tried to conjure her up, like the Witch of Endor?"

Paul said, "I was startled."

"Is that all?"

"When you're startled there isn't room for anything else."

"What about afterward, when you got over being startled?"

"She was as good as engaged, and that ended it as far as I was concerned."

"What about her?"

"What do you mean?"

"Was it ended as far as she was concerned?"

"I don't know; we didn't discuss it."

"Did you want to?"

"I told you I was startled; that was all I felt at the time."

"So that was the end of it?"

"That was the end."

"What effect did it have on you?"

"None, after it was over."

"Are you sure?"

"Yes. I'd been going in one direction for a long time. Thinking about her changed me a little, and after it was over I changed back to the way I had been going before."

"It was one time then when you might have fallen in love?"

"I might have."

"Tell me," Bailey said, "was she sweet?"

Paul said, "I thought she was."

"You should have seen Louise. She had a stout heart and good digestion and such good health she never mentioned it.

She was enthusiasm without effort. Everything in sight interested her, and she wanted to know how things worked, especially people. She was always having me tell about people I had known and the things they did. 'In my next incarnation I'm going to be a priest,' she would say; 'I'll listen to confessions for fifty years without saying anything, and then the penances may fall in strange places.' "

"I hadn't thought eastern girls would be like that," Paul remarked.

"I hardly noticed her at first," Bailey went on. "She would come into the book shop quiet as a mouse and make for the corner where I kept books on the dance; then when I looked that way she might be gone—or reading one of the books as if it belonged to her. She was studying modern dance, and she didn't have much money to spend, but when she found a book she really wanted she bought it. In her deliberate way she was a good customer, and she was loyal. The first time I realized that was when I was dealing with another sort of woman: a Continental who admired the little porcelain figures and animals, using a phrase from a different language for each one; picking them up and exclaiming how charming they were, and how reasonable—until you'd have thought she was going to buy the whole collection. Soon she began tapering off until I knew she was only killing time without intending to buy anything. Then I saw Louise at the counter with a book which she'd decided to buy. I don't know how long she'd been waiting, but finally she gave the woman a sidewise glance and said '*Hyas wawa; halo chickamun.*' It was so unexpected from a shy, exquisite little person, and the comment punctured the hot-air balloon like a pin."

"*Much talk, no money,*" Paul translated the phrase for himself. "But a New York girl wouldn't know Chinook Jargon!"

"She was from Hood Canal," Bailey said.

Paul instinctively looked towards the southwest, but his view of the peninsula was blocked by the high shore of Whidbey Island. "I thought she was a New York girl."

"That was your idea," Bailey said. "You were right, too. New York is made up of boys and girls from Hood Canal, Amarillo, Cedar Rapids, Scranton, Cheyenne, and Sandusky. The whole nation feeds that magnificent bonfire, that eternal light."

"Enough of them seem to get burned," Paul observed.

"You can't blame New York for that."

"I don't see why not."

"The boys and girls have New York in their hearts before they leave home," Bailey explained. "They pool their hearts and build New York in their own image."

"That's only partly true."

"Nothing is altogether true."

"Not even that," Paul said. "I see how New York could be exciting, but people never seem to have much to show for it."

"It's one life," Bailey said, "and you can't take any of it with you except things you can communicate to some one else who has loved New York."

A few miles from the town, Bailey sailed the sloop close in to the beach, then brought her up into the wind. His brother went forward to let the anchor go, and while he was still paying out line, Bailey joined him and took in the fluttering jib.

Before getting down the mainsail, the brothers stood near the mast a minute, looking towards the shore. Home Place looked quiet and deserted, with the homely brown-shingled house standing modestly behind trees and shrubs. The house was smaller than it had seemed in childhood, and everything else had grown. The Bing cherry tree spread as wide as the house, its top branches higher than the chimney; and the spindly little spruce Bailey and Tom had brought in from the woods was a great blue-green Christmas tree, with its top looking in the window of what had been Tom's room above the garage.

"The shrubs want cutting back," Paul said.

"That's part of Tag's job," Bailey said, "but maybe his wooden leg gives him a fellow feeling for the trees." Bailey had drunk nothing all day but a few stubbies of beer, but when his brother pulled the dingy alongside, he put in a quart of whiskey. "Tag will want a snort," he explained, but he was beginning to feel the need of one himself.

They had not seen any sign of life about the place, but when they were walking up the path from the beach they heard the sound of music. Bailey stopped, with the bottle of whiskey in one hand and a sack of canned goods in the other. "Tag's getting drunk to music."

A somber, triumphant voice came to them, like the tread of marching feet:

> I dreamed I saw Joe Hill last night,
> Alive as you and me.
> Says I, "But Joe, you're ten years dead."
> "I never died," said he.
> "I never died," said he.

"Joe Hill? He's the one we were talking about," said Paul.

Bailey nodded. "And in our stronghold, where the Old Man licked the Wobblies!"

"It's a good song. Whose is it?"

"Alfred Hayes wrote the words. The voice and music are Robinson; our own composer who wrote the music for *Ballad for Americans.*"

They waited for the end of the song, then went on up the path, among Tom Horton's trees, with Bailey singing like an echo: "I dreamed I saw Joe Hill last night, Alive as you and me——"

They tramped up the stairs of the garage, and Bailey pounded on the worn cedar door with the confidence of one bringing gifts.

The record player stopped near the middle of another song. "Who's there?"

"Deputies! Come out of there, you Wobbly!"

"Wait till I get my leg on."

"The hell with your leg." Bailey threw open the door. In the untidy room, Tag sat on the leather-covered sofa, strapping on his peg-leg. Beside him was the squat radio, topped by a bottle and glass, like a combination offer of wine and song. Tag was big and heavy-featured, with old blue eyes and wispy red hair turning gray, and the dumb, sly look of a drunk prepared to prove himself sober. When he saw who his visitors were he relaxed. "Find some chairs while I put on my leg."

Paul went over to stand beside the window. The room smelled of whiskey and stale tobacco and unwashed bedding and old magazines.

"We brought you some canned stuff," Bailey said, as proudly as if the caretaker sat and starved until the brothers had the happy thought of dropping in with food.

"You didn't need to," Tag answered; "the store delivers."

With his gift of food dwindled by lack of appreciation, Bailey presented the liquor. "I brought a bottle of whiskey, too."

"*Ja.*"

"Old Overholt."

"*Ja.*"

"It's good liquor."

"*Ja.*"

"That's what I like about you," Bailey said, "you're so God-damned appreciative! I bring you a bottle of Old Overholt, and you say '*Ja*.' It's good whiskey, I tell you."

"*Ja*," Tag said, "and you'll drink it."

"Why not? You've had too much already."

"I'll get you a glass." Tag got up and went over to the cupboard, his wooden leg thumping heavily on the thinly carpeted floor. Bailey took the corkscrew from among the litter in the ash tray and drew the cork. Filling the cloudy glass which Tag brought, he said, "Anyway, I'm washing one of your glasses. I hope you appreciate that."

"*Ja*."

"How about one for you?"

"No," Tag answered.

"The Swede knows two words—*ja* and *no*." Bailey moved phonograph records and a mail order catalogue out of Tom Horton's old Morris chair and sat down carefully. "This place is a dump."

"*Ja*."

"It isn't a dump and you're a nice housekeeper."

"No."

"Cheerful, isn't he, Paul?"

Tag said darkly, "You try losing a leg."

"That was twenty years ago."

"*Ja*. And what's worse—to be without a leg one year, or twenty?"

"You get more used to it in twenty."

"You don't get used to not going to the woods any more."

"You got a soft job out of it," Bailey reminded him. "And you were always a lazy bastard."

"Now I got nothing to look forward to." Morose and tousled, he stared at Paul's back and the closed window with the blue-green top of the spruce tree outside. "You boys come for something?"

"We came to hear your Wobbly songs," Bailey told him.

"I got no Wobbly songs."

Drinking straight whiskey, Bailey said, "You carry a Wobbly card, too; it's inside your left shoe."

"Yust try and find it." Tag pointed to his left leg, which was the wooden one. "There are no more Wobblies."

"Let's hear the Wobbly song, anyway; the one about Joe Hill."

"That's no Wobbly song."

"I suppose Joe Hill wasn't an I.W.W., either."

From the window Paul said, "Tag's right; it's just a song."

"A good one, too," Bailey added cheerfully. "That's why I want to hear it."

Putting the record on the player, Tag said, "I got it because Joe Hillstrom was a Swede."

"That's no reason," Bailey said. "Anyway, he didn't amount to anything until he took an American name—and was shot for it."

The argument was brushed aside by the singer's voice, touched with sadness, but confident and triumphant—singing of a rebel whose body died before a firing squad in a prison yard, while his spirit escaped to lead workingmen wherever they organized. The song ended, the voice of Joe Hill diminishing into the distance but clear to the last whispered word. *"I never died,"* said Joe.

"Propaganda," Bailey said.

Paul said, "It doesn't matter, if it's good."

"Joe Hill made good songs," Tag said; "the Swedes make good songs."

"They have bad manners, though," Bailey said. "Joe Hill was a working stiff who took what he needed. When he ran out of money in Salt Lake, he shot him a grocer—and got caught."

"*Ja*, he was shot—for being a Wobbly!" Tag shouted. "Because he made songs for working people! They framed him!"

The baiting had gone a little too far, and Bailey put his arm affectionately on Tag's great shoulder.

"See, Paul? He is a Wobbly! The Old Man cleaned them out of the woods, but he's never got them out of his own hair. Tom Horton was a Wobbly, too. Only he kept this room neat."

Tag did not seem to hear the slur on his housekeeping. His eyes had blazed at the mention of Tom Horton, and he cried, "*Ja, ja,* I knew Tom! He came to Pilchuck camp."

Paul asked, "What was he like, Tag?"

"His face was like Christ," Tag said; "he was like a pastor—a good pastor."

"Do you remember anything he said?"

"*Ja.* I was bull bucker, and I wanted to keep my yob. I didn't want to take out a Wobbly card and lose my yob. Then Tom Horton talked to me like I was his brother, and I didn't think about my yob any more. Tom put his hand on my shoulder and he said, 'Tag Sorenson, we are more than they. If we organize, there won't be any more talk of firing. These are our woods and this is our earth. We will share in the work and the good things. No one will say to his brother: *Go away; we don't need you any more.*'"

"Visionary," Bailey said.

"Tom was a good man. He loved people and he would die for them. Tom was a good man."

Paul went back to the window and opened it, letting in the smell of sun-warmed spruce.

Tag poured some of his own whiskey into his glass. "If you want something from the house, you know where the keys are."

"We are all coming up for the summer in a week or two," Bailey told him. "How do you like that?"

"*Ja*, it's your house; I never use it."

"Your hospitality leaves nothing—leaves nothing!"

Paul closed the window. "I'm going to try for some pictures in the orchard. There's one I've tried before, but it never came out right."

Bailey emptied his glass and got up. "There's something I left in the house the last time I was here—" He took the keys from where they hung on the antlers by the door and followed his brother down the stairs. "I'll be around somewhere when you get back."

"I won't be gone more than an hour. There's a tree by the creek—you'll see what I mean if it comes out right." He went away through the tall grass, easy and tall and abstracted, with his thick hair golden in the June sun.

VIII

G*OING INTO* the house was like opening the cover of an old book, airless and cool and dimly musty. The fireplace that smoked when the wind was in the south, and the furniture shabbier than when he had seen it last; but all in neat, humorless order. The smoke of a cigar was real and a little rude, like smoking in a museum. He went up the creaking stairs, sliding his hand along the banister, polished by the seat of childhood pants. Once he had gone too fast and proved the reality of the newel post; his legs collapsed like air when he got off the banister, and he howled his fright because there was no reassuring pain. While his mother telephoned the doctor, Tom Horton held him comfortingly in his arms. Then he hit Bailey lightly below each kneecap with the edge of his hand. The feet flew up of their own accord, and it was so interesting that Bailey stopped crying. Tom said: "You're all right; you can walk now." He walked a step, then ran; and the memory faded out as confidence in his legs returned and became a commonplace.

He had come for something, but he could not remember what at first because it was nothing tangible. It had to do with a house, and the nursery. But when he went in and pulled the shades, he could see nothing of it. The nursery windows looked out on the orchard and a bend of the creek, and there were no houses in sight. But the memory grew clearer. It was a white two-story house with dark oblong windows. Just beyond the house, against the sky, there were dark poplar trees. As long as the house and grove were there, no harm could come to any one; there would be no storms or pain or frightening things; only the sun and moon taking turns in the sky; the rising and falling of dew; changes that were like the music of a song out of deep peace.

The house on the hill, and the poplar trees, were probably from some old picture book, gone long ago, and nothing in themselves, only a symptom. What he had come back for was the feeling of security he had known in childhood—the comfort and peace. There wasn't much left to connect him with that state of mind; nothing in the room but his big maple crib, which had served variously as a ship on the high seas, a lion's cage, and finally as a place of refuge when sleep struck him down gently.

He went over and touched the dented maple railing that was like a little fence around the plot of mattress. Aloud he said, "The grave of the amiable child!" Standing there, amused at himself, he had a sudden idea—or perhaps it was what he had come for, without knowing. He went over to the window to make sure that Paul was away in the orchard. And he braced a chair against the door, with its back under the knob. Shame-faced, but determined, he let down the side of the crib and tried to crawl in. In one moment, he realized how enormous he had grown. It was a big crib and he had slept in it for years, but now there was no room for his great hulking legs. He solved part of the difficulty by draping his knees over the end railing, but he was immediately dizzy from the rush of blood to his head. A cushion from the armchair raised his head to a comfortable position, and the crib began to feel more natural. There was still the awkwardness of managing a cigar in cramped quarters, and he made another expedition around the nursery. An old toy box became a crib-side table, with a doll's dish for an ash tray. When he eased himself in again, the place was more like home. Through cigar smoke, he considered his gigantic legs, draped over the end of the crib, and thought, "I've learned to smoke since I slept here last." The taste of the cigar became unsuitable, and when it went out he put it aside.

But the stale aftersmell of tobacco belonged in the nursery. It was like his father's breath when he got home from camp and came upstairs to kiss Bailey good night. The car stopped in the drive under the nursery window, a friendly monster that pushed away silence and the dusk with its sweet, chuckling roar, and a glow of lights. The car door closed with a smooth, rich slam. The father's big voice said, "Take her away, Tom!" There was the soft sound of Tom's answer, and a great, soft rumble as the homing monster lumbered down the drive into its stall in the garage.

Bailey stood in his crib when he heard his parents on the stairs, and reached out his arms as his father came into the room. His father was big and solid, with thick hair and a thick moustache that tickled. Sometimes he smelled of pitchy smoke, and sometimes of fresh evergreens, and sometimes of whiskey. But there was always the reassuring smell of cigar smoke. He would kiss Bailey and lift him up on his shoulders, where he sat as securely as a squirrel on the branch of a great tree; he would feel Bailey's arm muscle and say, "Do you see that, Myra? He's almost strong enough to hold a peavey! He'll be the champion logger of Thunderbird County when he grows up."

The father was not supposed to take Bailey out of his crib and play with him; it excited him and kept him awake afterward, the mother said. But the father did what he pleased. He never stayed in the nursery long, and after a few minutes he would hoist the child back into his crib. "All right, boy, hit the hay." If Bailey had got into the mood for play and tried to slip out, his father caught him with a hand like iron that could break him in two, only it fitted so exactly that it did not hurt. "You stay there, boy; enough is enough!" Bailey stayed.

Bailey's father was always the same, but sometimes he noticed that his mother had changed from the way he remembered her. Once, when she seemed too thin in the face and full in the body, she tucked him in his crib and said, "Be a good boy, Bailey, and maybe I'll have that little brother for you."

Bailey had often asked for a little brother, but when he heard that he could expect one, he was not interested any more. He said, "Little brother, or no little brother, I want those little rabbits you promised me."

After that his mother was sick and went to the hospital, and things went badly at home. Bailey threw the cat down the laundry chute, and broke the glass in the cold frame, and put a silver spoon in the kitchen stove, and wet his bed every night.

The housekeeper was named Veronica; she had red cheeks and spectacles, and she could not understand why Bailey made so much trouble. He did not know, either, except that he wanted his mother home, and he did not like Veronica.

When the mother came home without a baby, Bailey was no more surprised than if some one had gone fishing without catching anything, and he thought no more about it. Later she provided the baby brother with much less fuss.

Paul seemed an impudence at first, but he was a good baby who did not ask for much. He would lie in his crib or carriage for hours, without making any more noise than a cooing pigeon. Instead of his being a bother, you wanted to watch what he was doing, and bring him things. Usually he was playing with a rose or a grape leaf, and talking to it. Tom had thought that Paul showed a special liking for such things, and it was his idea that he should always have flowers and leaves to play with. Bailey kept him supplied, after he had learned what things were safe even if Paul ate them. Safe things were roses without the thorns, violets, and nasturtiums, apple and grape and maple leaves, and little branches of fir. Things that were not safe were: salal leaves and laurel, nightshade and fennel and poppies and foxglove. Collecting things was about all he could do for Paul. His mother had learned from the newest baby book that babies should not be rocked or bounced or played with, or handled unnecessarily. Paul spent his infancy austerely, considering leaves and flowers. Once, to see what he would do, his mother gave him an artificial rose from one of her hats. He examined it for a minute, then pushed it out through the railing of his crib so it fell on the floor, and went back to playing with a cluster of white lilac. His mother said he was as wise as one of King Solomon's bees. Bailey thought it a small enough compliment. He had already decided Paul would be a fine brother and was not jealous of him any more.

There had been a wall of safety around the family; the new brother made a break in it, but after that the wall healed and he was safe and welcome inside. Bailey was rich in time; long days lengthened away into an eternal summer, and the years of life were beyond calculation. During that part of time, Tom would bring the father home while it was still daylight. The days were so long that even after Bailey had been sent to bed, night had not come. He would stand at the window in his pyjamas and look down into the garden. Everything there was visible, but softly, in a cool light that made no shadows. Voices, too, were soft and cool. Bailey, at the window, would listen to them without noticing what they said. Tom's voice had a kind of low vibration that seemed going away to meet the dusk; the mother's voice was clear, but quiet, like a bird that has left the sky because of the coming dark. The wings of her voice were folded, but you knew they would fly again. There were voices in the garden because there were things to plant or transplant —shrubs or little trees Tom had brought home from the woods, or things from other parts of the garden. He was going to leave them until next day, and so was the mother; she was only going to decide where this or that could go, and having decided, she would get a spade or trowel and begin to dig. Then Tom would come to help, and sometimes they would work until they became dim shapes in the dusk of the garden, with the earth driving them toward fulfillment.

Bailey's father never did any gardening, and he and his voice did not seem to change as much as the others in the evening. Tom would be holding a little tree upright in the earth, while the mother knelt, covering the roots, lovingly, and when one of them spoke and the other answered, you felt they were part of the earth and the dusk and the tree. Then Bailey's father would come striding through the garden leaving a trail of cigar smoke, and his big voice would sound, impatiently: 'Oh, give it up, Myra; you'll go blind working in that light! And you, Tom; I'm not paying you to work fourteen hours a day."

Even after the end of the gardening, the day did not always end. Sometimes, when the darkness was just showing itself, the moon thinned it out again until there was silver on all the little fruit trees, and the creek became a bright silver stream in the orchard. And Tom was still near; Bailey heard him playing his flute, softly, from his apartment above the garage. The mother came to tuck him in and kiss him good night. Before going downstairs, she would stand for a minute at the window, looking out and listening. That was when Bailey was awake. When he was asleep, everything was still there, securely: the kiss, and the moonlight, and the song of the flute.

Somewhere in those days and nights there was the picture of all security: the serene white house with dark oblong windows, and the grove of poplar trees against the sky.

All the time there were other things in the world, and other people. Only he did not notice them until they became angry or excited. One Sunday morning when Tom was driving Bailey to Sunday school, he stopped to pick up some loggers who were walking into town. The car was a seven-passenger Packard with bucket seats in front and an aisle between, so you could get into the front of the car and walk through to the back. When the folding seats were up there was room on the floor for two fifty-gallon drums of oil, or parts of a donkey-engine, or a few sides of beef for the cookhouse. It was a big car and the three loggers and their blanket rolls did not fill it. Bailey didn't pay much attention to them. One of them asked Tom about Iron Horse Camp, which Bailey's father owned. Tom said it was all right, and another logger said, "Highball, like all the others." Tom did not answer, and that was all the loggers said about camps. After a minute one of them seemed to remember it was Sunday and began singing a hymn tune. Then all three of them sang, sitting in a row with their blanket rolls propped up against their knees and swaying as the big car rumbled along. Their voices were rich and deep, like church, only they sounded a little mocking as they sang:

> "You'll get pie in the sky
> In the sweet bye and bye——"

It was Bailey's first acquaintance with the songs of Joe Hill. At the time he knew only that the words were interesting, and he marched into his Sunday school class singing the new hymn:

> "You'll get pie in the sky
> In the sweet bye and bye——"

"Bailey," his teacher said, "that isn't a very nice song for Sunday school."

He didn't see why, and on the way home he sang it again, sitting beside Tom, who neither joined him nor said it wasn't nice.

"We're going to have pie for dinner," Bailey said. "Veronica set them out to cool, and I stuck my finger in one; it was raspberry."

"Veronica makes good pies," Tom said.

"*Pie in the sky*—what does that mean?"

"Pie after you get to Heaven."

Bailey thought it over. "That's a long time to wait for dessert, isn't it?"

"I think so."

"Do some people really have to wait that long?"

Tom said, "It doesn't mean just pie; it means all the good things like having your own little farm, or a job as long as you want it; being able to marry, knowing your children won't suffer or go hungry or ignorant."

"—Pie in the sky in the sweet bye and bye. Are they sure of getting married then?"

" 'In Heaven there is neither marrying nor giving in marriage.' "

"Then it's a gyp!"

"That's what the song is trying to say."

Until they began to sing, there had been loggers just the way there were trees, and the only trouble that ever happened was when one of the trees fell on a logger, or a log or a cable did something to him. On Saturday nights loggers got drunk in town, and on the Fourth of July they got very drunk and stayed that way for several days, and there was no work done in the camps. Except for special times like those, you did not notice loggers much more than trees; they came and went as quietly as the seasons, by steamers or interurban or freight trains, or on foot with their blanket rolls on their backs. Those who went away by hearse went most quietly of all.

Loggers had been that way until they began to sing, and their voices reached the dining room. At dinner the father reported that the loggers were grumbling because there were no shower baths, which they had never had. They also complained about having to carry their blankets, which they had always carried. And they even thought the camp should provide them with clean sheets. The loggers did not get those luxuries, but thinking of them seemed to lead to other expensive tastes, and presently they talked about working eight hours a day and being paid more. By the end of the summer they had decided that the woods belonged to them as much as to the operators, and they should have their share in the profits. By fall they had decided that the operators were unnecessary and should have their lands and camps taken away to be run by the loggers.

Somewhere along the way Bailey learned that it was not really the loggers who were to blame. There were sinister people who stirred up trouble in the camps and harvest fields; wherever they went they made men dissatisfied. At first the troublemakers were known as the I.W.W., but soon they became "Wobblies," and were hardly ever spoken of by the older name.

Bailey's father had thick red-brown hair and a thick moustache, a full face that got red easily, and big shoulders and a big, confident voice. He knew just how Wobblies should be treated, but at that point the mother always checked him, because of Bailey.

The mother and Tom sometimes talked about the Wobblies, but they were not nearly so certain. Bailey remembered them talking one day while waiting at the interurban station for a guest: Tom sitting sidewise in one of the bucket seats of the car; Bailey and his mother among cool leather upholstery in the tonneau. Tom with his wavy hair tousled and one big arm hooked over the back of the seat. He was big and strong to protect the people he loved; his eyes had the look of seeing tomorrow's sunrise, while his smile was sad and gentle about today. The mother in the back seat: her hair was light brown and her eyes were gray, and the color in her face was delicate. There were no strong colors or anything sudden or surprising, but all delicate things together made something strong and cool and fine that was always there, quietly. You had to look twice to see how pretty she was.

The mother was saying, "I know the men should have shower baths and clean beds and more pay when the business can afford it, and more time for themselves. But it must stop somewhere; they can't have everything!"

Tom said, "They haven't anything yet; nothing of their own except their blanket rolls and bedbugs, and pride in the work they do for some one else."

"That isn't right," the mother said. "But neither are all the things they want. Suppose they got what was fair? Would they be satisfied?"

Tom said, "It would depend on whether they thought it was fair."

The mother said, "Suppose it was you. Would you do what you thought was fair if it was likely to ruin you?"

"It would depend on whether I cared most about doing what was right, or being comfortable."

"Then you would."

Tom said, "I hope I would."

Bailey heard his mother take a slow, deep breath. After a

minute she asked, "What do you think is right, Tom? How much of what they want?"

Tom didn't answer immediately. At last he said, "I don't know if their methods are right, but I believe all industry should be run by the people and for the people."

"That isn't the American way," the mother said; "in business, I mean."

"If it happens, it will be the American way. It is what men have learned in the woods and mines and harvest fields of America."

"If it happened," the mother said, "what would become of me—of us?"

Tom said, "Nothing bad will ever happen to you, Mrs. Dow —to people who want to be fair."

Bailey squirmed about on the back seat beside his mother. The talk was like blowing dust, and while he listened to the words, he did not understand their meaning. But he felt uneasy, and he sensed that parts of his fine, reliable world were crumbling and blowing away in dust. The only comfort was his impression that Tom would take care of his mother and himself.

Not long after that Bailey found the first colored leaves for Paul to play with in his crib, and the family went somewhere in the car and were on their way home at sunset. Bailey could not recall where they had been, or their home-coming. All he remembered was a moment of their journey. He was warm in the back seat of the car, between his big father and his mother, who held Paul on her lap. Tom was driving. The engine made a hungry, homing sound, and as the car soared up out of the valley you could see the round top and square shoulders of the big radiator dark against the dawn of headlights on the road. Then they were on high level ground, where there was still some daylight left. Away to the west, where the sun was gone, there was a clear yellow light in the sky, and cold purple clouds. Night and autumn were coming on, and it was cold outside the car, but inside everything was warm and safe. The ones Bailey loved were all there: his mother and the sleeping Paul, and his big warm father, rich with the smell of cigars; and Tom, who understood everything and could do everything, driving the big car as steadily as a star in its course. They were all together, travelling through the darkening, cold world in a safe and warm world of their own. That was all of the memory, one moment of a journey, and the feeling that no harm could come to them, no illness, or age, or trouble, or separation.

A few days or weeks after that, Tom Horton was gone. He went quietly, but he had been so much a part of everything that it felt as if a giant had walked out, tearing part of the wall and roof away and leaving the house open to the weather and the sky.

The new chauffeur was a spindly, fair-haired young man who read detective magazines, told Bailey dirty stories, and did not know one tree from another. Bailey was not the only one who noticed the difference. There was a flock of quail, like plump women with little feet and high plumes in their hats. The first morning they came around the garage, the window was opened as usual, but instead of scattering wheat, the new chauffeur began firing with a .22 rifle, and he killed one and wounded two others before they realized that the world had changed. That was the difference between Tom Horton and Jim.

Things away from home did not go well, either. The shingle weavers in town went on strike, and Bailey's father was always cranky. He said the mills were crippled just when the price of shingles was up and the owners had their chance to make a killing.

Jim, the new chauffeur, was not like Tom, and he thought a

little "sapping up" would end the trouble. Once, in the kitchen, Bailey heard him telling Veronica that the strike was as good as over. The police had driven the pickets onto the trestle bridge over the bay, where they met a party of strikebreakers with clubs. When they turned back they met more strikebreakers, and they had to take their sapping up or jump into the bay. Jim thought that was the end of it, but it was only the beginning. The next day the shingle weavers and their friends beat the strikebreakers. Then there was a "riot," and after that the Wobblies came to town.

The Wobblies and the police played a game. It was simple, but they were serious about it and people got hurt, and Bailey could not understand why they played it. The Wobbly who was *It* would get up on the corner at the Avenue and start to make a speech, and the sheriff would arrest him. Then another Wobbly would be *It*, and while the first one was being taken to jail, the second one would speak until it was his turn to be arrested. It seemed as if the Wobblies wanted the sheriff and his men to arrest as many of them as possible, though Bailey could not understand why any one should want to be arrested. When he asked about it, his father said the Wobblies hoped to fill the jail so full that they would have to be turned out again. But there were ways of handling that.

Bailey was going on seven, but that year ended one kind of childhood for him. At the beginning it was like a song: people were the words, and the music was the sun and moon and the weather, and things growing out of the earth. Before the year ended the music got thin, and the voices were everywhere, and out of tune: talking guardedly in the kitchen, arguing upstairs at night. Sometimes when he had been asleep for a long time, he woke and heard the angry buzz of voices from his parents' room. The words were never loud enough for him to hear, but they went on and on and would not let him sleep. The hateful sound usually went on until Paul began to cry. The mother would go to quiet him, and after that everything was still. Paul, who was two, was the only person in the house young enough to raise his voice against wrong.

That was Bailey's first year at school in town, and at school he also heard arguing and angry voices. One day at noon there was a fight between a shingle weaver's son and one of the big boys who said that all the strikers should be sapped up good. Bailey was scared by the fighting and the sight of blood, and he did not understand why they should fight about words. Afterward he learned that the smaller boy's father had been beaten in jail; the beating of the father only led to the beating of the son, who also had his face rubbed in the dirt of the playground. Meanwhile the game between the Wobblies and the deputies went on. Every time some one tried to speak at the corners of the Avenue, there was a bigger crowd to see him dragged from the platform.

Why did men want to do a thing that only led to jail and getting hurt? His mother told him not to worry himself about such things, but he kept on asking and finally she told him they were fighting for "freedom of speech," which was sacred to those who believed in it.

Bailey asked, "Do you believe in freedom of speech, Mother?"

She didn't answer right away, but when she did she said, "Yes. What the I.W.W.'s say is wrong, but they have the right to say it."

"Why should people be allowed to say things that are wrong?"

"There's a chance of their being right, Bailey. People can't be sure."

"You are."

"No," she said, "that's only what I think."

Jim came to school for Bailey every afternoon and drove back by way of the Avenue, where he usually stopped for a magazine, or on some other errand. If he had only Bailey in the car, and there was a crowd at the corner, Jim drove very fast and close to the curb where people were standing, and usually he tooted the horn. If Bailey's mother was in the car, Jim drove slowly and didn't make any noise.

One afternoon the crowd was so big that people were standing in the street, and there was not much room for cars to pass. Jim drove slowly until suddenly Bailey's mother leaned forward and called, "Stop, Jim!"

The car stopped in drizzling rain and Bailey looked at the backs of loggers in stag shirts and tin pants, and shingle weavers and their wives in their shabby best clothes. People were cheering, but Bailey did not know why, and he did not know why his mother wanted to stop. Then he saw Tom, whom he never expected to see again.

Tom was above the crowd, on a platform back from the sidewalk, and the people were cheering him. Bailey cried, "Tom! Tom! There's Tom!" and he began cheering, too. He felt his mother's hand on his arm, and thought she was going to stop him, but her hand just stayed there and she didn't say anything.

Tom was bare-headed, in overalls and a blue flannel shirt open at the neck, and he looked strong and gentle and sure of himself. He raised his hand and everything went still; then he began to speak about "industrial democracy." It sounded dry and Bailey was disappointed; but the cheering stopped him and he had to raise his hand so he could go on.

Then the cheering changed to booing and angry shouts. Bailey looked around in the drizzle of rain to see what was wrong, and when he looked back to the platform he saw a swirl of big men in Stetson hats and dangling clubs, and Tom was blotted out, except for the arm which he had raised for silence and could not get down again as he was swept from the platform.

Bailey did not remember thinking what he should do, but he remembered his mother pulling him back and reaching past him to close the door, which he had opened. The car was moving, with the shouting loggers and shingle weavers and their women sliding by like people on a moving platform. Then the car was rolling down the Avenue where people under black umbrellas were walking as if nothing had happened. Bailey hated them, and he was screaming: "Mother, we have to get Tom! They'll sap him up! Mother, make Jim go back!"

The mother soothed Bailey and she said that the sheriff's men wouldn't hurt Tom. He believed her at first, and was quieted. Then he had doubts. Every minute or two he asked: "Are you sure they won't hurt Tom?" and his mother would say, "I'm sure of it, Bailey; we won't let them!"

Bailey didn't know what was done about it, but in the morning when his mother woke him for school she looked easy and smiling. "They didn't hurt Tom," she said. "They just kept him at the jail a little while and let him go. No one tried to hurt him at all."

Bailey was glad of that, but he wasn't excited any more, and he just said, "That's good." Then he asked, "What are we having for breakfast?"

"Pancakes, with bacon and apple jelly."

Bailey said, "Oh, Boy!" No one else could make pancakes like Veronica, but his mother didn't let him have them often. While he was putting on his slippers to go to the bathroom, he thought of Tom again. "Will Tom come to see us?"

There was black rain outside, and his mother, standing at the window, did not look as happy as when she had first told him about Tom. "No," she said. "They made him take the inter-urban back to Seattle; they wouldn't let him stay."

"I don't see why he couldn't stay if he wanted to."

His mother did not answer.

"What would have happened if he had stayed?"

"They would have put him in jail," his mother said, "and he might have got hurt."

It was a good thing Tom didn't get sapped up, but the trouble wasn't over. A few afternoons later, Jim whispered to Bailey that he had something to show him. When they were in the garage, Jim opened the black tool box of the car and took out a new policeman's club, with a loop of rawhide for his wrist, and while Bailey was still feeling startled, he turned the lapel of his coat and flashed a badge. "Meet Deputy Sheriff Jim Collins."

Bailey said hopefully, "You aren't going to drive for us any more?"

"Sure," Jim said. "This is only part of my work. Every one on the right side has been sworn in. We have a whole army, with one company to watch the boats, and another the trains, and another to take care of strikers. Your Old Man and I are in the Flying Squadron that gets Wobblies out of town."

The "Flying Squadron" had an exciting sound, and Jim let Bailey hold the club, which was heavy at one end and light at the other. "It's loaded," Jim explained, and Bailey gave it back gingerly, under the impression that it might blow up.

At the age of seven Bailey could keep a secret; Jim asked him not to say anything about the Flying Squadron, and he did not mention it even to his own mother. But his mother must have known. Sometimes the father and Jim didn't get home until after Bailey was in bed, and sometimes they drove away after dinner and did not come back until late at night.

Around that time Veronica left, red-eyed and -nosed and angry. Bailey had never been fond of her, but the heart of the kitchen went with her and the Golden Age of cookery was over.

Veronica's departure was mixed up mysteriously with a letter from her brother, who was hurt and in Seattle. Some one had ruptured him with the muzzle of a revolver while threatening to shoot off something called his "personals." At least that was how Bailey understood it.

Veronica got the letter in the morning, and that evening Bailey's mother served a dinner which she had prepared. It was a good dinner, but the silence made it seem like eating pictures of food when you weren't hungry. Bailey's father did not like the silence. When they were almost through he cleared his throat and said,

"I'm sorry it happened, Myra, but he was a fool to come to town in working clothes."

The mother did not say anything.

"When you have five hundred deputies, there are bound to be mistakes."

The mother did not answer, and that was all of the conversation during dinner.

That was the fall Tom came back. There was some rain that night, but it was not raining when Bailey was awakened. His father and Jim drove away after dinner and came back some time during the night. Bailey half-woke when Jim was putting the car in the garage, and almost immediately the father came upstairs. Bailey heard him washing noisily in the bathroom, and making a spitting sound as if he was trying to get rid of some taste he didn't like. After that he went to the big bedroom; the boy heard him in the hall and once he gave a spitting grunt as if he hadn't been able to get rid of the taste.

Bailey supposed his mother was already in bed, but after a

while he heard her moving about downstairs. He had grown afraid that fall and insisted on having his door open a little, so light from the hall and the sounds in the house would come in. It wasn't exactly that he was afraid of the dark; he no longer trusted his parents to manage everything safely.

Some time after his father had gone to bed, he heard the kitchen doorbell, and then the sound of his mother's footsteps hurrying through the downstairs. He heard Jim's voice in the living room, not loud, but frightened. Bailey was terribly awake by then and he jumped out of bed and started downstairs.

There were lights in the living room and Bailey's mother and the chauffeur were there, talking. The mother was the way she had been at dinner, but Jim was dressed only at the ends, with his chauffeur's cap on his head and black shoes with dragging laces on his feet. In between he had a white night shirt spotted by rain. He was grasping a revolver in one hand and explaining: "I heard one of them try the door! First I thought the boss had left something in the car. I was going to let him in, and then I knew it was some one else. I looked out of the window, and I could just see him in the dark and rain, going away towards the back of the house."

The mother looked scared, but she was trying not to be scared, and she said, "It might have been some one who is lost."

"There were more of them," Jim said. "I waited until he was gone and then I circled around towards the front door. I just got around the corner when I heard one of them walking. I stopped and he must have seen me, because he dropped behind a bush. I heard him fall. Then I ran back the other way and got to the kitchen door."

"But what could they want?" the mother asked.

Jim said, "It's Wobblies; they have the house surrounded!"

The mother said, "I'll call Mr. Dow. I don't like to——"

Frozen on the stair landing, Bailey saw him shrink back and raise his revolver.

The sound was on the porch, like walking, only some of the steps were loud and others you did not hear at all. Then there was a heavy bump against the door, and the glass panes rattled.

"Keep back!" Jim called, but the mother had already pushed the switch of the porch light. "Who is it?"

Bailey, clinging to the stair railing, did not hear any answer, but his mother unlocked the door and opened it. "It's Tom!" Then she screamed and started back, while Jim got behind a chair with the revolver wavering in his hand.

The thing that staggered in was like the body of Tom, dug up out of muddy earth, but his face seemed to be gone, or hidden under long strands of woman's hair. The door was still open to the roar of rain and a cold draft came up the stairs and caught at the boy's ankles.

There was that moment of horror, and then Bailey's mother wasn't afraid any more. "He's been hurt!" she cried, and put one arm around the muddy shape, steadying him as she walked him to the davenport.

Bailey wasn't so much afraid now when his mother wasn't and he ran downstairs. The shape on the davenport was Tom all right, with stag shirt and overalls soaked with mud and rain. He had his face, too, only his nose was swollen and twisted to one side and clotted with blood. What had seemed like long strands of hair hanging down was blood; but now it ran sidewise across his forehead and through his hair and some of it went into his ear before running down on the brocaded cushions. One of his wounds was hardly bleeding at all and it was like his head being parted along with his hair, and you could see the pink bone underneath. The blood was from another wound, and Bailey's mother was trying to stop it with her handkerchief.

Tom's eyes were closed and he looked dead or asleep, but he began talking. Bailey could just hear him above the sound of rain that came in through the wide-open door. "It'll stop if you press the right place—somewhere up there. I had it stopped with a rock under my handkerchief. They came off when I fell —and I couldn't find them in the dark."

"I'm getting it stopped," the mother said. "Just rest, Tom." Then she said to Jim, "For pity's sake, put that gun away and close the door. Call Madge and wake Mr. Dow, and telephone for a doctor. Bring me some bandage first—you'll find a roll in the downstairs medicine cabinet."

When Jim had gone, Tom began talking again and he didn't seem to remember he wasn't the chauffeur any more. "I don't know where the car is," he said; "I don't remember having it out. I walked and I didn't know if I'd ever get home. I kept falling, but I knew if I got here I'd be all right. I was going to wash up—but the door was locked and I couldn't find my key."

"You got here, all right," the mother said; "you haven't anything to worry about."

Tom said, "They'd have killed me if I hadn't got away to the woods. At the end of the line they were clubbing us across the face from one side and across the back from the other. Then there was the cattle guard, where men were slipping through and breaking their ankles; but I got away into the woods."

"Don't talk about it now," the mother said. "Just rest, and we'll take care of you." She seemed to notice Bailey for the first time. "Go to bed, Dear. Tom's been hurt, but he'll be all right."

Madge, the new housekeeper, came in with bandages and a basin of water, and without saying anything she began washing the blood from Tom's face. Bailey moved to one side for her, but did not go away. He loved Tom and had been in terror of his getting sapped up; now he was broken and still and not very real. The boy was mostly interested in the wounds and the flow of blood, and what his mother was doing to stop it.

The father came downstairs, hurrying heavily. His hair was tousled, but he was dressed except for his coat, and he had a revolver in his hand.

Tom's face was pale after the blood had been washed away; his eyes were closed, and he looked dead or asleep. Bailey's father started and stared at him and asked, "How in hell did Tom get here?"

Tom's face twisted and his eyes came open, dark with terror. He threw up one crooked arm to protect his head, and his elbow knocked the basin from Madge's hands; it made a muffled ringing sound on the wet carpet. Shielding his head with his arm, Tom cried, "For God's sake, Dow, don't hit me again! I'm all broken!"

It was dreadful to see him cowering there, with things mixed up in his mind, where the beating and the healing got in each other's way. Then Bailey's mother put his arm down to his side again, gently. "It's all right, Tom. No one is going to hit you. Just lie still." She was tender and gentle and soothing until Madge had picked up the basin and gone to the kitchen. Then she turned towards her husband. Bailey thought she was going to speak, but she did not say anything, only looked. She was not looking at Bailey, but he felt the looking going past him like lightning that never stopped. He edged back, afraid of being seared, and watched his father anxiously. Once, on the school playground, he had seen one of the big boys focus light from a lens on another boy's coat until the cloth smoked and began to burn. He was afraid it might happen now, but his father only looked frightened and stuffed the revolver out of sight in his back pocket. His voice was frightened, too, when he said, "Christ, Myra, don't look at me like that!"

The mother did not say anything, but the look went on like white lightning that grew fiercer and fiercer until Bailey began to whimper softly, feeling it could only end in fire or an explosion.

"Myra," the father said, "it wasn't anything personal! There were two hundred of us, and forty of them, and we made them all run the gantlet. Tom had been warned to stay away and he was coming back to speak——"

Still the mother didn't say anything, only the lightning was dying down and she looked dazed and lost. Her look broke something inside Bailey and he sobbed wildly. The rest was not very clear, except that Madge put him to bed and sat with him, and after a little while he heard the doctor's car stop in the drive. Bailey let Madge go when she promised to leave his door open a little and that his mother would come up to see him as soon as she could. Then there was the steady roar of rain, footsteps and voices downstairs, and once the reassuring sound of the toilet being flushed.

He could not remember his mother coming to his room that night, but she came to see him other nights, after strange days. Madge had moved upstairs, and Tom was in her room downstairs, where Bailey was not allowed to see him. During those days Bailey was haunted by the feeling that it was not Tom who was in danger; it was the family that was sick and going through some crisis in which it might die. Sometimes in the middle of the night, and sometimes in the wet gray of morning, he woke and heard his parents' voices struggling; his mother's voice always accusing, or reckless and wild, and his father's voice explaining and pleading. The voices were in a struggle too desperate to be loud, and it was they who were going through the crisis—not Tom, who was sick with pneumonia. Bailey thought of the voices as the struggle between the body and the soul. His mother's swift voice was the soul. It wanted to leave the body, which was his father's heavy voice, and the body was trying to keep it from going away. Bailey wanted the body to win, so there would not be death, but he could feel how the soul felt; it was daring and swift and impatient, and leaving the body would not be death for it, but freedom and life.

Bailey thought of reasons for staying home, so he would be with his mother; but every day Jim took him to school, where he was not allowed to say anything about Tom, and Jim brought him home after school. Then Jim drove to camp. Later in the afternoon a Reo touring car would come through the bare orchard and stop in the drive. Men wearing Stetson hats and badges would get out, holding their rifles carefully. If it was not raining, they sat on the garden bench or ate apples in the orchard, or came to the kitchen door and joked with Madge. If it was raining, all but one of them would go to Jim's room over the garage and play poker. They could also make coffee there. But they were not allowed even in the kitchen of the big house; Bailey heard his mother say that to Madge. When the father and Jim got home, the deputies got back into the Reo touring car, handling their rifles carefully, and drove away, going very fast through the dark orchard.

It helped when the deputies were gone and his father was home; that meant the family was all together; even Tom was there in the house. But the feeling of illness was there, too, waiting to break out whenever the parents were by themselves downstairs after dinner, or upstairs after they had gone to bed, or in the gray hours of early morning; the struggle of the body and the soul that made you go through all the tiredness and troubles of dying. Paul hated the sound of struggle, too; he would wake and cry loudly in protest, and then the voices would be still for the night, or for a few hours.

One night, when the voices were still, Bailey opened his eyes and saw his mother sitting on the edge of his bed. He did not know whether she had wakened him or if it had been of his own accord. In the night light he saw her there, smiling mysteriously, like some one in a dream. Lately, he thought, she hardly slept at all; but she looked younger than she had ever looked before—young and reckless.

"Mother," Bailey whispered.

She kissed him and asked enticingly, "Bailey, would you like it if we went away from here—away from all the deputies and fighting and trouble?"

"Yes," Bailey said, but he knew his mother was being very young, and because of that he had to be wise. "Where would we go?"

"Maybe to a cabin on one of the islands," she said, "where we would do our own work and every one would help. We'd plant a garden and make things we needed with our own hands. We'd have a boat, and live mostly out of doors, and you and Paul would grow up to be strong and brave. We'd treat other people like brothers and help them all we could, and we'd never, never try to make money out of them."

"I'd like that," Bailey said. "Will you let me have a Savage .22 repeater?"

"When you are old enough—and if you'll always be careful." She was smiling because he was just a boy, but he was already thinking of more bothersome things.

"What about Father?" he asked. "He wouldn't care much for things like that. Is he going?"

"I don't know," she said. "I wanted to talk it over with you."

"What about Tom?"

His mother did not answer at first, then she asked, almost in a whisper, "Would you want him to be there?"

"It wouldn't work without him," Bailey decided; "we'd need Tom."

His mother gave the littlest smile and said, "That makes him rather important, doesn't it?"

Bailey nodded, sitting up in bed. "Did he say he'd go?"

"I didn't even say I was going to ask him," she said. "I was just asking if you wanted to go away to a place like that."

"It wouldn't be any good without Tom," Bailey said. "He isn't going to die, is he?"

"No, dear, I think he's going to be all right; he's getting stronger every day."

"That's good; we'd need him; but I don't know about Father."

"What do you mean?" she asked.

Bailey said, "I don't think he'd go, and if he did, he wouldn't like it. Not unless he could start a logging camp and boss everybody."

"That wouldn't be what we wanted, would it?"

"No," Bailey said, "but we can't change Father."

When his mother kissed him good night, she said, "This is just between you and me. I want you to think about it, but don't say anything to any one else."

Bailey never had, to his brother or any one else. Now there was no one to substantiate the conversation which had lain forgotten in his mind for over twenty years. It could be explained away as a dream, and it was—hers, not his. Bailey had been wiser than his mother that night when she sat on the edge of his bed—young and reckless with the bloom of a second spring that was only in her mind.

A few days after that Jim brought Bailey home from school in cool, bright autumn weather. When they turned into the drive, the boy saw Tom dressed and sitting on the garden bench with his mother and Paul. Paul was sitting on Tom's lap, as good as gold, delicately pulling the petals out of a rose, while Tom talked to the mother. When Bailey ran up, shouting over the miracle of convalescence, Tom put one arm around him and held him close while he went on talking. His clear face was bright in the sunshine and his hair had grown long and wavy and his eyes were bright. Bailey thought his mother had been crying, but that did not seem likely, and she looked proud and sweet while she listened to Tom.

Maybe what Tom was saying had started to be just for the mother, but it was too important to stop and it had enough love for every one who could gather around.

Tom was saying, "This was only a little of what should be. If things were right, no one who was with other human beings would ever be among strangers or enemies. No orphan or laborer's child would know fear and want. While he was little, he would have love and good care, which all babies understand. When he was able to understand more, he would be shown the richness and the beauty of the earth and he would be told, 'You were brought into this world as the rest of us were brought, and your right is equal to our right. You are one of the shareholders. Use your share for the profit of this great company of human beings, and your children and all children who are born will have the security of a fuller life on a richer earth.' "

Tom held Bailey while he was saying that, and the boy could feel the strength of his arm and the warmth of his heart. There was not as much warmth in the autumn sunshine that poured over them like cool rich color, and after a few minutes the mother made them all move indoors.

When Bailey got home from school next day the weather was still fine, but Tom Horton was gone. No one knew just when he had left or where he had gone, but a week or two later he was given a jail sentence in another county for leading an I.W.W. meeting. That was the last Bailey had heard of him.

With Tom gone, none of the family went to live in the wilderness; but that same fall they closed Home Place and moved to Seattle. Bailey knew his father did not like the move, but there was some alternative which he liked still less. The father was generous in defeat, and surprised his wife with the big house near Lake Washington. So the woman who had wanted a cabin on one of the islands went to live in a mansion in town. . . .

Bailey reached out of his crib and took his half-smoked cigar from the doll's dish. There was not elbow room enough to go through his pockets for matches, and when he got up he found he had no desire to get back into his crib. Instead he went downstairs and out through the kitchen door, which he locked again.

Paul was coming back through the orchard, easy and preoccupied, with his camera in one hand and a half-eaten yellow apple in the other. When he came up he said, "I suppose we'd better go on board and get under weigh."

Bailey said, "I think we should."

They were on their way to the beach when Paul asked, "Did you find what you were looking for in the house?"

"No," Bailey said. "It was never really there."

IX

THE DARLINGS were their first week-end guests at Home Place that summer, and there were different opinions about the occasion. Martin and Mrs. Darling and Violet said it had been splendid, although they decided late Sunday afternoon to go home that evening instead of staying over until Monday morning, as they had planned; and Mrs. Darling apologized to Marian for what she termed, "my daughter's rudeness." At the last moment, when the disgruntled Bertha was behind the wheel of the car, she thanked Marian for her hospitality but she did not say that she had enjoyed herself. Charlie, who always made a special effort where Martin Darling was concerned, was disappointed, and he blamed "that boy." Bailey also blamed Paul for anything the week end lacked—Paul, who was not there either to defend himself or to express an opinion. When they looked for him Sunday morning he was gone, leaving only a brief note, without explanation or excuses.

What Marian thought about the week end was in the nature of a confidential report to herself; there was no one with whom she could share it.

Saturday had been a fragment of the fine summer they had planned. They had a picnic and clam bake on their beach, with Paul managing the bake quietly and beautifully. Marian did her conscientious best as a hostess, and was only occasionally disturbed by fleeting reminders of her day with Paul under other circumstances on another beach. And Paul seemed less bothered

174

than she would have expected when Bertha monopolized him possessively by making herself his assistant. Bertha also persuaded him to take her for a sail in Bailey's sloop, but the plan fell flat because of a dead calm. Instead, they all went to the back lawn, where Martin had set up his archery target. The old financier, with his soft voice and pink baby face, sent one arrow after another into the target at the far side of the lawn, until there was a cluster of them in the bull's-eye. It looked enchantingly easy, but the others could hardly hit the target at all. Paul made some fair shots, and Bertha insisted on taking lessons from him, though her father was the expert and she had every opportunity to learn at home. Afterward, when the dusk was too deep for them to see the target well, Bertha took Paul with her to look for lost arrows. They stayed out until it was nearly dark, and Bertha was exasperated because Paul had done nothing but look for arrows.

That was a fair idea of Saturday, and there was nothing about the day, as Charlie and Bailey had seen it, to justify Paul's flight before any one was up next morning.

There was one other incident which they had not observed. The mild excitement of the day had been enough to keep Marian awake and restless with a feeling of unfulfillment. By a little after midnight the whole house was quiet, except for sounds of sleep. At length even Bailey's distant snoring died away. But, still later, the house had dreams.

The downstairs clock had struck two and she was just drifting towards sleep when she heard some one stirring. She heard a door open, and the sound of bare feet in the hall. People had got up before at night, and there seemed nothing unusual about it now. But the sound of the footsteps went on in her mind, light and slow and as even as if each one had been measured. Then she heard the faint rattle of a knob, and another door opening. Not the bathroom door, but far down the hall. It sounded more like the end room. Then the door closed again.

Marian was wide awake, but she had no intention of doing anything about it. It might be anything or nothing, and her guests were all of age; if they chose to call on each other at two in the morning, she was not supposed to be awake to hear them. But she was puzzled because it had sounded like the end room, and that was where Paul slept. . . .

From the far end of the house there came the sound of a faint scuffle, followed by the sound of the door opening again, and bare feet in the hall. This time the steps were heavier and less even. They came almost the length of the hall, hesitated, and turned back; then she heard them returning again, as if the feet could not make up their mind.

Some one was in trouble, and she got up quietly and went to the door. The dim hall light was on, and as she opened the door, Paul turned from where he was hesitating near the head of the stairs, and came towards her. He was in an old bathrobe, which looked as if he had put it on hastily, his thick yellow hair was tousled from sleep, and his face looked troubled. She stepped into the hall and closed the door behind her. "What is it?" she asked. "Is anything wrong?"

"It's Bertha," Paul whispered. "She's in my bed!"

Under other circumstances, Marian would have laughed at the ridiculous situation, but now she whispered solemnly, "Can't you get her out?"

"I'm afraid of waking her!"

"She's asleep?"

He nodded, gloomily. "She was walking in her sleep. I didn't want to wake her; it might frighten her."

She thought, and whispered, "It might be safest to leave her until morning." That still left the matter of where Paul would sleep. "You could sleep in her bed; that would be only fair."

Paul frowned, "I wouldn't like that, and it might embarrass Bertha."

Marian saw how that could be, particularly if some one else found her out of place in the morning.

He whispered, "I thought of waking her father and mother, but that would make a lot of fuss."

"It would." She thought again, and whispered, "Maybe we could get her to walk back without waking."

Paul looked hopeful. "You think we could?"

"We can try."

"I don't want to frighten her."

"I don't think we will." Marian felt confident. "Even if she wakes up, it won't be the same as finding herself on her feet. It'll be more like waking her from a normal sleep."

"I think you're right," he whispered. "Let's try."

When they had put the house in order for the summer, there had not been enough usable furniture to go round, and the end room had been skimped. Because it was the least desirable, or because of his Spartan tastes, Paul had chosen it for his room. Now, in the light of the old table lamp which he had turned on to identify the intruder, Bertha lay in Paul's bed like a visiting princess. Her white satin nightgown would have served for a bride, her face was sweetly composed, surrounded by waves of blond hair, and she slept with one finely groomed hand on her breast, and one smooth arm relaxed at her side. Marian had never liked Bertha, but she had to admit that she made an effective picture, and she whispered, "How pretty she is!"

Paul was more interested in getting her out of his bed. "How do we go about it?"

Sitting on the edge of the bed beside Bertha, Marian spoke

in a low, even voice: "Bertha will walk back to her room without waking. In the morning she won't remember anything about it, or she will remember it only as a dream."

Paul nodded encouragingly.

"Bertha is going back to her bed now."

Bertha did not seem to think so. She slept on sweetly, in white satin, with the faint fragrance of expensive perfume about her.

Marian took one of the girl's hands in hers. "Bertha is going back to her bed."

Still Bertha did not think so, and she slept on, breathing deeply and evenly.

Paul was beginning to look uneasy. Meeting Marian's eyes, he whispered, "It doesn't seem to work!"

Marian nodded, to say it would work. "Bertha will walk back to her bed." She pulled at the hand, gently, suggesting getting up. In answer the sleeping girl's face clouded with a look of annoyance, and the almost imperceptible frown lines between her eyebrows deepened. "In the morning she won't remember anything about it; it was only a dream." She stood up and took Bertha's other hand and pulled on both, gently. "Bertha will go back to her room now."

Bertha's look of annoyance deepened, but she rose slowly, until she was sitting up in the bed, with her breathing slow and even. "Bertha will walk back to her bed."

Bertha's feet slipped off the side of the bed to the floor, and she stood up slowly. Marian went on in the same voice, "Paul will walk on one side of Bertha, so she won't fall or bump into anything on the way."

With Paul supporting her on one side, and Marian on the other, she walked out of the end room and down the hall; her slow steps were as even as something mechanical.

The dressing-table light was burning in Bertha's room, where Paul drew back the covers and plumped the pillow considerately.

"Bertha will lie down now," Marian said.

Bertha lay down, obedient and relaxed, and Marian covered her and tucked her in. Her breathing was slow and measured and she had never opened her eyes, but the frown lines were clear between her eyebrows, and the look of annoyance and disappointment remained.

They went out quietly, on bare feet, and Marian closed the door behind them. She had an unreasonable feeling of triumph, and of being close to Paul. "We had an adventure!" she whispered, walking a little way down the hall with him.

"You were wonderful," he whispered; "you did a perfect job!" He, too, was feeling the excitement of their hushed adventure, and for once he was not shy with her—only human and companionable, and unconscious of their haphazard costumes—his battered old bathrobe and her candid nightgown. "You managed beautifully!"

"I just guessed at it," she whispered, "but it worked, didn't it?" It would be suitable, she felt, for them to go downstairs and make coffee and compare notes and talk it over until morning, or until they had found all its meanings. But the weight of a houseful of proper, sleeping people was against it.

Paul, too, wanted to talk it over. "Do you think she'll try to come back?"

"I'm sure she won't!" Then she added in a laughing whisper, "If she does, you know where to come for help!"

He saw the ridiculous side of it with her and laughed silently, "I wasn't thinking of myself!"

"Anyway, you can lock your door from the inside."

"I was surprised, I tell you!" Then he asked, "How do you suppose she happened to do it?"

"Acting out a dream," she whispered.

"You think she knew where she was going?"

"She knew."

"I never took any psychology."

"I've taken some, and I've read some."

"She won't remember about it in the morning?"

"She won't remember, except as a dream, perhaps."

"You managed her beautifully!"

She again had that unreasonable feeling of triumph and she whispered, "I suppose she'll hate me for it!"

His deep-set blue eyes looked startled. "But if she was asleep——"

"I mean subconsciously; you can hate people in dreams, as well as love them."

"I suppose so."

"More likely, she won't remember anything," Marian assured him.

"It would have been embarrassing without you."

I was glad to help, Paul."

She knew they should both be in bed, but since their first meeting they had never been as companionable, and he had never been as free from self-consciousness. Except for the danger of disturbing some sleeper with their whispering, she could have stood cheerfully in the hall in her bare feet until morning, going over their adventure.

He seemed as unwilling as she to end it, but after a few minutes he whispered, "I mustn't keep you up any longer."

"And I'm keeping you up."

"Thank you for helping me."

"It was no trouble. Good night, Paul."

"Good night," he said.

At the last moment the excitement of their adventure seemed

to ebb away from them as they said good night in the cold hall, with sleeping people all around them. Marian shivered a little, and Paul looked cold and gloomy. He stood for a moment longer, as if trying to say something. Then he turned abruptly and went back to his room.

She had known already that there was nothing more to say.

X

Monday MORNING at Home Place, Bailey woke up late, with every one but Marian and the servants gone.

He started breakfast at a few minutes after ten: Pink Arizona grapefruit, piece bacon sliced in the kitchen by Mrs. Wilkes, two poached eggs and toast which he had made for himself in an old-fashioned toaster. To go with the toast there was the usual butter, and English marmalade in a covered glass dish which he remembered from childhood.

Outside it was a mature and healthy summer morning and some of it came in to light up one wall of the room. The sunshine did not reach the table, but it was already cheerful with yellow breakfast dishes, and in the center there was a blue glass bowl with nasturtiums. They were freshly picked and made a fine splash of color, but Bailey disliked the hot orange ones which reminded him of a red-haired woman who had been too much for him. He started breakfast alone, but Marian came in after a little while and sat at the opposite side of the table and poured herself a cup of coffee. Bailey did not pay any more attention to the sun or the flowers on the table, but he was pleasantly conscious of them while he visited with his stepmother. She would be twenty-five later in the summer, and she gave the impression of being fresh and beautiful without any more effort than the summer morning. He felt special about her, the way he did about some one who was beautiful or who knew more than he did, or who had been notably successful.

182

Spreading marmalade, Bailey said to her, "I'm the dregs of the week end, waiting to be thrown out."

"You don't look it," she said. "You look fine."

He said, "I feel fine," and when he had said it he realized that he did. "It seems more like the beginning of a week end. If the Old Man and Paul and the others were here, we could really have a good time. We wouldn't, of course, but that's the way I feel. Do you know the kind I mean—when you know while it's happening that everything is right?"

"I know," she said, "though it doesn't happen very often."

He said, "You nearly always give the impression that everything is going beautifully. It's graciousness, I suppose, or being cheerfully resigned to everything."

"Resignation isn't as common as you might suppose," she said.

The quiet answer startled him. If her husband had been any one other than his father, he would have gone on to find out why she said that. And maybe, if the Old Man were to die— As it was, the idea tempted him only faintly and he did not think the statement was meant to encourage him. "It really was a good week end," he said.

"No." Then she said, "Almost, but it wasn't."

"You were lovely," Bailey said; "but I was no help, spending all my time with Violet."

Marian said, "It was noble of you; some one had to entertain her."

"And Paul didn't add to the sport by walking out on us Sunday morning."

Marian had to admit that.

"I never saw a girl more out of sorts than Bertha was the rest of the day."

"She was disappointed," Marian said. "You can't blame her."

"She can blame herself, some." Then he said, "I don't know how a girl would go about acquiring Paul, but she doesn't have the right method, being possessive with him when other people are around."

Marian said, "I don't know what the right method would be."

He said, "I've noticed that when a woman really wants a man, she's so damned clumsy that she defeats her purpose—but maybe I only notice the clumsy ones." When she remained quiet, he went on, "I was disappointed in Paul; there wasn't anything to justify his running out on us."

"I think people should do as they please," Marian said, "when it's possible."

Bailey said, a little jealously, "You're always excusing something Paul has done, or thinking about what would be good for him."

"I want to be a good stepmother," she said gravely; "I want him to be happy."

"You're my stepmother, too." Then he said, "I'm thinking about Paul, too, and what would be good for him. Sometimes I think you have more influence over him than the rest of us—or you could have if you tried. You could help break him of this running-away habit."

Marian shook her head, decisively. "I haven't any influence with him, and I wouldn't try."

"I have all kinds of plans," Bailey said. "We could all have a good life if we got together on it, instead of fragmenting in all directions."

"I know how you feel."

"Maybe it's the war in Europe," he said, "or maybe I'm getting old, but I want to come home. We haven't had much of a life since I was a child."

"All of us want to come home—in one way or another," Marian said.

"We could," he said; "but it has to center around some one; don't you understand, Marian? I'm proposing to you; I want you to be our mother."

All at once she was heartbreakingly lovely, smiling her acknowledgment. "I would like to be, but I'm not wise enough."

"Mothers never are when they start, but they learn after a while."

The telephone rang and there was the sound of Mrs. Wilkes going from the kitchen to answer it, as Marian said, "I've tried for years and you don't even know it."

"We haven't given you any support," Bailey said. "That's what I'm proposing now."

Mrs. Wilkes came in and said, "It's for you, Mrs. Dow; Seattle calling."

Marian said "Thank you," and "Excuse me, Bailey," and went away. From the still breakfast room Bailey heard her voice talking to some one in Seattle—soft and self-possessed, then growing puzzled as if the miracle of long distance had failed and she and Seattle found themselves talking in different languages. Then there was an open break and admission of failure. He heard her say, "No, I'm sorry," and her lowered voice said some one had passed away six years ago. Apparently she had been asked questions that could only be answered by the dead. "I'm sorry," her voice tapered towards hanging up, then it started again at the beginning. "Who is this speaking?" Then she said "Oh!" with unexpected interest, and, "Bailey is here now. Wouldn't you like to speak to him?" as if she wanted that.

She came back looking less alive but more excited. "It wasn't for me," she said; "it was for your mother."

"Who was it?" Bailey asked.

"Tom Horton."

"Tom Horton!"

"He's on the phone," she said. "I thought you might want to speak to him."

"You always think right," he said. "If I had missed him——"

"Why not ask him up for lunch?"

He was too excited to think clearly. "I don't know, but I've got to see him!" He had been convinced that he would recognize Tom's voice anywhere out of a thousand others, but after the telephone conversation he could not remember much but his own excitement and the absurdity of giving the former chauffeur directions. He told Marian, "It was a master stroke of yours, suggesting that I invite him up here. He came here almost at the beginning and planted the orchard and nearly all of the trees and shrubs that Tag neglects."

Marian seemed almost as excited as himself. "Then he is coming for lunch?"

"About one o'clock. I offered to go for him, but he said he has a car of sorts."

"Do you remember if he likes steak? We have some nice sirloin in the refrigerator."

"Anything you like, Marian. Steak would be fine. Tom's mostly interested in ideas, anyway." Trying to explain his excitement, he said, "I don't know how much you've heard about Tom, but he's a kind of saint in the family, except with the Old Man, of course. You've helped work a miracle, bringing him back. He's been only a legend for twenty-odd years."

Marian said, "He's been very real in a ghostly way. The first time I saw Paul he asked if I knew a Tom Horton who might be working in one of the camps. Paul didn't know what Tom looked like, but he seemed very real to him."

"He caught every one's imagination—every one but the Old Man."

Marian's eager face clouded. "Do you think he'll mind our inviting him here?"

"After all these years?" He still wasn't sure, but it seemed too improbable to think about. "Anyway, I'm the one who invited him." Then he said, "I must get Paul, too. Tom practically raised him for the first two years."

He called the house in Seattle, but got no answer, and could not think of any other place to call. When he gave up and reported to Marian in the back garden, he was still excited. "Tom practically raised Paul when he was a baby," he said. "I'd forgotten until last month when I was up here. When Mother brought him home from the hospital, she had one of the new baby books that say the baby mustn't be touched unnecessarily or picked up and loved. She followed the book religiously, and that may explain half of Paul. Tom explains the other half. It was his idea that no one is ever too young to appreciate beauty, and he trained me to bring Paul flowers and leaves. It worked so well that after a while he would cry if he didn't have them to play with. I can't think of a more likely infancy for a nature lover."

"Psychologists don't teach that any more," Marian said, "about not loving babies. They say the more they're loved, the better—just what the old timers believed."

"They're right, too. Just look what the intermediate school did for Paul. And I think you'd find a whole race of young Puritans who were brought up on books of the same school."

Marian said, "I was thinking it might be nice to have lunch out here under the trees. It's such a beautiful day."

Bailey said, "Nothing could be better."

She said, "Mrs. Wilkes makes a fuss about serving meals out

of doors, but she'll probably stand for one more. And you can help bring things out."

He was still excited and he could not remember what he had said a minute before. "Did I tell you I couldn't get Paul?"

"Yes. I didn't really expect he would be in."

"We must invite Tag!" he decided suddenly.

Marian looked surprised only for a moment. "All right. Better ask him now."

"We can't be undemocratic when Tom is here, and Tag worships him. He's still a Wobbly at heart, and Tom is the only idol he has left."

"He'll probably be more at ease with lunch out doors," she said. "And tell him he isn't expected to dress up. When he's in his Sunday clothes he always looks as if it had been such an effort."

Bailey said, "Did I tell you about the college Tom went to? They had the system of studying half the year and working at practical things the other half. Tom went out on a job in the wheat fields and forgot to go back."

Marian was laughing at him. "Bailey, I know just what you were like when you were a little boy! Now please go and invite Tag for lunch at one o'clock and give me a chance to plan things."

Bailey was unrebuked. "You could be my mother," he said. "She was beautiful, too."

"Please, Bailey!" Marian had the helpless look of not being sure whether she was dealing with a little boy, or a man who might make love to her.

On his way to find Tag, Bailey felt a little confused. Tom was coming home; Tom to whom his mother was still alive or only newly dead, and there had been a telephone call for her that morning. She seemed more nearly living than she had for a long time, and he could see her as she had been when he was a child, her fine, thin face and gray eyes, and her determined mouth and smooth white throat. She had been on the ascetic and intellectual side—the wrong kind of wife for his warm-blooded and unreflecting father. Marian would have been a more likely bet for his young days.

A few minutes or a few hours earlier he had seen Tag leave his wheelbarrow at the edge of the drive and stump into the garage. The wheelbarrow was still there and more than likely Tag hadn't gone any farther than Tom's old apartment. He ran up the stairs and found the door open, but Tag was not in. The windows should be open, too, he thought. Suppose Tom wants to see the old place in which he lived? This stinking junk house of old magazines and phonograph records, empty whiskey bottles and unemptied ash trays—Tag should at least let Mrs. Wilkes clean the place. Among the mess on the table, Bailey recognized his old aquarium, resurrected from somewhere and covered with a dirty tablecloth. He stared at what seemed to be the ghost of a fish swimming on the other side of the dusty glass, and took off the cloth.

The aquarium was filled with water and there were living things swimming in it; not fish—tadpoles. You wouldn't have expected it of Tag—wanting pets to fuss over. Big fellow, you've been in an accident! Then Bailey noticed something odd: each tadpole was minus a left hind leg! He covered the aquarium and went downstairs quietly. On the way he heard Tag's wooden leg thumping on the concrete drive.

They met at the garage door: Bailey uncomfortable because he had stumbled onto a minor gruesome secret which he did not understand, and because he was consciously keeping his eyes away from the covered tin pail which the caretaker was carrying; Tag uncombed and frowsy-bearded, with bleary eyes and a deferential look that was like a carelessly slapped-on mask which did not hide his scorn.

Bailey said, "I was looking for you, Tag. We want you to have lunch with us."

"I don't want to have lunch with you."

"It's special; we're having company."

"*Ja*? If you have company, you don't need me."

"It's an old friend of yours."

Tag said bitterly: "I have no friends."

"What about Tom Horton?"

"What about him?"

"He's coming to lunch."

Tag's face changed; the mock deference and the defiant look went away, and he was a defenseless human being, lonely for something in which he could believe. "*Ja?*" he said with gentle scepticism. "Is Joe Hill coming, too?"

Bailey said, "Joe Hill is dead, but Tom Horton telephoned a little while ago and he's coming out here for lunch."

Tag did not even pretend not to believe any more. He set the tin pail inside the garage as if he were afraid of spilling his secret, then stumped over to sit on the running board of Marian's car.

"You're not fooling me, Bailey?"

Bailey sat beside him and said, "I wouldn't fool about Tom. When he phoned from Seattle I was as much surprised as you are. He can't have been in this part of the country, because he thought we'd been living here all the time and he didn't know Mother was dead."

"Yust last month, after we were talking about him, I dreamed he came back. His face was like good news happening everywhere, and he put his hand on my shoulder the way he did once; I could feel it, strong and big, and he said, '*Tag, we are more than they!'* I don't know what else he said, but when I woke up I felt so light I could yump to the moon. I didn't know at first it was a dream."

"It isn't, now," Bailey said.

"You know what he's doing?"

"Fighting for some lost cause, probably; he didn't say."

"*Ja.* Tom would be out there fighting somewhere."

Bailey got up from the running board. "You're having lunch with us, aren't you?"

"What time?"

"One o'clock; we're going to eat on the lawn."

"I'll mow it, first."

"It doesn't matter." Then he said, "Maybe you'll want to tidy things upstairs. Tom might want to see his old room."

"*Ja,* it looks like a crap house, because I didn't care." He stumped towards the stairs, then turned back for the mysterious tin, which he had almost forgotten.

In the impulse, Bailey said, "When I was upstairs looking for you, I noticed your polywogs."

Tag was not as resentful as he might have been half an hour earlier. "*Ja,* foolishness. Now I feed them."

"Think it's a good idea to cut off their legs?"

Tag said defensively, "It doesn't hurt them."

"To have only three legs?"

"They grow new ones."

"Is that why you do it?"

"*Ja*; maybe I find out how."

Bailey thought it over. "Well, good luck!" he said.

"You won't tell?"

"No, but I hope you don't have to do it all the time."

"Thank you. They might not understand." Tag went thumping up the stairs.

The table was set on the back lawn, which Tag had mowed, in the light shade of the mountain ash and the big dogwood tree. Beyond the table, the lawn went away under trees and around islands of rose bushes and rhododendrons until it met the deep grass and trees of the orchard. It was not a hot day, but it was warm and the air and the earth and everything on it was filled with summer. Like a blessing, a small breeze off the Sound brought the smell of salt and a dim blue haze of evergreen smoke, as light as remembered incense.

They brought out a serving table and put the chairs around the table under the big trees that Tom Horton had planted. Marian said, "I think that's everything for now." Bailey looked at his wrist watch; it was a minute of one o'clock. Tag Sorenson fumbled at his necktie; he had disobeyed instructions about not dressing up and put on his good suit and a celluloid collar and a dark blue tie striped with broken lines of white. The collar chafed him, while the inexperienced tie kept turning wrong side to, and the blue serge of his left trouser leg was crumpled miserably between his stump and the wooden leg. He looked like an old pirate condemned to observe the Sabbath, but he was happy in his misery and eager to help. "Could I do anything?" he asked. "Is there anything more to bring? Maybe I should cut some flowers."

Marian said, "There isn't anything more, Tag, and Tom has already provided the flowers; they're all around us. But you can let me fix your tie." Bailey saw the old ruffian's breathing stop, beatifically, while the girl's smooth fingers worked with his tie. "What a way to put on a tie!" she said. "I'm going to untie it and start all over. I told you not to dress up. Tom will probably be wearing waist overalls and a leather belt and a flannel shirt open at the neck, the way men should dress."

"*Ja*, I'll do that next time." A few hours before, Tag had been a dirty and rebellious old man, messing about his chores in the background of things. Now he was one of the family, with Marian's laughing, excited face near his own and her beautiful young fingers caressing his tie. Tag had come home a little because his prophet was coming home. This redemption was the meaning of Tom Horton who had preached the gospel of love and democracy in all things.

Bailey was in the house for cigarettes when he heard a car stop in the drive; by the time he got outside a stranger was getting out of a black Buick coupe with a Colorado license plate. Marian was hurrying to greet him, with Tag stumping along behind her, but Bailey felt there was some mistake. He remembered Tom as a big man, and the stranger was of medium size, in a conservative business suit, with a solemn hat in his left hand and a superfluous topcoat over his arm.

It was not a mistake. The stranger was saying, "Thank you, Mrs. Dow; this place means so much to me!" She said, "You are ever so welcome, Mr. Horton; here's Bailey now." Then the stranger was shaking hands with Bailey, warmly, while his kindly eyes looked through rimless pince-nez glasses, trying to gaze away the years. "Bailey, I don't know if you remember me; you were a little boy when I saw you last."

With Tom's hand still gripping his, Bailey said, "I remember you perfectly." Then he turned towards Tag, "Here's an old friend and admirer of yours, Tag Sorenson."

Tom shook hands with him and said, "Yes, I remember; it's good to see you, Tag." But Bailey was the one he wanted to see just then, and after a minute he excused himself from the others and he and Bailey were walking across the lawn in the shade and in bright sunshine. "How the trees have grown!" Tom said. "How time has passed and how much has changed!"

"There have been changes," Bailey said. "You would notice them more, coming on them suddenly."

Tom said, "Your mother—I didn't know until this morning."

"She died six years ago this spring."

"And I was so certain of finding her here! She died young, didn't she?"

"Comparatively. She was fifty-one."

"I can only think of her as beautiful and young."

"She didn't change much," Bailey said; "not until her last illness——"

"Don't tell me about it," Tom said, "I couldn't bear to hear!"

Walking slowly, they passed into the shade of the big maple tree. "I could cry," Tom said. His kindly gray eyes were bright behind his pince-nez glasses. Then he said, "How this tree has grown! It was a little sapling when we planted it."

They passed out of its wide, dappled circle of shade into the sunshine.

Bailey said, "Look at that spruce by the garage; it's the one I found at camp and you helped me plant it. Now it's up to the second story window."

Tom remembered, and asked, "Where's the baby—Paul?"

"In Seattle," Bailey said. "He's a big fellow now, six feet one, and quite handsome. He would be here. only I couldn't get him on the phone."

"I would like to have seen him; he was a beautiful baby, always playing with flowers and leaves." After a while he asked, "Were there any other children?"

"Paul was the last," Bailey said.

Tom took the handkerchief from his breast pocket and wiped his bald, shiny forehead. "Having children is one of the things you don't regret," he said. "Mrs. Horton and I have three— two girls and a boy. We would have had more if we could have afforded them."

Bailey said, "It's very warm; wouldn't you like to take off your coat?"

"No, thank you," Tom said, "I'm quite comfortable." When

they had walked a little farther, he said, "It was on the impulse that I called up this morning——"

"I'm glad you did."

"I've been in Seattle occasionally in late years, and each time I thought of coming up here——"

"You wouldn't have had to do that," Bailey said. "We moved to Seattle the winter after you left. We're only up here for the summer."

Tom said, "It was always such a flying trip, and it was already such a long time. I didn't know——"

"You were quite a hero of Mother's and of ours. She always wondered what had become of you."

"God bless her; she was the noblest woman I ever knew. Was she happy? Did life treat her well?"

Bailey didn't know. She hadn't had the life she had wanted, but he wasn't sure another kind would have turned out any better. "Yes, she had a good life."

"Thank God for that," Tom said. "She deserved the best!"

On the other side of the lawn, Tag was sitting alone near the table, like the last pirate, with his wooden leg crossed jauntily over the good one, and Marian and Mrs. Wilkes were carrying dishes out from the kitchen.

"Lunch is on the way," Bailey said. "Maybe you'd like to wash up."

"No, thank you; I stopped at a service station on the way."

At lunch it was Marian who got him to loosen up a little. Sitting like a pretty young mother at the head of the table, with Tom on her right and Tag on the left, she said, "You're holding out on us, Mr. Horton. I suppose you've told Bailey everything, but Tag and I want to hear. Ever since I've been in this family you've been a kind of mystery man, and now you're more of a mystery than ever. I expected a scholar-gypsy, or a romantic bindle stiff—and you roll up in a big car, looking like a successful businessman!"

Tom smiled, and was flattered. "I was a rolling stone, Mrs. Dow, but that's all past. I've been in Denver sixteen years, except for business trips."

"Then you are a businessman!"

"In a small way," he said. "I got to Denver, riding the rods of a freight, with a quarter in my pocket, and I expected to take the next train out—instead, I've been there ever since."

Filling his glass with Burgundy, Marian said, "You must have invested the quarter in good securities!"

Tom said, "I was going to invest part of it in doughnuts and coffee, but near the freight yards I ran into an old college friend——"

"I'll remember that," Bailey said. "I bet any time I'm down on my luck I could go to the freight yards and find a Yale man —but he'd probably be worse off than I."

Tom smiled and paused to polish his glasses with his handkerchief. "As it happened," he said, "I was worse off than Leonard, and he took me to a restaurant for dinner. He had a small furniture repair place on Curtis Street, and I stayed over a few days to help. One thing led to another and the upshot of it was that we formed a partnership."

"It sounds exciting," Marian said; "the beginning of a success story!"

Tom smiled at her warmly, "You might say it was; last year it was written up, with photographs, in the Denver Business Magazine—but I don't suppose any of you would have seen that."

None of them had. "We'd rather hear it from you, anyway," Marian said. "I'll bet it wasn't a hole-in-the-wall concern for long."

Tom said modestly, "Chance had a good deal to do with it, and I'd had experience as a handy man. But what helped most was my handicaps. I'd been in nearly every jail in the West on account of my I.W.W. activities, and I was middle-aged when I hit Denver. I knew that life was real and earnest, and I didn't have much time left to make good."

Marian smiled. "I would say you made good with time to spare!"

"I haven't done badly," Tom admitted. "But the thing that put me across was feeling there wasn't much time left. I put a truck together out of junk parts and drummed up business, and then I'd work on it until two or three in the morning. It was like a cause, and I never felt tired until I dropped on the cot in the back of the shop and was asleep. It wasn't long before we had to move to larger quarters."

"I should think not," Marian said. "Right now we have two houses full of broken and sprained furniture. A repair man with a good sales talk could get enough to keep busy for a year."

"It took salesmanship," Tom said, "and good work afterward. But the repair business was only a beginning; I got the idea of handling some new furniture and after a few years the business had grown to where repairs were only a side line."

Bailey said, "It was a good day for your partner when he met you in the freight yard."

"It turned out well for both of us," Tom said. "Leonard's health was never too good, and in later years I was the active partner. He passed on in 1934, and recently I bought his interest in the business from his widow."

"You're a capitalist now," Bailey said.

"In a modest way," Tom said. "It was all slower and more uphill than it sounds. But now I have a nice store on Larimer Street and the best-known repairs department in Denver. We know our furniture from the inside out, and I draw on my knowledge of repairs in selecting merchandise; everything we touch is glued and screwed."

"Do you have any trouble with your employees?" Bailey asked.

Marian said, "Let me give you some steak, Tag; and how about a little more wine?"

"*Ja*, wine," Tag pushed his empty glass towards her; "no more steak."

Tom asked, "Why should any one have trouble with his employees?"

When no one answered, Tag raised his trembling glass, like a toast, "Capital and Labor have nothing in common!"

Tom smiled benignly at the familiar slogan. "I wouldn't say that, Tag. My employees and I get along very, very nicely. They do a good day's work and I pay them well. At Thanksgiving there is a turkey for each one, and at Christmas each one gets a check, the size depending on how long he has been with me. Some of the checks run into three figures."

Marian said, "I know you would be a good employer; you've seen life from both sides."

Gray and full-faced, with kindly eyes behind his rimless pincenez, Tom nodded slowly in assent. His hair was all gone, except for a nicely barbered fringe of gray around the base of his head, and his polished dome was marked with the thick white scars of clubs and a pistol butt—long white scars and a right-angled one, with the corner bitten in deeply. "I have seen both sides," he said, "and I try to be fair." Then, as if he might be giving the wrong impression, he said, "Of course, I don't take any nonsense from my employees; when a few of them wanted me to give every one a share in the business, I told them, 'This is Denver, not Utopia! I sweated blood to build up this business, and I'm not going to see other people tear it down and carry the pieces away.' "

"They built it, too!" Tag muttered, but Tom did not seem to hear him.

Bailey said, "We've always thought of you in connection with the Wobblies, Tom. I don't know how you feel, but if you care to talk about those days, we'd like to hear."

"*Ja*," Tag said; "the days when we lived!"

Mrs. Wilkes had cleared the table and served the dessert and gone away again, and they were at their ease over their coffee.

"I'd be glad to talk about them," Tom said. Then he asked, "Does smoke bother you, Mrs. Dow?"

Marian smiled and gestured with her lighted cigarette.

Tom took three cigars from the vest pocket of his gray business suit and gave one each to Bailey and Tag. Cutting the end of his own with a pearl-handled penknife, he said, "Those were the most exciting days of my life. So much happened that I don't know where to start."

Bailey smiled and said, "This time at least you didn't have any trouble getting into Thunderbird County in daylight."

"Did you, ever?" Marian asked.

Tom smiled. "Often. After a while I couldn't even get in after dark."

"Really, Tom?"

"As I remember, I made it once and got as far as the Avenue, where I started to make a speech, and I was dragged off the platform——"

"I remember that," Bailey said. "Our car had stopped at the edge of the crowd, and when the deputies grabbed you I tried to jump out and help you. I was about seven. We were all heroes in those days!"

"You were always loyal," Tom said affectionately. "You'll never know how often I thought of you afterward. Well, that time I was taken to jail and then deported——"

"For what?" Marian asked.

"For trying to exercise the right of free speech," Tom said. "The next time several of us tried to get in after dark on a freight train, but it stopped at a water tower on this side of town and Storm Troopers came out from everywhere—each with a white handkerchief tied round his arm, so they wouldn't make a mistake and club their own men in the dark. They dragged all of us off the train and put us in cars and threw us out on the other side of the county line. We got off easy, except one young Jew. When they were putting him in the car, they tried to make him say he would not come back, and he kept saying he would exercise his right of free speech wherever he pleased. Well, that was the second time——"

"What happened to the young Jew?" Marian asked.

Tom said delicately, "He suffered, but he got over it and kept his promise about going back. The third time forty of us tried going by steamer, but we were surrounded at the dock and taken across the county line in cars. That time they made us run the gantlet and we didn't get off so easy. Some of us got away into the woods, and I don't remember much after that except being alone and walking in the rain and falling. I had some head wounds and I would have bled to death if I hadn't got to a house where I had friends——"

Marian looked so incredulous that Bailey leaned over and said, "You don't remember the dark age in which you were born!"

She said, "Charlie has told me in a general way that it was a rough time; but wasn't there any one to prevent that kind of thing?"

"If there was," Tom said, "we never found him. As far as I

observed, no one who was a Wobbly, or mistaken for one, had any redress for anything that happened to him."

"But that was anarchy!" Marian said. "A man could have been robbed or murdered—and nothing done about it!"

Tom smiled benignly. "Quite so. But that's what we were up against. Probably that's why we had so many youngsters. I saw boys of eighteen and nineteen take beatings—but never mind. It took young men with stout hearts—and they grew older after a while."

Bailey said, "You're far enough away for perspective. What about the Wobbly organizers and leaders; how do you see them now?"

"I knew them all," Tom said. "They fought and suffered and went hungry, and never asked anything for themselves. All of us were arrested times without number, on charges too flimsy to hold together until they reached the court room. The only one they ever made stick was preaching the brotherhood of man."

Tom polished the lenses of his glasses thoughtfully and clamped them on his nose again. "A good deal of water has flowed under the bridge since then, but when I remember that band of heroes, it is like suddenly coming on my youth again. There was Jim Rowan, whom they nearly flogged to death, and who came back before his wounds had healed; Walker Smith, who spoke and wrote and thought so clearly; Gurley Flynn, with her flaming red tie and flaming beauty; there was Charlie Ashleigh, who was on the *Verona* during the affair at the dock. He was the one who wrote that verse:

> Song on his lips he came;
> Song on his lips he went——

"*Ja, Ja!*" Tag cried, with his eyes blazing. "It was about a Swede, Yohnson! I was there, wounded, with a pile of dead and wounded men; the deputies were firing into them——"

Bailey touched the old man's arm, "Tag, not now——"

"I was there!" Tag shouted. "The boy, Gerlot, was there; he climbed the flagpole and waved when we came in, singing. They shot him down like a cub out of a tree. Rabinowitz was there—the New York Jew who said he would come back."

Tom Horton put his hand on Tag's shoulder. "Please," he said, "Mrs. Dow is here——"

Tag could not stop. "That was the last time he came back. He was there—I saw him—with the back of his head shot off."

Marian got up quickly and bent over Tag, with her arm on his shoulder. "Tag, you're upsetting the others!"

"*Ja, ja*, certainly, certainly," his shouting voice softened and dwindled. "The rest is beautiful. We were singing 'Hold the Fort,' when the steamer came in to the dock and those things happened. Yohnson was near me and he was hit. Soon he said, 'Hold me up, Comrades, I want to finish the song.'

"They were shooting from the warehouse and from the other dock, and from a tug, but after he said that I wasn't afraid any more. We held him up and he sang 'Fierce and long the battle rages—' Bullets and buckshot hitting all around, but they didn't hit us. Yohnson was a big logger with yellow hair, and he had a big voice. Soon we all were singing. The song was like a flag, with the guns shooting holes in it, but the flag was there all the time, waving. Yohnson's voice was the strongest when we came to the last line, 'Cheer, my comrades, cheer!' He held the last note so long you thought he would never stop. Then something burst inside and blood came out of his nose and mouth, all over us—and he was dead."

It was still at the table, but overhead the breath of summer went through the big trees that Tom Horton had planted. Marian said, "Thank you, Tag; you told that beautifully."

Tom said, "You see how men had to die in the old days for freedom of speech."

"When we all believe in it," Bailey said, "we shouldn't have tried to stop Tag."

"We shouldn't, really," Marian said.

Bailey said cheerfully, "Men don't get hurt any more, either, for belonging to labor unions."

"They're more likely to get in trouble if they don't," Tom said.

Tag asked, "When will we have One Big Union, like we used to talk about?"

"That was a dream," Tom said.

"The ones we have do pretty well," Bailey said.

Tom was unsympathetic; relighting his cigar he said, "I'm inclined to agree with Westbrook Pegler; he may not always be fair to organized labor, but I think his attitude is sound."

Bailey said to himself: I think I'll sit this one out.

Marian was smiling, with the look of being away somewhere, and Tag was hurt and puzzled because every one had gone to his own corner, where he saw the same thing from a different angle and was too polite to say so. Bailey tried to bring them back.

"Well, Tom," he said, "the I.W.W. lost out here, but you must get some satisfaction from seeing the idea work out somewhere else on a tremendous scale."

Tom was still cool and out of reach. "Where?"

"Russia, of course. I can't see any real difference between your old program and theirs."

Tom looked hurt to the quick. "They have nothing in common!" he snapped. Then he said, "I'm sorry, Bailey, but I feel so strongly on the subject. Possibly they look somewhat alike on the surface; a few of our old leaders were misled into going to Russia, and they were thoroughly disillusioned."

Bailey asked, "Wasn't 'The Red Flag' a Wobbly song?"

"With us 'The Red Flag' was the symbol of the revolutionary spirit—the liberation of the working class. The Russians have desecrated it."

Marian asked, "But, Tom, don't you think they have accomplished wonderful things?"

"I'm sorry that you seem to have been misled by propaganda," Tom said. "Personally, I can see no good in the Russian experiment. I don't think too well of the Nazis, either, but their conquest of Russia will do more good than harm."

Faintly exasperated, Bailey said, "Even Father has decided that the Russians have something; and you know what an old die-hard he was."

"I know," Tom said; "it has reached every walk of life; I have even had some sharp differences of opinion on the subject with my banker."

When they gave up controversial subjects, they did not find anything on which they could get together, and Tom Horton left soon afterward.

They said their final good-byes beside his Buick coupe on the drive. Tom gripped Bailey's hand warmly, with his eyes bright behind his rimless pince-nez glasses. "God bless you, Bailey!" To Marian he said, "I can't tell you how much this has meant to me, coming back here and being made so welcome." Tag had disappeared, but Tom Horton did not seem to notice. He swung the car around the circle and drove away, going fast through the orchard of big trees.

Marian's voice said, "He's nice, isn't he?"

Bailey agreed.

"I don't think I ever met a kinder person."

"Wasn't he terrible?"

"He wasn't what I expected," Marian admitted; "but he was very nice."

Bailey was going to get his bag and start back to Seattle, but he couldn't go indoors just then; there wouldn't be enough air in the house. They drifted back to where they had had lunch under the trees. Bailey lay on the grass, and Marian sat near him, smiling absently.

"Let's get drunk!" Bailey suggested.

"I would like to." But the tone said she wouldn't.

"Two is all it takes."

She shook her head regretfully.

"Tag would help us, if we needed it."

Marian shook her head again, still smiling, with a breath of wind stirring her light summer dress.

"Where is Tag?" he asked.

"He went to his room, I think."

"Probably getting drunk by himself. Why shouldn't we?"

"We'd only have to get sober again."

"I never think of that."

"I do," she said. But the day had thawed something virginal in her, and she looked soft and warm and waiting. Bailey reached out and took her hand. "You're lovely today," he said.

She gave his hand a squeeze and took hers away.

"You've seen Tom Horton's ghost," he said.

"I wonder why he didn't call up one of the other times he was in Seattle?

"Vanity, I suppose. He wanted to own his own business and drive a good car. He wanted Mother to see that he was a success."

"I don't think your mother would have cared much for that kind of success."

"She wouldn't," Bailey said. "She would have been terribly disappointed in Tom, but how could you expect him to remember that? Life gangs up on you; every one with something to sell."

"He's so proud of his business———"

"He and his precious furniture: everything glued and screwed! Well, better the furniture than the customer." After a minute he came to Tom's defense, although he was the one who had been critical. "You can't laugh at him for wanting to do something for himself. If he'd gone on bleeding and going to jail for other people, who would have cared about him?"

"Only the few who loved him," she said.

"Unless you're a standard success, it's hard to feel that you're anything but a failure."

She said, "That's what Mother is always preaching. I hate it, but what can you say? It's just as if she said, 'You have to take your galoshes and umbrella; it's a rainy day.' You hate it, but you can't contradict her, because it is."

Bailey was still afraid she might have a bad opinion of Tom. "He didn't give up easily. By then, he'd given more than any one should be expected to give. Did you see the scars?"

She nodded. "That was the only thing that made it possible to believe."

Yes, it was even difficult to believe that this sunny lawn had once been part of the Dark Ages, where Tom had stumbled in circles, dazed and bleeding and falling.

Marian asked, "But what kind of men could have done that to a gentle person like Tom?"

He shrugged. "The average kind, bent on hanging onto what they had." Then, without intending to, he said brutally, "I think it was the Old Man who left the mark of the pistol butt." He saw her wince and bite her lower lip, and he said hastily, "I'm sorry I told you that."

"You wouldn't have, if it weren't true."

But what had made him say that? He couldn't think of any reason, unless it was to damage the Old Man. And why should he want to do that? Then he saw the pattern and felt vaguely ill. "I'm sorry I invited Tom," he said.

"I'm not." Then she asked. "Do you think your father will be upset?"

"I don't suppose so," he said, though he wasn't as sure about it now. "If you like, I'll wait until he comes home."

"No, it isn't necessary," she said. "It would be better for me to tell him, anyway."

The day was spoiled and there wasn't anything else to stay for.

When he was leaving he heard Tag's record player from the room above the garage:

> I dreamed I saw Joe Hill last night,
>   Alive as you and me.
> Says I, "But Joe, you're ten years dead."
>   "I never died," said he.
>   "I never died," said he.

Joe had lived by dying. A reliable method, Bailey thought. There could be a special camera for people who wanted to be heroes. You struck your favorite pose and the bulb fired off the pistol in the camera.

XI

THEY JUST made the eight o'clock ferry at Ballard. On board, space was plentiful, even though time had run out.

Bailey drove to the port side almost 'midships, and stopped behind a car from Jefferson County and beside a panel truck. As he shut off the motor, a deck hand began putting blocks behind the rear wheels. Drivers in other cars had already relaxed: in the high-topped sedan ahead, children were eating bananas and cookies, while a big woman with frowsy hair kept them in order with her elbows, and poured milk from a bottle into paper cups. Drivers and passengers up ahead were getting out of cars, and the panel truck beside Bailey was already deserted.

Before he had time to light a cigarette, the gong clanged and the ferry quivered to the hissing trample of its engines; clusters of piling slid by the windows, and between the files of cars up ahead he saw the incoming ferry dawdling offshore, waiting for the berth which the *Klickitat* was just leaving.

Violet said, "I wish we were up in front where we could see everything."

"We can go on deck," Bailey said; "the view is better up there."

"Maybe after a while." She took out a vanity case and powdered her nose delicately. "It isn't the same, though. It's always windy in the front of a boat." She began touching up her mouth with lipstick. "Can you get anything on the radio, Bailey?"

"I'm afraid you're out of luck," he said.

"Why? Is it broken?"

"I don't have one."

"Oh!" But she didn't understand why he didn't have a car radio.

He laughed at her. "Look, Violet, I'm taking you for a car ride and a boat ride at the same time, and you want the double-header buttered with a concert."

"No," she said, "I just thought if you had a radio you could get the Morning Syncopade. I always turn it on when I'm dressing."

"You're dressed now."

"I know, but this is the time."

This outing was Bailey's reaction to Tom Horton's visit. He had planned only a gloomy drinking party, but after thinking it over, he made it more comfortable by persuading Violet away from Martin Darling's office. The girl had never known Tom, and therefore did not share Bailey's disillusionment; but she was good company when he did not want to think.

Settling down beside him, she asked, "Will there be any place to dance at Lake Crescent?"

He thought there would be. "And I'll get you a room with a radio in it."

"You make it sound as if I was going to stay in the room by myself."

"No, but I might have to rent two for appearances."

"I know, Bailey." She took his hand, almost absent-mindedly, and held it beside her, with their wrists touching. "We're going to have a nice time."

"Any time you like, we can go up and have some breakfast."

"Pretty soon," she said, "but it's nice here, even if you don't have a radio. I like boat trips, if the boat's big enough. It isn't that I'm afraid of small ones, but when you see the water it seems too kind of personal."

The boat ride went on like a garage full of cars gone adrift in the gentle trembling of an earthquake. The door of the sedan ahead opened and the big woman with the untidy hair billowed out, gripping a small boy by the arm. Other children followed like links in a chain. The last one banged the door shut, earnestly, with both hands, and the procession trailed away between the cars and up the stairs. Two Indians in blue serge suits got out of another car to examine a white-walled tire, and the driver of the panel truck came back—a straight, easy-moving young woman, bare-headed, in an old, unbuttoned polo coat. Bailey saw the level look of her brown eyes and her amused half-smile as she passed the front fender of his car and turned towards the truck. He opened his door and floundered out to meet her.

"Louise!"

The look in her eyes became more level, like warm sunlight from the horizon, and her amused half-smile woke and was alive. "Bailey, to think of meeting you in our own country!" Her hands felt tough and good; she was thinner than when he had seen her last and very much tanned.

"Louise!" he said again. He wanted to carry her away—but there was Violet waiting in the car at his elbow. He would have to get his sins together under one roof. "We're neighbors," he said, indicating his car and Violet, who was just finishing powdering her nose again.

He introduced the girls and said, "Come in, Louise, and tell us how things are in New York!" When she hesitated about getting between him and Violet, he got in first and Louise followed him. Sitting between them, he said, "You two have New York in common. Any one who has been there likes to tell about it, and any one who hasn't, likes to hear."

"That's so," Violet said.

He said, "When I had a book store in New York, Louise was one of my best customers."

"You're exaggerating," she said; "I bought only books about dancing."

"So I knew the kind to stock."

Violet asked, "Is New York much harder to get around in than Seattle?"

"It's easier, really."

"If you stay out of the Bronx," Bailey added.

"And Brooklyn!"

"By all means stay out of Brooklyn!"

Violet said, "You two have been in New York. You can talk about it better than I can ask."

"We can work it both ways," Bailey said. "I'll ask Louise questions and you can interrupt whenever anything isn't clear."

Louise said, "I'll try, but I won't be very good at it; I only noticed things that interested me."

Bailey asked, "Is it true that they've torn down the Sixth Avenue El?"

"Yes, it was all torn down before I left."

"What's an El?"

"Elevated Railroad," Bailey explained. "It ran above the street, level with the second-story windows. It was dirty and old, and it blighted everything in its shade."

"But when it's gone, it's something to remember," Louise said.

"The cars were made in the time of the Civil War," Bailey went on. "They were wooden with open platforms at the ends and a curved overhang roof. The platforms had pitted iron gates and hand-brakes with horizontal wheels."

"They were electric trains," Louise said. "The early ones were drawn by locomotives, and in dry weather cinders would fall and set fire to the awnings of the stores below."

"I don't remember that," Bailey said.

"They were before my time," Louise admitted. "I only heard about them."

"It must be funny—seeing trains moving in the air," Violet said.

"It is. When you are far enough away, the trains look like children's cut-outs in motion."

"When they stop, you expect to see Union soldiers get out," Bailey said.

"Where they run through the tenement district, women open their windows in summer and put pillows on the sills for their elbows; they lean there all summer, watching the trains go by. In winter you can see their faces behind the closed windows. I don't know what they'll look at when the El's are all torn down."

"Maybe they'll see the sun sometimes," Bailey suggested.

"They deserve to go," Louise admitted. "But the stations were nice, though; especially those on the Third Avenue line. My favorite was at Fifty-third Street; it was like a silly little Swiss chalet with lots of gingerbread and open stairways. It was nicest in winter, with big flakes of snow falling and people going up and down the stairways. You had the feeling that there were as many people as there were flakes and that they would be coming down the stairways for as long. I don't know where they all came from or where they were all going; and they couldn't have, either, or they would have got there long ago. Sometimes I came down those stairs and I didn't know where I was going—but it was exciting just to be there."

Sitting between the two girls, Bailey found Louise's hand and held it quietly while he said to Violet, "That answers your question about whether it's easy to get lost in New York."

"They weren't really lost, were they?"

"Beautifully, and they didn't care. That's what makes a city. In Seattle, people know what they want and where they're going. At the end of the day they say to themselves: 'We didn't make a city of it today, but we'll come back and give it hell tomorrow.' They do, but they haven't made a city of it yet. Every day, after five o'clock, downtown is like a construction job with workmen's tools dropped where they were being used when the whistle blew. People can't save their own souls and give a city one."

Louise said, "I never thought of it that way before, but that's the difference."

Violet was still thinking about getting around in New York. "How will people travel when they take away all the El's?"

"Underground," Bailey told her. "There's a city underneath the city—tracks and trains and platforms and stores and restaurants. A person could spend a lifetime there without ever seeing the light of day. Some people probably do."

"Ugh! I wouldn't like to."

Changing the subject, Bailey asked: "Does Emily still serve popovers for lunch on Tuesdays?"

"She did when I was there last, and some days Sally Lunn. On Fridays the place was always extra clean and smelling of coal oil."

"Who is Emily?" Violet asked.

"She ran a restaurant on Greenwich Avenue; not big or famous, but very nice."

"Do the horses still gather around the horses' Christmas tree at Seventh Avenue?"

"I couldn't get to see it last Christmas, but it was there the year before. One horse picked his own present off the tree—a big carrot."

Violet asked, "What is a horses' Christmas tree?"

"Just that," Bailey said. "Every Christmas there was a tree near the watering trough at the corner of Thirteenth Street, hung with apples and carrots for the neighborhood horses. Visiting fire horses used to be welcome, too, but that was before my time."

"What a funny idea! Who thought of doing that?"

Bailey said, "I never heard it explained, but it was probably some sentimental member of the humane society."

Louise said, "The horses were so solemn and well-behaved, I used to think they were Christian descendants of the ones who knelt around the manger."

"She's a mystic," Bailey explained to Violet, "and you can never prove that she's wrong."

Violet slid her left hand into his right one, which was free. "I suppose horses are all descendants of each other."

"How was the weather in New York?" Bailey asked.

"About as usual, and the newspapers made the most of it. Every day that was hot or cold or wet or dry broke some record, and days that were just moderate broke all records for moderation." After a minute she recalled, "There weren't any more ice storms."

"What's an ice storm like?"

Bailey said, "It's when sleet freezes as it falls. There was one when the trees iced up to where a twig as thin as a pencil looked like a glass baseball bat. It happened at night and in the morning Louise—telephoned me and we went to Central Park. It was like a glass forest—crystal trees bigger than any that had ever been there——"

"It was something you accepted, but it was never quite real,"

Louise said. "The sky was gray, but light seemed to come from somewhere and the glass branches had colors in them. And all the time you thought, *it isn't real, it can't last!*"

"It didn't," Bailey said; "not when every tree was loaded down with tons of ice. While we were looking, a wind came up and the glass forest crashed and began to fall——"

"We were near a big tree and Bailey pulled me out of the way of a limb that came down just where we'd been standing. It must have weighed a ton."

"Half a ton, at least," Bailey said. "It was the only rescue I ever accomplished in the woods—saving a rubber-necking New Yorker from an ice tree in Central Park."

"Thank you just the same." She gave his left hand a light, quick squeeze.

Violet withdrew her hand from his unresponsive right one. "It must have done the trees a lot of damage."

"It made a wreck of them," Bailey said. "It was the most expensive beauty I ever saw, and it lasted only a few hours. It showed that nature is feminine, with no instinct for mechanics. A glass forest!"

"It was wonderful while it lasted," Louise said. "And nature has been managing for longer than you have."

"I worship nature," he said, "but she hasn't much sense of mechanics."

Violet stirred and said, "You two have a lot to talk about. I think I'll go upstairs and find the Ladies' Room."

Bailey said hastily, "We can all go."

"To the Ladies' Room?" Louise asked.

Violet had opened the door and was getting out. "Don't hurry on my account." She closed the door and went away.

When he looked at Louise she was still laughing. "Bailey, you're so funny!"

He held her hand savagely.

"I'm not really laughing at you," she said. "You manage very well."

"Manage what?"

"Carrying water on both shoulders."

He couldn't even have the satisfaction of saying anything disparaging about Violet, whom he had invited to be his overnight guest.

Louise said, "I hope you were holding her hand, to make things even."

"No."

"Then I hope she was holding yours."

"No." It wasn't true, but it was none of her business, which was the same thing.

"I wasn't prying; I only wanted to be fair." She looked at him and laughed again. "You're almost monogamous, Bailey. You looked as if you'd have been happier with only one of us in the car, but I couldn't tell which one."

"You know," he said.

"So long as you leave it that way, you're still playing fair." Then she said, "You're with me now and you certainly don't look happier."

"Louise!"

When he tried to kiss her, she drew away definitely. "Bailey, if you have a serious date with that girl, you haven't any right to be flirting while she goes to the Ladies' Room."

"You make me sound like a barnyard animal!" Then he said, "You turn me adrift and laugh at me when you see me out with a girl two years later!"

She was not laughing any more. "Did I do that?"

"You did." Then he said, "You know me better than any one else; you know that as long as we were together I never made a pass at any other woman."

"Didn't you?"

"You know I didn't."

She smiled absently and shook her head. "I never even thought about it."

"That's better than knowing," he said, "that's you." Then he asked, "Well, what are you doing for a sex life?"

She seemed surprised at the question. "Why, I live in chastity, just like you."

"I hope not."

"That's ambiguous." Then she said gravely, "I'm almost becoming a virgin." She looked it, and she looked very nice and thoughtful and a little away somewhere. He couldn't decide whether she was happy or not, but he didn't think she wanted him to be too personal or possessive.

"When did you get back?" he asked.

"This May; the last part of the month."

"I wish you had let me know."

"I thought about it."

"That was kind of you."

"Oh, it was no trouble."

He let it go, and asked, "Did you come back for the summer?"

"No, I just came back."

"How is the dancing?"

"I'm a failure," she said.

He didn't believe it. "You were wonderful!"

"I'm pretty good, but not good enough; or I didn't click."

"What are you doing now?"

"Helping on the farm."

"I might have known; you're as tanned as a haymaker."

"I helped with the haying—drove a hay wagon. Now I'm driving a truck." She inclined her brown head towards the panel truck. "I delivered a load of strawberries to the public market this morning."

He added and subtracted hours. "You must have started at daybreak."

"A little before; I caught the first ferry."

"You make me feel ashamed." Then he asked, "Could you use a good farm hand?"

She looked amused, "After all the farm-hand stories I've heard this summer, no!"

"Do you like farming?"

"I love it," she said. "Our farm is almost in the shadow of a mountain and on the other side the meadows go away to the flats at the mouth of the river; then there's the canal and the end of the Toandos, and the coast on the other side. It was lovely from the top of a load of hay, with meadow larks singing everywhere."

"Do you like picking strawberries?"

"Not so much. We let the Indians do that."

"Do you talk to them in Chinook Jargon?"

"They prefer English."

He said, "The first time I knew you were from this part of the world was when you spoke Jargon. That international windbag was dazzling me with all the known languages, and you needled her with one she didn't know."

"I remember. It was rude of me."

"It was nicely done and it saved me from being bored to death." Then he felt depressed, because it had been the first sign of her loyalty to him. Since then everything had happened and come to nothing. Now he didn't know where he stood, and at the moment he was in an embarrassing fix with Violet on his hands.

"Did you ever pick strawberries?" she asked.

"No; but I will even do that for you."

"Thank you, but they're mostly picked. I asked because you sounded as if you had tried it."

"I got the impression from my stepmother, Marian. She grew up near Ilihee."

"Is she the young and beautiful one?"

"Yes, and she has more beauty than ever; I don't know what she does with it all."

"I don't blame any one for not liking to pick strawberries."

"Marian didn't seem to take to farming the way you do. They cleared the land as they went along and raised some of everything."

"That would discourage any one. We raise hay mostly and keep some stock. The berries are only a side line. We don't make any money, but we live; it's a help to have capable brothers."

Bailey said, "You always made them sound like heroes."

"They're nice," she said. "They didn't bother going to the University, but they have a good-natured tolerance of culture. When I needed money for my dancing, they worked in logging camps and went to Alaska with the fishing fleet—all that without having been asked to and for something they probably thought was crazy."

"Are you going to stay on the farm?"

"For the summer, anyway. Maybe in the fall I'll open a studio in Seattle. When you're not good enough, you teach others."

"I'll be one of your pupils."

"No. I'll have only small children at first."

"Then I'll have children and send them to you."

"I don't want to hurry you, but it isn't long until fall." Then she said, "Don't you think you should find Violet before she feels too slighted?"

"I suppose so. Louise, when am I going to see you again?"

"I told you where we live. If you want to call——"

"When are you free?"

"Now." She was amused again. "When will you be?"

"Almost any time; maybe this afternoon."

"That would be rushing things, and you haven't anything to rush for."

"Any time you'll let me; any time you're free."

"I'll never be too free again, if that's what you're thinking of."

"I'm not." Then he blurted, "I got you into a jam and I've been sorry——"

"Don't boast," she said quickly; "don't exaggerate! You talk as if I didn't count for anything! It takes two, and that's why there are men and women."

"I always say the wrong thing."

Louise said, "Now you must go and find Violet." She opened the door on her side and got out.

"Don't you want to come on deck?"

"No, thank you." She peered ahead between the files of cars. "We're almost there; we've passed Point No Point, and there's Foulweather Bluff."

"Good-bye, then," he held out his hand. "And I'm coming to see you, Louise."

"You'll be welcome," she told him, shaking hands. "And bring Violet."

He felt outraged, but there was no help for it. "If I were doing that, I'd follow you home; maybe I will."

"You mustn't," she said. "I'm sure that's not where you were going."

"I won't follow you if you don't want me to, but I am coming to see you."

"All right, Bailey, and bring——"

"Never mind," he said.

She looked rebuffed. "You don't know what I was asking you to bring!"

"What, Louise?"

"Never mind," she said.

He found Violet sitting at the counter in the restaurant, finishing a sandwich and a glass of milk. She looked unnecessarily dressed-up and made-up, as if some one had sold her a bill of goods by misrepresenting life as a chic affair. He took the stool beside her and she looked up in a matter-of-fact way. "I was hungry," she said.

"I'm sorry. When you get talking with some one you haven't seen for a long time——"

"You weren't very long."

"I thought I was."

"I didn't think so. Anyway, I said not to hurry on my account."

"That was generous of you."

"Are you going to have anything?"

"No. We're almost there. If you like, we'll go out on deck when you're through."

"I'm through now." She had finished while they were talking, and she picked up her shiny new handbag and her check from the counter and slid off the stool.

He took the check from her and paid it, and they went out on deck.

The *Klickitat* had passed Foulweather Bluff and was heading to pass to starboard of the black light buoy at the harbor entrance, a flat boat trundling over a flat sea. Ahead there was the low shore and what was left of the town.

"Port Ludlow used to be the capital of a lumber empire," Bailey said.

"It isn't much now, is it?"

It wasn't anything but a ferry dock and a village of neat, fading houses.

"It's nothing," Bailey said, "but it was history. Any one who's been in Maine could tell where the first big-time lumber men came from. Closer up you can see the big beams under the eaves of the town hall and the company store; that construction belongs to Maine."

"Is that where the lumber men came from?"

"The Popes and Talbots were from East Machias; Cyrus Walker, who ran things here, was from Skowhegan."

"That's a funny name."

"Almost as funny as Snohomish or Snoqualmie."

"Do you think they're funny?"

"Don't you?"

"It isn't much of a town, is it?" Violet went on.

"No, but it was when the mill was here. That stack is all that's left."

"Why did they take the mill away?"

"They ran out of trees," he answered.

"Do you think we should go downstairs?"

They were almost the last to go below, and even on the car deck the *Klickitat* had the feeling of being deserted. People had gone back into the shells of their cars and there was only the empty sound of gongs in the engine room; the ferry slip looming towards them and tension of being ready to start. It broke with a grind of starters and a roar of motors as the ferry was made fast, and the lines of cars moved off, joint by joint.

Louise got the signal first, and as she passed she smiled and waved. Then there were cars from the other side, and when it was Bailey's turn the panel truck was out of sight.

In another half minute he was out of the village and driving slowly through second-growth fir and gravel country in bright sunshine.

Beside him Violet asked, "Was all that true about New York?"

"That, and much more."

"I liked the part about the glass forest."

"It doesn't happen very often."

"Was the ice all colors?"

"Not exactly. It broke up the light and reflected colors, but all the time it was as clear as glass."

"It must have been beautiful."

"It was—while it lasted."

"Did it really happen that way when the wind blew?"

"Yes. When the sun got warm and the wind blew, it crashed and fell to pieces."

She didn't find anything more to say about it and he drove in silence along the secondary highway at less than thirty miles an hour. In a few more minutes, he thought, Louise would reach the Quilcene cutoff to the Loop Highway and turn south towards the Canal. When he reached the same intersection, he would continue north. They would go in opposite directions, and all the time she would be laughing at him: Bailey carrying water on both shoulders. Bailey on the motor ferry *Klickitat*, with his hair parted in the middle, holding hands with a girl on each side. Bailey stooging for a parable of Sacred and Profane Love. Bailey being interviewed by body and soul. That was libel on Louise, who could burn, body and soul, in clear flame——

Violet stirred beside him and asked, "How far is it to Lake Crescent?"

He thought, and said, "Sixty miles."

"Louise is nice, isn't she?"

He glanced sideways at her pretty, unrevealing face. "Yes, I always liked her." He was driving slowly in bright sunshine, with his hands almost idle on the plastic and chromium steering wheel. For some reason the wheel made him think of old Jim Donaldson's pearl-handled revolver. Was it his idea of elegance, or was it all he had left when Martin Darling was through with him? Bailey didn't know. The Old Man had got along with Martin for years——

Violet stirred again and uncrossed her neat legs. "You aren't talking to me, Bailey."

"I guess I wasn't."

"Usually you talk and tell me about things; it's almost like the radio."

He said, "I'll have to get one; they're more reliable."

"You know so much," she said. "You could go on 'Information, Please.' Remember the time we were listening to my radio? The *New Yorker* fellow would ask questions and you would answer, and the men on the radio would answer, and their answers were the same as yours; except once Christopher Morley said something different, and he was wrong."

"I wasn't really that good."

"First I thought you were wrong and I pointed at you and I had to pay a forfeit."

"Yes."

"You used to kid me about that. It was the first time——"

"Yes."

"You don't want to talk about things now."

"I'm sorry," he said; "I was thinking."

"What were you thinking, Bailey?"

"Just now I was thinking about an old logging operator who shot himself."

"Ugh! I'd never shoot myself!"

"It isn't a good idea."

"No." Then she remembered, "Once I said the same thing about not shooting myself and you said maybe somebody else wouldn't feel the same way about me. Now you don't kid me about things."

"I'm sorry." He drove on slowly.

After a while Violet said, "Bailey, you don't have to take me to Lake Crescent."

He looked at her. "I asked you to go."

"That was different; you wanted to, then."

"Lake Crescent is a nice place," he said. "I've always liked it."

"It isn't the lake," she said, "it's me."

"You're a nice girl; I've always liked you."

"Louise is nicer," she said. "Wherever she is, it would be nicer."

He drove more slowly. "I don't see what Louise has to do with it. I invited you to go to the lake with me, and we're going."

"That's only because of me. You don't want it now."

"I didn't say that."

"I don't want to go now. It would be like seducing you when you didn't want to be."

"You make me sound very pure."

"I guess everybody is pure, in a way."

"At least every one would like to be, in a way."

"I wouldn't do anything that was wrong. Going with you now would be like going out with a married man—I mean if he and his wife loved each other. I have principles."

"You're a fine girl," he said.

"I want you to turn around, Bailey; we aren't going to the lake."

Driving at twenty miles an hour, he said, "But I invited you. We could have dinner there, anyway. We wouldn't have to stay if you didn't want to."

"It wouldn't be right," she insisted. "Going there meant something different. I want you to turn around."

"All right, if you want me to." He drove on until there was a gravel side road going away into the sparse second growth. He turned into the side road and stopped, then backed onto the narrow highway and drove slowly towards Port Ludlow.

"I feel better now," Violet said; "I feel fine."

He, too, felt fine and generous. "Where would you like to go, Violet?"

"I want to go home." Then she said, "You can put me on the ferry and go to see Louise."

"Don't be ridiculous."

"That way she'll know that we didn't go anywhere together. She'll know that she's the only one you care about."

More likely she would think that *he* was the only one he cared about. "I'm not doing anything of the sort. This is our day."

"It isn't any more," she said, "but it's nice of you to say it is."

"It's our day," he said, "and we'll go where you like and do anything you want."

"We'll have lunch on the ferry," she said, "and you can tell me about things. You can talk about Louise if you want to, and I won't be jealous. I liked her, too."

"You're a fine, generous girl." He put his hand on her arm, approvingly.

"I only want to do what's right." Then she slumped down and put her face against his hand and began to cry. He felt the warmth of her face and of her breath and the wet warmth of tears on his hand, and he was upset. He had known her for a year, on and off, and they had done everything usual, and there hadn't been any special tenderness between them. Now she was very human and warm and he felt more affection for her than he ever had when he was making love to her. "Don't cry, Violet," he said; "please don't cry." He wanted to stop the car and comfort her, but the rough, brushy country came to the edge of the road and there was no place where he could safely stop. Trying to comfort her, he drove back along the narrow road in bright sunshine.

XII

CHARLIE had been sensible about Tom Horton's visit. At a few minutes after six on Monday afternoon, Marian had met him at the door, as she was expected to, and kissed him, and taken his hat. When she asked him how things were at camp, he said, "We're logging now," which meant that everything was going the way it was intended.

When they were in the living room, and she was mixing a highball for him, he asked, as he always did, "Anything happen today?"

Marian said, "Bailey stayed over for lunch; we had company."

"That's good."

She gave him his drink, with a coaster to go under the glass.

"Was there any mail?"

She said, "Nothing important, I think," and gave him what there was.

The mail did not amount to anything. He glanced at it, and put it aside and asked, "Tag getting any work done?"

"Oh, yes. Among other things, he mowed the back lawn."

Belatedly, Charlie asked, "Who was the company?"

"Some one you once knew: a Mr. Horton."

"Horton?" He drank and looked puzzled, going over a card file in his mind. Apparently he didn't find anything until he got to the T's; then he swung his head and shoulders towards her, abruptly. "Not Tom Horton?"

"Yes. He used to work for you."

"What was he doing here?"

"He was passing through Seattle and he telephoned. I knew he'd done a lot of work on the place and I invited him to come to lunch."

Charlie thought it over. "It wasn't Bailey's doing?"

She sipped her drink and said, "No; but he thought it was all right."

"What did Tom Horton want?"

"Nothing," she said, "except to see the place."

"He wasn't after help of some kind?"

She laughed, "You should have seen him; he's quite the prosperous businessman!"

Charlie drank and said. "I wouldn't have expected it. What's he doing?"

"He has a furniture business in Denver; he's been there for sixteen years."

"Is he staying around here long?"

"He's on his way back," she said; "he was going to Portland tonight."

Her husband grunted and finished his drink. "I suppose I have time to change before dinner?"

"Yes; we won't be eating for half an hour."

It had gone as simply as that. It did not occur to Marian that in Charlie's mind there were various depths, and it would take longer for the echo to come back from some of them. On Wednesday afternoon, Marian saw him come home precisely as he had on Monday.

In his vigorous young days, Charlie had a chauffeur to take him about. Now, when he was older in a less stuffy age, he drove his own car home and put it in the garage. Then he walked methodically to the house. His walk had become more deliberate in the last year or two, but he was still straight, and his shoulders were so big that there was hardly any impression of paunchiness about his figure. His business suit might have been made by the same tailor as Tom Horton's, but it had suffered indefinably from the woods, and his wide hat and thick-soled shoes gave him the appearance of a seasoned county sheriff.

Marian met him at the door and kissed him and took his hat. "How did things go today, Charlie?"

"They're going all right, Girl; we're logging now."

They went on to the living room, where she had the tray ready with whiskey and ice and water. He settled himself in his chair and asked, "Anything happen today?"

Mixing his highball, she said, "Nothing special. I tried to call Bailey about the week end, but he was over on the Peninsula. Egil said he might be gone a day or two."

Charlie grunted and accepted his drink. "Tag getting any work done?"

"I think so," she said. But she could not have told anything that Tag had accomplished. During the last two days he had been working less and apparently drinking more than usual. "There was some mail," she said; "there's a letter from Paul."

Charlie drank and asked, "What did he say?"

"It's for you." She gave him the letter with the other mail and the heavy brass letter opener.

He put on his horn-rimmed glasses, opened the letter and read it, and with an annoyed grunt passed it on to Marian.

The letter was on stationery of the Forest Fire Association, and it was written from a lookout station in the Cascades. Paul said that he had got restless doing nothing, and had taken a job with the Association. He would be on lookout for the rest of the fire season, and that would give him time to think over what he was going to do after that.

Marian folded the letter and said, "I suppose Paul has been away for so long that he was homesick for the mountains."

"He certainly wasn't homesick for home." Marian knew that her husband was disappointed, though he did not say anything more at the time.

But he came back to it when they were going to bed. He sat near the tile fireplace, looking at the *Seattle Times* and getting cigar ashes on his pyjamas. Marian was at the old-fashioned walnut dressing table, working on her smooth face with cleansing tissues and cream and thinking restless treason: If you don't have to work enough to get your skin dirty, you're expected to work extra hard cleaning it. Men have better complexions, age for age, without doing anything but washing their faces. If you were living, you wouldn't be plastered with everybody's preparations, like handbills on a vacant shed. Beauty is made to be played with and loved; if your life is incomplete, you act out a little of what is missing. But that is not being a woman; it is not having a man. You would give it up in one swift moment for a life where you never saw your reflection except in a tin basin of water or a pool in the woods. . . . She rubbed the beauty cream from her face as if she were drying it with a rough towel, and got up restlessly and went to the window. Outside there was starlight over the orchard and on the lawn. The big trees stood silently in the night, with deep shadows under them.

Charlie stirred in his chair and put his newspaper aside. "I don't see why Tom Horton had to come here!"

Marian had supposed the incident was already in the past. "I'm sorry," she said, "I suggested it on the impulse."

"I don't blame you," he said, "but why did he have to turn up, after all these years. He was always a signal for bad luck—and now Paul is gone."

"Paul went before he came."

"Just the same, there's a connection," he said; "that damned radical!"

His wife smiled faintly. "He's certainly not a radical now."

"He was when it did me the most harm."

She had supposed the damage was the other way. "I don't see what difference it made."

"You would if you knew."

"How is that?" she asked.

"Sit down, Girl," he said, "and I'll try to tell you what I mean."

She sat on the arm of the other chair. He looked more paunchy than when he was dressed, but he was impressive in a big, bumbling way in his pyjamas and slippers and horn-rimmed glasses. "I'm nothing but an old timber beast," he said. "I've been tough in my day and I can still get tough. But there are things I can't bring myself to do: one of them's gossiping."

"I know that," she said.

"I feel the same whether it's one of the neighbors today, or something about people who are in their graves. If I don't tell you everything, it's because I still think I can manage my own affairs, or because it's none of my business."

"I think I understand."

"And I don't talk more than I have to about business matters or things I've had to do to protect my interests."

"I know that."

"Once I helped give Tom Horton and forty other men a hell of a beating. Did he tell you about that?"

She said, "He told about being beaten, but he didn't mention names."

"He wasn't one to gossip, either," Charlie said; "but there were other things I didn't like. Anyway, it was a hell of a beating; it's a wonder to me we didn't kill some of them."

"I saw the scars."

"He must be bald-headed for you to see them."

"He is." Then she asked, "What had the men done?"

"Didn't he tell you?"

"He said they were going into town to speak."

"That was it; and we had given them fair warning to keep out."

She asked, "Would it have done so much harm for them to give their side of the case?"

"We had strikes everywhere and we weren't going to have them stir up more trouble."

"You didn't really have the right to stop them, did you?"

"It was our mills and our timber and our business; we owned the county and paid the taxes. Just like this house," he said. "It's my house and I have a right to throw any one out of it, or burn it down if I like."

"You didn't feel that the men had any rights?"

"The ones who had homes and families here, yes. Not the Wobblies; they didn't own anything and they didn't believe we had a right to our own timber. When people threaten what you have, you crush them any way you can."

Sitting on the upholstered arm of the chair in her dressing gown, she said, "I see how you felt."

"Good." Clearly he wasn't interested in how she felt about something that wasn't her business. "That's past now. You know, I took Tom out of the woods to be my chauffeur and gardener. I wouldn't have done it if I hadn't trusted him. And I found he couldn't be trusted."

Marian was surprised. "He didn't——"

"Wait," Charlie said. "I'm not trying to say anything against Myra. When I married her I was a wild young man and she was a high-minded school teacher. I suppose that's why I wanted her, and she was never anything but high-minded. That was the trouble, maybe; and she was stubborn. When I brought Tom here I hadn't any idea he was a Wobbly. That was before college men and ministers began helping them, and they were just working stiffs.

"Myra looked up to Tom, in a way, because he'd been to college. That was her business, I thought, as long as she remembered he was the chauffeur. Then I found he'd given her all kinds of radical ideas. By the time he went to join the Wobblies, she was almost one herself."

Marian nodded. "I see how it could happen."

"I don't," he said. "Tom didn't have anything to lose, but Myra should have been able to see that her interests were on the other side. She wanted me to do things that would have ruined us, and when I told her so it didn't make any difference. She would only say, 'Do what is right and never mind the consequences.'"

Marian smiled and said, "You wanted a high-minded wife—and you got one."

"I got rather too much of it," he said. "I hadn't supposed she would try to interfere in my business. But it was Tom who turned her head with ideas about Industrial Democracy."

"You must have been relieved when he left."

Charlie gave a big sigh that puffed out his red-veined cheeks. "Sometimes I've wondered if he ever did leave. Before there was time for it to help, he came back this way in the free speech fight and got hurt. For a while after that it was worse than ever. Then Myra and I fixed up a truce and moved to Seattle. Tom dropped out of sight—the last we heard of him he was in jail somewhere—and I was willing to forget him. I wasn't going to hit a man when he was down, but Myra was always holding him up as an example to the boys; it was Tom this and Tom that; he was out somewhere fighting for working men and poor women and children who didn't have enough. She made a saint out of him, the kind boys might have hated; but they had a stake in him because he'd been here watching over them when they were children. I don't think she ever told them anything that wasn't true, even if it all gave the wrong idea."

"I should think he would have faded out after a while."

"He did. But by that time the damage was done. Ever since the trouble started up here, the family's been split; not wide open, but clean through." He puffed out his cheeks again and sighed. "I have fine boys, but they aren't much use to me."

"I'm sorry it happened that way."

He recalled, "In her last year or two, when Myra got more religious, she began thinking about Tom again and the time we beat him up. She made a fuss over having found thorns in his forehead."

"Thorns? You mean she imagined——"

"The thorns were there all right," Charlie said; "spines, anyway. When the Wobblies ran the gantlet, some of our squadron used sticks of Devil's club. Any one who got hit would have spines in him; but that didn't make a Jesus out of a Wobbly!" He sighed again. "What business did you say he's in?"

"Furniture."

"And she was always trying to live up to his ideas about doing things for others. If she hadn't started working on the hospital drive before she was over the flu——"

Marian thought, "She would be alive today—and so would I."

"Tom's making out well, eh?"

"He seems to be quite a success."

"That's something," he said. "Myra didn't make a fool of herself over a failure."

It's a matter of opinion, the girl thought. I could feel bitter if I hadn't seen the scars.

Charlie yawned. "Well, Girl, how about going to bed?"

"I don't know," she said; "I don't think I could sleep."

"Anything bothering you?"

"Nothing special."

"Anything you want?"

"I have too much already."

He thought that over. "Anything you want to do?"

"People always want to do something."

"Well, what about you?"

"I want to live."

"What are you doing now?"

"Sitting on the arm of a chair."

He smiled faintly under his thick, gray moustache. "That is a half-way measure. Why don't you stand, or sit in the chair?"

She got up and went over to the window again.

"You're restless, Marian."

She didn't deny it.

He said, "I thought you wouldn't be as restless up here as you were in Seattle."

"So did I. But there I was able to take long walks. Here there isn't any place but the beach when the tide is out. Anyway, what's the good of walking?" She took a cigarette from the box on the table and struck a light. Charlie was holding a flaming kitchen match, and when he saw that it wasn't wanted, he threw it into the fireplace. "Walking only builds up your health so you have to walk more."

"Sit down, Girl," he said again.

Obediently, she sat in the chair.

"You said you wanted to do something. If it's within reason, you only have to tell me."

"It would cost less than nothing. I want to do something useful; work at a job where I wouldn't have to think about myself, only about getting work done."

They had been over that often, and it was always the same. "Your work's here, Girl, looking after me and the house. I couldn't get along without you."

"You wouldn't have to; I'd be here whenever you were."

He smiled indulgently and patted her silk-covered knee with his thick hand. "You wouldn't really be here any of the time; you'd be thinking about your job."

"I wouldn't give it a thought while I was here, and my disposition would be better; you'd see."

"I know what won't work," he said; "and I don't complain about your disposition. It's good—like your health and everything else about you."

"Thank you, but it isn't guaranteed forever if I always have to be thinking about it and about myself."

"I can't have my wife working at a job. We wouldn't have any kind of a life if you did."

They were back where they had started, and he began offering substitutes. "Do you want to take a trip?"

"Alone?"

"Do you want to go alone?"

"I didn't say I wanted to go anywhere."

"You have to make up your mind, you know."

He seemed to think she was being wilfully difficult, when she was trying to be cold-blooded with herself. . . . You look at yourself as one of a family; give every one the same value and try to see what you should do. What you want is something you threw away long ago. When your mother was telling you all the advantages of marrying Charlie, she would say, "As you make your bed, so you lie in it." It was the right house, but the wrong bed, and you knew it. Now you can sleep in it gracefully and be considerate of your partner. . . .

She said, "I hadn't thought of going anywhere, and I don't see much point in going alone."

"I thought you might want to get away for a week or two."

"Of course, if you would like it——"

He covered her hand with his. "I don't make a lot of fuss over you, Girl, but I miss you after a day."

She said with an effort, "Maybe we should be together more, instead of less."

"I've always wanted that," he said. "Do you remember the first time I saw you? That morning in the pasture?"

She remembered very well.

"The light on your face, and your eyes, and your smile! I thought then that you were the most beautiful thing I'd ever seen in my life; I still think so. I told myself then, 'You mustn't let any one as beautiful as that get away from you,' and I didn't."

Marian thought back, trying to find something in the experience that both of them could share. "You had just come ashore from the *Camano*," she said. "The best times we ever had were on that old tug."

"It was good, wasn't it?"

"When we were going to Seattle you sent the mate out of the pilot house and took charge. It seemed to me you could do everything."

"I should have been able to, with my sea-going background."

"You let me take the wheel; I sat on the high stool and steered for hours and was never tired."

"You learned fast," he said.

"After I got the hang of it, about all you had to do was

tell me how far to keep away from the points of land. I'd never steered any kind of boat much, and it gave me such a feeling of power, being up so high and making the *Camano* do just what I wanted."

"You were all right."

"We were steaming close to green islands and high yellow bluffs and shores where there wasn't anything but maybe one boat pulled up on the beach. Everything looked new and clean; it didn't seem to have been really discovered. I had seen it all when the steamers were running, but they were taken off while I was still a little girl. It was like a picture book that had been closed—and that morning on the *Camano* it was like opening the book again and finding the pictures fresher and more beautiful than ever."

"It was a good trip," Charlie said, "and I was a pretty good doctor, thinking a sea voyage would be good for your mother. You remember she'd been an invalid all summer and you were doing the cooking and half the work on the farm. By the time we got to Seattle, she was full of ambition and she's been pretty well ever since."

"She keeps well," Marian said. Then she asked, "Do you remember the seagull? He would stand on the ball at the top of the mast with his wings spread like the American eagle. He would pose like that for maybe five minutes, then fly around and come back again. Each time he'd pose the same way and keep so still that I could hardly remember he wasn't something carved. You said you'd get a can of gold paint and make him a permanent ornament."

His eyes twinkled. "I'd have done it, too, if you'd given me the word!"

"We had other good trips in the *Camano*," she said; "and then you sold her."

"She was idle most of the time and it was cheaper to hire some one else to do our towing. I never realized how much you enjoyed her."

"I didn't, either, until now when I got to thinking it over."

"If you want me to, Girl, I'll buy her back."

"I wasn't thinking of that. I was thinking generally about things we had enjoyed. You liked the *Camano*, too, didn't you?"

"I travelled that way whenever I had an excuse. And I can see now that you never belonged to me as much as you did when we were on board."

"It might be worth trying again," she said. "It doesn't have to be the *Camano*, but if we got a boat we could afford we could have good times. We could go around all the inlets and islands of the upper sound, and we could go to the San Juans and explore them—" she stopped, puzzled, because the torrent of new ideas seemed to be rushing through a channel that was familiar at every turn.

"Go on," Charlie encouraged her.

"I thought it was a new idea," she said, "but it isn't. When I was small and Jerry was alive, Father planned to build a little ship. We were going to build her on our own beach and spend a whole summer around the Sound and the islands. We were going to anchor where we pleased and stay as long as we liked, and hunt and fish and explore and visit settlers. Things went wrong and we were never able to do it—but it was a good idea."

"It's the right idea!"

"I don't know what it would do to your plans——"

He said, "There's the two weeks' shut-down after the Fourth—that's only a few days away. If I can't take my girl on a vacation then, I might as well jump in the bay."

"We planned things other years," she said, "and something always came up—a forest fire, or a contract——"

"Nothing is going to interfere this time."

"When do you think we can go?"

"As soon as we can get ready. This is Wednesday—say, a week from today."

It was like having something the minute you began thinking about it. "Can we go that soon?"

"If you can be ready."

"My preparations won't take more than two days—but you have a lot to think about."

He said, "Anything I can't do in a week, can't be done at all. And Bailey can be of some use this time. I'll call him in the morning and have him find a boat for us. And I'll go over things with Johnson. Any one ought to be able to look after a camp when it's down—" He was almost young again, making plans and decisions. He hadn't been that way for a long time, and Marian had grown accustomed to the change which she supposed was permanent. Now it was gone and he was the driving, omnipotent Charlie who had once overwhelmed her objections.

"How long do you think we'll be gone?" she asked.

"Two weeks, at least—that's in the clear—and probably a little longer. I'd make it all summer if I didn't have a hunch that we're set for a killing this year. We'll take two weeks anyway, and I'll keep in touch with things and see what happens. If everything goes right and we find these waters too tame, we'll work up in the lee of Vancouver Island— maybe follow the inside passage to Alaska—" He began to sound like a boy dreaming, and instinctively Marian became more conservative.

"When we're sure of everything," she said, "I'll give Mrs.

Wilkes a vacation; she's talked so long about visiting her daughter in Montana. Tag looks on us all as nuisances, anyway. Bailey knows where the keys are if he wants to make any use of the place; Paul, too, if he changes his mind and comes back."

"Write to Paul and tell him we're off to hell-and-gone," he said. "We'll see Bailey, anyway. Maybe he'll want to come along."

"I don't think he should, this time; this is our voyage."

Charlie said, "That's the spirit; we have to straighten ourselves out first. Now suppose we get some sleep, Girl."

In the big old walnut bed he held her in his arms and petted her for a minute, calling her his girl and his bride, and he reminded her again of their first meeting in the pasture. When he recalled it, the girl fancied she could see herself as she had been at that moment, walking swiftly along the skidroad trail, with the light of morning and the light of first love on her face, and around her the rocks and grass and spider webs sparkled with imperishable dew.

For him the moment was still there in two dimensions, like a painting which he held securely in his arms. For her there were other dimensions in the picture, and she had gone back there to start over. In the distance, at the foot of the pasture, the *Camano* loomed out of the burning mist; by finding that fourth dimension of motion, she was able to escape with the one she had been trying to escape. . . .

Charlie's imprisoning arm relaxed and he rolled away with a great, impatient snore that was like renouncing the earth and all its works for the night. She was glad to be alone, but she was still excited from the thrill of planning and there was nothing to bring her flying mind safely home to her body for the night.

She was awake a long time before parts of her mind began falling asleep. In what was left, she hurried along the skid-road with a fragile feeling of joy. Then the trail dipped into a valley between waking and sleep, and only her mind and eyes were there. High on the hill on the other side, against white clouds and a blue sky, swinging towards her, was a walking statue, or a naked bronze woman with her face hidden by a cloud, her tireless bright body walking over the earth, walking and walking forever.

XIII

BAILEY'S moorings were on Northlake Avenue near the University bridge. Charlie had not been there for so long that he stopped at the wrong place. Most of them had the owners' names familiarized with "Jim" or "Walt" or "Herb," like a politician reminding voters that he is a servant of the people. But a few had only the address, and Bailey's place had a vague name which his father could not recall readily. Then he saw "*Avalon Moorings*" over a gate, and remembered at once. It was not far enough from where he had stopped to bother moving his car. He went through the gate and down the wooden steps with some of the feeling of being already on vacation.

On the left a willow tree overhung the fresh-water beach where a little boy and girl were playing, and old boats were hauled out to rot while their owners dreamed of repairing them. From the right, two girls and a boy of college age came out of Bailey's headquarters, carrying life jackets and paddles and an outboard motor. Near the foot of the steps they turned and went out on the narrow pier that extended into the lake between a second-growth forest of masts.

In the shop of *Avalon Moorings* he found Bailey's assistant, Egil Hanson, uncrating a reverse gear while he smoked a cigarette and told a woman customer a long list of repairs that were needed on her boat. The young Norwegian was big and blue-eyed and robustly cynical, and he seemed able to do any number of things at once without losing his poise. Probably any one who worked with Bailey would have to be very good at everything. While the woman was being shocked at the condition of her boat and having no idea, Egil found time to recognize Charlie.

"Hi, Mr. Dow," he said. "You got the right idea at last. I've tried logging—and a new strut bearing, Mrs. Pearson. Better get one of the rubber ones—I drove a logging truck with a trailer a block long and no brakes. We came down a hill like a power dive, grazing trees—and a vent pipe for your gas tank, or seal off the one you have—I yelled to my partner to keep his head inside the cab, but he didn't hear me, or he'd lost it already. When we got to the foot of the hill, his brains were all over my right shoulder—Better none at all, Ma'am, than what you have; it ends up under the deck instead of going overboard—I stopped her there and climbed out and said, 'You can have your God-damned truck and your God-damned logging.' I haven't been back to the woods since—It means just this, Mrs. Pearson: one of these times you'll strike a match and your cigarette'll light before the match gets to it—Bailey has a boat for you. He'll be back in a few minutes, or you'll find him out at the end of the pier, putting gas in a cruiser—No, it'll only cost a couple of bucks; I'd rather do it for nothing than see a nice-looking woman like you get blown up—He picked a good one for you, Mr. Dow; built like a brick outhouse, with all the comfort you can have in a boat, and it don't try to get in the ones you can't—It'll all cost you about ninety bucks, Mrs. Pearson, thirty for material and the rest for labor. You can try somewhere else; I don't know if I'd have the time."

Charlie walked out of the shop and along the pier in the cool breeze and warm sunshine. Mallard ducks that had once been wild made a sudden frightened churning on the water as he approached, then subsided and rode at ease when they saw it was only a man. On board the boats young people and some older ones were preparing to get under weigh, or they were contentedly scraping and painting and varnishing for some future voyage. Charlie had never felt that way about boats, but evidently to the hard-bitten a boat was a boat at any time. A few seemed to have given up the idea of going anywhere, or they had never heard of it. On one dingy sloop with no sails bent, a frowsy old man in pyjamas and bathrobe was slumped in an armchair in the cockpit. He seemed to be dozing, but as Charlie passed he raised one arm in salute, then let it fall slowly to his knee again. On one fine new sailboat hull a young woman with a basin of wash was hanging tea towels on a line strung from the galley stovepipe to a flagstaff. She looked pretty, even with clothespins in her mouth, and she did not seem to mind at all that the schooner had no masts.

By the time he reached the right-angle turn at the end of the pier, the boat that had stopped for gas was throbbing out into the stream, headed towards the Locks. Bailey stood near the red gas pump, restowing bills in his wallet. Then he looked and smiled. "Well, Father, I knew I'd have you for a customer one of these times." He was wearing a white shirt and stained duck trousers and his yachting cap was at a rakish angle, but he was sober and looked as if he had been having enough sleep. He was a fine-looking boy with his husky physique and his warm ironic grin, and he evidently thought well of running a parking lot and filling station for boats.

Charlie said, "Your business seems to be doing all right."

"It's better this season," Bailey stuffed his wallet into his hip pocket. "In September I think I can pay you another thousand."

"Hell, you don't have to," Charlie said. "I only thought of it as something for you to play with."

"Might as well be in the clear." They started back towards the turn of the pier. "If I were to get married, I'd want to be on my own feet."

Charlie was startled, but he only smiled and asked, "Is she any one I know?"

"Nothing that definite," Bailey said. "Only an abstract proposition." Then he said, "I have the boat for you; she's all right."

"Egil told me. It was lucky you had one on tap."

"We didn't have her; she was at Barker's, beyond Fremont. I had her catalogued in my mind; she seemed to be the boat for you, charter price and all."

"Let's go and see her."

"She's here," Bailey said. "We brought her up last night. They didn't want to let her go, but I told them you were a big shot who expected service."

"I could have gone there."

Bailey said, "I wanted to try her out myself, and last night Egil and I went over her like G-men looking for trouble. She's good, and the inventory's complete."

"When will she be ready to go?"

"Any time," Bailey said. "The captain isn't here, but we can get him any time by phoning. Here she is." They stopped beside a cruiser that Charlie had noticed in a general way in passing. The boat wasn't impressive, but it was less colorless than most cruisers, with a black hull and an honest cabin instead of the usual raised deck with flaring sides, pop-eyed with portholes.

"She's not very big, is she?"

"Forty-three feet," Bailey said. "As big as I'd advise, unless you wanted something a lot bigger. If she were forty-five or a little over, you wouldn't like it, with a sea running on the Sound. She'd have her chin on one wave and her tail on the next, without much support in between." He spoke with easy assurance. "Of course, selecting a boat for some one else is about like choosing a wife for him."

Charlie said, "At least I'd trust you to pick something interesting."

On board it felt better. There was deck enough so you could walk around the cabin, and the appearance of bulwarks, though they were only a foot high. There was also a cockpit that would do for fishing, and the glassed-in bridge deck was almost roomy, with a settee and table and two wicker chairs. At the pretty mahogany-and-brass steering wheel there was a lunch-counter type of seat with a comfortable back. That at least would remind Marian of the high stool in the pilot house of the *Camano*.

Below, on one side of the companion stairs, there was a miniature bathroom, with everything including the tub in reduced size; on the other side there was a compact galley which seemed to have everything needed, in aggressively white and bright enamel and stainless steel. Forward there was a cabin with two wide berths, hanging closets, and a chest of drawers.

"The berths are six-feet-two," Bailey said. "That ought to be long enough for you."

"Long enough."

Bailey said, "The crew's quarters are forward of the bulkhead. They have their own toilet and a hatch to the deck. There are berths for two paid hands, if you want them. That would leave you and Marian free to do as you please."

"I'll think about it," Charlie said. It seemed to him that if there weren't something they had to do, they would be in a bad way.

"You think she'll do all right?" Bailey rather looked as if he expected to be congratulated.

"Do? Yes, I think she'll do fine," Charlie said. It wasn't the kind of boat he would have chosen for himself, but she wasn't really for himself. And the cruiser had more comforts, if not more comfort, than you have on a tug. His only real objection was that nearly everything seemed too pretty and toy-like. But then, if you're playing, you can't reasonably object to toys.

"She'll do fine." Then he said, "I wasted some time trying to buy back the *Camano*, but they'd put a new Atlas diesel in her and they wanted more than I had sold her for. And when I figured the cost of operating a tug without doing any towing——"

"It wouldn't work. Things are only economical when you use them for what they're intended."

Charlie agreed with him, but he didn't want to stay any longer. With Marian on board, and some of their own possessions around and somewhere to go, the boat would come to life; but now he only felt caged and uneasy. "She's all right," he said. "Can we settle the deal now?"

"I have the charter papers in the office. If you want to sign them, I'll do the rest."

"How about my check?"

"Yes, you can give me that, too."

When the business was settled, Charlie suddenly felt relieved and younger. Beyond a few minutes of routine business with Martin, there was nothing between him and his voyage with Marian. For once she wouldn't be able to say that logging had wrecked all the plans they ever made. He looked at his watch; it was not quite ten-thirty. "Have the captain and a paid hand on board by two," he said. "I'll take her home this evening." Then, knowing from a lifetime of experience that nothing ever went quite as smoothly as it did in the planning, he said, "Or, if anything comes up, I'll take her tomorrow."

Bailey said, "If I'm not here tomorrow, Egil will see to anything you want. I might have to go over to the Canal. In case I don't see you, how about a drink to your voyage?"

"I want to be downtown before noon— Hell, it's a bad day when I haven't time to drink with my own son!" Following Bailey upstairs, he said, "You see I need a vacation."

Bailey's room above the shop was not like Bailey. Except for shelves of books, it was almost as bare as a bunkhouse, and the only touch of luxury was a full-sized bed. When Charlie had seen the place a year before, he supposed the boy was going to furnish it. But evidently he had never got around to it, or he considered it furnished already. The only good thing Charlie could say about it was that he felt as much at home as in a logging camp. He put his hat on the floor and leaned back in his chair, with his feet comfortably on the unpainted wooden table. Bailey brought out a bottle of whiskey and glasses, and they drank and looked out of the window at Bailey's pier and the boats that almost interlaced with boats at other piers.

"Your cruiser isn't as big as a tug," Bailey said, "but you'll find her more comfortable. And she's bigger than the schooner out there, built to sail around the world."

"Which one?"

"That new one, with the wash line and no sticks in her."

"I saw the girl hanging out the wash, and I wondered if somebody had forgotten the masts."

Bailey said, "They know what they want, she and her husband. They came here to build a boat and sail around the world. They built a good one, too, but they ran out of money by the time she was launched."

"Tough, eh?"

"They're tough, too," Bailey said. "They met it by giving up their house and moving on board. Now he's working in the plywood factory, earning money to finish the boat. He'll do it, too, and they'll sail around the world, if there's any of it left by then."

"They know what they want, eh?"

"And they're only a sample. This city is made up of people who've come here to build boats and sail around the world alone, or the equivalent. That's what makes Seattle such a friendly and cohesive place! If the people could ever relax enough to exchange ideas, this would be the richest and most exciting city in the world."

Charlie asked, "What about the old man in pyjamas I saw on one of the boats? Is he going around the world, too?"

Bailey shook his head gravely. "He's been around, I don't know how many times, and he knows better; he knows that it always leads to the same place. He's going to cruise on Hood Canal: fish and dig clams and pick berries; live off the land."

"That's more sensible," Charlie said. "He hasn't far to go."

"But he'll never get there."

"How's that?"

"Dying," Bailey said. "Something the matter with his legs. When he was a boy he was in a lumber vessel that didn't have a slop chest, and he had no boots. He had to stand wheel-watch off Cape Horn in bare feet, in snow up to his knees. It started some trouble in his legs, and now they swell up like barrels."

"That's what comes of forgetting your boots."

"He didn't have much choice," Bailey said. "He was shang-haied."

"Tough, eh?"

"He divides his time between his boat and the Marine Hospital, but they can't do anything for him. One of these times he won't come back, or he'll die on my hands. I don't collect rent from him, either. I'm helping pay for the delivery of a cargo of lumber in the 'Eighties, but it's nothing to what he's paying."

It seemed to Charlie that if you are going to live at all, you have to take a lot for granted. One of the things his generation had accepted was the fact that some men have luck, and others don't. Bailey's concern for the under-dog seemed freakish, and it stood for some barrier between them. There was something else—then he remembered. "I hear you had a visit from our old chauffeur."

"Tom Horton. Yes." Bailey looked uncomfortable. "I invited him to Home Place for lunch. I hope you don't mind."

"I mightn't have done it myself, but it was all right."

"It seemed the least I could do."

"The place is yours as much as mine; you can do as you please."

"It wasn't really Tom, anyway, only his ghost."

Charlie looked at him sharply. "What do you mean?"

"He's gray and conventional and prosperous; he's gone back on all the things he used to believe."

"No more radical stuff, eh?"

"You make a better showing than he, Father; you've at least been consistent."

Charlie only grunted and took his feet from the table and

his hat from the floor, but inside him something was thawing in the warmth of a belated spring. After all these years under the spell of Tom Horton, Bailey admitted that his father was the better man.

XIV

TEN MINUTES away from the quiet backwater of the moorings, Charlie took the elevator in the Western Life Building. His interview with Martin would probably be nothing more than listening to a little dry advice, or accepting an archery set as a bon voyage present. It would be nothing—but he wished it were over, and he felt chagrined about having talked and drunk so long with Bailey. It was six minutes past noon, and Martin might already have gone out for lunch. If he had, that would mean a foolish gap of an hour or two in which he had to live, but could not act. And then he would start at a disadvantage, if advantages and disadvantages were being handed out. . . .

He was in a rush, but the elevator went up too fast to suit him. The elevator itself did not suit him. It was one of those things you had to accept in a mechanical world. They shut you up in a steel cage, or take you ten thousand feet into the sky, or put you asleep so thoroughly that they could cut your heart out without your knowing it—and you can only trust to the clever young men to bring you back safely. They usually do it, too, but inside you always hate the times when you are made to be a helpless baby, or a piece of freight, or an animal shut up in a steel cage. There were other people in the cage with him: men holding their hats piously in front of their chests, and a few young women—no one he recognized, but one of them seemed to know him. When he was getting out at the eighteenth floor, he heard her say, "Timber Baron." The elevator door clashed shut and he walked briskly down the gray marble corridor.

He had been uneasy, thinking that Martin might have gone to lunch; but lunch had come to Martin, as nearly everything did. At the switchboard, Joyce said, "Mr. Darling is having lunch in his office; he said for you to go right in." She had transparent-looking skin and prominent, glassy eyes, and she wore long transparent ear-pendants. As she delivered the message, she tapped her pencil against one of them, and it gave off a glassy "clank." She looked as if she would clank anywhere she was touched, but Charlie had no wish to make the experiment. He said, "Thank you, Joyce," and went through the office and opened the flat mahogany door.

In the inner office, Martin sat behind his black-and-chromium desk, with a dinner napkin around his neck and a sandwich and a pint bottle of milk in front of him. With his smooth pink face and pink bald head, and a bib around his neck, he looked younger than his eighty years; you almost expected to see a nipple on the bottle of milk. "Ho, Charlie," he said softly, with a cut of sandwich in his hand. "Let me send out for a lunch for you."

"No, thanks, Martin; I don't eat till later."

"How about a drink?"

"Of milk?" Charlie asked, taking a chair.

"Milk would be good for you," Martin said, "but I wouldn't try to change another man's habits." He opened a drawer and set a bottle of Scotch and one whiskey glass on the desk. "There is a theory that any habit is good so long as it is regular."

Charlie poured a drink and resigned himself to Martin's soft-voiced lecture. "I try to make this a regular habit."

Martin sipped his milk and said, "Half of it is true, anyway, but I want to make sure of all of it by making a habit of what is good for me. There is some question of what is good. Regularity is the important thing. If I could lead a perfectly regular life, I would be as good at a hundred as I am today. But even in the best-run office there are minor irregularities and irritations."

"You ought to try logging," Charlie said, "where nothing is ever the same twice."

"For instance, I am never sick," Martin rapped delicately against mahogany, with his white fist making the sound of a distant woodpecker. "But just the other day our Violet was home sick. That upset the whole office in ways you'd never notice on the surface. The next day she was back, but she was out of sorts; and that, too, put everything a little out of gear."

Charlie said, "Wait till your men go on a Fourth of July drunk, or a forest fire runs through your office!"

"It's something I have to fight against," Martin said, "being jealous of little irritations that interrupt the regular flow of life. I have even found myself annoyed in archery because no two arrows ever behave exactly alike——"

That's what comes of having money, Charlie thought. You can talk the god-damnedest rot and people have to listen to you! He poured himself a consolation drink. They even have to hear about archery!

"I condition myself against it, though," Martin said; "I do reasonably well. I try to plan ahead so there won't be any major dislocations of my routine. It might not be the one for some one else, but it is the one I am used to. If I miss going to church on Sunday, or moving my bowels after breakfast, I suffer for it."

O Lord, that, too! Charlie thought. He was unreasonably irritated by people who talked about moving their bowels, as if it was something they were just learning, or talked about not being able to.

"It's the secret of life," Martin said. "We'll talk some more about it another time. I understand you're going on a vacation."

Charlie said, "I'm planning to take the boat up to Home Place this afternoon."

"You need relaxation." Martin set his empty milk glass beside the empty pint bottle, and raised the corner of his bib to wipe his lips. "Of course, you should be relaxed all the time, but that's difficult. Relaxing periodically is better than nothing." He reached up with his short arms and untied the napkin from around his neck, and pushed a button on the desk. "I never have to go anywhere, because I take a vacation every day the weather permits." The door opened and Joyce came in and took away the tray with the bottle and glass and napkin. The only sound was one light, glassy clink as she went out, but that somehow startled Charlie. The door closed and Martin's voice went on, as if it were something fragile which he did not want to strain and break. "I have my own archery range on the lawn, and that is my vacation land." His pink baby face beamed with the wisdom of self-satisfaction. "But every man to his own habits. How far do you plan to go?"

"Not far enough to be out of touch," Charlie said. "We'll knock around the upper Sound, where Marian grew up, and work north towards the San Juans."

Martin said, "I have something for you—a little going-away present." He got up and went softly to the corner where the coat rack stood, and came back with a slender carton. "This isn't all of it; the target——"

"An archery set!"

Martin beamed. "The secret is out now. You don't think

much of archery, but I want you to give it a trial. You and Mrs. Dow can set the target up on the beach almost anywhere, and have as long a range as you wish. You'll find it giving you endless satisfaction."

The interview had been just what Charlie expected; nothing worse, and only a little more tedious. "All right, I'll try it, Martin." Then he said, "It's almost in the family, anyway. Father used to tell about the first time he tried to look over the timber on the Skagit; he ran into a camp of Siwashes, and they chased him out with bows and arrows." He got up to go. "If we run into Indians, we'll be able to talk their language."

"Yes, yes," Martin said. "I have several native bows, and some of their arrows." He took a ledger from a drawer and put it down silently where his luncheon tray had stood. "I've tried them out and found them very crude compared with modern equipment."

"We'll have the edge on them, eh?"

Martin said, "Before you go, we want to be sure everything is in order. I had a memorandum about your mortgages."

Something in the lumberman's mind gave a sickening lurch. "Mortgages," he said; "what about them?"

"Yes, Charlie, here we are!" Martin nodded at the open ledger as if he had found something that would save both of them a great deal of trouble. "Yes, the chattel mortgage on your logging equipment, and the mortgages on your timberland. Do you recall, offhand, how much I've put into the business?"

"For this season?"

"No, altogether."

Charlie calculated. "It would scale around three hundred and twenty thousand; but——"

"Three hundred and eighteen thousand. That's a lot of money."

"Not in big-time logging," Charlie said. "In a year of the kind we had in the early Twenties, I'd have it all paid off."

"It's a great deal for me," Martin said. "I don't know how I justified it to myself."

Charlie said, "You knew that sooner or later I'd hit the jackpot. You gambled along with me, only you weren't risking anything."

"I was risking three hundred and eighteen thousand——"

"Yes, on security worth close to a million."

"If you can get that much for your properties, I would certainly advise you to sell them."

"I'll get a damned sight more without selling, and you know it! The upswing has only started, and Camp Two is putting close to three hundred thousand feet of logs into the salt chuck. As soon as it's justified, I'll give her the other barrel with Camp Three, and bring it up to six hundred thousand feet a day."

"You're logging on speculation," Martin said. "You had hopes other years, and talked about upswings, and I went along with you and made up the losses out of my pocket."

"Sure, you were gambling with me on what's happening now, and this isn't the time to get cold feet."

"You may be right," Martin said; "but last year you were sure the upswing had started; it looked as if it had—and then the market went flat again."

Charlie said, "Nothing ever happens as clear-cut as you expect, but everything happens, just the same."

Martin beamed at him, softly, "You loggers are all gamblers, full of hunches, with faith in gamblers' luck. I don't know how I ever came to be doing business with you. I don't know anything about hunches or luck. Do you remember Patrick Henry's oration?"

Charlie did not.

"We had to learn it in school: 'I have but one lamp by which my feet are guided, and that is the lamp of experience; I have no way of judging the future but by the past—' Beautifully clear, isn't it? Nothing about hunches, or luck." He touched the ledger page with a soft white hand that had not done a day's work in eighty years. "Here is the light of experience; here is the record of the past: the record of ten years of logging at a net loss of over three hundred thousand dollars. Before you started borrowing from me, you probably used up cash on hand, and sold equipment to the junk boys."

Charlie poured himself a drink. "Sure," he said; "I did what I could to stick. I've stuck this far, and I'll be in at the finish, by God! Fifteen years is a long dry spell. Maybe I can't put my finger on the day when it'll start raining, but I know it's going to rain like hell!"

"That's another hunch; you don't know the future, and neither do I. The Bible says there are three things which no man knoweth——"

The logger thumped the desk with his big fist. "Let's get down to business, Martin! What have you got in mind?"

Martin looked gently surprised. "I thought I had made myself clear. I have to close down on you, unless, of course, you can meet your obligations."

Charlie blinked, and could not believe it. "Is it a joke, or are you out to ruin me?"

"Neither," Martin said, "but if you can't meet your obligations, you're probably ruined already."

"But you said we'd let it ride!"

"That was almost a year ago. I've let it ride too long already."

Charlie still could not believe that the senseless blow had fallen. "But a man has to live!"

"I wouldn't say that."

The logger stared in wonder at the pink cherub face. "What do you mean?"

"Living is a luxury, for those who can afford it."

Slowly it came to him that he was nothing to Martin. No one was anything to Martin. All that mattered was his smooth routine; living a long time and gathering more money, getting pinker and fatter, like a fat pink wood tick on a rabbit. Staring at him, he realized that he had always hated Martin, the pink tick who had never got a log out of the woods in his life, or done any other honest work. He had always hated him, but he hadn't even let himself know it because he had accepted Martin as a saviour. Martin had money, which he stupidly supposed could be of help to him. So he had sealed off his contempt and looked up to Martin, and listened to his twaddle, when he might just as well have kicked him at the beginning. The first time he met Martin was when they were pallbearers at Jim Donaldson's funeral. Jim, the great logger, who had gone into a partnership with Martin—and shot himself. That should have been warning enough to any fool. But Martin had millions of precious money when other men were going to the wall. Money as alluring as a woman's beauty to a reckless young man. It had been like that: the beauty of money which you must have, or die. Martin's wealth had been like a beautiful widow at a funeral, burying one lover, and looking for the next. It had been so dazzling that Charlie saw no warning in the dead face of his friend, who had fallen under the same spell. Charlie and Martin shook hands over Jim's coffin, and walked down the aisle together. . . . He didn't know how long he had been silent, staring at Martin without seeing him, but he blinked and brought him back into sight. "So it's a luxury for those who can afford it! I suppose you told Jim Donaldson that!"

Martin was gently surprised. "It never came to me clearly until now. And I don't see what Jim has to do with this."

"I suppose you gave him the pearl-handled revolver!"

"Dear, no," Martin said. "I did what I could for him, and carried him longer than sound business justified."

Charlie was shaking with anger. "God damn you, Martin, I see how you work! You let me sweat blood; you let me high-ball and kill men, keeping in the game, and when I draw a winning hand, you take it away from me and take the jackpot!"

"You're being unreasonable," Martin said. "I've carried you longer than a bank would, and I'm not asking for anything more than you agreed to pay. And you're at liberty to get some other financing, if you can. But you would save yourself trouble if you just went on your vacation and forgot about it. Relax. All you ever got out of it was a living. Perhaps, when you get back, we can work something out——"

"Yes, you'll own everything, and I'll work for you for wages!"

"Other men have done worse," Martin said. "Think it over."

"You don't own me yet; you aren't telling me what to think!" He reached the rack in three strides and snatched his hat. Stopping beside Martin on his way out, he said, "When I come back, I'll do the telling! I'll give you your small change, and tell you where you can put it."

"You're excited and unreasonable," Martin said. "You make an agreement, and go into a temper when you're expected to keep it. All I am asking for is my small change, as you call it. I wish you luck in finding it, Charlie. I know what you'll do. You'll over-exert yourself racing around the country, trying to prove that two and two make something else. You'll burn up a lot of energy, and maybe damage your heart, and you'll have your labor for your pains. You would do better to sit down and look at a few figures in black and white, instead of trying to run away from them."

On the way down in the elevator, Charlie kept telling himself: "I'm in a jam. It's up to me, now. I have to work fast. It's going to take everything I have." But he didn't feel the full force of the blow until he was on the street, in the bright mid-day sunshine. Then he saw the sharp, unfamiliar look on faces, and about the cars and taxis passing in the street. People went by, close to him, but they seemed to be at a distance, or he was invisible. He wasn't in the world he saw, and he would be alone until he found his way back. The world had lurched suddenly, and he had fallen overboard. He was swimming alone, and no one gave a damn about him. His own family would. Marian. . . . Whatever happened, he mustn't see her until he was out of the jam. If he couldn't manage his own affairs; if he had to limp back to her for sympathy, he might as well shoot himself. He had his self-respect, and he had to keep clear of every one who would be sorry for him. But Marian was expecting him home this evening. He would have to get in touch with her to cut himself off from her.

He telephoned from a drugstore, standing in a booth that was like a coffin with connections to the land of the living. Dropping coins in slots, and looking at scribblings on the wall, he thought: It'll be easier if Marian is out and Mrs. Wilkes takes the message; it'll sound more inevitable that way——

Then he heard Marian's voice, unsurprised by its own naturalness. "Mrs. Dow speaking."

"Hello, Girl. This is Charlie." He wouldn't have said that if he hadn't needed to reassure himself. . . .

"Is everything all right? Did you get the boat?"

"I got the boat," he said.

"I knew you would! What's it like?"

"It's all right; it's fine. But, Marian——"

"Yes, Charlie?"

"Something came up at the last minute. Business——"

"Oh!" Then she said, "I'm sorry."

Not as sorry as I am, he thought.

"Nothing is wrong, is it?"

"No, Girl; just a contract, but I have to get it straightened out."

"Do you think we can leave tomorrow?"

"I don't know; I'm afraid not; it may be a day or two."

"We can't help that, can we?"

"We can't help it, Girl."

"Will you be late getting home?"

"I'm not coming home; I'm going to stick here until it's finished. I'll be through quicker that way."

"It isn't necessary, on my account."

"I think I'd better," he said.

The conversation was reassuring; questions and answers that fitted each other; but everything else in the world was haywire. Time and locations had changed their meaning, and they didn't make sense any more. Half an hour later, on Highway 99, he passed a side road he had once known. He had driven out of there long ago; this morning—but that didn't make sense. The way it used to be, if he turned onto the side road and drove for a few minutes, he would come down the hill to the orchard. The lawn and house were just beyond the orchard, and beyond them was the Sound, where he had planned to bring the cruiser that was eating its head off in Seattle, with two paid hands on board since God knows when. No, he had chartered her only this morning, if he could make himself believe that. It used to be that a few minutes' driving on that side road would bring him to Marian. Marian, who would always be as young and as pretty as that time he met her in the pasture. Marian, who was a secret, or discovery. She was so much younger than he that as long as he lived she would be young and fresh and desirable—like more money than he could spend in a lifetime. . . . Mustn't think about her now. The orchard and the house and lawn and the salt water beyond are a lost country. He wouldn't find them on that side road. The way to get there is through hell and back, and it might take everything he had.

In the Lumber Empire Bank, part of the reasonable world returned. Horace, the president, was an old friend, big and heavy and gray, with a big, steady hand and kindly eyes. "I'm never too busy to see an old friend," he said. "If you will wait a few minutes—" Then he looked at Charlie's face more closely. "I had an appointment, but it can wait. Come in." In the private office he drew up a leather-covered chair beside his own and took a bottle of Scotch and glasses from his desk, and poured two drinks, and waited.

"I'm in a jam," Charlie said.

Horace said, "I'm sorry to hear that. It isn't money, is it?"

"That's what it comes to."

"Somehow I didn't expect it," Horace said. "I've always pointed you out as one old-timer who always kept his chin above water. Is it Martin Darling?"

"It's Martin, God damn him!"

"Is he putting the squeeze on you?"

"Yes, just when I'm set for a killing."

"I'm sorry to hear that," Horace said. "I always thought you were making a mistake by not financing through us."

Charlie nodded. There was no use reminding Horace that he had gone to Martin in the depression, after the Lumber Empire had turned him down. Horace had told him then, "We wouldn't dare to risk twenty thousand on all the timber on the second bench."

"Maybe we can help you out," Horace said.

"You can, and you won't be hurting yourselves, either. With this upswing——"

"How do you stand with Darling? How much are you in for?"

"A little over three hundred thousand; it isn't——"

Horace made a whistling sound that was like a skyrocket going up forever. "You're in pretty deep, aren't you, Charlie?"

"I don't see it that way," Charlie said. "You know the property; it's worth close to a million. I'll get more than that out of it. I'm ready to open up Camp Three, and I'll be getting out six hundred thousand feet——"

"I think I have the general picture," Horace said. "It's just a question of what you want us to do for you."

The logger jumped up and shook hands with him. "By God, Horace, that's the kind of talk I like to hear!" He went on shaking hands until he saw that the banker looked embarrassed. He let go the reluctant hand and said, "I'm not asking much: all I want you to do is take over my mortgages from Martin. You won't be risking anything, and inside a year——"

"Sit down, Charlie," Horace said, "sit down and let's think this over."

Charlie sat, obediently. He felt the way he had when Doctor Williamson lectured him about his heart, and made him listen through the stethoscope. That time he had been frightened, as he was now. He had quit drinking and done everything else he was told, until he suddenly felt well again, and would not have anything more to do with Williamson's advice.

Horace said, "I see it this way, Charlie; if I were in Darling's place, I certainly wouldn't clamp down on you now, when the picture's rather brighter than it's been for years——"

"I know that!" Charlie said. "I know you'll give me a break, and I won't forget it, by God! When I've made a killing——"

Horace said, "I certainly wouldn't clamp down on you now; but the fact is, Darling has lent a healthy amount on your security."

"It's nothing to what I'll get out of it in two good years; it's small change——"

Horace said, "I wouldn't pretend that it's the full potential value of the property, but it seems to be rather more than would be considered sound banking practice."

Charlie felt stunned. "Then you won't do anything for me——"

"I wouldn't say that, Charlie. We're old friends, and I've handled your pay-roll account for a good many years. I value you, and if there's any way of straining a point to help you——"

"I won't ever forget it!"

Horace said, "We'll have to go over your holdings and all that another day. I can't make any offhand promises, but I don't want to see Darling ream you. I'm only thinking out loud now, but suppose we could strain a point and buy Darling out?"

The logger jumped up again and shook hands with him. "God love you, Horace! If you could do that—if you could do that——" Again he felt the embarrassed unresponsiveness of the banker's hand. He let it go, and sat down, feeling uneasy and a little foolish.

"Mind, I'm only thinking out loud," Horace said. "It would probably mean taking your property over, but you would still run it, at a good salary. We might even——"

Charlie was not frightened any more, but suddenly angry, pounding the desk. "Horace, God damn it, I came here to save my property, not to lose it!"

"I was only thinking out loud," Horace said. "We might

be able to do a little better. What do you say I call in Edwards? He's a clever young man and I value his suggestions."

The clever young man plunged into the problem with the air of knowing just what he was after, but the three of them talked until after banking hours, without arranging anything except that Charlie should come back another day. When Horace let him out of the side door, he had the feeling of being alone again, cut off from the world until he found his way back. Again, time and location were all haywire. Home Place and Marian were a thousand miles away, and he had found no way back, but for the girl it was still only a few minutes' drive to town. He might meet her at any turn, and she would not understand that they were in different worlds; she would speak to him, believing it was only a few hours since he had left her, and that he would go home with her. That meeting could happen, but it seemed so impossible to him that he had no idea what he would do. If he had his revolver, he would want to shoot her because he loved her and she must not know of his humiliation, and she had no right to see him when they were in different worlds.

He found his car and got in, as furtively as if he were stealing it. Driving through town, he told himself, "I'm in a jam. I have to work fast. It's going to take everything I have." Then his mind put it into the past, and began telling about it as if it were over and he was telling about it afterward. "I was in the God-damndest jam that time! I was afraid of meeting my own wife on the street. I was desperate, because I didn't know where to turn, and I couldn't see any way out of the jam." It seemed to help a little, telling it that way, because he could only half remember that he was still in the jam and could see no way out.

He was driving north out of town, feeling cold and frightened. "I'm scared to death because I don't see any way out of this," he told himself. "Tomorrow I'll call on the bankers I know in Seattle. One of them will know a proposition when he sees it. Crane, of the Pioneer Exchange—I could have seen him today, if Horace hadn't kept me so long with his twaddle. I don't know where I'm going now——"

The last meal he had eaten was with Marian, in another world. A person is supposed to eat three times a day, and he had lived half a lifetime on breakfast. The whiskey he had drunk was wearing off without having any effect, and he felt weak and crumpled. He stopped at a restaurant and ate everything the waiter brought him. One of the things was a T-bone steak. It looked all right, but there was some trick about it and all the rest of the food. It was in one world, and he was in another, and it didn't do him any good. When he had finished, he was still hungry; he couldn't eat enough now to keep himself from being hungry when he was on the rocks, and that hunger was already gutting him. The waiter said they weren't allowed to serve liquor; the world was full of crazy regulations. He bought a bottle of whiskey at the liquor store, and when he got to his car he couldn't open the bottle; he had to go to a hardware store for a corkscrew. The whiskey was hot and reassuring at first; then it went down like water and it didn't do him any good.

He drove out of town thinking: I'm in a jam; I've got to get out of this; it's going to take everything I've got. Horace, damn him; he hadn't been much different from Martin, trying to put the same cold tongs into him with warmer hands. Suppose all bankers are alike? Suppose it's like going to a chain store for a custom-built car? You could go to their downtown store, and in the University district, and up in Bellingham, and down in Tacoma, and they'd all tell you the same thing. When

you're in a jam, you don't want a banker; you want a friend.
A banker's a good friend as long as you don't need one. What
you need is somebody who's been in the game and understands,
and has the money to help you. . . .

In his mind, he went over the old-time operators: Harry
Parker, who started logging with a bull team and ended with
giant skidders. He had made and lost money, and pulled out
when he had broken a little more than even, after fifty years.
Old Man North was dead, and his logging camps and mills
and shingle mills were in the hands of a receiver; Humphries
had been working for Weyerhauser ten years; Roberts is dead,
and Larry Jones is starting over again with a haywire outfit
on the Peninsula; Jim Donaldson shot himself, and the banks
took Morrow over, long ago. . . . Names and faces came towards him, like signboards along the highway, loomed up and
were real for a moment, then flashed by. None of them was
what he was looking for. Who was the old-timer who had kept
in the game and beaten the depression and was sitting pretty?
Horace said, "I've always pointed you out as one old-timer who
always kept his head above water." It had been near enough
true to look that way. He had done better than any of them,
but now he was in a jam; a hell of a jam. . . . "I was desperate
that time, I tell you. I didn't know where to turn, and I couldn't
see any way out of it." He couldn't see any way now, but he
knew that some day he would be saying that because he always
got out of jams, somehow.

The land through which he was driving disappeared on the
left, and he was on a magnificent white road, blasted out of a
mountainside. Below him, and going away forever to the west,
the left side of the world was blue air and sparkling blue water,
filled with islands that went away to the horizon and were a
darker blue against the late afternoon sun. He hadn't expected

to be in any such place, and he was puzzled. Then he knew that he was on Chuckanut Mountain. But what was he doing up near Bellingham? Nothing. Looking for something that he had to get out of himself. He turned the car around at an observation point, took a drink out of the bottle and started back. Time and locations were all haywire. Those blue islands out there were the San Juans. He and Marian were going to cruise among them. They hadn't expected to work up that far until the middle of the month, and he had got there in a few minutes, without thinking about it. In the other world, it would have been a long, happy voyage. In the world where he was caught, it was like picking up a map and looking at a place—and there you were. And that was all the good it did you. . . .

The highway swung inland and the islands and the dancing blue water went away. He did not notice anything more until he was driving through gravel uplands, scattered with second-growth fir. On the right, in the summer dusk, there was a side road that went away to some remote and improbable land. It had nothing to do with him now, and he roared by on the main highway.

In Seattle, he went directly home to the closed-up house. With the shades of the library drawn, he sat at his desk and rumpled through papers, and figured profits that made him rich, and poured himself drinks. Sometimes his hand shook, or he took his eyes off the bottle while he was pouring and the whiskey ran under the papers. But his mind was clear, and it would talk about now as if it were telling about something in the past. "It's funny how you are in a jam like that. I drank whiskey like water; I poured it down; and I never got drunk. My mind was clear all the time."

Later he had the fear that Bailey might come to the house for something, or that Marian might suspect trouble and drive down to see if he were there. But he looked at his watch and it was near midnight. "Nobody's going to bother me tonight," he decided. "In the morning I'll pack up and go to a hotel. None of them can help me, and I don't want to see them until I'm out of this jam."

When he felt more certain of not being disturbed, he made coffee in the kitchen and carried the pot and a cup to the library. He started figuring what property he could sell, and how much he was likely to get for it, and when he tasted his coffee, it was cold. The pot was cold, too, although he seemed to have brought it in only a few minutes before. He took it to the kitchen to heat, and brought it back and set down a few figures —and it was stone cold again. He took it back to the kitchen and heated it until it boiled, and after what seemed a few minutes, it was cold again. That happened four or five times, without his finding out what the trick was. He knew by its taste that the coffee had boiled several times, and when he had spilled a little of it on his way from the kitchen, it was burning hot through his shoe. Finally he gave up and drank the cold coffee out of the pot, pouring the dreadful stuff down his throat like water. "Have to get some sleep," he told himself; "it must be nearly one o'clock." When he looked at his watch, it was after four in the morning, although he had set down only a few figures on paper.

He stumbled to the couch and was asleep, but while he slept he was like a busy city at night, and he got no rest. He could feel time and distances changing and getting mixed up, opening and closing like accordions that were attached to him. Faces came out of the dark and looked at him, and when they were close they were no bigger than when they had been a long way off. They were sad, meagre faces the size of a fist; Indian faces from totem poles, carved out of wood. They came up close, and looked at him without any change in their pinched features that were beyond further grief for themselves, or pity for the man at whom they were looking. One after another they came up and looked at him, and went away. The last face of all was the face of a sorrowful nun. It, too, was carved out of wood, no bigger than an apple, but its shrunken size only intensified its grief. The face looked at him for a long time without any change of expression, but he felt exhausted by a struggle that was going on; she was trying to overcome her sorrow so she could be sorry for him. She tried for a long time, and then went away. There had been no change in her expression, but at the last moment her grief seemed to become more burning because she had failed. After she had gone, he wondered if it had been Myra. But the face had been so pinched and meagre that there wasn't room in it for anything but grief.

XV

BEFORE THEY were married, Marian assumed in a general way that Charlie owned the earth and was master of it. Actually, he owned a good deal of it and a bewildering amount of machinery; or maybe it owned him. It was a kind of marriage that gave him responsibilities. It was almost inevitable that his business would demand a new hat, or begin having a baby, as he was about to leave it for a while. Marian might have known that, but she made all her preparations on schedule, and took Mrs. Wilkes and her baggage to the Great Northern station and saw her on board the nine o'clock train. Driving home, she thought: It will be just like Charlie to hit a snag and leave me to do my own housekeeping for a while. And it was. He telephoned while she was eating lunch, and estimated a delay of a day or two, which might mean anything up to a week.

She was disappointed at first, and then she decided she had no reason for disappointment. It was summer, she had the house, the orchard and the beach—enough for a dozen happy people—and until Charlie got through with his business she would have the luxury of being alone. She had thought and done all she could about being some kind of wife, and now there was an interval of freedom in which she did not have to think at all. These perfect summer days were no time for thinking. They were the time to live, or to dream about living, if that was all you were allowed. And even when you only dreamed, the warm fact of summer was there with its promise of fulfillment.

When she promised herself the luxury of being alone, that was only partly true. Tag was also there, being alone after his own fashion. Since Tom Horton's visit, he had been nursing some private grief, and doing almost nothing around the place. Mornings and evenings, Charlie had been too full of plans to pay much attention to him, and Mrs. Wilkes, departing for Montana, had given up scolding him. As for Marian, she wasn't sure it mattered. Tag had been there twenty years, and who was she to judge his usefulness by part of one summer? If he did not feel like doing great deeds these days, neither did she. He was there if she needed help, and he was not intruding. It seemed quite possible that each of them could spend the whole summer alone at Home Place without getting in each other's way.

The afternoon Charlie telephoned, she saw Tag just once, and they talked only because she asked him for a ladder. The Bing cherries were ripe on the big tree in front of the house, and she had the sudden idea of making jam. When she saw Tag stumping toward the garage, with a covered tin pail in his hand, she ran out and asked him if he would bring a ladder round to the tree. The old man had not shaved for days, and he smelled of whiskey and looked as if he did not care to be bothered about trifles, but he listened to her patiently. After thinking it over, he decided the request was reasonable. "A ladder? *Ja,* certainly, certainly."

He brought a ladder from the garage to the unmowed front lawn, where he stood for a few seconds lost in contemplation. Then he said, like giving her grudging permission, "*Ja,* it's your ladder and your tree; pick your cherries." He set the upper end of the ladder against a branch, and the lower end firmly on the lawn.

"Thank you, Tag." Then she said, "It's your tree as much as mine."

He shook his head gloomily: "Capital and labor have nothing in common."

She laughed. "Not even cherry jam? I'll give you some when it's made."

"*Ja*, thank you." But he still looked gloomy, reaching up to pick a cluster of cherries from a lower branch. "Tom Horton planted this tree when he was a young man," he said; "when he loved poor people and would die for them. Now he is old and fat, and he forgets. Does that make the tree good, or bad?"

Marian had known in a general way that Tag had been disillusioned by Tom's visit, but she was only beginning to see how deeply he was troubled. She said, "The tree is good, of course. Planting is what mattered. After a tree is planted, nothing makes any difference except the earth and the rain and the sun."

Tag was not so sure. Picking a few more cherries, he said, "You don't know. Tom was like a holy man, close to God. He told us about Paradise on earth—we were going to see it. Twenty years I waited for him to come back—and he is fat and sells furniture and he has glasses that go on his nose like this—" he pinched the bridge of his nose contemptuously. "Whether he puts them on or takes them off, he sees nothing."

"Some of the things Tom fought for were a union and the eight-hour day and better pay and clean beds. The loggers have those things now."

"*Hah!* the C.I.O.!" He made a spitting sound. "Workers are still slaves."

"Everything is much better for them than it was," Marian

said. "Tom helped make it that way; and one man can only do so much." She was standing beside the ladder, looking idly at Tag's hands moving among the green branches and shining fruit of the tree. When he moved about, his ugly wooden leg punched holes in the lawn, but above him everything was beautiful, and his hands reached up among leaves and fruit that had a classical perfection, like the meaning of all fruit and foliage. "There certainly is nothing wrong with the tree," she told him. "It is part of the Paradise on earth that Tom promised you. Paradise is on earth now, only people make such horrible messes of their lives."

She was thinking mostly of her own life, but Tag took it personally and began defending himself. "*Ja*, sure, you think I look like an old bum, too dirty to come in the house, and I want Paradise——"

"I wasn't thinking of you at all; I was thinking——"

"A drunk, dirty old bum, with a peg-leg, making holes in the lawn I forgot to mow; *Ja*, I saw you looking!"

She said, "I wasn't thinking of your leg at all, but since you've spoken about it, why not get an artificial one; the good kind? If it's the cost, I'm sure Mr. Dow——"

"*Ja*, certainly, certainly," he chanted, "and cover it up with my overalls so Mr. Dow won't have to remember he made me lose my leg!"

"But, Tag, you would be more comfortable with one!"

"*Ja, Ja*, certainly, certainly!" He stopped his aggravating chant and became confidential. "You want to know why I won't get a store leg, Mrs. Dow?"

"Yes, Tag. Why?"

"*Capital and labor have nothing in common.*"

"We were talking about artificial legs," she reminded him.

"Certainly, certainly; that's yust what I was talking about. That's why I won't have one."

Marian was puzzled. "Because capital and labor——"

"Have nothing in common," he finished for her.

"I thought that is what you said, but I don't understand——"

"I won't make peace with them," he explained. "I won't give in! Capital made me lose my leg, and capital can look at it!"

"But, Tag, it hurts you worse than it does them."

"It's principle," he said. "I won't give in; I keep myself this way. I keep myself miserable to spite them!"

"I wish you wouldn't," she said. "It hurts you, and it's silly."

"*Ja,* you think it's yust a lot of foolishness. It's principle. I got no other way to fight them. I don't forget, like Tom Horton. I still fight!" He stumped away, like an irreconcilable old pirate, punching holes in the lawn with his peg-leg.

Marian wondered if she hadn't exaggerated to herself when she thought that she and Tag could get along harmoniously for a whole summer—but then, she had broken the rules by asking him to do something she could have managed for herself.

The next day she saw Tag only twice when he was within speaking distance. The first time they said, "Good morning"; the second time she was going into town on an errand and she stopped the car beside him at the edge of the orchard and asked if there was anything she could bring him. There was nothing, and she drove on. When she came home she heard the record player in his room above the garage, but she did not see him the rest of the day.

When she did not bother Tag, he faded into the background and was less of a distraction than any one else she could think of. Almost at once she had become jealous of her aloneness. If she had been asked to explain, she would have said that she stayed in town only half an hour because there might be a telephone call from her husband at any time, and she did not go to see any of her friends for the same reason. And she did not try to telephone Charlie because he was tied up with important business and had indicated that he did not want to be disturbed. Those things were true, but it was also true that she wanted them to be that way, and when she might have telephoned for temporary help, or company, she did not.

On the morning of the third day of her being alone, she dreamed about Paul. It was not the usual kind of dream she had about him. She was on a hill, in a field, and around her there was dry grass, and flowers with thin dry stems. It was in bright sunshine and dry air, and the edge of the hill ended a few feet away, against a blue sky. Paul came to her, and he was the way she had seen him first, in old corduroy trousers, oxfords without socks, and a faded blue shirt. He was young and stern and shy. He looked at her, and asked, "Where are the others?"

She said, "I sent them all away."

He took her hand and they walked over the hill in the sunshine, among the dry-stemmed flowers. Paul did not tell her where they were going, and she hardly felt his hand; it held hers so lightly; but she was full of joy and a feeling of sacredness for the dry field and the thin-stemmed flowers in the sunshine. Then they were in the arboretum, beside the boulevard, and there were dandelions with stems knee-high. Some of them were in bloom, and others had gone to seed, so it was like looking over a Milky Way of bright yellow suns and pale moons.

They stopped at the edge and Paul said, "The seeds were mixed up when they came from the nursery."

She said, "It wouldn't have happened if Tag had mowed the lawn," and she took up a stick and began knocking off the white, airy globes of the ones that had gone to seed. She felt happily wicked, but Paul was uneasy. He said, "We haven't time," and they went on into the woods, among the enormous columns of fir trees. When they sighted their lean-to of fir boughs, their fire was burning in front of the shelter, with blue smoke gliding up among the trees, but there was a great deal of noise going on.

Paul said, "I must have forgotten to turn off the radio."

The noise grew louder and louder, and she woke and heard Tag's record player blaring in through the open window. I've slept late, she thought, but the room was half dark and dawn was just coming into the sky. Tag was playing his favorite record, about the martyred Joe Hill whose vision appeared at some one's bedside in Salt Lake City; the singer's voice was diminishing into the distance and the dawn: *"I never died," said Joe*——

There was no denying it was effective at that hour and in the house that had been divided by the battle with Joe Hill and his fellows. Marian shivered and was glad it was over. But it was only over that once, and in a few seconds it began again, full force:

> I dreamed I saw Joe Hill last night,
>   Alive as you and me.
> Says I, "But Joe, you're ten years dead——"

Tag must be drunk, Marian thought. Before, he had always played his records at considerate hours, and so softly that no one ever complained. Now he was certainly drunk, on whiskey, or music—both, probably, and more. It was the storm that had been boiling up inside him ever since Tom Horton's visit. He had to get it out of his system, and who was she to try to stop him? Poor Tag, she thought; like an angry child; like a child angry at the gods.

The record player blared on, and in quieter moments she heard Tag's wooden leg thumping the floor of his room as he walked up and down—one unbalanced, giant footstep, like a tree walking.

She was not ashamed of having locked the downstairs doors and windows so carefully. Before, it had seemed like a slur on Tag, who had no treachery in him. There was no treachery about him now, but a storm was a storm, even if it was in the maimed shape of a giant logger.

It was hard on the nerves, listening to the racket; but she was doubly safe as long as she was in one building and Tag was in the other. She did not think any one was in danger unless Tag accidentally set fire to his room. It would be safer if she could watch the garage. There was the end room, with a window facing in that direction. . . .

She had not opened the door in all the time she had been alone in the house. When she opened it now, in the light of early morning, the austerity of the room seemed to continue the youthful sternness of Paul as he had appeared in her dream. To make his nearness more real, there were a few of his possessions that had been left behind in his flight; an old camera case and a tripod, a geologist's hammer, and clothes that had since come back from the laundry—shirts, some underwear, and a few pairs of socks. Mrs. Wilkes had arranged everything neatly on the table like an exhibit: relics of Paul who wore these garments and used these articles; who was here, and went away. Marian thought the scarred old camera case was the one he had had the day they met in the pasture, and it seemed like part of her dream. She picked it up, like a relic; it was heavy; the camera was still there. She thought: when it is daylight, I can make sure if it is the one. Now there was only the dim light and the chill of dawn in the room, and the echo of Tag's uproar.

Through the curtained end window she had a clear view of

the garage. The light was on in the upstairs room, but the shades were drawn and all she saw was Tag's gigantic shadow which loomed against the shades and disappeared again as he stumped up and down to the loud music of "Joe Hill."

Sleep was impossible, but she could at least be comfortable. She went over to the bed and drew back the covers. By the faintly crumpled look of the linen, she knew that Mrs. Wilkes had made up the bed as Paul had slept in it last. Her first impulse was to be displeased; then she had a strange feeling of triumph, which she did not put into thoughts. The sheets and pillow were cold, and then they responded to the warmth of her body. . . .

She did not really sleep, but she came back from a half-dream when the uproar across the way changed to another key. The record player stopped and there was a clatter of pans, as if Tag were getting breakfast. He had taken over the singing and was bellowing:

> See our numbers still increasing;
> Hear the bugle blow:
> By our union we shall triumph
> Over every foe.

With the change of a few words, it might have been a hymn from the Methodist Church at Illihee. For the first time she understood why Bailey insisted that the Woobly cause had been a religion. But she was confused about the heresies. The union of which Tag bellowed had been driven out of existence with clubs and rifles and rifle fire—and now the loggers had another which seemed to do very well by them. You would expect Tag to be satisfied, but he spat contemptuously when she mentioned it, and would not accept any substitute for the true faith.

Fierce and long the battle rages,
    But we will not fear,
Help will come whene'er it's needed.
    Cheer, my comrades, cheer!

She remembered his account of the shooting at the dock—
Tag, behind a pile of wounded and dead men, holding up a
dying logger who sang, "Cheer, my comrades, cheer!"—holding the last note forever. Tag had been there at the Trial of
the Faith, and it was no use expecting him to forget what others
had burned into his memory. . . .

The sun had risen and the room was growing light. Now she
was hardly afraid at all and she thought it a good sign that
Tag was doing his own singing.

After a few minutes the singing stopped and she heard the
clash of cutlery and the sound of dishes—Tag was eating his
breakfast, she thought. The storm had worn itself out and
she was not afraid any more.

Standing out of the line of the window, she took off her
nightgown and began to dress. She was not coming back to the
room after she left it, but she wanted to stay as long as possible.
It did not count when she went to the big room for things
she had forgotten, and she put up her red banner of hair in
front of Paul's small, heavy-framed mirror. That seemed quite
proper: she had once given him some of her hair, and his
mirror was welcome to it all. She looked very well, for a woman
who had withstood an imaginary siege. Well, and something
more. Perhaps it was the light of early morning, or the cleansing
effect of the storm, or the room, but there was a look she had
never seen before, a look of compassion and fulfillment. Smiling
a little, she said, "Some one could have a nice wife."

Then the uproar began again in the room over the garage.

Tag was marching up and down, shouting a song, and every few beats his wooden leg thumped on the floor:

> Song on his lips he came;
> Song on his lips he went;—
> This be the token we bear of him,—
> Soldier of Discontent!

There were other verses of which she caught only a few words; mostly they were like the muttered rumble of marching men. The first seemed to be his favorite, and in a little while he came back to it: the first two lines with an inevitable marching swing, the third—*This be the token we bear of him*—was an impassioned shout, like banners above marching men, and the last—*Soldier of Discontent!*—took up the inevitable march.

Marian found herself caught by the fierce, marching energy of the song, which she repeated to herself, and she no longer wanted to stand still. Perhaps the Wobblies had been a threat to the overly comfortable, after all!

There was a clatter of hardware, then the sound of the wooden leg thumping down the garage stairs. "Now, what?" she asked, running to the window.

The side door of the garage opened and Tag came out, dressed in his best suit, with a burden on his back. When he turned to close the door, Marian saw that it was a blanket roll, and attached to the rope harness was a frying pan and a small tin pail. There was more meaning in his marching song than she had guessed.

She had a moment of panic when she saw him start in the direction of the kitchen door—and then she was running out of the room and downstairs. If he were to knock furiously on the door while she was still inside, she might disgrace herself by being afraid to open it.

They met in the drive, and she said somewhat breathlessly, "Good morning, Tag!"

He said, "You're yust in time to say good-bye."

"You're leaving us?"

"I don't do this to mow the lawn." He had been drinking, but he was not as drunk as she had expected, and his usual look of brooding was gone.

"I'm sorry you're leaving," she said.

He said, "You ought to be sorry for yourself."

"Why, Tag?"

"You're staying."

She did not know whether he had insight or was only being difficult. "What about your wages?"

"*Hah,* you people, always talking about money, money!"

"But if we owe you anything, Tag——"

"You don't owe me anything," he said. "Charlie owes me one leg."

"I'm sorry," she said.

"*Ja,* so am I."

He was drunk, and probably a little crazy, but she got up her courage and asked, "Could I take you anywhere in the car?"

"*Ja,* certainly, certainly!" His voice was mocking. "Where do you suggest?"

"But you must know where you are going."

He thought it over. "Is it a law?"

"No. But you must have an idea of where you're going."

"*Ja?* I must?"

"Why are you leaving, if you aren't going anywhere?"

He said, "I don't want to rot here."

That, at least, was an answer. "What about food?" she asked. "If there's anything——"

"That's not why I came to the back door!"

Her face was suddenly warm. "You misunderstand everything I say!"

"*Ja*, certainly, certainly."

"But why, Tag?"

"Capital and labor have nothing in common."

She made one more effort. "You may not need anything, Tag, but I respect you, and when you respect people you want to show it."

"*Ja*, certainly."

"Well, is there anything I can do?"

"*Ja*, don't keep me standing here all day with this bindle on my back."

She put out her hand. "Good-bye, Tag."

He shook her hand, a little mockingly.

At the last moment she remembered their conversation of a few days before, about Paradise on earth, which he had once expected to see. "I hope you find Paradise!" she said.

"*Ja*." He gave his blanket roll a hitch. "You'll never know."

She stood in the drive in the morning sunshine, looking after him as he stumped away, with the frying pan and tin pail swinging at his back. Near the corner of the orchard he turned and called something to her. It sounded warm and friendly, but it was in Swedish and she did not know the language. Then he went on and did not look back again. The last she saw of him was his broad back, lurching along the orchard road, and the tin pail flashing in the sun, and the sound of his defiant voice came back to her:

> Song on his lips he came;
> Song on his lips he went; —
> This be the token we bear of him, —
> Soldier of Discontent!

All the rest of the morning she felt cleansed by the storm that had swept Tag away; cleansed and restless with energy for which she wanted to find some immediate use, but could not. Walking about the grounds she told herself: Tag thinks I'm a parasite, and I am. I used to prove it was Charlie's fault because he would never let me take a job or do anything useful. But after I proved it, it was still a lie. No one can stop another from doing what she really wants to do. In a few days of being alone I've become a human being; he can never take that away from me, and if he doesn't like it, it's his own fault. I have to go on this trip because it was partly my idea, but I won't be the same person and the trip will mean something different. Long ago he brushed me aside when I told him I loved Paul. He brushed me aside and said all the girls had a crush on the boy. All his life he's been brushing people aside or overriding them —or using a club or a gun when they stood up to him and refused to be overridden. I've never been honest enough before to let myself think about that. He doesn't do brutal things like that now, but it's because times have changed rather than because he has. He got what he wanted because people let themselves be brushed aside the way I did—the way I won't! He's had his way because he is what he is, and he's convinced that he's right. When I'm myself and have some conviction, I'll make out all right.

For the first time she saw Charlie and herself from all sides and saw what could be done. He would come back, expecting everything to be the same because he had been away only a few days. But, in a way, he would never really come back, because she was no longer the same person. She was no longer afraid of him, or willing to be brushed aside. She would have a life of her own, and if it led to clashes or separation, it would only prove what she had known all along—that they had nothing in common.

She thought: To hear me any one would think I'm willing to wreck a home for the sake of a career! I never wanted one. The only career worth anything is loving some one, but when you don't have that, you must have something. . . . There was that personnel job I could have had, if I hadn't let him brush me aside. I could certainly find another one like it. If you can't love some one and be loved, you can at least love and understand people. . . .

In the afternoon she walked again about the unmowed lawn, under the trees Tom Horton had planted, and along the orchard road, following the half-man footprints of the Soldier of Discontent; she walked back again, and down to the shore and along the rocky beach, where the tide was beginning to go out. Her mind was clear now, and she thought affectionately of Tag and his unconquerable spirit and cleansing bitterness. At the last moment, when he had called back to her in Swedish, his voice had been warm and friendly, and she chose to think that it was a blessing. She was sending him a blessing anyway, and she said aloud: "I hope you find Paradise!" Though he was not likely to find more than a hobo jungle, or a few of the faithful in a dusty Wobbly hall. And she added, "I hope your spree does you as much good as it has done me."

But it was more than Tag, even though his storm had been responsible. While things turned and changed and became clear in her mind, there had been the recurring image of an unfamiliar, compassionate face in the heavily framed small mirror. She could admit it to herself now; it was Paul's wife, who had got up from his bed and dressed in his poor room, and was fixing her hair before his mirror. . . .

Her body went on walking after it was tired, and her mind went on working after she was through with thinking for a while. It was like the nights when she wanted to sleep, but the excitement of the day went on and on, and there was nothing to bring her flying mind safely home to her body for the night. At last, when she could not walk any more, she lay down in the long, dry grass of the orchard and stared up at the pale sky, touched with the tender green of apple leaves. As she lay there, the calm warmth of the earth came through the crumpled grass and through her light summer dress, to her body; her shuddering breath grew quiet and her clenched hands relaxed. . . . She did not even hear the car that came along the orchard road and blotted out her restless footprints.

Paul had the small, square letter buttoned in the breast pocket of his shirt. He had saved it partly because of the handwriting; he had not noticed before that Marian wrote so beautifully. The letter itself did not have much in it. It said that his father had asked her to write. They were leaving on a trip the following Wednesday and would be gone for at least two weeks, possibly for the whole summer. She hoped he was enjoying his work, and that he would take good care of himself. She signed it, "Sincerely, Marian."

He had given them three days extra, to allow for possible delays, and then he arranged a half-day off to come to Home Place for the things he had left. He did not particularly need any of them, but there was something there that he wanted.

The garage door was unlocked, and for a moment he was surprised to see Marian's car. Then he realized it could hardly be anywhere else, because you don't take a car along on a small boat.

When he ran up the stairs to get the key, Tag's door was standing open and he was startled by the mess inside. The room had always been bad enough, but after the air of the mountains it stank belligerently and it looked as if it had been the setting for a drunken search. The bureau drawers were open, the mattress and bedding were pulled half off the bed, and the floor was littered with pieces of broken phonograph records, pint whiskey bottles and clothes, and an empty aquarium.

"Tag's been on a drunk," Paul said to himself. He reached for the keys that hung on the deer antlers and did not find them. "Maybe he's gone to the house to sleep it off," although he had never heard of Tag doing anything like that.

The kitchen door was unlocked and he went in; everything was clean and peaceful and put away, except for a few dishes in the drying basket, and a tweed coat that Marian sometimes wore was hung over the back of a chair. The coat seemed to have something to do with his return, and he stood for a few seconds with his hand on its shoulder, trying to remember. The honest cloth was good under his hand; then he felt the dull edge of the chair underneath, and took his hand away.

In the dining room everything was put away except for one place set with silverware, and nasturtiums in the blue glass globe. The nasturtiums were not quite fresh, but they were less than three days old, probably not much more than one. He had been right in allowing extra time for delays. He went through the living room, where everything was in order except for a book open on the sofa, and up the creaking stairs. On one of the steps was a bathing cap and suit, folded, on a folded bath towel. He thought the cap and suit were Marian's, and it looked as if she might have forgotten them in packing, but she probably had others. He went on up to his end room, and smiled faintly at the neat display of his possessions on the table.

The bed was less neat, with the covers thrown back as he had left them. The bed was not quite as he had left it: tossed on the foot was something of ivory-colored silk, and when he picked it up he saw it was a nightgown. His first thought was of Bertha, but she had worn white satin. Then he seemed to remember that Marian had worn something that color on the night of the sleep-walking. But why was it here? It didn't seem likely that the room would have been used unless there had been a houseful of overnight company. He moved the pillow to see if anything had been left there and found a crumpled handkerchief with an embroidered M. He sat on the bed, holding the handkerchief in one uncertain hand and the nightgown in the other, searching for an explanation which he could not find.

He got up and walked about the room, and saw Marian's hairbrush on the chest of drawers under the old mirror. But why? He went back and sat on the bed, shaken by some great and dim excitement. The dishes for one in the kitchen drier; Marian's coat; the one place set in the dining room; the almost fresh flowers; these things in his room. . . . He stuffed the handkerchief into his pocket and went out. One after another he found the other rooms unoccupied, and in order.

There was still the big bedroom which he had left to the last, and he had an unreasonable distaste for going in there at all. The big, ugly walnut bed had the covers thrown back on one side, preserving the gesture of some one getting up, and the pillow on the other side was smooth and undented. Only one person had slept there—probably his father—and his dislike of the room became a little less. Then he noticed a thin dark object on the crumpled pillow, and picked up a hairpin. He could not decide anything from the room and he did not want to stay. He went back to his own and put the hairpin on his dresser, beside Marian's hairbrush—then he wondered why he had done that.

Standing at the front window, with one hand holding back the curtain, he stared out at the Bing cherry tree and the blue water beyond—trying to piece things together in his mind. . . .

The tree was close to the window, and he looked into its world of sharp, oval, drooping leaves. Out of the mass of the tree, long branch ends reached up like blind heavy vines, with their secret red fruit still among the trembling leaves. In the distance of the blue water, the outgoing tide moved like a dream through the mind of the sleeping world. . . .

At first he could decide nothing except that Marian had been living in the house alone until the last day or two; and for some obscure reason she had moved to the end room. Then, staring at the tree, he had the overwhelming certainty that she was still here, somewhere about the place. Even now he might be able to collect his belongings and go away unnoticed.

He was bunching his things together when he remembered the wreckage of Tag's room—and Tag was gone! Then he was running downstairs, around the house, and down to the beach, where she had gone but apparently returned, and back again. . . .

Marian half-woke and heard some one calling her. She opened her eyes; Paul was kneeling beside her, golden in the late afternoon sun, and tiger-striped by thin shadows of orchard grass. He looked wild and sweet and very dear, and his blue eyes were frightened. She was only half awake and she was not sure he was real; he had come to her so often, in different guises, at the strange turns of dreams. But she felt that he would not go away as long as she lay still, smiling up at him. Then she felt his hand on her shoulder.

"Marian," he was saying, "Marian, are you all right?"

"I'm all right, Paul." She sat up. "I must have been asleep." Then she said, "You look frightened, Paul!"

"I was," he said. He had been kneeling, and now he sat beside her on the grass that had been pressed down by her body. "I saw that you had been alone—and I saw Tag's room, and he was gone——"

"He got on a spree, and went away with a blanket roll on his back."

"He didn't bother you, Marian?"

She shook her head, smiling tenderly. "He was like an old hero! All these years he'd believed Tom Horton was out fighting for the poor and the oppressed, and then Tom came back——"

"Tom came back here?"

"Last week," Marian said. "And he was such a disappointment to poor Tag. He's in the furniture business in Denver, and he's fat and smug and conservative, and he wears pince-nez glasses! I'm not making fun of him, Paul. He was really so dear and kindly. I can understand how it was: he'd given so much that there wasn't anything left. And you could see the terrible scars, Paul! I saw them——" She had not cried in all the upheaval of the past days, but suddenly her eyes overflowed and her tears pelted down while she said, "I saw them—and I can understand!" After a while she continued, "But Tag couldn't accept it; he was disillusioned because his hero had failed him. Then he got over it in one grand spree of drinking and singing—and he went out to take Tom's place."

"I hope he makes out all right," Paul said gently.

"I hope he finds Paradise!"

In the world of afternoon sun and tall grass, the memory of Tag became dim and went away, and they came back to themselves. Paul said, "You wrote that you were leaving on Wednesday."

"There have been delays," Marian said; "business."

"You've been here alone?"

"Yes."

When they talked, they both avoided mentioning Charlie.

"I thought you would be gone when I got here," Paul said.

She looked at him, smiling faintly. "You didn't want to see me?"

His eyes were somber. "I didn't think I should."

Marian looked away without answering; she hadn't thought they should, either. But Paul seemed to think she was offended; she felt the touch of his hand; it was trembling and she took it in hers to steady it.

"I tried too, Paul. That was why I planned this trip."

He said, "I waited three days."

"That is the time they allow the dead, before they are buried."

Paul's hand still trembled, and he said, "It's like being dead, being away from you."

It had been very much like that for her, and this was an afterward which found both of them unprepared and without defense against each other. She told herself, "We buried our love, and on the third day it rose from the dead." It did not seem blasphemy, but rather like something sacred, like Easter and the return of spring: seeing the earth blossom again, after you have been dead.

Paul said, "I went away because I love you."

She said, "I love you dearly."

He must have known that, but she felt a shiver go through him, and his voice was a whispered cry, *"Marian!"*

When she looked at him, he was staring straight ahead, at the tall, waving grass. To make up for not meeting his eyes, she put her cheek softly against his. They stayed that way for a long time, in the light, calm afterward, where there was only the feeling of well-being and tenderness.

After a while, he said, "I loved you, but I was too slow, and then it was too late. I couldn't love easily; it meant too much to me. It means everything: life, and the meaning of nature, and immortality."

"It means all those things, and more, Paul!" Then she said, "But I didn't find it hard to love you. That first time, when you made a fire with the bow drill; when we went into the woods, and you tasted a mushroom that I thought was poisonous—we'd been together only an hour, but I ate some of it too because if it was poisonous, I wanted to die with you."

He put his arm around her, so gently that at first she did not feel its strength. "I've thought of that day so often," he said, "and there was always something new about it; something I hadn't noticed before. It was only this summer that I really saw its meaning, or thought I did."

She asked, "What meaning did you find?"

"It isn't easy to explain," he said, "only, it seemed to me it was a kind of mating. We met in the field in the morning, without any one having done anything about it, and we went away together, through the woods and to the beach and into the water. We discovered the world, and started making use of it—we should have been allowed to go on with it. Living shouldn't be so complicated that people forget what it means; if anything grows up to hide one of the meanings of life, it should be cut down. Somehow, we should have gone on with it together——"

She told him, "I knew it then, Paul! If you had asked me, I would have gone right then to live with you in the woods. Maybe it couldn't have been quite that way, but it should have been something like that."

"It should have been like that," he said. "It should have been like this." He put both arms around her and held her against him. His strength surrounded her, and she could feel his heart thudding against her, and his kisses on her hair, and the sweetness of their bodies answering each other.

She didn't want to think any more, but things from earlier in the day kept shining in her mind. The feeling of being Paul's wife—she almost was now—but that brought responsibilities she hadn't foreseen. Now she had to find the way for both of them when all of her wanted to be lost in the warm darkness of being. With her face muffled against him, she said, "You shouldn't have loved me, Paul, you would have been so much happier if you hadn't!"

"I tried not to," he said, "but I couldn't help it; I can't help it now!"

"You might have," she said, "if I hadn't wanted you all the time; if I hadn't wanted you to love me."

In answer, he held her more searchingly, but the admission made her feel guilty, and she drew away from him. "It was my doing," she said, "and it wasn't fair!"

He looked at her, with his eyes wonderful, and his face golden and tiger-striped by shadows of grass. "Why are you trying to hurt yourself now by being fair?"

"Because you love me." That was what she hadn't foreseen: that his loving her would bring responsibilities. But it also brought more love in return, and made responsibilities difficult to remember. . . . There was one destroying word, and she had to use it quickly, before he took her back into his arms, where she longed to be. She said, "I can't be fair to any one without being fair to your father."

His face changed, and for the first time he looked guilty. "I suppose not."

She said, painfully, "I was free to chose when I took the job of being your stepmother. I'm not free now, and I have to go on with it."

When he did not answer, she said, "We'll have to think about what we have, and not what we can't have."

He said, "But I won't have anything if I don't have you! Most of my life I've been out in the cold, and it'll be that way more than ever."

She was crying inside for the warmth and security of love that she could give him, but that was something to forget, not to remember. "At least we can be honest with each other," she said. "We know that we love each other, and we have to decide what we are going to do about it."

His voice was cheerless as he said, "I don't see how we can do anything about it."

"We have to decide where we're going to face it," she said. "I haven't any choice; I'm afraid it comes down to a question of where you'd rather be."

"Where I'd rather be, or where I think I should be?"

"Where you think you should be."

He said, "I know I shouldn't be here."

"I don't want to drive you away from home, Paul."

Meeting her eyes, he said, "If it weren't for you, there wouldn't be any reason for coming home!"

She thought, "Oh, Paul, if it weren't for you, there would never have been any reason for my being here!" But saying that would not help. She said, "Then I suppose you'll have to be somewhere else. But it mustn't be just running away from me; isn't there some place you'd like to go?"

He said, "Uncle Phil wants me to come to Alaska. He thinks I could be useful at the mine."

"That would please Frances and Ginger," Marian said.

"They'll like it, all right."

She smiled with him, and said, "I don't feel sorry for you at all. You'll be doing something useful, and that seems a luxury."

"Why do you say that?" he asked. "You're always doing something useful; you're the most important person in this house!"

She shook her head. "I'm little better than a parasite. Even Tag, who was old and crippled, got tired of leading an easy life here." She was being sorry for herself, and that wasn't fair to Paul. She asked, "Do you have to go back to the look-out station, first?"

"I'll have to, until they get some one in my place. Then I'll pack up and go north."

"You'll be gone by the time we get back from our trip?"

"Yes." Then he asked, "Will you write to me sometime?"

"Not very personally," she said. "And not at all if you're going to look for things that aren't there." She had felt her letter in the pocket of his shirt, and she knew that letters can be cruel and exhausting, keeping unreasonable hopes alive. "I'll probably write when your father asks me to."

They sat together a few minutes longer, then he said, "I think I should go now."

"You should, Paul." She didn't want him to find out how frail her good resolutions were; they might have broken under a word or a touch, and just being with him in silence made it harder to remember what they should do, and easier to think of what she wanted to do.

He helped her up, and as they went back through the orchard, the sun was flooding among the trees like a golden tide, level with the earth; she could feel its richness on her face, and when she looked at Paul, his face was golden. She thought of the morning when they had first met, and walked together in a new-seeming world, with the light of the rising sun on their faces. . . . Now it was sunset, and it seemed to her that between the rising and the setting of the sun they had lost the world, but whether it was through fault or misfortune, she did not know.

When they were in the shadow of the house, standing beside Paul's car in the driveway, she reminded him of the things he had left.

"It doesn't matter," he said. "I can get them later." He did not look or sound as if anything mattered.

At the last moment, he took her in his arms again, and said, "I don't like to leave you here alone."

"It won't be for long," she said, "and I would rather it was that way."

He said, "Promise that you won't stay here alone tonight."

"I promise," she said. "Good-bye, Paul."

"Good-bye, Marian."

Paul was gone, and she felt alone for the first time. Before, when she was by herself, Home Place had been alive with something she had not even put into thoughts. Now everything was hollow and dead, and she never wanted to be there again.

XVI

HIS MIND kept putting things into the past, like telling about events that had already happened. "I was desperate," his mind said. "For three days I'd been going around Seattle, Hewitt, Tacoma, seeing people I knew; trying to borrow, or beg, or sell. Nobody would help me. I was in a jam, I tell you. I was up against a wall and I couldn't get around it or over it. I moved to the Savoy Hotel, where none of the family would think of looking for me. I slept there—what sleeping I did; I drank straight whiskey; I poured it down like water and never got drunk; my mind was clear all the time. I was in a jam and I couldn't see any way out; but I knew there was some way, if I could only find it.

"I didn't find it until the afternoon of the third day. I was walking up and down in my room at the hotel, pouring whiskey down like water. I could hear the traffic on Second Avenue, and once the whistle of the Alaska steamer on the waterfront. Everything like that was in a different world.

"All at once I saw it! I poured the rest of the whiskey down the basin in the bathroom. When I shaved my hand was steady; I cut myself only once. I put on a clean shirt, packed my things, and checked out. My car was at a parking garage, but I took a taxi. I could have driven all right, but I didn't want the bother when I had important business.

"When I got to the house, I went upstairs to our room and unlocked the little drawer in the right-hand side of my bureau.

. . . I hadn't carried it since Wobbly days, and then I'd used mostly the butt end. I'd oiled it before I put it away, and it was still loaded, and there was also a box of cartridges. I broke it down and cleaned it, and loaded it with cartridges from the box. They were as old as the ones I'd taken out, but I wouldn't have felt comfortable if I'd used the others. I loaded all six chambers, though I didn't need that many. I locked the drawer and washed my hands and went downstairs."

That brought him up to the present. He went into the library and switched on the lights, because the shades were drawn. He stood for a minute, with a cigar between his teeth, his arms behind him, and his feet far apart, looking at the group of photographs on the wall: Myra when she was a young woman, in a shirtwaist with a high neck, and her hair piled up high— after a while you can only be young in a photograph by looking old-fashioned—Myra with her thin, high-minded face, something like Paul's, only not outdoors and golden. Myra was in her grave. She had been a good woman, even if they hadn't had much of a life together. He bowed to her. . . . Bailey in a photograph from a Christmas or two ago. Bailey confidently close to the camera, with sad eyes and a faint grin, and underneath it what his mother used to call a determined jaw. He didn't know what Bailey had ever determined on, unless it was not to work in the woods. Bailey with that large head so full of ideas that he was like a shopper with so many packages he could never get them home. . . . Paul in an enlarged snapshot, taken when he was twenty. The boy had taken so many photographs, but there were hardly any of him, and since he was grown they'd never been able to get one of him with a collar and tie. The picture was taken in a mountain meadow, with the slope of Mount Olympus behind him; Paul bare-headed, in old hiking clothes you hardly noticed more than you would the coat of a deer; Paul with his mother's fine face, and his own deep-set eyes. The boy hadn't been any more use than Bailey, but when some one is enough of something, you let him go his own way. . . . Marian in half-profile, with light touching her hair and a touch of smile that didn't change the calm of her face. Beautiful, calm Marian, when she wasn't restless. Bailey was right that a good painter should do her portrait, but it wouldn't be right unless it had the wild, sweet, breathless look of the moment of their first meeting. A painter wasn't likely to get that; he'd never seen it since, though in his mind he could see her with that look of ecstasy. . . .

There they were, his wives and sons, looking from the wall as if they expected him to say something appropriate. He saluted them with his hat and said, "Here goes Charlie!"

The glassy Joyce at the switchboard said that Mr. Darling was in. Charlie said, "Thank you, Joyce," and went through the office, where the unshrinking Violet looked up sullenly, then stared as if there were something odd about him. He said, "Hello, Violet," and went on and opened the flat mahogany door.

Martin was sitting behind his black and chromium desk, reading a typewritten report—sheets stapled together. His round pink baby-face looked up. "Hello, Charlie."

"Hello, Martin."

Martin put down the report. "Sit down."

Charlie sat down, holding his hat on his knee.

"Don't you want to hang up your hat and make yourself comfortable?"

"I'm not staying long," Charlie said.

"How about a drink?" Martin opened a drawer, then paused. "Or would it be superfluous?"

"Keep it," Charlie said.

But Martin set the bottle of Scotch and one whiskey glass on the desk.

"Keep it."

Martin said, "It's a bad sign when you clamp down suddenly on a habit; it's as much of a shock as over-indulgence. It's the same thing, of course; clamping down is the other half."

"Go on," Charlie said.

Martin said, "I was only going to add that it's best to make a habit of what's good for you; then there's no reason for stopping." He beamed a little to himself, enjoying the rest of it like a self-satisfied speaker chuckling over the notes for a lecture which he was not allowed to give. Then he said, "Well, Charlie, I see you've been doing just what I warned you against."

"What is that?"

"Racing all over kingdom come, seeing bankers who wouldn't do as much for you as I have done; drinking like a fish and paying no attention to what you eat, and neglecting your sleep——"

"What I do is none of your business!"

"Certainly not," Martin said softly. "I was only telling you what you've been doing—and you've aged yourself ten years in the process."

"Is that any skin off your back?"

"Dear, no. I was only—" Then he said. "It is my business to ask how you made out. Did you find any of the banks willing to do more than I have done?"

"They all said that in your place, with this upswing, they wouldn't shut down on me."

Martin said, "I could be generous, too, with other people's money. I could give you the First National Bank, in hot air."

"You could," Charlie said.

"Did any of them give you anything more than hot air?"

"They all said that with this upswing in lumbering, you should let me go on——"

"Of course, and I could say that with this upswing, it's the banks' duty to finance you."

"They would, too, if you didn't have me by the balls!"

Martin chuckled. "You make me sound like a pawn-shop operator!"

"Sound like it! What else are you, for Christ's sake? You and the bankers! You gamble by lending five dollars on a fifty-dollar watch. Your only gamble is whether you get back your money with interest—or get a fifty-dollar watch for five bucks!"

Martin beamed, like a pink tick. "Charlie, isn't it rather late in life for you to try to change the banking system?" Then he said, "It's a comfort to know that none of them could do more for you than I have done."

"They said that in your place——"

Martin said, "I'd advise you to see your doctor, and go home and sleep—then go on your vacation. I still have your archery set——"

"You know where you can put it," Charlie said.

"—and when you get back, we'll arrange something——"

"I want to arrange it now," Charlie said; "you have to give me one more year."

"I've been giving you one more year for ten years."

"Those were bad years," Charlie said, "and you know it. You have to give me this one good one."

"You don't know whether it's going to be fat or lean. Go on your vacation—you need it—and when you come back, we'll see what we can arrange——"

"Sure, you'll arrange to take the works—and have me run it and make a fortune for you!"

"I've been thinking it over, Charlie," Martin's voice was almost kindly. "We might do better than that."

"If it's anything reasonable," Charlie said, "I can be reasonable, too."

"I don't want to be hard on you," Martin said. "I'm only doing the business thing; but I might manage something better. Suppose we could work out something so I didn't have to take you over——"

Charlie held himself back from getting up and shaking hands with his enemy. "Go on; if it's anything within reason——"

"There's your son, Paul," Martin said. "He's a fine boy!"

"I know it."

"And he has the making of a good logger——"

"If he'd log," Charlie said.

"If he could be persuaded to get into the game seriously——"

Charlie said, "By God, I'm with you there! I've done all I could to make him see it. If any one else can do it——"

Martin beamed at him. "I've never said much about it before; I didn't think it was quite my affair; but I've always felt there was something lacking in your business: continuity. Even if you could go on the way you've been going, the minute anything happened to you, the whole enterprise would go up in smoke. That would be the end of it."

"Unless the boys snapped out of it——"

Martin said, "With all the other gambles in logging, you don't want to gamble on a miracle. Continuity is what the business needs. If you could encourage Paul——"

"God knows, I've tried," Charlie said. "If any one else——"

"Don't you think Paul would feel differently about it if he knew it was a matter of saving the fat out of the fire?"

Charlie hadn't thought about it that way. "He might, though I hate to put it up to him that way; it's like holding a gun to his head——"

Martin chuckled. "There are times when you're justified in holding a gun to some one's head. Don't you think he'd feel worse if you lost everything and he found out later that he could have saved it by doing what any good son would do?"

"He would, all right," Charlie said. "I'll put the cards on the table and he can decide." Then he said. "I want to get this straight: you're going to let me go on if Paul will come in with me——"

"That's part of it," Martin said; "but both of us have children. There's my daughter, Bertha; I want to provide for her as much as you want to provide for Paul——"

"Sure," Charlie said, "and she won't lose anything by your giving me this chance; she'll be better off——"

Martin said, "You know she's in love with Paul——"

"Sure, all the girls are."

"She and Paul went to college together, and they have other ties——"

"I don't see what that has to do with business."

"Bertha has been in love with Paul for years—too long for it to be good for her. And it's time Paul married; he's almost twenty-five, isn't he?"

"He is twenty-five."

Martin went on softly, "If Paul and Bertha were to marry——"

"No one is stopping them," Charlie said, pouring himself a drink. He was beginning to have waves of feeling sick and gutted, and he wanted Martin to finish with their business, so he could go home. "Paul and Bertha can do as they please," he said. "Let's get back to your terms for my going on."

Martin cleared his throat. "I don't seem to have made myself plain, and I haven't finished."

"Go ahead then, and let's stick to business."

"This is business," Martin said. "Both of us have a stake in this business, and you have a son and I have a daughter. If Paul and Bertha married, I would write off everything I've advanced you, if you would make the business over to Paul and Bertha after your death. Until then, it would be yours, and if there were a few of the good years you expect, you could make plenty of provision for the rest of your family. Isn't that reasonable, Charlie?"

"Sure," Charlie said, "it's fair enough. But there's a hell of a canyon in the middle of your plan, and no trestle over it. You talk as if those two were going to get married tomorrow, and I've never seen any sign of it ever happening. Bertha's willing all right, but what about Paul?"

Martin said, "Bertha's a fine, intelligent girl; she would be a good wife for any man. And Paul has to marry sometime if he's going to amount to anything——"

"I know all that," Charlie said, "but what in hell makes you think Paul is going to up and marry your daughter?"

Martin was soft and pink and beaming, "It's only a wish, Charlie; but if Paul were to know that besides getting a fine wife he was saving you and the business——"

Suddenly Charlie began laughing. He laughed, and could not stop for a long time. While he was still laughing, he took out his handkerchief, which smelled of whiskey, and soaked up the tears that were running from his eyes. "Martin," he said at last, "Why didn't I recognize you before? You and your pink baby face and your archery! Why don't you take off your clothes and run around with your bow and arrows? O, Jesus, you were Cupid all the time, and I didn't know you!"

When he finally stopped, Martin said, "Laughing is good for you; it exercises muscles that aren't ordinarily used, chiefly the diaphram. I try to laugh at least once every day; it prolongs life; but it isn't getting us any farther in our business."

Charlie dried his eyes with his whiskey-smelling handkerchief. "O, Jesus, was that business we were talking? Where were we?"

Martin said, "I had given you my terms and I suggested that you explain them to Paul." He was cold and not beaming any more.

Charlie said, "You want me to tell Paul this rigamarole?"

"I think you'd better," Martin said, "for your own good, and his."

"I'll be God-damned if I do anything of the kind!"

Martin did not believe him. "What harm is there in telling him?"

"No harm, Cupid, no harm at all; only he might feel he had to do it."

"Bertha loves him, and she's a fine, intelligent girl——"

"Sure," Charlie said, "she's all right—she takes after her mother. I'd as soon it was Bertha as anybody else——"

"I approve of Paul, too," Martin said; "and Bertha has her heart set on him. I'm only asking you to tell him——"

"And I won't."

"It's for every one's good," Martin said. "I don't see why not."

Charlie said, "Because I don't mix business with family affairs. When Paul gets around to it, he'll choose his own wife."

"You won't think it over?"

"There's nothing to think over."

Martin said, "That brings us back to where we started. You might as well go on your vacation. When you get back, we'll settle up. You don't have to decide now, but I'll be glad to have you stay on the job. If you have any reasonable suggestion about salary——"

"By God, I'll never run my business for your profit, Martin! You have to give me one more year; I'm set for a killing——"

Martin said, "I've lent you more than any bank would, and then offered it as a present, on a silver platter. That's enough!"

"You have to give me one more year——"

"Go on your vacation, Charlie. I don't have to give you anything——"

"But you do, Martin," Charlie heard his own voice, clear and steady, "and I'll tell you how you can live to be a hundred, maybe."

Martin suddenly looked frightened, "How is that?"

"Keep clear of those push-buttons," Charlie said; "they might be the death of you."

Martin was shaking, "I won't touch them, Charlie; but if any one should come in——"

"Tell them you're busy. You can say it's a life and death matter."

"I'll certainly send them out," Martin said. "But if any one should see that, and call the police——"

"It wouldn't do you any good, Martin. But nobody'll see it; I'll put my hat over it, like this; that's why I didn't hang it up."

Martin was white and panting. "So that's what you came for!"

"I knew there was a way," Charlie said; "there always is—though it took three days to figure it out." His mind was clear, and he was firmly in the present.

"You'd better put that away, Charlie. You're drunk and crazy, or you'd know that kind of thing won't do you any good."

"I knew there was a way," Charlie repeated, "if I could only think of it; there always is——"

"A hold-up!" Martin said. "Any thug——"

"It's the difference between you and me. You're fat and soft and eighty, and you want to see a hundred because you've never lived; you've never had a belly-full of it, and you've never been in a jam that gutted you so that the only belly you had left was a burnt-out taste. The only chances you ever took were the pawn-shop kind, where you couldn't lose. You didn't even take a chance on leaving Illinois until the railroad was built. Then you came in a parlor car: a fat, soft young man who was going to make his pile out of the men who did the work and took the chances. You've been a miser ever since; a God-damned pack rat, storing away money, and then storing away time so you'd have enough to be a hundred. Now I'm sitting on your pack-rat cache of time with a gun in my hand!"

One of Martin's hands was resting on the typewritten report, and its trembling rustled the pages with a sound like a pack rat among dry leaves. He murmured, "If you weren't drunk and crazy, you would want to live, too—outside the penitentiary!"

"The hell I would!" Charlie said. "If I was like you, I wouldn't be doing this; I'd be afraid of losing. I've got nothing to lose. I'm nothing but an old timber beast, high-balling and killing men and breaking my ass, trying to break even in the bad years, waiting for the good ones. I've seen enough years, good and bad, and I've done everything, good and bad, and I don't give a damn! But I have a wife and sons to provide for—and I'm not going to see any pack rat run off with the provisions!"

Martin asked faintly, "What do you expect to gain from this hold-up?"

"If you want my terms," Charlie said, "I'll give them to you without driveling you to death: You can give me another year to pay you off, or there'll be two dead men carried out of this office."

"I understand," Martin said. "But it's no way to do business, Charlie."

"I tried the other ways first," Charlie said. "Well, what are you going to do?"

Martin had stopped shivering, and he was only a little pale. "I have no choice. I'll give you your year, if you think it'll do you any good."

"It'll do fine."

"But don't expect to come back asking for another one—with or without a gun."

"You have my word for it," Charlie said.

"And you have my word about the year. Is that good enough for you?"

Charlie let his body ride over a wave of dizziness. "Your word is enough for me, Martin, but something might happen to one or the other of us. Better have it in writing."

"It'll have to be in longhand."

It mightn't look so good if it was questioned—shaky longhand, with no witnesses. "Call Violet in," Charlie said; "dictate it to her and have her type it. She can witness our signatures."

Martin looked doubtful, "If she were to see that, and scream——"

"She won't see it—I'll keep it under my hat."

"You want me to ring for her now?"

"Go ahead. I want to get this over with."

"I'm going to push the button."

"That's what I told you to do. If you dictate anything I don't like, I'll tell you."

Martin was as good as gold, dictating the memorandum of agreement, and Violet took it down in her notebook, sitting with her fine legs crossed and her face pious and unsmiling. She always had that Sunday look in the office, and you didn't know if she ever had any week-days, or what she would be like then; or what she would be like if you pressed the trigger and a Colt .38 roared beside her. But she was calm and unsmiling, taking down the memorandum and reading it back from her shorthand notes.

Martin said, "Make two copies at once, and bring them in for our signatures."

"Yes, Mr. Darling." Violet went out silently. Martin insisted on rubber heels for his help, and noiseless typewriters, and well-oiled hinges. The memorandum business went on skids he had already greased.

Martin sighed and leaned back in his chair; he did not look as if there was any fight in him. Charlie watched him, dully, while he rode over another wave of dizziness. He recrossed his legs, which had pins and needles in them, shifting his hat and revolver to the other knee.

Martin said, "You don't have to keep that thing pointed at me; I agreed, and that ought to be enough."

"I know," Charlie said; "it's just a reminder."

"You're heartless."

"You're heartless, too, in your own way," Charlie said. They didn't sound quarrelsome; they were two tired old men, waiting for papers they had to sign before they could get away from each other. The business had taken the pink out of Martin's face, and given him the shakes. Charlie, who was twenty years younger, felt old enough, riding over waves of nausea, with pins and needles in his legs and pains in his upper arms and chest.

Once the telephone rang and Martin made the beginning of a gesture towards it, then drew his hand back, as if he had started to pick up a rattlesnake.

"You can answer it," Charlie said, "in the right way."

Martin answered. He said he was sorry, it was late and he had an appointment. Tomorrow, maybe. Good-bye, Bertha.

They were still avoiding each other's eyes when Violet came back with the agreement.

Martin said, "You can witness our signatures, Violet, if it's satisfactory."

Charlie read the carbon copy, with one eye on Martin and the other on the letters dancing on the page. "All right." He put it down. He was holding his hat and revolver in his right hand, and he had to shift them awkwardly to his left before he could accept the pen which Violet offered him. Martin was already signing. They exchanged and signed again, and Violet wrote her name four times as witness, sitting with her legs crossed and writing her name neatly, with the look of signing a Sunday-school register.

When she was gone, Charlie folded his copy with one hand and put it away in his inside coat pocket. "I guess that's all."

"I hope so!" Martin said softly.

Charlie stood on his cramped legs. "Don't try to telephone, or raise a fuss."

Martin looked pained. "Dear, no!" he sighed. "I'm going to sit here and compose myself; this has been a bad day!"

At the door Charlie drew himself up straight and looked back. Martin's face was still pale, and he had not stirred in his chair; he was still composing himself, and looked as if he might be some time about it. Charlie slid the revolver into its arm-pit holster and went out through the flat mahogany door, which closed silently behind him.

In the outer office, Violet was looking at him over her noiseless typewriter, and she beckoned to him with her neat, dark head. She was the first person he had seen since his escape from the world in which he had been alone, and she might have been an angel doing clerical work at the gate of heaven. He leaned over and chucked her under the chin. "Well, Violet!"

Her eyes met his a little sullenly. "Remember me to Bailey," she said. Then she lowered her voice: "I didn't see anything, but you'd better get rid of that revolver."

XVII

*B*AILEY had had a good time on the Canal. He stayed overnight with the Smiths, and came home chiefly because he did not like to leave Egil for too long with everything to look after.

Louise's parents were all right, and her brothers, George and Harry, were as good as you could find anywhere. To look at, they were just farm boys in their twenties—husky and shy and sunburned. But they were men of the world in their own way. They had been everywhere in what they looked on as their world, which was Puget Sound and Alaska. Between spells of farming, they had worked in the woods, in big-time camps and haywire ones; they had gone out in the salmon fleet, where they took their part in big hauls and big chances. And they had observed things in their travels. In Alaska, they climbed a mountain which had hot springs at the top, and a sporting house beside the trail at the bottom. Their companions stayed down, and when George and Harry were starting up, a phonograph was playing in the sporting house and girls were waving to them out of the windows. The boys said the hot springs were well worth seeing, and the water was really too hot to put your hand in. Bailey knew one of the reasons for their temperate and sometimes hazardous adventures, but knowing the boys even a little, he knew they would never mention having financed Louise in New York.

The brothers accepted Bailey because he was their sister's

friend, and they welcomed him on their own account when they found him willing to discuss endlessly the designing and building of boats.

Bailey had arrived in his sloop, and in the afternoon, when a summer northerly came up, the brothers knocked off work and they and Louise and Bailey went sailing. Actually, George and Harry did the sailing. It was their first experience with a boat that was rated non-capsizable and unsinkable, and they gave Bailey all the thrills of flying with test pilots in a new plane.

They anchored in the lee of Tabook Point and built a fire on the beach of high and lonely Toandos Peninsula, golden in the late afternoon sunshine. Beside their fire, the brothers told of helping pirate an Alaska fish trap at night, with their faces blackened, and the trap-tenders covered by rifles and cheerfully helping brail up the trap and load the boat, which had canvas battened over its name and number.

Apparently the brothers had never told of the adventure before. Louise did not approve, and she said somewhat sadly, "I am a sister to pirates!"

George said, "It wasn't our idea—we were only part of the crew—but it was a good haul."

Harry said, "They shouldn't allow fish traps, anyhow. You'd never think of robbing a boat that got its fish honestly."

To the brothers the piracy was only the passing adventure of an Alaskan night and a few minutes of entertainment around a campfire at home. Their real interests were more serious, and with Bailey they started planning a fifty-foot ketch for a voyage to the Central American coast. Bailey and Paul were to be included in the party. They even considered taking Louise, but could not decide in one afternoon.

Bailey made out well with the brothers, and when he was

leaving he commented on the fact. On the night of the picnic they had anchored the sloop in Pleasant Harbor and walked back to the farm; in the morning Louise took him back to the harbor in the panel truck. It was one of the few times on his visit when they were alone, but he did not get much comfort out of it. When he was saying good-bye, she let him kiss her once, which was little enough from a girl with whom he had lived two years. She looked tough and tan and lovely, and she was very nice; but as for any feeling of being closer to her, he might as well have had Violet along. And he knew Louise well enough not to try to break through her wall of reserve. When she had loved him, there had never been any room for doubt, or need for any one else. Before that time, and after it was over, there might as well have been plate glass between them.

Except for a fishing boat and an old cruiser at the far end, Bailey's white sloop was the only boat in the little oval harbor. It was edged by low, rocky cliffs and a steep, tree-covered shore on the far side, and a rocky beach and less steep but tree-covered shore on the near side. Louise had stopped the truck on the weed-grown sandspit that narrowed the harbor entrance to a few fathoms. The sloop was white, with a white reflection, in the harbor that was deep green with the reflection of trees; the tide was rippling out through the entrance, and beyond that the Canal opened away to a seven-mile width of sunlit waters that were divided by the blue-green cape of Oak Head at the end of Toandos.

Bailey wondered how far his father and Marian had got on their voyage. It was a fine morning to be afloat, but it was not so fine leaving Louise, and he sat in the truck beside her a few minutes longer, though he knew he might as well go. "If you don't appreciate me," he said, "I know my place."

Louise was interested, "Where is that?"

"At your farm," he said. "I'll move in and be your brothers' brother."

"You can be mine, too."

"Never!" he said. "One must draw the line somewhere. This hasn't anything to do with you. We'll build our big ketch and cruise to Alaska, and to the Gulf of California for black pearls, and to Guatemala and Honduras prospecting and looking for ruins——"

Her eyes were sparkling like the outgoing tide in the morning light. "You do make it sound exciting. I could marry almost any one, to do things like that!"

"Could you marry me?"

"Well, no," she said reluctantly. "One must draw the line somewhere."

When he reached the moorings in the middle of the afternoon, Egil came out on the pier and helped him with the mooring lines. There was not much going on, after all.

Egil said, "Your father hasn't showed up yet."

"I noticed that." The cruiser was still at her berth, with the paid captain reading a magazine in the cockpit, and the young crew of one polishing brass. "I expected them to have left," Bailey said, "but when the Old Man gets going on business, he's hard to stop."

He called Home Place to check with Marian, but got no answer. Then he began to feel uneasy, and telephoned around town. There was no fresh news of his father until he called Martin Darling's office. Joyce said he had been there, but had left a little while before.

His mind was at peace again and he went back to tidying up the office-shop and reviewing his visit to the Canal, where he had made out so well with every one except Louise. It seemed unreasonable that a girl should have a passionate and candid love affair with him for nearly two years—and then refuse to do anything but flirt; or laugh at him, which was worse. He thought it was because she had grown more serious, though that sounded contradictory. Even if it were true, it did not seem to help.

A few minutes after five, when he was writing up a gas sale, an old man staggered into the office, carrying a long white package. In Bailey's first instant of impression, he knew it was some relative, though he could not place him. Then he turned for a clear look, and the old man said, "Bailey, I got here, by God!"

Bailey stared at his father, and was shocked. If it was his father. The old man and his clothes looked as if he had been on a week's drunk, and the dark semicircles under his eyes looked like something he had put on deliberately and could take off if he chose. There were other things about him which left only a confused impression.

Bailey put a chair under him and took the long florist's box which he was carrying and laid it on the desk. "For Christ's sake," he said, "where have you been?"

The father asked, "Is the boat here? I'm ready to go." Then he said, "I've been in hell, but I got out; I always do!" He was in a cheerful mood, and after sitting for a few seconds, he said, "I came here as soon as I was through; I didn't stop for anything except to get Marian some flowers. You know how women are; she's going to be sore because I'm late."

Bailey said, "The boat's ready. But you'd better go up to my room and lie down for a while. I'll call Doctor Morrow and he'll give you something to straighten you out."

"To hell with the doctor," his father said. "I'm all right. I'm going home now; I've earned it. Wait till I tell you!" He looked ghastly, and when he leaned back, with his arms hooked over the back of the chair, his coat slipped and showed the butt of a revolver under his armpit.

"Better let me have that." Bailey eased the weapon out of its holster and slipped it into his trouser pocket.

"Careful," his father said, "it's loaded."

Bailey said, "I don't know what you've been up to, but maybe you should get out of town! I'll go with you, if you'll turn in as soon as we're on board."

"I want you to be with me," Charlie said. "I was sick most of the way in the taxi, but I'm all right now. I'm set for a killing. Wait till I tell you——"

"You can tell me when we're on board." Bailey was conscious of the solid weight of the revolver in his pocket, and his ears were tuned for the wail of a prowler-car siren.

"I'll call Marian first," Charlie said. "I don't want her to be worrying." He started to get up, but his son made him sit down again.

Bailey got long distance and gave the number, and waited for several minutes, with one ear listening for Mrs. Wilkes or Marian, and the other for the wail of a siren. He did not hear either, and the operator said, "Your party does not answer. Shall I keep ringing?" Bailey hung up. "They must be out; they don't answer."

"Let's go, then," Charlie said. "It'll be more of a surprise that way."

Everything felt safer and better when they were in the comfortable cabin, hearing the faint, smooth sound of the motors and the rush of passing water. Charlie said, "This is better, having some one else look after things; I've earned it. Wait till you hear how!" He was half-lying on the starboard berth, with his big shoulders propped against the bulkhead, and he would not take off his clothes. "I might be sick again if I did," he said. "I feel fine now, and they help hold me together. I need a drink, though; there must be plenty somewhere: I ordered a case."

Bailey had helped stow the supplies and he knew where the whiskey was, but he did not know if it was a good idea. "Haven't you had about enough?"

"I've got to have one," Charlie said; "I'll take it easy. I've been pouring it down like water for days—and I never got drunk; my mind was clear all the time."

Bailey said, "You can have one, if you'll take an aspirin with it and turn in." He got the whiskey from its locker and the aspirin bottle from the medicine chest, and his father poured half a dozen tablets into his hand and gulped them down with a swallow of whiskey.

"You shouldn't take more than two," Bailey said.

Charlie said, "I can eat them by the handful—they never bother me. I can drink, too. I poured it down like water—" While he talked, Bailey tried to readjust his father in his mind. The man who was talking sounded like his father, and recognized him as his son, and that troubled Bailey as much as it reassured him. It seemed unreal that any one could be so changed and still recognize other people. He was so wound up from his adventure that the only thing to do was to let him go, and try to make him comfortable as he unwound.

He helped his father off with his vomit-stained coat and took the holster from around his left shoulder. His father winced and admitted having pains in his arms, though he insisted that he had not fallen or been in a fight. "I used my head," he explained. "All the time I knew there was some way out—if I could only think of it——"

Bailey took the embarrassing revolver from his own pocket, mated it with the holster, and put them on the other berth beside the long, white florist's box—as strange bedfellows as Beauty and the Beast. When he was hanging up the evil-smelling coat, his father remembered, violently, that there was a precious document in the pocket, and he insisted that Bailey take it out and read it to him. To Bailey, the agreement was a shock, and he realized that his father was a long way from shore, on thin ice; but he said it was a wonderful document and he folded it away respectfully in his father's wallet.

"I went to hell to get that," Charlie said; "I had a good look at it and I can tell you what it's like." He began telling of his adventure, and though it had started only two days before, it sounded like something he had told over and over again, and there were phrases that he kept repeating. "I told myself, 'I'm in a jam. It's up to me, now. I have to work fast. It's going to take all I have.' It was just as if the world had given a sudden lurch and I had fallen overboard and couldn't get back on. I was swimming alone and nobody gave a damn about me. People passed close by but they didn't see me. I wasn't in the world they were in, and I wouldn't be until I found my way back. Once I got to worrying about this boat and the paid hands eating their heads off at the dock for weeks; then I remembered I'd chartered the boat only that morning. . . ."

The boat stopped a few minutes, waiting to enter the Canal lock, then it crept ahead, and stopped again. Bailey heard the thud of lines being thrown ashore and the lock gates closing behind them, while his father's story unwound. "Time and places were all haywire. I hadn't more than got out of Seattle when I saw a side road that looked familiar; it was the road to Home Place. If I'd been in the right world, I could have been home in ten minutes. But I told myself, 'Home is a thousand miles away. You'll never find it on that side road. The only way there is through hell and back—if you ever get back—'" The lock was emptying, with the cruiser descending smoothly towards sea level on the liquid elevator. "I was scared to death because I might never get back—" He stopped with a look of terror in his eyes that were staring up at the oval cabin windows and the wet, earth-colored wall of the lock sliding by as they were lowered into deepening shadows, out of the sunlight. "*Christ, where am I?*" He started up, but Bailey put his hands on his shoulders and held him.

"Steady," Bailey said; "it's all right. They're just emptying the lock."

His father leaned back against the mahogany bulkhead and wiped the sweat from his white forehead. "I looked up suddenly and I thought——"

Bailey switched on the light above his father's head. "We'll be out of it in a minute, on our way home." The downward motion slowed and stopped, and he heard the cough and rumble of motors coming to life. They were opening the lock gates.

When Charlie knew where they were, he forgot his fright and his story went on unwinding. "Horace said, 'Is Martin putting the squeeze on you?' and then he said, 'It would probably mean taking over your property, but you could still run it, at a good salary.' 'God damn it, Horace,' I said, 'I came here to save my property, not to give it away!'

"When I got outside, things were all haywire again. It was a thousand miles to Home Place, but it was only ten minutes' drive for Marian. I might meet her anywhere on the street, and that thought almost made me crazy. She would speak to me and I couldn't stand it, because we were in different worlds. If that happened, I'd want to kill her——"

"Why, Father, you could have told her and she would have made things a lot easier. If she'd ever stick by a man, it would be when he was in trouble. If you could have talked to her, things wouldn't have seemed nearly as bad——"

"I couldn't have talked to her," Charlie said. "I'd have killed her first! Marian never had anything to do with my business. She probably thought no matter how much money I lost, I always had plenty more. I gave her the idea; I always thought Martin would let me go on gambling until I hit the jackpot. Anyway, if I couldn't look after her without her having to worry about things that were my business, I was a failure. . . . When I ate, there was some trick about the food. I was in one world and it was in another, and it didn't do me any good. I couldn't eat enough to keep from being hungry when I didn't have anything—and that hunger was gnawing at my guts all the time. I bought a bottle of whiskey and it went down like water, and it didn't do me any good. . . ."

Bailey watched his father's crumpled face and the excited light burning behind his burnt-out eyes, and he held him steadyingly by the shoulders. "You've been pouring it down, all right; you've had a hell of an adventure. Why not turn in now; and get some sleep?"

But his father's mind was wound up. He had been shaken terribly awake by his adventure, and his adventure had been so tremendous that he marveled at having come out of it alive, and he could not stop from telling about it. "I was in a jam, I tell you. I was desperate. I didn't know which way to turn, and I couldn't see any way out. . . . I drove and didn't think where I was going, and I found myself on Chuckanut Mountain, looking at the San Juans. Marian and I were going there in the boat I'd chartered; we were going to take a week to it. I got there in no time, without thinking about it, and it didn't do me any good. . . . I went out to the Seattle house and worked in the library. I poured whiskey down like water, and never got drunk. I made coffee and took it to the library and poured a cup, and when I picked it up, it was stone cold. I took it to the kitchen and heated it till it boiled, and brought it back, and after a minute it was stone cold again. I did that till it was morning——"

"That's what comes of concentrating," Bailey said.

"I was desperate; nobody would help me, not even my lawyer. He said, 'It doesn't look as if we can do anything but let Martin foreclose and save what pieces we can.' He was like Horace; he called in his smart young partner and they talked a lot of rigamarole and Allen said, 'It looks as if Martin has you by the knockers, all right.' I said, 'I don't have to pay any God-damned lawyer to tell me that! I came here to find out how to make him let go.' Allen said, 'A contract is a contract. There isn't any way, unless we can talk him into changing his mind.' And the smart young man gave me his legal advice: 'Martin has you by the knockers, all right.' I said, 'Martin has knockers, too, if I can figure out how to get a hold of them.' I didn't see any way, then. . . ."

By the increased speed of the boat, they were out of the dredged channel in Shilshole Bay, and then there was the mournful iron clang of the bell buoy. Bailey got up and looked out of an oval cabin window, across the wide reach of the Sound to the blue shore of Bainbridge Island, and the paler Olympics beyond. "You and Marian should have fine weather for your trip," he said. "I hope you make the most of it. Why don't you lie down and get a little sleep?" The Old Man looked ghastly and flabby, and Bailey thought grimly of Marian's shock when she saw what he was bringing home to her. "You don't want to worry Marian," he said; "get some rest; it'll be better for both of you."

But Charlie went on struggling with his adventure. It was coiled around him like a snake, and he had to get free of it before he could rest. "I was desperate. For three days I'd been going around—Seattle, Hewitt, Tacoma—nobody would help me. I moved to the Savoy on Second Avenue; I slept there— what sleeping I did—and drank straight whiskey, and my mind was clear all the time. There was some way, if I could only find it. . . . I didn't find it until the afternoon of the third day. Then I poured the whiskey down the basin and checked out. . . . I went to the house and unlocked the little drawer in my bureau. There it was—I hadn't carried it since Wobbly days. I loaded it with cartridges from the box. Then I went to the library. There you all were, living and dead, looking at me from the wall. I took off my hat and said, 'Here goes Charlie!' I didn't know if I was going to come out of it alive. . . .

"Martin said, 'Paul's a fine boy.' I said, 'I know that.' He said, 'Bertha's a fine, intelligent girl.' I said, 'She's all right; she takes after her mother.' He said, 'If Paul was to know that besides getting a fine wife he was saving you and the business—' I laughed. 'O, Jesus, Martin, why didn't I recognize you before? You and your archery!' He asked, 'What's the harm in telling Paul?' I said, 'No harm at all, Cupid, only he might feel he had to. He'll choose his own girl when he gets around to it.'

"Martin froze up. 'I don't have to give you anything, Charlie.' 'You do, Martin. There's a way; I knew there was all the time. . . . I've got nothing to lose; I'm nothing but an old timber beast. You're a God-damned old pack rat, storing away money and storing away time. Now I'm sitting on your pack-rat cache of time with a gun in my hand. . . . You can give me another year, or there'll be two dead men carried out of this office. . . .' We didn't quarrel. . . . I had pains in my arms and chest and my legs had pins and needles, and I was getting sick. . . . Violet said, 'Remember me to Bailey' and then she said, 'I didn't see anything, but you'd better get rid of that revolver.' "

The last coils of his adventure were falling from him, and he slid down on the berth with his head on the pillow. "The whole thing would have failed if it hadn't been for Violet. Bailey gets around, eh?" Then he said, "You'd better be good to her."

"I'll be as good as I can," Bailey said; "but I have another girl."

"Only one?"

"Only one."

"Better not let Violet know."

Bailey said, "She knows."

"And she did it, anyway!"

"Maybe because of that."

"I don't see why."

"Being noble, maybe."

"People do things like that. I've never been able to afford it, myself. It was high-ball all the time. If anybody gets in your way, slug him down. I had to stick through the bad years, so I'd be there for the killing. I'm set for one now."

Bailey said, "You're going to need help, Father. I have my limitations, but I think I can be of some use. I'll even work in the woods. I think Paul will, too, when he knows how things are."

"You're fine boys," Charlie said, and took his hand, "even if you have too many ideas. It's a great game, logging. You roll the dice a dozen times, and lose every time—and a dozen years are gone and you're an old man. Then if you can keep in the game and you're lucky, maybe you hit the jackpot. Maybe it's a hell of a thing to be proud of," he said after a minute, "but I've felt better ever since that time you said I was a better man than Tom Horton."

It had been only the day before yesterday, but Charlie spoke as if it had been long ago; it was not quite what Bailey had said, but he let it pass. "You've been consistent," he said.

When his father was asleep at last, Bailey covered him with a blanket and went up on deck. It was past sunset, but light still seemed to come from the sky and the water, and it was like a softer day.

The young captain was perched on the seat of the wheel, steering thoughtfully, and he asked, "Is your father feeling better?"

"He's sleeping," Bailey said. "He needed it." Then he said, "You might cut her down a little; I want him to get as much sleep as he can."

"Why not?" He throttled the motors down to an easy speed. "We have all the time in the world."

Bailey went aft to the cockpit and closed the door behind him. Then he took the heavy revolver in its holster from under his coat and let it slide over the stern into the lazily boiling wake. "Editing Father's life," he said. "If you don't look at his face, he makes a nice picture in the cabin, sleeping like a baby, with the long white florist's box for company." He didn't approve of the hypocrisy, but there was the chance that the police might be waiting for them when they landed. Father's life isn't complete without the revolver, he thought; the butt end for labor, and the muzzle for financiers. Father is what he is, and makes no bones about it; he'd never want a whitewashing, because he approves of himself the way he is.

He hadn't got rid of the revolver for hypocrisy, and only a little because of the police. Dropping it overboard was a symbol: he was pledged to go into the logging game with his father, who was getting old, and who might never come all the

way back from his adventure. I'm going to have some say as an
employer, and we won't say it with brute force. I won't highball and I won't walk over people. At first he could only find
things he would not do, and a cloud of good intentions. Then
he went deeper and found words: *If things were right, no one
who was with other human beings would ever be among
strangers or enemies. No child would ever know fear or want.
When he was old enough to understand, he would be shown
the riches and the beauty of the earth; he would be told: 'You
were brought into this world as the rest of us were brought, and
your right is equal to our right. You are one of the shareholders. Use your share wisely, for the profit of this geat company of human beings——"*

It was the first time he had let even himself know just where
he stood, but his creed came out strong and clear. He stopped
because the words sounded too familiar for a first utterance.
He had heard those words before—on a bright autumn afternoon, when he was a child, with Tom Horton's arm around
him: Tom, sitting on a garden bench; the baby Paul on his lap,
pulling a rose to pieces. Bailey's mother was there and she
looked proud and sweet, listening to Tom. . . . Bailey thought
ruefully: I don't know how much help I'll be to the Old
Man——

They had passed Possession Point and were coming up to
Mukilteo light, to starboard, in the long summer dusk, when
he heard a shrill, trumpeting sound, voices, and the scuffle of
feet. He jerked open the door and felt the boat surge ahead as
the revolutions of the motors went up. In the dusk of the bridge
deck, Bailey saw the young crew's frightened face in the light
of the binnacle. "What is it?"

"Down there." The boy pointed to the companionway. "It
sounded like a horse whinnying!"

As he rushed down the companion stairs, he heard nothing

but a loud snoring. The light was on in the cabin, and the young captain was bending over the berth. His first, erratic impression was that his father had shot himself. Then he thought: That's impossible; I dropped the revolver overboard. "For Christ's sake, what happened?"

"Stroke," the captain said. "You watch him while I get some ice." The captain was younger than the frightened Bailey, but he was efficient, and a great comfort.

Charlie's eyes were open, with one pupil smaller than the other, giving the impression of a wink; but he seemed to be unconscious, with his red face twisted and his cheeks puffing out with his loud snoring. Bailey took his hand and said "Father!" But the hand was limp, and there was no answer but the stentorious breathing. He put the limp hand down, feeling as alone and helpless as his father.

It was better when the captain came back from the galley. He had the ice tied in a dish towel, and he put the improvised pack on the old man's head. "When it hit him," he said, referring to the stroke, "he made a sound just like the whinnying of a horse."

Bailey said, "We've got to get him to a doctor. Can you get any more speed out of her?"

"Motors are wide open now," the Captain said. "I'm keeping on for Hewitt."

"That's right," Bailey said. "Can we do anything more for him?"

"Nothing that I know of." Then he said, "It hit him hard, and he went out like that. He made a noise just like the whinnying of a horse." It seemed an important point to establish.

"He'd been tearing himself to pieces for days," Bailey said. "I didn't know."

"He'd better go easy after this," the captain said. "A couple more good ones will finish him." He sounded very sure of his knowledge, but he did not know what the old man had been through.

Charlie Dow died in the hospital that night.

Marian was there, but they were not able to reach Paul at the lookout station until morning. If it made any difference. Charlie had been unconscious ever since he fell asleep after his adventure.

XVIII

IT WAS BEGINNING to drizzle as they left Seattle, and when they reached Home Place the still house was cold in the driving autumn rain. Bailey lit the furnace, and he could hear its roar above the blower. The sound of the rain, and the cold cellar under the earth, made him think of his father, who had been dead three months; but when he went upstairs again, he was in the land of the living.

The stairs led to the kitchen, and Louise was already working, without having paused to take off her coat. She had the kettle on and was unpacking the groceries they had brought. She was quick-moving and lovely, with her light brown hair and dark eyes, and a dash of color in her thin face that was still tanned from summer. The week end was Paul's and Bailey's first entertaining at Home Place, and Louise, who was one of the guests, had laughed Bailey out of hiring help.

Admiring her, he said, "There's nothing like having a woman around the place!"

She said, "You might turn on the refrigerator, Bailey, and put in the steak and things."

While he was obeying, he complained, "You didn't even hear what I said!"

"You said there was nothing like having a woman around the place, and I asked you to help; that's just what a woman around the place does."

"You're certainly an efficient wife."

331

"I'm not very efficient," she said; "and I'm not any one's wife."

"I was only judging by appearances. Any one who happened in here——"

"You don't have to judge by appearances," she said. "I may be here under false pretenses. but there has to be a woman around the place."

"I'm glad you understand that."

"I understand more than you might think."

"I doubt that."

"What wouldn't I understand?"

"That while you are around the place, you might be more of a woman."

For a moment her eyes had the warm, level look that used to be there so often. "I might even understand that."

But when he reached for her, the look was gone, and she was difficult again. She let him kiss her once, and that was all. When the kitchen was in order, he said, "You can knock off long enough to take your things upstairs. You haven't even seen the house."

Bailey carried her suitcase, and she followed him. "It's a big house, isn't it?"

He said, boastfully, "You should have seen our mansion in Seattle, the one we sold. If we'd moved it to the University district, we could have auctioned it off for a frat house."

"I was there once," she reminded him. "I met Marian there for the first time, soon after the funeral."

"It was a fine place to get rid of." He paused on the upstairs landing and indicated the length of the hall with its many doors. "You can almost have your choice of rooms; they all have furniture now, with what we salvaged from the other house."

She asked, "Which are the ones I can't have? They interest me most."

"There aren't any you can't have," he said. "Paul uses this end room when he's down from camp, but I know he'll be glad to give it up to you."

"I wouldn't think of it!" she said.

"This is my room—you're welcome to stay in here."

"I wouldn't think of having you move out."

"I wasn't intending to."

She said, "I think you'd better show me something else."

"Here's another one." He opened a door. "It has two beds; you're welcome to both, though I thought it might do for your brothers."

"It will," she said. "It's a fine room, and I don't need anything as large."

"I think this is the one for you." He opened the door of the master bedroom, with its gloomy walnut furniture. "The bed is ten feet wide—and I hope to hell you get lost in it!"

Her clear laugh rang in the somber room. "You're such a gracious host, Bailey!"

"I took lessons from Tag." Then he said, "I'm sorry you didn't know him."

"Was he the one who was killed on the highway?"

"A few miles from here," he said. "I think he was coming home—but we never knew."

"Marian told me about him," she said, "how he went out to look for Paradise. But he couldn't have found it—because he was coming back."

Bailey said, "Maybe he realized it was here."

"I'll be more respectful." Her eyes were deep and serious. "Anywhere we are might be Paradise, without our knowing it."

"Father planned this place as something of the sort, but he

lost out on it. He used to say that he had never enjoyed it the way he had hoped to. But that doesn't make it any less."

"It's a fine place," Louise said. "People could have a good life here." Then she asked, "Have you any other rooms to show?"

He said, "Any one could tell that you had lugged your suitcase around the Village and the Chelsea district, looking at furnished rooms!"

"You're lugging my suitcase this time," she reminded him.

"I should make you carry it yourself, then you wouldn't be so particular." He opened the door to the small bedroom. "I can't tell you much about this one, except that Bertha Darling once slept here—and went home mad."

Louise said, "I don't think it would affect me that way; I'll take it if it isn't too expensive."

He put her suitcase down. "If there's anything you need, I'll at least look for it."

"Thank you, Bailey," she said. "It's much more complete than what I'm used to on the farm." When he was about to leave, she asked, "Have I seen all the rooms now?"

"There's still the nursery, if you'd be interested."

"Has it a bed?"

"It has a crib," he said, "if you don't mind slats."

"Is it big enough for me?"

He said, "It ought to be; I've slept there myself."

"Bailey," she said, "your crib! I must see it!"

"If you'll be quiet." He took her by the hand and led her to the nursery. There wasn't much there that had belonged to children; a few discarded toys of Ginger's, the old play table, and his battered maple crib. It was made up with a hopeful white spread, and they stood looking at it respectfully. Bailey said, "The grave of the amiable child!"

She looked at the little white plot, with her eyes bright. "You must have been very nice, when you were a little boy!"

He accepted the belated compliment. "I was a cherub."

She turned away from the crib and sat on the low play table. He sat beside her, looking out at the autumn rain driving down on the lawn, and on Tom Horton's trees, and on the wet tattered orchard, where some last yellow apples were hanging on high branches. She said, "You must have had a fine time here when you were small!"

He said, "I started to, and then the world went haywire. It wasn't the fault of the place, but none of us had any luck here. Father discovered the valley on the Dark Day—and afterward we had the Dark Age, and Mother hustled us out. But that doesn't alter the fact that the place has a lot to give. It's just never known the right people."

Louise said, "Marian liked it here."

"But she didn't have any luck, either," Bailey said. "This was going to be our first summer here together—and Paul went away on his own, and I began going to Hood Canal——"

"I've already contributed to the ruin of the place," she said.

"I didn't have to go and see you."

"No, why did you?"

"God knows, for all the good it did me." Then he said, "Yes, it did; I got to be your brothers' brother, and the business got a fine head loader and second loader out of it when we started up Camp Three."

"We're a versatile family," she said; "if you just keep your patience, and shop around, one of us is sure to be able to help you."

He said, "It wasn't a help to the kind of summer we'd planned, but it didn't make much difference, with Father cracking up about that time."

"Marian certainly bore up well."

Bailey said, "By now, you probably know her better than I do. She's practically divorced the family since Father died."

"It isn't because she doesn't like you and Paul."

Bailey asked, "She's really getting along all right?"

"Yes, she likes her job and she likes living alone; but most of all, I think, she likes being herself."

"What is herself really like?"

"I didn't know her before," she said, "and I can't imagine her having been any different. She's a lovely, quiet person, with so much warmth, and a nice sense of perspective. The kind of woman you could build a family around."

"And it was her luck not to have children." Then he said, "I'm grateful to her in all kinds of ways. She could have wrecked everything by demanding even a part of what was coming to her; instead she didn't even want a house to live in. It was she who insisted on our selling the Seattle place—and she got out and supported herself."

"She's a fine girl, Bailey."

He hesitated, then asked, "Did she tell you that she's waived her right to her share of the estate?"

"All of it, Bailey?"

"Everything," he said. "In her letter she argued that we were bankrupt when Father died—and if Paul and I save anything, it belongs to us."

"You aren't going to accept that, are you?"

"I haven't talked it over with Paul," he said; "but I'm certainly against it. What I can't figure is why she took that stand—unless she's that glad to be rid of us."

"I know it isn't that; she told me that she was very fond of both of you."

Bailey said, "She didn't tell you why she was waiving her share?"

"I didn't know she had, and I'm not very good at guessing." She thought a while and said, "Maybe it's because she is fond of you and Paul."

He said, "It's a strange way to show it—cutting loose from us altogether."

"Maybe she doesn't want to be a relative, or some one to whom you owe money. Suppose she just wants to be herself, so you can accept her or let her go on her merits?"

Bailey said, "We're the ones who aren't accepted, when we can't even get her to come up here!"

"She talked to me about this week end," Louise said. "I think she really wanted to be here, but she was afraid her job would make her too late for dinner. And she feels obliged to spend her week ends with her parents."

"That is noble of her."

"Why?" Louise asked.

"Marian hasn't told you about her parents?"

Louise shook her head. "Only that her father was hurt in a runaway, and is laid up with a broken back."

Bailey said, "He and the Old Lady seem to have had a stormy life—mostly because he liked the farm and she didn't, or thought she didn't—and she let every one know it. He didn't give in until he got hurt and was told he mightn't be able to work for years. That was late last summer, when things had begun to boom around Illihee, and he agreed to sell out and move to town. But instead of taking him up, the Old Lady went into a tantrum. She said they'd spent their lives making the best farm in the county, and they weren't going to throw it all away. So she's nursing him along, and running the place with the help of a hired man."

"The mother sounds like quite a character."

"She is, and I'm not sure I'd like to spend a week end in her company—but Marian seems able to take such things in her quiet stride."

Louise said, "Mother or no mother, I'll hold you responsible for seeing that Marian gets something out of the estate."

"I'll see to it," Bailey said.

She looked at him thoughtfully. "It's too soon to talk out loud about such things, Bailey, but if you're any judge of women, you won't let Marian get away."

He smiled a little grimly at the rain-driven landscape beyond the window. "I probably wouldn't, if it weren't for you."

"I don't see why I should make you hesitate."

"I don't, either," he said. "Do you know what you are?"

"I don't know what you think I am."

"You're just a memory."

"I hope I'm a pleasant one."

"That's the hell of it," he said. "If I start thinking about it, I won't be responsible for what happens. When we talk about ourselves, you just laugh at me. I'm getting to be a successful logging operator, and you just laugh, and take the heart out of it, and leave it hollow."

Sitting beside him on the table, she put her slender brown hand in his. "I'm sorry, Bailey." She sounded penitent, but he did not trust her to stay that way. "I'm glad the logging is going well—not just for your sake; there's Marian; and George and Harry; they think you're the best operator that ever logged and they're so anxious for you to make a go of it——"

Bailey said, "We're making a go of it, all right. Since we started up Camp Three, we've been averaging better than half a million feet of logs a day, without high-balling. And the logs are sold before they hit the salt chuck. We're logging, now, Louise; we're making money!"

"I'm glad you're not running a high-ball outfit, Bailey."

"I couldn't do that," he said. "Your brothers are there, and my brother, and a lot of other people's—and I'm responsible for them. The hardest work I have is seeing that they don't take chances. We haven't killed any one yet, though it's bound to happen sooner or later; but it won't be because they were pushed."

"I know it won't," she said.

Bailey said, "I've figured that with a decent fall and winter, we'll be able to pay Martin off by summer."

"That will be wonderful; you'll feel as if you owned the world."

"I'll at least feel as if we owned the business," he said. "Figuring as pessimistically as I can, I don't see how we can miss owning it before long. Even if we can't quite pay Martin off, we'll be so nearly in the clear that it won't be any trouble getting a bank loan to make up the difference. That's why I wanted to celebrate this week end—I'm so certain of it."

"You're a great success!" she said.

"It isn't anything I've done," he said; "it's a matter of having the timber and fairly good equipment at the right time, and having a good logging superintendent, and a good crew. You can't miss when you have everything, and the log market is booming. It's the killing Father was waiting for, and he killed himself, hanging on and dragging the ladder to the tree. All I have to do is climb up and pick the apples."

Louise said, "You're making a good job of it; don't belittle yourself."

He still felt gloomy, looking out at the autumn rain and the tattered orchard. "Even if I am doing all right, it's still hollow."

"Why, Bailey?"

"You know what's making it a success—defense orders. Half

the world is burning up now, and the fire is coming our way. There was good money in logging during the last war, and it's happening again—and there wasn't even a living in it between wars. In a decent world, people would be building all the time. You wouldn't have to wait for a disaster every generation, so you could make a living out of it all in one bunch. If we can't do better after this one, we're all through, anyway."

"I'm glad you see that."

He said, "There's a chance of something better, too. In the last war, everything was torn to pieces with labor troubles. Before we were in it, we had what amounted to civil war and a reign of terror. I don't see any sign of trouble this time. The loggers are more reasonable, and the operators are more reasonable, and there isn't any friction. It seems like saner people in a madder world. Maybe enough people realize the game is up for all of us unless we can work out something better."

She said, "You're the best kind of a success when you can see behind it!"

"There isn't much satisfaction in being a success that's part of a failure; succeeding in a world that's already dead."

"There isn't, Bailey."

"But I believe in people," he said, "more than ever. The only comfort I get is from other people: your brothers, and Paul, and Marian when I see her, and our logging crews——"

Louise said, "You make me feel very guilty!"

"God knows, I don't get much comfort out of you!"

"I would like you to."

When he looked at her, her eyes were very bright.

"I would like to be some comfort to you," she said, "but we've already tried that. We lived together, and I gave myself, you know how completely—and nothing came of it, Bailey, nothing!"

"I got you into a jam——"

"We got me into a jam!" Her eyes flashed at him out of her brown face. "It took two of us."

"And I bought you an abortion," he went on. "I remember feeling proud of myself at the moment, being able to buy that miracle of modern science, the perfect abortion! I don't feel so fine about it now, when I realize that that is all civilization in our time has produced." He got up and walked around the table, with his head down and his hands in his pockets. "A baby would have been much more of a miracle, and it would have done us more good; it would have kept us together. We'd have had some hold on the future. Don't you see, Louise? The skids are under our generation: they're under your brothers and my brother and me, and all of us. We have to pin our hopes, like diapers, on another generation——"

Louise said, "Do you have to keep walking round the table?" Then she said, "You can if you want to, Bailey. You can do anything that's any comfort to you!"

His mind was still full of things he was going to say, but when he stopped beside her, she was crying, and he felt confused. "What do you want me to do?"

She said, "You could hold me—if you want to."

He gathered her up easily and sat on the old sofa, holding her. He was still distrustful of her, but she rested sweetly in his arms, smiling at him with her eyes still wet. "May I kiss you?" he asked.

"Yes, Bailey."

She responded to his kiss with light gentleness that somehow changed and ran through him in waves of wild, sweet flame, searching and tender. When he stopped at last, he no longer felt distrustful of her, only dazed and wondering.

"What is it, Bailey?"

"You've changed so!"

"I'm only being myself," she said.

"But how did you get to be yourself again?"

She told him, "It was something you said a little while ago; something that made me realize you've grown up."

"May I kiss you again?" he asked.

She smiled at him, with the warm level look of her eyes flooding through him. "Bailey, you can do anything that will be of any comfort to you. You're grown up now and can take the consequences."

He had just started to kiss her again when they heard the car droning towards them along the orchard road.

Louise started up out of his arms. "And I was going to have dinner ready when they got here!"

"It was my fault," he said.

"Don't boast!" She kissed him quickly. "I had something to do with it."

As they went downstairs, he said, "Anyway, they can't fire you."

"They ought to, Bailey. Why not?"

"We'll tell them you're the lady of the house, or going to be. We'll invite them to our wedding, and that will shame them out of firing you."

Louise and Bailey stood at the open door as their brothers came in from the garage, where they had left the old sedan: Louise's brothers, husky and quick-moving, with quiet, self-reliant faces, and Paul, tall and tough and shy-faced. They were still in their logging clothes, but George and Harry had their suitcases. They came back almost leisurely, joking with each other, indifferent to the driving rain, with the steel calks of their boots biting at the wet gravel of the driveway. At the door they stopped respectfully, and their stiff "tin" pants crackled as they sat on the steps taking off their boots. Explaining their clothes, Paul said over his shoulder, "We came down on the speeder, and the canopy doesn't help much with a south wind."

George said, "Paul almost caught up with the main-line locie."

Bailey said, "You be careful with those damned things!"

Paul said, "I know I'm not going to meet anything with a log train ahead of me."

"We really took her easy," Harry said.

Paul said, "I wanted to look things over before I left."

George said solemnly, "He was getting a block watchman for our side."

"It's forest-fire weather, all right!" Bailey said, above the sound of rain.

"That was the trouble," George said; "the rain kept getting in the watchman's water tank."

"You're accomplished liars," Bailey said, "and when you come in, you can all have a drink."

Taking off his second boot, Paul asked, "Do we have any company?"

"Just the family," Bailey said. "We tried to get Marian, but she couldn't make it."

Paul did not comment, and the three came in in their stocking feet, leaving their savage boots in a row outside.

When the door was closed, the sound of rain became fainter, and the kitchen was pleasant with good faces and human warmth. George looked admiringly at the whiskey and soda and glasses that Bailey was setting out. "I didn't know you allowed your loggers to drink!"

"It's a long time till Monday morning." Then he said to Louise, "You see, I'm getting the reputation of a damned old woman! Well, I can't help it. One can't be too careful with his brothers."

Harry said, "You're swell, Bailey!"

George said, "I wouldn't kid you if I didn't think so."

"You really are my brothers," Bailey said; "Louise and I are going into partnership."

George looked puzzled for a moment. "You mean you're going to tie the old logging chain around your necks?"

"That's the idea," Bailey said.

In the confusion of handshaking and congratulation, the room seemed full of warm-hearted people, and Bailey was the only one who forgot to kiss Louise.

The glow lasted through dinner, when Bailey remembered another piece of news. He told his brother, "Today, we had a good offer from United for the Illihee tract."

Paul asked, "Do they want the stumpage or the land?"

"Both. They'll probably cut it up into stump ranches when it's logged off."

"Do you think we ought to sell?"

"Sell, or log it ourselves," Bailey said. "All our lives it's been a question mark, with taxes attached."

Paul nodded, gravely. Then he said, "There's a lot of good piling in there, close to salt water."

"I looked over the cruise on it today, and it isn't bad. And we have a right-of-way through the Clark place."

Paul said, "It follows an old skidroad through the pasture."

"If we don't sell, we ought to bring in a couple of 'cats' next spring, and log it ourselves."

"It would be worth trying," Paul said.

"It'll be a small-time operation, but it should be profitable if we have a good man on the job."

Paul said, quietly, "I don't know how good I am, but I'd like to have a try at it myself."

Bailey was startled, but as he thought it over, and looked at his brother's determined face, he was less surprised. "Why not?"

he asked. "You're on your way to being a timber beast, and that's a good place to see what you can do on your own."

Louise had been wondering how they could talk about logging around the Clark farm, without any mention of Marian. Then it occurred to her, quietly, that they were talking about her now.